A TEMPEST OF TEA

PRAISE FOR HAFSAH FAIZAL

WE HUNT THE FLAME:

An Ignyte Award Winner
A *TIME* Magazine Top 100 Fantasy Book of All Time
A *Teen Vogue* Book Club Pick
A Barnes & Noble Teen Book Club Pick
A *Paste Magazine* Best YA Book
A *PopSugar* Best YA Book

★ "A fresh and gripping story."
—*Booklist*, starred review

★ "A debut series not to be missed."
—*School Library Journal*, starred review

★ "Zafira's courage will teach readers the power of the human spirit."
—*VOYA*, starred review

★ "Impressive world building, stellar cast, and intricate story."
—*The Bulletin of the Center for Children's Books*, starred review

"Faizal creates a dazzling and beautiful world that will make you not
want to put this book down."
—*Seventeen*

"Delivers on all fronts."
—*Entertainment Weekly*

"Spellbinding."
—Kerri Maniscalco, #1 *New York Times*–bestselling author of the
Stalking Jack the Ripper series

"Dazzling and magical."
—Kiersten White, *New York Times*–bestselling author

WE FREE THE STARS:

★ "A memorable story at the height of the fantasy genre."
—*Booklist*, starred review

"This Sands of Arawiya duology closer will not disappoint readers . . .
Faizal's prose truly shines."
—*Kirkus Reviews*

"Those who were left breathless by the previous installment will heave
a sigh of relief."
—*Bulletin of the Center for Children's Books*

ALSO BY HAFSAH FAIZAL

We Hunt the Flame
We Free the Stars

A
TEMPEST
OF TEA

HAFSAH FAIZAL

FARRAR STRAUS GIROUX

NEW YORK

Farrar Straus Giroux Books for Young Readers
An imprint of Macmillan Publishing Group, LLC
120 Broadway, New York, NY 10271 • fiercereads.com

Our books may be purchased in bulk for promotional, educational, or
business use. Please contact your local bookseller or the Macmillan Corporate
and Premium Sales Department at (800) 221-7945 ext. 5442 or by email at
MacmillanSpecialMarkets@macmillan.com.

Library of Congress Cataloging-in-Publication Data is available.

First edition, 2024
Book design by Aurora Parlagreco
Printed in the United States of America

ISBN 978-0-374-38940-6 (hardcover)
ISBN 978-0-374-39265-9 (special edition)
ISBN 978-0-374-39264-2 (special edition)
1   3   5   7   9   10   8   6   4   2

TO ASMA,
because you are my sister
but more often than not, my sanity

PALACE

PENN'S HOUSE

IMPERIAL SQUARE

THE ATHEREUM

OCK TOWER

IVYLOCK STREET

WHITE ROARING SQUARE

COFFEEHOUSE

ADMIRAL GROVE

WHITE ROARING

A TEMPEST
OF TEA

right wing

left wing

rooms

vault

offices
& rooms

auction
hall

parlor

prison

locked
& guarded

glass
chutes

dormer
guard

stair

guards

guard
house

mori...
vivos
docent

locate the
the wretched
way over her
is why I didn't
ly dreadful, she

Athereum
marker

numerical
code
inside

A

left wing

vaults

offices & rooms

right wing

stone wall →

parlor

auction hall

rooms (mostly debauchery)

prison

locked & guarded

marker archives

dormer guard

glass chutes

'winsome' sketch of a female vampire

gardens

ACT I

VENGEANCE NEVER DIES

Athereum List

- Edward Prior
- Sanjay Bhatt
- Oliver Tan
- Daisy Vincent
- Clayton Lambard
- Ronnie Humphries
- Faulk

ARTHIE didn't let me finish adding roses

1

ARTHIE

The streets of White Roaring grew fangs at night. When the moon dragged a claw and the shop fronts cut dim and those who craved blood walked bold. Arthie Casimir couldn't be bothered. By the cold, by the dark, by the vampires.

Business never stopped.

It was long past midnight and the foundries were silent. The sparks that lit the evening now simmered in coals left to cool, and dirty aprons had been cast aside as workmen hobbled into hovels. Coffeehouses, butchers, and betting shops slumbered in preparation for dawn, the capital kept alive by sin and a tearoom nestled at the crossroads of slum and wealth.

Spindrift, it was called.

Arthie's pride and joy, with its gleaming wood floors and the aroma of fresh tea as it filled a sparkling pot, in turn filling the coffers of her crew. The snobbery of her patrons was amended by the secrets they spilled in front of a staff of orphans who *most certainly* wouldn't understand the refined tongue of the rich.

She'd much rather be there than here, in the late autumn chill.

"I could go alone," Jin said, slowing his pace to match hers. His hair fell straight and sharp as a knife, his umbrella as elegant and clean-cut as he was, all lean limbs and broad shoulders sauntering down the gaslight-peppered streets.

"So I can come looking at dawn to find you nattering away with him?" Arthie didn't make a habit of visiting patrons who were racking up tabs, but this one had turned away too many of her crew.

"With *the* Matteo Andoni?" he asked, as if the idea were preposterous. "Really, Arthie."

Jin was the sort of charming even a king would draw a chair for if he flashed the right smile—and he knew it, so she didn't bother with an answer. They crossed down to the quieter Alms Place, where dirt was nowhere to be seen and the houses were posh and brick-faced.

A carriage trundled past the uniformed men standing guard at the top of the street, horses snorting under the coachman's direction. Ettenia's capital of White Roaring rarely slept, and with the recent vampire disappearances, whispers kept the city ever more awake; not because the people cared for the welfare of vampires, but because if something nefarious could happen to *them*, how would weaker human-folk fare?

As alarming as the disappearances were, Arthie disliked the increase in the Ram's Horned Guard even more. They were everywhere, keeping watch. It was unfair for the masked Ram to see so much when the people of Ettenia couldn't even see the face of the monarch that ruled them.

Arthie tucked a fold of paper into her vest and stopped before an imposing black fence. "Here we are. 337 Alms Place."

Jin whistled at the mansion set behind a trim lawn. "Now that's what we call money."

The estate demanded attention, from the frills along the windows to the fervent red of the front door. Fitting. Men lauded Matteo Andoni's name on the streets, women whispered it into their sheets—though very rarely with him in them.

"No, that's what we call too much. Look sharp." She didn't care if

Matteo Andoni was the country's beloved paint slinger. If you couldn't pay, you shouldn't drink.

They stepped through the gate and made their way up the wide steps. Arthie rapped with the iron knocker, and Jin leaned back against the porch wall, his grip loose around the black umbrella.

The door opened to a thin man with a thinning scalp; whatever hair that might have once been on his head had now relocated to the thick mustache curling above his lip.

"Yes?"

Arthie tucked her hands into her trouser pockets, the pistol in her holster glinting in the light. She'd rather not shoot the thing, but it was the only one of its kind and she sure as blood wouldn't keep it hidden away. "Paying a visit."

"Don't mind the hour," Jin added with a grin.

The butler looked from Arthie's mauve hair and brown Ceylani skin to Jin's monolid eyes and back to Arthie, glancing from the short crop of her hair to the lapels of her open jacket, then to the shine of the chain that led to the watch in her vest.

Look all you want, bugger. He'd find no slum in them. Her crew might have hailed from the worst of White Roaring, but what Arthie lacked in status she made up for in dignity, thank you very much.

"Weapons?" the butler asked, palm outstretched.

"No, thank you." Arthie smiled. "I have my own."

"What we'd really like is a kettle on the stove," Jin said. "It's quite the chill you're letting us linger in."

The butler looked chagrined. Jin rapped his umbrella on the ground and invited himself inside, his frame engulfing the narrow hall. "Much obliged, good sir. Come along, Arthie."

She tipped her hat and followed Jin into a receiving room with brocaded walls and shadowy shelves, most of the lamps banked low so the coffee table gleamed the same crimson as the rug.

"You—" The butler worked himself into a fit behind them. "You cannot—"

"It's quite all right, Ivor," someone said in a smooth voice.

A match hissed, and a bob of light illuminated a man lounging on a settee with one arm slung across its back, sleeves rolled to his forearms. His shirt was untucked and open at the collar, the loose strings framing a vee of cream down to his navel. The ruffles looked like petals kissing his skin. It was far more flesh than Arthie was accustomed to seeing from members of high society.

Jin coughed, throwing out a word in the midst of it. "*Ogling.*"

She was not.

"Matteo Andoni," said Arthie, ignoring Jin.

He had the fine aristocratic features unique to the neighboring country of Velance, making him as much an immigrant as she and Jin, but without the struggle.

"Arthie Casimir." He matched her slow drawl. Onyx and brass rings glittered from his fingers. His hair was dark and long, a carefully arranged mess. "Ivor and I have been making bets. He believed you'd show twenty duvin ago. How many of the Casimir crew had dropped by my doorstep at that point, Ivor? Three?"

"Six, sire."

Matteo waved a hand. "Never been fond of numbers, me."

If his prowess in the arts wasn't evident from the faint smudge of color on his fingers and every fool crowing it on the streets, it was overwhelmingly so from the way he observed. There was a greed in his gaze, as if he feared missing the world by giving in to a blink.

"Needless to say, Ivor lost." His smile carved a dimple in his cheek, and she was irritated that she noticed.

"And now you can use those winnings to settle your accounts," Jin said.

Arthie nodded. "All two hundred and twenty-four duvin."

"Hefty," Matteo noted, and his brief pause told her this was the moment of truth, of answer. "You know, for the longest time, I've wondered if those of us who come and drink tea can taste the blood you serve in those very same cups."

And there it was.

Since learning the name of the patron who was leaving tabs unpaid, Arthie had known something was amiss. He wasn't short on money. No, he'd set his lure, and she'd come to see why, armed with a little information of her own.

"Not that you drink much tea at Spindrift," she said, holding Matteo's gaze and making her implication clear.

"Come now, Arthie," he drawled, regarding her a little more intently and a little more seriously. "I only wanted to meet you."

"Look at you wooing the men," Jin cooed at her, then he snapped his fingers at Matteo and held out his hand. "Our money, if you please."

Jin tightened his grip on his umbrella when Matteo leaned forward, but he was only withdrawing a purse from the table at his side. The man had the money waiting.

He tossed it at Jin and frowned when he slipped it in his pocket. "Aren't you going to count it?"

"No, and if I have to come here again, you will regret it," Arthie said. "You're not as out of reach as you think."

Matteo sat back. The emerald of his eyes went flat, a forest at dark. "We all have our secrets or the world would be out of currency. Isn't that right, darling?"

The lamp flickered on the table, reflecting off the glass cabinets behind him.

Every aristocrat had their fair share of dark secrets, from affairs and extortion to distasteful dealings that built the ladder upon which high society had climbed so high. In that regard, Matteo Andoni almost *was* out of reach—*almost*.

"You know it more than any of us, dropping notes in official mailboxes, whispering private affairs to prim ladies," Matteo said. "Stirring up chaos."

"Vengeance," corrected Arthie. "I have no interest in chaos." Not directly. Nor did she have any reservations about making her intentions clear.

"Semantics," he replied with a shrug.

Arthie kept her seething to herself.

Matteo took that as permission to continue. "And your offerings? Vampires can easily find thralls on the streets, especially when there's nothing quite like the euphoria of being pierced by their fangs. You decided to take what's freely available and turn a profit. Thievery at its finest."

"Innovation," Arthie corrected again, flint in her bones. Before Spindrift, before her pistol, she was nothing. An orphan on the street, picking pockets and nicking blankets with a stumbling tongue and fumbling hands, eyes round as the moon and just as hungry. "Or is it a sin when it's me and an achievement to be applauded when it's those in power? When it's that wretched trading company leeching resources from the east?"

Matteo blinked. "You know, I mostly *was* applauding you."

"You'd do well to remember," Arthie said, ignoring him and turning to leave, "that some secrets are worth more than others."

Matteo hummed. "You know it more than anyone, Arthie, the girl who pulled pistol from stone."

Arthie didn't flinch. All of White Roaring knew about Calibore, the breechloader that no one but she had been able to pull free. It was nothing. Only a few more seconds and she would have left, money in her hand and brittle peace in her mind, but Matteo wasn't finished.

"Arthie, the girl who came to Ettenia in a boat full of blood."

She froze and turned back.

Matteo was on his feet now, and that damned dimple made another appearance. But it wasn't because he was gloating. No, something unnerving sparkled in his gaze, as if he could understand what she'd been through. As if he was on her side.

She couldn't let that stand. She refused. Arthie stepped closer. Close enough to rile Ivor, and she heard Jin hold the butler back with a soft *tsk*.

"I've always wondered why you never visit Spindrift after hours," Arthie said, shifting the conversation away from herself. She wanted him to know she had been watching long enough to figure him out. "We both know you have no appetite for tea."

Yes, Matteo Andoni was almost out of reach except for one glaring secret.

Jin drew a quick breath. "You—you're a vampire."

Matteo said nothing. He was young, too young for his work to have spread so far and so wide without immortality on his side.

"Most artists only ever see success long after they've rotted in their graves. But here you are, early twenties and a household name. Imagine what White Roaring would think," Arthie mused, "if they knew their beloved painter wasn't even alive. Terrible for business, really. You might not even have a place in society anymore."

"Yet you won't tell a soul," the vampire said quietly, not at all alarmed.

"And why's that?" But it was true. Arthie didn't sell her goods for cheap. Secrets were meant to ferment; they aged well. The longer they sat, the higher their value.

"Because you can't resist the power of a threat. I, on the other hand," he continued, drawing attention to his fingers, which were twisting a Spindrift syringe sparkling with blood, "only need to shout about your illicit affairs, and I promise you the guard at the top of the street won't hesitate before galloping over. It's funny how quickly they can move when you least want them to."

It would take more than a syringe to bring her down, but Arthie was nothing if not careful.

"Jin," Arthie said.

Jin sighed, recognizing the tone. "As you wish, little sister." In one move, he tossed his umbrella to his other hand and snatched up the revolver she'd told him—several times—to pack.

Matteo's gaze widened. She liked her men a little afraid of her.

"I do think we can talk—" he started.

Jin squeezed the trigger.

The sound of the gunshot blasted in the chamber. Matteo crumpled to the ground with a surprised yelp, and Arthie shook away the ringing in her ears.

The vampire started quivering. Arthie frowned until he fell back, laughter rattling the glass of the cabinets behind him. Thick blood oozed from his wound, darker than crimson against his pale, ivory skin. Dead skin. Dead blood. "I liked this shirt."

The butler cried out in anguish.

"Oh don't worry, old boy," Matteo said, carefully extracting the bronze bullet with two slender fingers and a grimace. The skin around the wound was bruised a deathly shade. She almost felt sorry for him, until he looked up at her and winked slowly, with vanity. "Every good love story starts with a bullet to the heart."

Arthie didn't like the way those words shot through her veins. She picked up the syringe. "Next time I'll make sure you stay dead."

"I abhor violence!" Matteo called after her.

She shoved out into the night, Jin at her side. She knew before she looked to the top of the street that the uniformed men would no longer be there, not because she believed Matteo Andoni had any sway over them, but because she recognized the footsteps of her young runner pounding through the darkness, approaching 337 Alms Place.

Chester emerged from the fog, breathless and panting, gripping the gate from the street side. His blond head was bright in the moonlight.

"Horned Guard on the way to Spindrift. There's going to be a raid."

2

JIN

"Welcome to Spindrift. Here's what you need to know," Jin had said to the new recruit before they opened that morning. "At seven bells, the tearoom doors lock shut. No patrons in, everyone out. No exceptions, no matter how dashing the smile. Slide the shutters over the glass and come round to the back. Now, shuffle this bookcase and take down those frames. Will you look at that, the bloodhouse is nearly open for business."

The new girl shivered. Jin couldn't blame her.

"Make your way to the booths," he continued. He had enough to do, but no one else could show her the workings better than the one who had made it all, bit by bit, idea by idea. "Take that vase off. Set it on the table that unfolds from the right. Come back to the shelf, reach for the latches on either side, and a bed will unfold. Better if you don't think about what happens in here, eh? Unless that's your thing." He winked. "Step out. That gap between the stall wall? Reach in, pull out the door, angle it closed."

He paused to take in her awe. "Now our booth is a bedroom. Do it again, and again, and again. Oh, and make sure you have your uniforms ready. One's for serving our prim, aristocratic patrons, and the other's a little more alluring for our vampire friends who come from all walks of life."

She followed him out to the floor, where the tables were set with small bowls of depleting sugar cubes and cream pots to be cleaned. The smell of tea clung to the air. Jin plucked a tray from a passing server and shoved it in the new girl's hands, sweeping the ceramics onto it.

"Every other table folds away. First in half, then directly into the floor, like so. Slide the chairs to the wall and while you're there, push on this lever and sit back—a settee will come out and meet you."

Jin fell back, slipping through air as the sofa unfolded and cocooned him in a plush cushion. He propped up his legs and lifted his eyebrows. "That's Spindrift. Tearoom by light, bloodhouse by dark."

Now, hours later, it was time to do the reverse.

As the clock tower struck two, Jin and Arthie burst through the back doors of Spindrift, sign as sharp as its owner, bricks as bright as her ambition. The place couldn't have been more alive. Jin paused as he always did, allowing himself to savor its warm embrace.

Arthie glanced at her pocket watch. "Seventeen minutes until the peace posse arrives."

They only needed nine. Four to clear the floor and five to transform the place. They had this mastered.

The lights were down low, softening the edges to a bewitching glow over the midnight crowd: the undead who came to feast and the blood merchants who came to get paid. The crew bustled among tables, decanters glittering as they topped off teacups full of red. Vampires lounged, their conversations hushed, laughter dulcet and deep. Some relaxed with the day's papers while others converged near the dark wainscot walls, slips of shadow against the floral damask decorating the upper half. At the far end, a vampire and a blood merchant tucked into one of the private rooms as another pair exited the room beside it.

These weren't the vampires with exclusive access to the elite society of snobbery known as the Athereum, but they dressed and acted as if they were lords and ladies anyway, and it made Jin even more proud of Spindrift and the allure he and Arthie had created.

Spindrift was more than a business. It was a safe place, and not just for their crew of orphans and castaways. In Ettenia, vampires had lived for decades in relative secrecy, indistinguishable from the living, until a massacre had thrown their existence into sudden blinding light.

Twenty years ago, the Wolf of White Roaring brutalized the streets, ripping out throats until rivulets of red ran down the district. Though the Wolf did not drink from his victims so much as he mauled them, survivors spoke of fangs and a scarlet stare. He was a vampire, though no one had known at the time, and it was strange they'd never found the one responsible.

"Almost as if the attack had been created for a purpose," Arthie would sometimes say.

After all, fear became hate when it festered long enough. The world always teemed with darkness, Ettenia had just given it a new name.

A far from difficult task, for vampires were predators to begin with and it was almost too easy. A mysterious man murdering women for hire? Blame it on vampires. A woman who up and decided to kill her cheating husband? She had to be undead. It didn't matter if the majority of vampires acted with decorum, and though the richer vampires could assimilate into high society with no one the wiser, the commonalty had no place but the shadows and, thus, rare access to blood.

Vampires might have to exercise restraint when feeding so as not to drain their marks, but they weren't rabid. They didn't go on killing sprees when they could quietly slip their fangs into their victims for a treat. The

Wolf of White Roaring, at the time of his attack, was different—a half vampire, torn between the living and the dead.

Traditionally, a vampire was born when a person on the brink of death ingested vampire blood. Whether they were exsanguinated by an undead or died of other means, the process was the same: Drink an adequate amount of vampire blood in those precious seconds, and the deed was done.

Half vampires were different. They were fed vampire blood while they were still alive, and often against their will, giving them all the energy of the living and *then some*, enough to unleash their pain upon the innocent without even realizing it.

They were weaker than their counterparts, but still able to become full vampires the same way humans could. Both full and half vampires drank blood to survive, both bore no reflection in a mirror. Full vampires cast no shadow, half ones did. Unlike full vampires who were frozen at the age they were turned, half vampires matured at a pace much slower than humans until they eventually stopped.

Regardless, here in Spindrift, vampires could be themselves for a while. Jin struck his umbrella on the floorboards, drawing the room's attention. Crimson eyes turned his way, the sign of vampires who had gorged their fill.

"Wrap it up," Arthie announced. "Spindrift closes in ten."

The din rose to a soft buzz. Vampires were a quiet lot, fazed by little. With heightened hearing and increased speed, it only made sense. Several flagged down last-minute teacups of blood—many asking for Jin's signature coconut-blood blend, which Spindrift had been out of for quite some time—and others departed with satisfied sighs, retracted fangs, and chaste kisses to the backs of one another's hands.

Jin and Arthie got to work.

"You want to tell me what that was back there at Matteo Andoni's house?" Jin asked her, dragging the shutters down.

She spotted a dark spill and tossed someone a mop. "You shot him."

"Because you used the tone," Jin said, and Arthie tipped her head at one of their more popular and scantily dressed blood merchants.

Though most blood merchants filled large glass syringes and called it a day, this one offered her services in the private rooms, where a vampire could drink directly from the source. The euphoria from a vampire's fangs and whatever else transpired in a room had its perks, Jin supposed.

"What tone?" Arthie asked, picking up a decanter. Her eyes reflected the scarlet of its contents.

Jin lifted his eyebrows. "The one that says, 'Jin, please shoot the pretty man.'"

"Well then, you can't blame me for your lack of morales."

"Morals. The word you're looking for—"

"You know I can say all that and more in two other languages, both of which have far more letters than Ettenian, so don't patronize me, Jin," she snapped. He jerked back and paused. Arthie paused too before grabbing a rag. "Don't look at me like that."

"Matteo really has you riled up, doesn't he?" Jin asked, holding in a laugh. It was cute, he had to admit, Arthie being all worked up because Matteo had flaunted a dimple and taunted her with the suggestion of a love story.

She snapped her pocket watch closed with a muttered *riled*.

Jin clapped his hands and addressed the room. "Sorry to cut the night short, good friends, but if you would kindly leave the premises, I would be much obliged."

Chairs were pushed back, coins clinked. The last of the vampires stepped through the back doors with nods, waves, and hat tips. Everyone had a heartbeat, a flush to their skin. Well-fed vampires were as close to living as they could get.

It took three minutes and forty-nine seconds for the floor to clear, and then the true chaos erupted.

"Reni!" Arthie yelled. "Tea!"

Reni brewed good tea. Always the right steep, the perfect shade. It was the only reason Arthie let him wander the floor during morning hours, considering he preferred blood himself. An odd fellow. Fresh kettles thudded onto stovetops, ready ones whistled, and before long, steady hands were pouring steaming tea into bowls to mask the stench of blood.

It was a rhythm in Jin's veins.

"Pick up the pace," Arthie shouted, sliding the bookcase in place and sealing the back door. "Leave that, unlock the front. Chester, the glasses. You three get in uniform, and the rest of you out of sight."

Spindrift being a bloodhouse was no secret. White Roaring knew it. The crew knew it. Every member of the Horned Guard knew it. The difference was in the proof: None existed. Except for that syringe Matteo had, of course. Jin still didn't know how he'd managed to pilfer it. Only the crew was allowed to handle the supplies used for bloodletting, and they were instructed to do so with care and precaution.

"Felix, fetch the mirrors," Arthie ordered as Jin passed her the tubes full of blood and sterilized bundles of surgical instruments to tuck underneath the floorboards in the front.

Every few weeks, the Horned Guard would try something new: elaborate raids, claiming incorrect paperwork to stall shipments of tea and coconuts, all but defaming Spindrift in the newspapers.

"Maybe we ought to hide your pistol," Jin suggested, wiping down the counter. Sure, everyone knew about it, but there was a difference between knowing about it and having it shoved in your face. He glanced at its grip etched in black filigree that gave it an ethereal look, once smeared with the fingerprints of those who had tried to pull it free using chisels and axes and everything in between.

Really, all they'd needed were the small hands of a small girl from a small island far, far away. A girl who had been wronged, cheated, stolen.

Arthie tucked away the night's invoices and looked at him like he'd dropped his wits on the run here. "They're regular old guards, Jin. Since when are we afraid of them?"

But Matteo's words had struck a little too close. Something about this night had riled *him* too, and it wasn't the artist's dimple.

"They send a higher-ranked guard with every new raid," he said.

Arthie did that thing with her face, a dismissal that pulled back one side of her mouth. "Don't start doubting your handiwork now."

Everyone took the slip, slide, and click transformation of Spindrift for granted. Not Arthie. She never forgot the weeks it took to make it work, and the strain it had put on Jin. Arthie didn't forget anything.

When Jin was seven he'd wished for a sister. When he was eleven Arthie had pulled him out of death's embrace. Jin still remembered squinting up at her ratty and dirty figure, the kind of person his father, dressed in the finest wool and the shiniest shoes, would point out to him from the carriage window and say, "See, these are the people you will help one day, little heron."

His father hadn't been there to witness the roles reversed.

She was, simply put, a tempest in a bottle, tiny and simmering and ready to obliterate. White Roaring had whittled her sharp as a blade and her wits just the same.

How far she'd come from the girl in rags to a master in a tailored suit, baker boy hat pulled over the swoops of her mauve hair, a pinstripe waistcoat snug over her crisp shirt, cuffs neat, collar popped, suit jacket always open *because I'm no straightlace.* The jacket matched the belt slung low and angled on her hips, pistol on full display.

"Any news on the coconut?" Arthie asked when Jin grabbed a coir brush for a stubborn patch of blood. Coconut husks really did make the best brushes.

Spindrift's imports consisted of tea and coconuts from Arthie's homeland of Ceylan, but with a blight affecting crops across the island, they hadn't replenished their coconut stores in months.

Jin shook his head. He could have sworn the light in her eyes dimmed a little as she rearranged their various tins of loose-leaf tea, from plain and robust black teas to delicate white teas and curated blends infused with fruit and other flavors—though Arthie refused to brew any atrocity at Spindrift that wasn't truly *tea*, like chamomile or peppermint.

"At least our tea's safe, eh?" he said. Without it, they'd have no tearoom. Coconut, on the other hand, they only used to enhance the experience of the bloodhouse. "And still no word from our palace snitchers. Pol heard today that they might be on lockdown."

They had a network of maids and stewards and household staff willing to trade whispers for coin but hadn't heard from anyone in the palace in nearly two weeks.

"The *palace* might be on lockdown?" Arthie asked, lifting her brows in surprise.

Jin nodded. He didn't know if that meant the Ram was worried about someone getting in or out.

"They're almost here!" the lookout shouted over the ruckus of sliding tables and clinking teacups. Jin tensed.

"*Dulce periculum*, brother," Arthie reminded him, holding up her left arm.

He knocked the back of his right hand against the back of hers. Their knuckles rapped. "We were made for trouble, you and me."

Figures silhouetted through the frosted glass of Spindrift's doors as the last settee folded into the wall and the rest of the crew disappeared. Jin yanked up the flip-top table and stepped behind it. Arthie was in front of him.

The doors flew open without a knock, and five uniformed guards stepped inside. The outline of a head with wicked horns was emblazoned on their breasts in silver thread. The badge of the Ram, Ettenia's latest masked monarch.

A server scampered forward. "Hello, sirs. Can I interest you in a cup of White Roaring's best tea? Royal Ettenian's my favorite."

The guards looked perplexed. No self-respecting tearoom would be open this late, but Arthie liked to swamp them, get the men a little dazed and distracted, taunt them with what they already knew—especially when the alternative was awkward silence.

"Try the Ceylani Supreme. Best tea in the country, really," another crew member called, looking up from the sink. "Never mind the capital."

"Always go with the Crimson Gem myself," said a third, leaning close. "Nothing beats a good spiced pekoe."

If Arthie was a tea, that was what she would be. It was brewed with care and steeped with just the right amount of spices that brought out earthy, smoky undertones as the leaves unfolded. It demanded perfection, conferred the best, and punished anything that wasn't with downright bitterness.

"Gentlemen." She inclined her head on cue. Jin could only see the back of Arthie's mauve head, but he knew her smile was the edge of a razor. "Noise complaint? I understand the clinking of teacups can be a little . . . aggressive at two in the morning. Always a lot to clean and prepare for our morning guests."

The one in charge of the lot puffed out his chest and stomped closer. His livery was a light gray and stood in contrast to the solid black of the others. If only he knew that every last bit of proof the clods needed was underneath the floorboards at his feet. "You think you're a king, Casimir. Defying the law."

"Did you hear that, Jin? I'm King Arthie now." She turned back to the guards. "Laws enacted by men like you scrawling words they believe they might understand? Laws vilifying anyone who isn't as peaky as you?" She leaned back, slinging a hand across the bar top. He really did look peaky in the light: pale and an almost sickly white. "No, Sergeant. Can't defy a law that doesn't include me."

She was right. Ettenian laws were created for the white man, usually at the expense of anyone who didn't share their pallor. This was how someone like Matteo Andoni could live a markedly different life than someone like Arthie.

The sergeant's gaze lit up eagerly. "Touchy subject, is it? Having trouble keeping up with rent, I heard. That's the problem when folk like you come to a place where we have rules. I hear it's only a matter of time before they evict you and your lot."

Jin's brow furrowed. They made every payment for the building— on time.

"Time to get your ears cleaned then," Arthie said, betraying nothing.

"Then why do you look like you want to kill me?" the sergeant asked with a smirk.

"Oh, that's just my face," Arthie replied. "One gets a taste for blood when you have to lick your own wounds, you see."

The sergeant stared for a minute, very likely trying to find something to say, before he jerked his head at the others. "Start looking."

Jin flinched as a table and chair struck the far wall, followed by several stools. The men treated the tearoom like a pen to play in, tearing up the floors near the private rooms that were now secluded booths, one of them ducking his head and coming up empty.

"I didn't say ruin the place," the sergeant said tiredly. "If you're going to pull up the floors, find wherever it's hollow."

"How considerate," Jin commented, and lowered his voice to ask Arthie, "What's he on about us being behind on payments?"

Arthie said nothing. Something shattered.

Jin sighed and lifted his chin to the men ransacking the place. "Need some help over there?"

With a sneer, one of them crouched by the front doors and rapped his knuckles on the wood. Even here behind the counter, Jin could hear that damning echo.

The sergeant looked to Arthie.

Arthie looked back. "Have at it. I won't stop you."

Jin wanted to stop him. He wanted his life unscathed. He wanted *Spindrift* unscathed, and they were the same thing. The sergeant wedged his knife beneath the worn floorboards.

"Blow switch two," Arthie murmured to Jin.

Matteo Andoni had clearly shaken her if she thought that would tip anything in their favor. Blowing a bulb was the oldest trick in the book. The silliest. The most amateur.

"*Jin,*" she bit out.

One of these days she was going to get him killed, and he'd be too dead to whine about it.

He pressed down on the faulty power switch he had long ago put together under the counter, cursing a stray spark. Above them, one of the many suspended bulbs popped and hissed. The men looked up as the light bloomed brighter and made an alarming buzzing noise before it shattered, raining glass down on them. The length of wire swayed, bereft, and the sergeant shook the shards off and returned to work.

Some bloody good that did. The light had dimmed the space, nothing else.

"Patience, Jin," Arthie said when he glanced at her with exasperation. To the men, she said casually, "Apologies. You know how it is on this side of White Roaring. Power can be quite fickle around here."

This was the side of White Roaring that society had discarded, where the sound of a gunshot was as commonplace as a horse's whinny. Spindrift sat on the edge of it, half outcast, half gentry, rising from the rubble of its surroundings through sheer force of will. With every new secret a patron let slip, Arthie tucked some official or another into her arsenal, turning the slums into a kingdom of their own with Spindrift as their crown.

And the Ram, as the increasing number of raids made clear, was painfully aware of it.

Yet, with the guards seconds away from enough proof to hang them all, Arthie had never looked more at ease.

The sergeant yanked the floorboard out of place. There was a long pause and a murmur before he and the others rose, and Jin saw that the hollow beneath the floorboard was . . . hollow. Not a syringe or blood vial in sight, though he had watched Arthie putting both down that very hole mere moments ago.

"Seems you lost a good night's sleep over nothing," Jin goaded, setting his chin in his hands.

"Told you," one of the Horned Guards said, yawning loudly.

The sergeant shot him a dirty look and fixed the same on Arthie. "You think you're—"

Arthie cut him short by swinging open the door. "Whatever you're about to say, Sergeant, I don't think it, I know it."

Power was indeed fickle, and in the ever-changing landscape of White Roaring, the Casimirs were untouchable.

3
ARTHIE

Spilled tea and chipped cups were better than a prison cell, and the mood was celebratory as the crew began cleanup. Arthie locked the doors, watching the smudge of the Horned Guard's retreating carriage through the frosted glass.

"Do you want to tell us what happened to our stuff?" Jin asked, dark green coat slung over his arm. Someone handed him a cup of tea, and he breathed in the bold aroma infused with the sweet, sharp tang of bergamot and soft lavender. Lady Slate was his favorite. It suited him, as elegant and put together as he was.

"Yeah, boss, where'd everything go?" Chester echoed, and the others paused their work to listen. He'd been with Arthie and Jin ever since he was toddling about, and Spindrift was all he knew.

"Still here." Arthie picked up the floorboard and popped out Felix's mirrors from either side of the hollowed-out space. Behind them, tucked farther inside, was the bloodhouse stash. Arthie showed them the panels. "Remember?"

"You didn't tell me," Jin said with a frown, setting the cup on the saucer in his other hand. She resisted the urge to roll her eyes when he took another dainty sip with his pinky raised.

"Then why bust the bulb?" Reni asked, morose and quiet as ever.

Arthie passed him the panels. "Because any guard worth his salt knows a mirror when he sees one, but when the light buzzed they looked up, blinding them just enough to obscure the mirrors."

Baffled nods went around.

"Those cabbage hats got close!" Chester exclaimed. It was getting worse. No one said it, but everyone in the crew knew it.

Though Ettenia had grown from a kingdom to an empire, its ruling body remained the same. No one knew how the council decided to appoint the masked monarchs, and no one knew the faces behind each mask. Before the Ram was the Eagle, before him the Fox, always with unchecked, untrammeled, unbridled power.

The Ram was different, allying with the people over their fear of vampires, amending and reinforcing vampire-human laws, speaking aloud what every Ettenian was worried about. It was as simple as acknowledging the existence of vampires when the prior monarchs were content not to. Ettenians had never been happier to allow someone they didn't know to wear a crown and command a country that was slowly leashing the world.

But Arthie wouldn't allow the Ram to control Spindrift the way Ettenia controlled its colonies.

"No one's going to take Spindrift from us." She met Jin's eyes, knowing the reason for his concern. "And no, Jin, not even our proprietor."

That was a hiccup she would settle tonight.

Spindrift was but one part of her retribution for what this country had done to her. She'd spun a business out of tea leaves because the Ettenians had found her tiny island of Ceylan and cultivated it to their liking. What lives the Ettenian soldiers in red uniforms hadn't stolen were claimed either by disease or deforestation that spawned landslides and floods in a country unprepared for such wrath, simply because they wanted to make room for crops like rubber and tea.

They took Ceylan and called it a *colony* as if it was an honorable title, when they'd really made chattels out of both people and land, praising themselves for their villainy before doing it again and again and again.

If the peakies wanted to harvest the blood of her people for profit, she would make them pay for it in their own country, pocketing their secrets and wreaking as much havoc as they had in whatever form she could.

She supposed Spindrift wasn't simply *part* of her retribution, but the core of it—though Calibore came close.

For as long as Ettenia could remember a pistol had been lodged immovably in a plinth at the center of the busy White Roaring Square, time and age adhering legends and rumors to its ever-shining surface. They were fairy tales, really, carried on desperate tongues, born out of despair.

The one who draws Calibore free is our savior. The one who wields Calibore is Ettenia's right and true leader.

Arthie was neither of those things, only a girl who paid attention. It was hard to believe in fairy tales when she'd lived a nightmare, and it just so happened that legends were good for business.

The pistol had created a new market in Ettenia's economy, with merchants selling everything from luck charms to ointments promising a good grip. But it wasn't until Arthie tracked one such merchant through a shadowy alley to an official's grand manor that she realized the monarchy was involved.

A flocking crowd meant money spent and taxes paid, and in this scheme Ettenia was the ultimate puppeteer. With Jin in tow, Arthie had watched and waited until White Roaring Square was cordoned off by the Horned Guard, and the pistol effortlessly pulled from a disguised contraption by a pair of men for what was clearly maintenance. Calibore was a hoax: The pistol had been artificially fixed in place to exploit hopeful Ettenians. Still, the pistol *was* special: silver and strange, with a single bullet in a pristine chamber. Otherworldly, yes, but there was no legend holding it in place.

If Arthie hadn't seen firsthand what Ettenia had done to her people, she might have felt as betrayed as Jin had upon the revelation. Instead, she'd felt a glee so poignant, so acute, that even today, nearly a decade later, she remembered it.

Arthie wasn't like Jin, whose parents had done the immigrating for him, softening the thorns beneath his shoes and blunting the daggers that came with being different. She had come to Ettenia on a boat more than a decade ago. Alone and hungry, unable to communicate in any of the languages she knew. All she could do was observe.

It had taken weeks to learn the ropes of a swindle, to play the game that every man with polished shoes and muttonchops called good business. She was still a child, but when you saw the cruelty of the world firsthand, you became a little cruel yourself.

A great number of people had to be involved to uphold a false legend as complex as Calibore, and Arthie found enough loose lips and clandestine pasts to barter for what she needed: information on the years-old scheme. Jin took care of the rest, telling her why a particular angle was better in the morning than the afternoon, shoving a coconut with a straw into her hands while he perfected their timeline.

After days of plotting, White Roaring Square became her first mark, and she would never forget the way the people looked at her in the afternoon light.

The girl who pulled a pistol from plaster. She was dusty and dirty, but she didn't care. She'd found purpose that day. The Horned Guard stationed around Calibore looked as if they wanted to apprehend her, but there was no law stipulating that it had to be returned when it was finally pulled free.

The pistol was hers.

It wasn't waiting for a divine grip. It hadn't been left there by a long-forgotten enchanter for a future king. It was simply one of the many artifacts in Ettenia's possession. They collected trophies for *civilizing* countries that had never asked for a redefinition of the word.

Arthie, like her dead family, dead neighbors, and ravaged country, could tell you a tale or two about that. It started with trade, but every Ettenian was born with a mind-boggling, delusional sense of supremacy, and for them, the word *trade* translated to *take*. Ettenia conquered, and the EJC came in after, snatching up whatever it liked.

Without the hoax of Calibore, Arthie would never have found her true calling: vengeance. Without it, she would have remained trapped in her own skin, unable to escape her pain, to unleash her anger. Every day since, the Horned Guard waited for her to slip, to shoot the wrong man or steal the right document, anything to take her in and lock her up.

But she didn't abide by the law so much as she bent it. She didn't carry a weapon so much as her defiance—and weren't they one and the same?

Jin picked up his umbrella and handed Arthie her coat.

"Time to pay our proprietor a visit?" she asked.

He nodded. "We ought to ask him a few questions."

Arthie pulled up her collar as the doors swung shut behind them, muting the racket inside Spindrift.

Jin tugged on his favorite open-back gloves and sighed wistfully when they passed the abandoned warehouse at the end of the road where their forger used to take up residence, a two-story structure tee-tering toward the sea like a weed in search of sunlight.

Under the gaslights across the street, tarts waited for a sale, smoke curling from their cigars, hoopless skirts as starved as most on this side of White Roaring. Boys with caps pulled low meandered in the late crowds, swindling duvin. Arthie spotted four bloodhouse regulars blending in.

Spindrift stopped them from hunting on the streets and risking their victims dying or, even worse, waking up from the haze that came with a bite and lodging a complaint with the Horned Guard for drink-ing without consent. At Spindrift, vampires paid humans for their services.

Transactions, Arthie had learned, always made things easier. No one did anything for nothing, and neither would she.

Whether it was dangling a secret affair to ensure an unlicensed shipment got through, or reminding an official about his bastard child so she was given a warning before a raid. Arthie's pockets were full—of coin, of secrets, of people, and it aggrieved anyone on the shinier side of White Roaring.

"How's the new girl?" she asked. A banner announcing the open-ing of yet another new store ruffled in the breeze.

"Catching on," Jin replied. "I think she'll be good."

"Pretty doesn't mean good. Stay alert."

"You know, you should get out and see someone," Jin said even-tually. A decade ago, he wouldn't have spoken this way. Being a high society brat, he had been scandalized to walk about unchap-eroned with nine-year-old Arthie simply because she was a girl. But the world spun differently on this side of White Roaring. "Have a dally."

Arthie gave him a look. She wasn't like him. She didn't go around breaking hearts; she broke other things, like laws and contracts and bones.

"As the peakies like to say, you *are* pretty for a foreigner. Matteo seemed to like—"

Her face warmed. "Not. Another. Word."

Jin laughed, and when she didn't comment, he softened. "Ease up, Arthie. Whatever the Ram throws at us, we'll dodge it. We don't do the worrying. We create it."

"And if the proprietor's been compromised?" She got this far because she played a different game, but what happened when others decided to play it too? When the Ram got tired of sending sergeant after sergeant?

"The proprietor's had our back for five years," Jin reminded her.

Clouds wrapped the moon in gauze, and smoke snaked out of a nearby window, brawling with the salt breeze beyond. Arthie knew what it took to win in this country, the probabilities and the costs, every last tally rounding out in her head like the books she kept in her office.

Jin led her between two rickety flats over to the next street so they wouldn't have to squeeze past the fires the tarts lit in empty barrels to keep warm. He glanced at her. No one else could read her so well, and she felt lighter when he pretended to squint into the shadows only to turn and dangle a pocket watch on a chain in front of her. Arthie patted at her vest. *Her* pocket watch.

"Did you—"

Jin laughed and threw it at her. "Come on, you snail," he said, already loping ahead. "Race you to the docks?"

4

JIN

Jin loved the sea. The *hush hush* of the waves, the lazy sway of the moored boats. He loved its lie, the calm that masked strength like a beast unprovoked.

It reminded him of Arthie, who was already waiting as he passed the dry dock where the skeletons of vessels stuck out every which way, all broken bones and sorry masts. The windows of the port agencies against the cliff face were dark, but closer inland, the proprietor's usual late-night haunt, Eden Teahouse, was still lit like a lighthouse at sea.

Jin stuck his hands in his pockets, ignoring the way his limbs seized at the sight of a fire flickering in a bin by the steps. *Yellow. Orange. Red. RED.* The glint of a pocket watch pulled him free, followed by Arthie's comforting scent of coconut and a dark blend of tea that reminded him of a midsummer's night.

Arthie glanced at the flames and then at him before deciding against whatever she'd wanted to say, brushing hair out of her eyes. "Let's get this over with, shall we?"

They crossed the dock where the stone was shot through with dark mold. Arthie swept her hand down her side in reassurance. She treated Calibore like a lucky charm, though she'd never admit to it being one. Jin could understand that; she'd only ever had herself to rely on.

"Mister Proprietor," Arthie called, climbing the trio of weepy steps to the open porch where their landlord was seated at one of the tables exposed to the salty air. The teahouse was three stories made of soggy wood instead of brick and coated in sea rot instead of lacquer. Eden—both the place and the drinks it served—was a disgrace to tea.

"Casimir!" The proprietor's voice cracked in surprise. He was a polished older gentleman with a tiny mustache and specs as round as his bowler hat. He also happened to be one of the few people Arthie didn't mind seeing every month to hand off a wad of duvin.

"Long night?" she asked, because she didn't know small talk.

"Quite," the proprietor replied, flinching when Arthie dragged one of the chairs along the ground to sit opposite him. Jin leaned against the post near her and rapped on the grimy glass window. He would have preferred to have this meeting indoors, but he suspected Eden wouldn't be much better inside.

The door jangled open and a slender man glided out. "Welcome to Eden. Where our tea sends you to heaven—" He stopped when he saw Jin and Arthie, who cocked their brows at each other, and turned his attention to the proprietor. "Can I get you anything else, sir?"

Jin wasn't sure if he should be insulted that they weren't asked or honored to be spared.

"Oh, we won't be drinking, but thank you for asking," Arthie said anyway. She refused to drink tea that wasn't loose-leaf Ceylani. "My friend here will indeed have another cup. Jasmine, if you will?"

The man looked to the proprietor, who had the good sense to nod.

"Steeped extra well," Arthie added. Jin held back a snort. Jasmine was fickle, it had to be steeped for an exact number of seconds before it became too bitter to stomach. The man hesitated, but Jin silenced him with a look.

Lips pinched, the server disappeared inside, and the proprietor glanced from one Casimir to the other. Was he thinking about all the years they'd seen together? How they'd changed his life as much as he'd changed theirs?

Before their building was Spindrift, it was a museum known as the Curio, glittering from its prime location at the top of Stoker Lane, boasting artifacts from the colonies that the residents of White Roaring turned a pretty penny to see. That is, until Arthie decided those artifacts had to disappear and, worse, be mysteriously replaced with private collections stolen from thirteen homes in the capital's richest neighborhoods.

Of course, they'd have to do the stealing.

"Why?" Jin had wanted to know. It was ambitious: two weeks' worth of work in a night, and if they were sloppy, they'd rot in prison for the rest of their lives.

"Did they ask that when they came to take what was mine?" she replied. Those artifacts had been brought to Ettenia on East Jeevant Company ships.

Jin had called it theft.

"Reclamation," Arthie had said, her Ceylani tongue stumbling across the word. By then, Jin had taught her letters using old newspapers and her iron will.

The atrocity was on the cover of every paper the next day, destroying the Curio's reputation overnight. With headlines ranging from How Could They Do Such a Thing? to Did the Curio Believe No One Would Notice?

It was ironic the same questions were never asked when Ettenia did that elsewhere.

Still, no one believed the Curio would have destroyed its own artifacts, let alone stolen from someplace else. Only a curse could have caused such a thing to happen. And so, the building sat vacant for months because potential buyers feared falling under the same hex.

Jin still remembered stepping up to the proprietor's house one night beside Arthie. She was fourteen, Jin two years older.

"It's cursed," she'd reminded the proprietor. *Cursed by the Casimirs,* neither she nor Jin said aloud. "And you know as well as I do that you'll have no takers."

The proprietor, Arthie had learned, was running short on money, enough that he looked at them and then lingered on her pistol before he finally asked, "What do you suggest I do?"

"Give us six weeks," she said.

"We'll turn the place around and give you a cut of our profits," Jin continued. He pretended to think. "Say, ten percent?"

"Fifteen," the proprietor shot back immediately, exactly as Arthie had said he would.

She grinned and countered. "Thirteen. Only right for a cursed place."

It was the pistol, Arthie would later tell Jin after hammering out the finer details, and not the proprietor's desperation that made him accept her offer. There was a little bit of fairy tale in it, after all. She might not be White Roaring's savior, but she had its respect, however begrudging.

Eden Teahouse's bells jangled as the man returned with a tray. The proprietor took his first sip and immediately spat it back out while Jin watched his misfortune with pity.

Arthie was all teeth. "Not to your liking, Mister Proprietor?"

Jin could have sworn she grew in height by a few inches whenever she was scornful. To heaven indeed.

"Thank—" The proprietor cleared his throat, face twisting as he pushed his cup across the table. Jin bit his tongue. The sea beat at the rocks, laughing. "Thank you."

Jin leaned over and snapped a biscuit in two. "It's on us."

"Now"—Arthie stared at the proprietor until the man looked away—"we're not ones for gossip, but we've been hearing whispers."

"Correct me if I'm wrong, but it seems Spindrift is behind on our dues," Jin said.

The proprietor said nothing, but he wrung his hands and couldn't meet either of their eyes. That was enough proof of his guilt.

"Five years now. Not a single missed payment," Jin continued, quiet and slow.

"Each one bigger than the last," Arthie added.

The proprietor scratched at his head with a laugh that rattled like dice in a drunk man's cup.

Jin gripped his umbrella. "What's with the laugh?"

He mopped at his brow, muttering incoherently. Their proprietor had indeed been compromised.

"Next time, I'm placing a bet," Arthie told Jin.

"I was only trying to be optimistic," he replied. He'd expected more from the man. If Jin was being honest, he was even hurt by the betrayal.

In one sharp move, Arthie snatched the specs off the proprietor's face and slammed them on the table. The lenses shattered but remained in place. One loose stone made for an imperfect foundation, and the proprietor was faulty mortar in her empire. He sputtered in surprise.

"Put them on," said Arthie.

The proprietor didn't move.

"*Put them on*," Arthie repeated, voice as quiet as the night. "Or Jin will help you."

Jin scanned the dry dock and the surrounding offices. Behind the glass of Eden Teahouse, the thin man was smart enough not to obtrude. The proprietor reached for the specs with trembling hands, hesitating before putting them back on his face.

"Do you see how the world looks when you wrong me?" she asked. This was why Arthie didn't need dead bodies littering the streets of White Roaring. She had her ways. They kept her clean and the whispers rolling.

He clutched at the specs and nodded.

"Let's try this again," Arthie said. "Why is the Horned Guard speaking of eviction when we've abided by our agreement for half a decade?"

"I might have even thought we were friends," Jin said with a sad laugh.

The proprietor . . . stopped. He stopped trembling, he stopped wringing his hands. Jin thought he might have stopped breathing too.

"They threatened my family," he finally said. The admission was a whisper on the breeze. "I know what the pair of you are capable of, but I also know your limits. You might threaten me, you might threaten to run my coffers dry or never let my daughters marry, but you will not kill them."

Arthie went still.

"Our arrangement is no longer because in two weeks the building will no longer be mine. I—I am deeply sorry."

She flinched at the kindness in his tone, the pity. Jin didn't know how to react. If the building no longer belonged to the proprietor, who *did* it belong to, and what did that mean for them and Spindrift?

"Who are 'they'?" Arthie asked.

The proprietor pulled a letter from his coat and set it on the table. The wind ripped at its edges, but he held it in place. Jin pushed away from the post and looked over Arthie's shoulder, his stomach sinking at the sight of that insignia with horns that curled like those of the devil.

The Ram was kicking them out. In two weeks.

Arthie looked down at the proprietor. "Leave White Roaring."

The man's head snapped up. His eyes were fractionated and comical behind the shattered lenses. "But—but my properties."

"Properties?" Arthie laughed, low and humorless. "The only one that mattered was Spindrift, and it's no longer yours. If you set foot in the district again, I will fit you in a box and ship you off. Your occupation is the least of your concerns."

She might not hurt his family, but a slight was a slight, and Arthie did not forgive any more than she forgot.

People are afraid of you, Jin remembered saying once, feeling a little afraid himself.

That's not true, but it will be, she'd replied. She was always pushing the limit, reaching for more, prodding beasts with sticks when she was in the cage with them.

At last the proprietor nodded.

"Now," she commanded.

"But—how?" he protested. "The vampires outside the city!"

"We're holding your life in our hands, and you're worried about someone taking a sip out of you?" Jin asked.

Vampires were victims just as much as humans lately, disappearing without a trace. There was a new report this morning, a new ripple of disquiet through the underworld because despite inquiries and investigations, there was nothing to be found on those who had gone missing. No proof of a struggle, no bodies or weapons, no ransom notes.

Given Jin's early education, he had an extensive vocabulary of words he'd use to describe vampires. They were deadly, cruel, sibylline, and powerful. Bestial and sanguisuge. Beautiful and vicious. *Endangered* had never been one of those words.

For being undead, they had quite the physique, with some rumored to have fascinating gifts, such as the ability to manipulate the elements or even control minds. It was dangerous and frightening and really quite unfair, but they were well-nigh impossible to kill, which made their disappearances extra troubling.

The proprietor hiccuped and nodded, at last, in what could only be understanding.

Jin tilted his head. "This is the part where you grab your hat and make a run for it."

The man nodded again, hastening out of his chair. He tripped on one of the legs as he staggered down the wooden steps like a boulder rolling about and took off without a backward glance.

The waves crashed against the cliff face, angry and restless, heaving a new weight into the proprietor's absence. In the five years since opening its doors, not once had they ever truly feared Spindrift might close.

Arthie set a trio of duvin on the table for the tea and turned to Jin.

"I—" he started.

"Home?" she asked.

She was calm. Too calm. But Jin was too frazzled to question it. *Two weeks.* He simply nodded, wondering how much longer Spindrift could be defined as home.

5

ARTHIE

Back in Spindrift, Arthie slung her coat over her arm and headed up the stairs to tally the day's invoices in her office. *Too tired to sleep*, she'd told Jin. The numbers would help her clear the fog in her mind.

Seeing the glee of her rivals would feel even worse than losing Spindrift itself. If there was anyone outside the Ram who would rejoice, it would be the Athereum. The underworld was home to White Roaring's elite vampires, a society standing by its own rules and regulations. It was just as powerful as the monarchy, even if unofficially.

Most notably, the Athereum wasn't fond of Arthie's catering to the common vampire any more than she was fond of their pretension.

With a sigh, Arthie closed the glass-paneled doors behind her and settled in her chair, not bothering with the light. She cracked open the cabinet by her desk and took out her slowly diminishing decanter of coconut water. The liquid inside sloshed as she poured exactly a quarter of a cup and drained it, clarity returning when she set down her glass.

That was when she realized two things: There was a breeze coming in from the window she had closed hours ago, and a figure was silhouetted on the sill.

She slammed on the light switch under her desk, dousing her intruder in hazy gold.

A boy. *A Horned Guard.*

He sat against the window frame with far more gall than he should have had the sense to display. In her office. In her *home*.

"The great Arthie Casimir." His voice lilted in an accent that hinted of elsewhere, and his white hair sat stark against his brow. He couldn't have been much older than her.

The Horned Guard was large, with numerous ranks to enforce Ettenian law on every level. The lighter a guard's uniform was in color, the higher they were ranked.

His uniform was snow white. A captain.

Arthie lunged out of her chair, finding a grip on the checkered scarf he had draped around his shoulders. They staggered, shoes scuffing the floorboards, until she threw him up against the wall.

"Give me one good reason why I shouldn't flay you," Arthie hissed, pressing her knife against his neck. He might have been a head taller, and she might have been alone, but she didn't care.

"Because I can give you what you need," he said, and she took pride in the strain in his voice.

"All I need right now is a shovel to dig your grave," Arthie seethed.

His chest heaved. His features were rugged, a ruthless sort of beautiful.

"Tell me," he said softly, tilting closer until his throat bobbed against her blade, "do you remember what it's like to live?"

She stumbled back, releasing his shirt. Her mind and limbs were slow to communicate. His eyes clutched hers, knocking her off-kilter, and she saw herself in them. An unshakable pain. An endless torment.

He straightened his clothes, severing the connection, and before he could blink, she cocked her pistol and the night went quiet. The shutters ceased their creaking, and a restless silence crowded through the window.

"Such vain weapons, guns. Loud. Violent. Jarring," he mused before his voice fell flat. "Put that away."

"You forget, guard," Arthie murmured. "Spindrift is my home, and you've set foot in the wrong den."

"Oh, but I hear that in a fortnight Spindrift will be brought to the ground and your cargo blown back to the sea," he said, unaffected by the barrel pointing at his chest. "We'll have ourselves a tempest of tea on the horizon."

Arthie took a step closer to him, her aim steady. "Now you're simply begging to die."

"I will not beg for what's been promised." He took an equal step closer, and the barrel of her gun settled over his heart. She felt the warmth of his exhale, the cool sting of mint on his breath.

He lowered his chin.

"I'd like to propose an alliance." There was something dark in the timbre of his voice when he said it. "The palace is in lockdown, leaving staff and many officials trapped, because the Ram is in a frenzy. Confidential documents have gone missing. Specifically, a ledger."

The Ram, in a frenzy. If only Arthie could rejoice. But at least now she knew why she hadn't heard from her snitchers. The palace really was under lockdown.

"It's damning enough to threaten royal rule," he continued. "The Council could oust the Ram."

The Council was as arcane as the way they chose their monarchs and the masks they hid behind. By all appearances, they offered so little resistance that the Ram ruled the empire autocratically. If it could spur the Council into action, the ledger was damning indeed.

"And how do you know this?" she asked.

He gave her a look. "I work for the Ram."

"Every Horned Guard does." She wouldn't let him get away with half-truths, especially when his uniform was nothing like a typical guard's.

He hesitated a beat. "I'm one of several high captains sworn to act with discretion because the Ram doesn't want the disappearance known."

She'd heard of high captains but had never seen one to know they really existed.

"Known by whom?" Arthie asked, sensing that he was choosing his words with great care.

"Officials, advisers," he said, then worked his jaw. "Potentially other countries. A confidential ledger does mean illicit transactions."

Which meant this was trade related, possibly even connected to the East Jeevant Company. Her distaste for both the Ram and the EJC only continued to grow.

But things like that didn't just go missing. No, it was stolen by someone who knew exactly what they were doing.

"And you've been tasked with retrieving it," she surmised. With a mirthless laugh, she dug the barrel into his rib cage, forcing him back against the wall. "Do you think I'm desperate enough to work for the Ram?"

"Do you think I'm reckless enough to confide in White Roaring's favorite criminal?"

What a compliment.

He looked like he was trying to calm himself. "We might be on opposite sides of the law, Casimir, but we can both agree the Ram has too much power."

This boy just might be the first Horned Guard she ever agreed with.

"And I have no intention of handing over the ledger to anyone," he continued. "I want to take the Ram down with it."

"Treasonous words, but I have no desire to get involved with politics," Arthie replied.

"No? Not even if you can leverage that ledger to save Spindrift first?"

He might even be the first Horned Guard to leave her speechless. To give her *hope*.

"If I use the ledger to save Spindrift," she said, "you lose any chance of toppling the Ram with it."

The boy grinned. "Oh, but you're smart enough to do both."

She wouldn't give in to his flattery. She might have been smart enough to do both, but that didn't mean she would. As much as she'd love to see the Ram gone, Arthie preferred her method of chaos. She couldn't blackmail someone she'd nixed. She couldn't be a thorn in someone's side if they no longer existed.

The high captain didn't need to know that. Besides, she had no reason to fix a country that wasn't hers.

She pulled back, holstering her pistol. "And why should I believe you?"

He could easily make use of Arthie and her crew's resources, steal the ledger, and turn tail. He could go even further and claim *Arthie* had stolen it and lock them up for good. They might agree about the Ram's reign, but that didn't change the fact that the boy in front of her worked for the monarch.

And nothing good ever came from partnering with the enemy.

"You holstered your pistol because you've already decided you don't have to," he said.

He was perceptive.

"But I doubt I'm the only high captain who thought you might be of use. I'm offering you a deal. The others won't be so friendly."

She knew cunning when she saw it. "I don't like being threatened."

"Then don't let them threaten you."

If what he said about the other captains was true, they'd no sooner discuss their plans with the Ram than come directly to Arthie.

"All right," she said, gathering the invoices on her desk. "Where was it last seen?"

"In the Athereum."

The Athereum. That all-powerful vampire society where entrance was restricted to those with dedicated markers, and trespassers were killed with a stake through the heart. She couldn't waltz in. No one could.

"White Roaring is full of petty crooks. Take your pick. The Horned Guard seizing Spindrift doesn't make me a criminal any more than it makes you a saint, so enjoy your tea. I wish I could say it was a pleasure, but I'm not one to lie."

She started for the door to see him out.

"Are you aware of what happened to the museum known as the Curio?" he said from behind her.

She paused.

"Priceless artifacts stolen and replaced with those from the private collections of White Roaring's elites, all in a single night. They still haven't caught the robbers or the relics they stole from the museum that stood where your establishment does now. Such an odd coincidence, isn't it?"

It wasn't coincidence. It was her and Jin, and he knew it. Arthie chewed the inside of her cheek. He'd somehow sniffed them out. But how?

"Did you know there were rumors of a young brown girl in the museum that very morning?" he asked. "Foreigners aren't known to peruse colonizer collections."

She wouldn't indulge him. "And because I was in the museum before the theft happened, you believe I'm capable of thievery."

The guard almost looked amused. "You only need to be present in the room when the ledger goes missing again. This isn't a job for a pickpocket. Whoever infiltrates the notorious society has to have the right connections and knowledge of vampires. That's you."

Arthie wished Jin were here to hear all this praise. She returned to her desk and shuffled the mess on top of it.

"And once we worm our way into the Athereum, are we to grab every book we see until we find it?"

"It's a bound ledger. Violet ribbon, standard leather casing. Nothing out of the ordinary, but it's in the possession of a man named Penn Arundel who hasn't been seen outside the Athereum in weeks."

Sheets slipped out of her grasp and floated to the ground. Disquiet quivered through her at the name, but she couldn't let him see it.

"And," she started, stringing words together, "does the Ram know it's in the Athereum?"

"Not to my knowledge," the high captain said, and she wondered just how many guards with ears all over the city reported to him—and how much of those reports never made it to the Ram. "Otherwise we might have seen an army storming the place."

Arthie didn't think that would do any good, and the Ram had to have known as much. Vampires were a force to be reckoned with, but Athereum vampires with bottomless resources on hand? The Ram wouldn't stand a chance. Still, Arthie couldn't tell if the captain was certain the Ram didn't know, or if he was assuming as much *because* no one had yet stormed the place.

"If only you weren't so good at what you do, Casimir." He gave the room a slow perusal, pausing at the double doors when laughter rose from the lower floor, free and unrestrained. She thought she heard sympathy in his voice. "Spindrift might never have grown to the point where it threatened the Ram's ego."

The Ram's ego. That was a good way to put it. Arthie wasn't a menace to society, she wasn't ruining the economy. Spindrift wasn't loud or brash or an eyesore. She, a lower-class immigrant, was successful, and that made people mad.

"Seems you're on a quick path to becoming a criminal yourself," Arthie said, refusing to let him get through to her.

He gave her a soft smile. "I'm no criminal. I still work for the law that you break by breathing."

"Did you learn that from the little handbook the Horned Guard gives every recruit?" Arthie asked with a laugh. "What's in it for you? The Ram might need a reckoning, but by allying with me, you're risking your life."

"Is that not the duty of a guard?" he asked.

Self-righteous sod. She didn't believe him, but what he offered was enough to make her overlook it. For now.

When she said nothing, he tilted his head. "I take it you agree to the job then?"

She pinched her lips. She didn't even know his name. "Have you ever seen a lion? The people you work for sometimes snatch them along with the tea, spices, and everything else they steal."

He looked down at his wrist, and she saw that it was wrapped in a gauntlet with a blade along the inside. "I lived past the reign of one."

For the sake of this job, Arthie hoped he was being figurative.

"One," Arthie repeated with a mocking laugh. "And here you're asking me to infiltrate the Athereum, very much a *den* of lions, and bring something back. No, for a job like that, I'll need—"

"Duvin?" He looked disappointed.

Arthie scoffed. "I like my money hard-earned, thank you. I'll need to put together a crew."

She eyed him. He had sprung in through her second-story window. He was lithe and light-footed. Not only had he scaled the building, but he moved soundlessly too. And having a high captain of the Horned Guard on her side might prove useful.

If he *was* on her side. Yet another reason to keep him close.

"And if I'm breaking into the Athereum, you're coming with me,"

Arthie said. "Once I get that ledger, you will get me in front of the Ram."

That particular bit was a lie. Once she had it, the captain would be her biggest threat—he'd be close enough to nick it from her *and* close enough to report her whereabouts to the Ram, if it turned out he actually was in an alliance with the monarch.

He'd be close enough to slit her throat.

No, Arthie told herself. There was no room for risk. She would take him with her into the Athereum and leave him there, then figure out a way to get in front of the Ram on her own.

"Fair enough," he said, oblivious, then held out his hand.

She stared at it. "I'm not swapping spit."

"I was going to formally introduce myself." He strode to the window, climbing onto the ledge with an agility that rivaled a cat's. When he turned back to her, his eyes were intent as if they shared a secret. "Laith Sayaad of Arawiya. I wish I could say it was a pleasure, but I'm not one to lie."

And then he disappeared into the night.

6

JIN

Jin joylessly finished the last of his blackberry jam tart and downed the rest of his tea. A lost shipment, stalled paperwork, rival tearooms—all momentary setbacks that he and Arthie could and would and *had* recovered from. He wasn't usually so glum. If he rubbed at his soul hard enough to get past the grime of the streets, he might even find optimism. Not now.

In his thoughts, the Ram rose like a shadow from the flames. First Jin's parents, now Spindrift.

Once upon a time, Jin was the Adley Academy for Boys' brightest. He knew because he would not have been accepted otherwise. He was eight years old when his parents took him to enroll. It didn't matter that they had the exact amount of duvin for tuition counted and ready in a purse. The secretary had taken one look at their foreign skin and frowned distastefully.

Jin would have liked to leave, but when his mother brandished his reports from his previous school, he had watched in fascination as the man's odium slowly gave way to enthusiasm, growing when he learned they lived in one of White Roaring's best neighborhoods, Admiral Grove. That massive estate with its gabled roof and bricks the color of milk tea inspired more respect than they did.

He had begun life at the academy the same week, his mother stressing the importance of his grades and his father stressing the importance of his clothes. He became his studies, learning words, multiplying figures, recording facts until he murmured them in his sleep.

While he was immersed in his education, his parents were immersed in their research. They had an array of resources at their disposal, provided through grants from the previous monarch. He had heard the story countless times: The Eagle had been impressed with their advances in science, to the point where he'd commended Jin's parents in a private meeting.

Jin's mother and father didn't take such praise and provisions lightly, even after the Eagle's rule came to an end and the Ram sat in his stead. His mother kept an eye under the microscope; his father, the dreamer, kept an eye to the skies. *On the cusp of a discovery*, his father would say, even as he worked on other things—specifically, vampiric things. He was fascinated by the world of the living, enamored by the concept of the undead, and wanted to make life better for all.

Jin fancied that his father's compulsion lived on in his veins.

When he was eleven and three-quarters, his world crumbled. He had been counting down the days until his twelfth birthday, when he would be old enough to visit the gentlemen's club with his father. The Adley carriage trundled to a halt at the top of Admiral Grove, unleashing the boys with their grass-stained knees, loose ties, and hungry mouths. Jin had slung his bag over his shoulder and began the walk home alone as the others laughed and joked with a camaraderie Jin often admired. He heaved a sigh, thinking it odd that he could smell smoke. Admiral Grove wasn't the Little East—a decent drive from here—where smoke was synonymous with good food.

He still remembered his last thought before he saw his house: He was hungry, and it was the end of the week, which meant the cook was making one of his mother's favorite dishes.

But the Siwang Residence was ablaze.

Smoke spilled from the double windows in his father's study and tore from the balcony in his mother's dressing room. Flames rose like angry jaws. His confusion gave way to shock, shock made room for fear, and before that fear could cripple him, courage ripped through him.

And so, Jin ran for the house.

He hurried up the steps to the front door. It was unlocked, swinging open and immediately throwing him into a coughing fit. He looked out at the street, wishing there was an adult nearby, someone bigger than him who would know what to do. But there was only a little girl, staring from the shadows across the street.

"Ma! Pa!" he yelled and immediately resumed coughing. Fire burned. Smoke was worse, he remembered learning at the academy, but only if he breathed it in. Jin swallowed as much air as his eleven-year-old lungs could hold and rushed inside.

The foyer stretched longer in the chaos. Fallen beams and broken furniture littered the floor in shades of orange and yellow, obscured by smoke. The flutter of a striped shawl hanging from what remained of the staircase caught his attention, but the maid it belonged to was nowhere to be seen. It looked forlorn, a bright ribbon against the emptiness. A sob lodged in his throat.

"Ma!" Jin shouted again, a crack in his voice. "Pa!"

What if his parents were trapped? He hurried toward the kitchens, where the smoke wasn't as thick because the windows were blown open, glass remnants like jagged teeth.

It reminded him, oddly, of the front door, and how strange it was for it to have been unlocked and ajar. Something about it felt wrong, though he couldn't place why. His mother had often told him about how easily research could be abused, how imperative it was that their secrets remained secret.

"Bad people like to do bad things," she would say.

"Like who, Mother?" he asked once.

His mother had peeled the gloves from her hands and wiped them on her coat. "Hmm? There are far too many to list. Anyone is capable of malevolence, from our colleagues at the hospital to the Ram on the throne."

"The Ram?" Jin asked. Like history and geography, he read about the monarchs in school and in newspapers. Sure, his parents had met with one themselves, but that was long before Jin.

Jin's father had cleared his throat, drawing his mother's attention. Jin was too slow to catch the exchange, but now he wished he had. What if someone had broken in and his parents were in danger? They were fairly well-known in White Roaring. Jin would know—he had used his parents' name to get to the front of the line at an ice cream parlor before. There were bound to be people who weren't fond of them. Or what if it was the Ram his parents didn't seem to like? Jin needed to save them. He needed—Jin looked around—he needed a weapon.

Now panic was starting to build, squeezing his lungs and his eyesight. He didn't like guns because his father didn't like guns. He needed a knife. Where did the cooks leave the knives? Jin dug around, coming up empty. He tried to move faster. He thought very hard. He had kept all his parents' secrets, right?

His mother and father hadn't seemed any different, but now Jin thought his father had been worried about something the night before. Maybe because of their weekly visitor—an older man with a kind face and a gold ring piercing his ear. His father liked the man, and so Jin had been surprised when their voices rose in his office and the gentleman left without giving Jin one of the clove rocks that he'd come to love.

There. In his rush to find a knife, Jin had found something else. *In addition to making you happy, coconuts make for excellent weapons,* his father once said to him. He had been developing a theory involving the fruit, and so the house was full of them. Jin grabbed one out of the bin, the smooth green shell cool to the touch, and gulped down another lungful of fresh air from the open window before hurrying back into the foyer.

"Ma!" he yelled, venturing toward the staircase. Reason warned him that it was not safe, that this was not what his mother would have wanted, that she would have disliked this the same way she disliked when he called her *ma* instead of *mother*.

Jin didn't listen. He scoured the second floor of the house, tripping more than once, the coconut clutched to his chest. Fear beat beneath his skin. The smoke was making it harder and harder to breathe and see. He needed fresh air. He tumbled down the stairs as a wooden beam separated from the ceiling with a deafening crack. The following silence was just as deafening, until Jin heard what he thought was the shuffle of footsteps.

"Pa?"

He heard a scratching sound, distinct enough to ripple through the thundering smoke. *A matchstick.* Jin peered into the shadows, certain he saw the shape of a man. There was a figure beside it, more shapely. *Ma!* A heavy thud drew his attention to another figure, this one more imposing. Terror gripped him. *The Ram!* He couldn't see past the smoke to fully tell, but it didn't matter. Jin had to warn them. Save them. He called out, yelling as loud as he could, but he was too late.

An explosion shook the house, throwing him back. Flames erupted around him anew. He held the coconut against himself like a shield, somehow finding it within him to be embarrassed by his weakness. He was going to be all grown up soon.

He couldn't be afraid.

The fire roared, ripping wood from the walls and portraits from their hooks. It ate and ate and ate, growing and gasping as it devoured the house. The foyer was miles away, the door a shining rectangle of light out of reach.

Jin was very, very afraid.

He needed to escape. Fire caught on his trousers when he floundered into the receiving room, but he grabbed his father's umbrella from the stand, doing his best to bat it away. Embers fell in his hair, but he shook them off. He was trapped between two flaming walls when a curtain fell from its rod, striking his arm and lighting him ablaze.

Jin screamed. He had never smelled burned flesh before. He didn't know where he was going, only that his legs were carrying him. And when he begged for his ma and his pa, for anyone, *someone*, he didn't expect to see her.

The little girl from across the street.

The fire parted for her. Her face was void of emotion, her eyes vivid black. She slapped something across his arm, putting out the fire before shoving it into his mouth. A rag. *Breathe*, he thought she said, but his vision was tunneling.

And then Jin was outside. It happened so fast; he only recalled collapsing onto the grass in relief, his body a broken motor, his thoughts frenzied like someone had dropped a boulder in a pile of feathers. He heaved cough after cough, his lungs burning as if the fire was inside of him. The girl gave him water. Gray flecks floated on the surface, but he drank it all, handing her the grimy cup as if she had more to give.

"I'm Arthie," she said in a clear, strong voice with an accent he couldn't place.

"Jin," he wheezed. He felt numb, as if his mind and his body hadn't registered what had just happened. *Shock*. The explosion. *His parents*.

His arm throbbed with blistering pain, so much so that he thought it would be easier if he chopped it off. Arthie dropped to her knees, pulling various odds and ends and numerous ointments from her shabby satchel before she scrunched her face and treated the burn. It hurt more when she was finished. She shrugged. "No time. I'll do a gooder job later."

Jin was staring at the house. *The Ram*. The Ram had done this. He swiped at his face and his hand came away wet. He was crying.

"But what if they're still in there? Alive?" he asked, even though he knew, deep down, that they weren't. *Denial*, he would later learn it was called.

"They're not," she said, with all the emotion of reading an advertisement from a newspaper.

Jin sobbed wholeheartedly now. She pulled out a dusty bag from behind a bush. There were pastries inside, and she handed him one. It tasted fresh, just like the ones his mother would hand him after he did particularly well on an exam. The food turned to ash on his tongue.

The girl was watching him. He didn't know why she was being kind to him or why she had saved him. She stood up, and he didn't know what would happen next, but he didn't want to be left alone.

"Can you run?" she asked.

Over the crackling of the fire, Jin heard shouts from the end of the street: *There she is!* He nodded.

She tucked a silver pin into her pocket. "Good. Because I took this from a mean man and we need to run really fast or we will die. Badly."

Jin grabbed his umbrella, and she held his hand as if she'd done it a thousand times before and dragged him through the streets. He had never known anyone so fearless, the line of her spine as sharp as a blade. Yet she'd seen something worth saving in him. This sharp-eyed stranger who knew nothing of him suddenly knew him better than anyone else, and because of it, he clung to her. Her fight to survive morphed into his. He became addicted to anything that distracted him from the reminder of his existence. Anything that kept him from spiraling into the dark grave that had nearly claimed him. It wasn't purpose, but it was close.

Until Spindrift.

It became the beating heart of their bond, long after Arthie had found a surname in a book and declared it their own. It consumed him. The tearoom, the bloodhouse. Fitting pipes and cutting glass and twisting wires to light a bulb. He furnished rooms where a vampire and human could have their privacy while they transacted blood, he concocted a blend with coconut to give them something new.

A door slammed upstairs, bringing Jin back to the present. Spindrift had given him that purpose he sought, throwing a blanket over the simmering embers from the fire of his past. He would rather die than return to it. He looked up to find Arthie staring at him. She looked too bright and too excited for the news they'd just received from the proprietor.

"Stop thinking so much," she said, almost kindly. "It'll get you killed one day."

He didn't think so. Forget what day of the week it was? Perhaps. Forget he'd already had six cups of tea? Even more likely. But kill him? Nope.

"I know how we'll save Spindrift," she said.

7

ARTHIE

Arthie rubbed at her temples and rubbed them some more before slamming her books shut and propping her elbows on the desk. Outside her window, a lazy sun inched toward the soggy remains of the night.

"It's in the Athereum," Jin repeated for the thirteenth time. His hair stuck up every which way, tinted blue by the fading moonlight.

Arthie pushed a brand-new tin of bourbon biscuits across her desk. Jin stopped his pacing and set down his jacket and umbrella. It was his weapon of choice—elegant, clean, and very him. Knife fight? Jin's umbrella made an appearance. Confrontation? Umbrella. Stroll down the street? Umbrella. Unless Arthie made him pack a gun too.

"And yet, you agreed," he said, opening the tin.

"I seemed to have agreed, yes."

"Arthie," Jin chastised.

"What, Jin? Did you see us having much of a choice?"

"He wants us to break into the *Athereum*." Jin went back to paving a trench into the floorboards of her office. "We can save Spindrift some other way that doesn't involve shaking hands with a shady Horned Guard."

Laith wasn't just any other Horned Guard. There were his treasonous words, of course, but also the venom with which he spoke them, and his conviction that the Ram had grown too powerful.

Still, Arthie wasn't fond of the way her mind had recorded so much

of him, like that he looked nothing like a peaky, despite his fair color-
ing and light hair. Or how his eyes were rimmed in the same kohl she
sometimes saw on sailors, and how the twin flecks of black above the
curve of his left eyebrow threatened to mesmerize her.

"And how's that?" she asked, tidying her desk to distract herself.

"You have dirt on—"

"If we had dirt on half the people you're thinking of, we would
have buried them already." She gave him a look. "This is the only way
to ensure Spindrift isn't threatened again. No more raids, no more
proprietor."

It was a small price to pay when the alternative would cost the Ram
that mask of a crown. The very idea of the Ram lying awake because
Arthie held something over the wretched monarch was enough to turn
this night around.

"We've wanted to get at the Ram even before we were threatened
with eviction," Arthie added. Jin had hated the Ram since the fire all
those years ago. "Why the cold feet?"

Jin rolled up the sleeves of his dark shirt to his forearms, gripping the back of a chair with a huff. The leathery skin along his right
arm gleamed. "That was also before we learned that *getting at the Ram*
requires breaking into the Athereum and trusting our enemies."

"We're working with the enemy, not trusting him. There's a
difference."

Jin dragged a hand down his face.

"Spit it out," she said, leaning back in her chair.

"You do realize that whoever is in possession of that ledger might
want the Ram gone entirely, yes?" he asked, cracking open the window.
She didn't tell him that she knew who that was. "They're not going to
say, 'pip pip cheerio, here you are!' This is bigger than us. We blackmail
to get what we want. We don't usurp thrones and get in the way of

people *trying* to usurp thrones. And your Horned Guard who waltzed in through your window and provided us with a way out of our predicament *right* when we fell into it will be there with us, waiting to double-cross you." He stopped and looked at her. "What? Don't give me that smug face."

Arthie knew all this, of course. "We'll just have to double-cross him first."

"Wh—are you listening to yourself?" Jin asked. "That means letting him take the fall. The Athereum will kill the bloke."

Arthie shrugged. "It's either him or us at that point."

Jin heaved a breath. "But we need him to get us *to* the Ram. What do you plan to do if you find the ledger? Walk up to the masked monarch yourself?"

"*When* we find it, it'll give us a footstool to the throne. One, we'll have our palace informants to help us, and two, if your parents could use their profession to get an audience with the Eagle, I'm sure we can, too."

Jin was staring at her like she'd gone wild. "And what's our profession, exactly?"

"Professional criminals, of course," she said matter-of-factly.

A weary half-laugh broke out of him.

"When will you acknowledge that you're in way over your head? All right. Fine. Let's hear your astounding, top-notch plan for breaking into the Athereum so we can tell Reni what to carve on our tombstones when it all goes down terribly," he said.

"Adventure?" she asked.

His brow furrowed. "What?"

"For our tombstones."

"As if you'll stay in your grave like a proper dead girl." He knew her so well.

"Ambition keeps the heart pumping," she said. "As for our plan, the Athereum's annual display of altruism is around the corner. It'll be an easy job. In and out."

"The auction? Are you trying to get us in as blood companions on the Festival of Night?" Jin asked, like she'd lost her mind.

As ideal as that would have been, the Athereum didn't work that way. Everyone and their uncle wanted a glimpse of the underworld, and the process of becoming a blood companion to an Athereum member was strenuous and complicated. There was no way Arthie and Jin of all people would pass that screening, no matter how much blackmail and bribery they pulled.

"No," Arthie admitted.

"Which means we'll need appointed markers to get in, and they don't hand those out like candy," he said, trying to prove a point. "It's already impossible. We have *two weeks*, Arthie."

"Matteo will have a marker," she said. She'd stumbled on that realization quite recently, and something about their meeting tonight made her think he wouldn't be that difficult to get on board. "Acquire his, and then we can forge the rest. Flick can forge them."

Something shifted in his gaze at the mention of the forger.

"Hm," Jin said reluctantly. "And if one of us really needed to slip in as a blood companion, I do have a favor to call in."

"Precisely. We can do this, Jin."

He knew she was right, just as she knew he was concerned. His reluctance wasn't disregard, it was the opposite. There were days when she thought Spindrift meant more to him than to her. His expression was distant, and Arthie wondered if he was picturing his family estate. This was about more than Spindrift for him. Going down this path meant confronting his past too, which was a level of danger he didn't want to face.

He heaved a heavy exhale.

"We'll leverage the ledger for Spindrift and then some," Arthie said, thinking about Jin's parents. At this rate, ousting the Ram as Laith wanted would be horrible for business. "Vengeance never dies."

"I want to live. I don't want vengeance," he said, shaking his head so vigorously she feared it would rattle right off. But she'd struck a chord—he too was thinking about his parents. "The ledger for Spindrift, and then we're done."

But Arthie was already putting together their crew in her mind. She'd need Jin, of course, and their forger. She'd need Laith's ability to blend with the shadows, and they would certainly need an inside man.

Five people. She did like odd numbers.

She rose from her seat. "Rest up, brother. I want it enough for the both of us."

8

FLICK

Flick tugged on a lavender beret in front of her bedroom window with a happy sigh. There was no other way to regard such a view—from the fetching houses to the swaying trees dappled in jeweled hues, it was a sight no forger could ever replicate.

She couldn't remember the last time she'd held a parasol or felt sun-warmed cobblestones beneath her shoes, but oh, she was being dramatic. It had only been forty-three days since her crime had confined her to the Linden Estate here in Admiral Grove, not a lifetime.

Her maid entered with a light knock. *Miss Felicity is under house arrest*, she had whispered to the other staff when it happened because no proper Ettenian lady could be arrested. Flick often let her curls fall over her ears to make them think she couldn't hear their gossip.

The woman next door is a vampire. She was not—she had just given birth a month ago, which vampires could not do.

Miss Felicity is Lady Linden's illegitimate child. Flick was not—she really had been adopted.

Miss Felicity committed a heinous act. Forgery! Now that was true, though Flick wouldn't call what she'd done *heinous* by any means.

"Morning, Miss Felicity," said her maid, dismayed that Flick had dressed herself again.

"A very delightful morning indeed," Flick replied, tucking away her lighter. It was a gift from her mother for her tenth birthday, brass and delicate but capable of so much more if only one took the time to light it.

Like you, her mother had said then, skirts wide and bright as her golden hair. *My little spark.*

The maids thought her strange for not being glum, but this predicament was her own fault. Her mother had every right to be angry, and any sorrow that stirred beneath Flick's contentment was of the devil. She had forged enough to know how to forge happiness.

"How is my mother?" she asked.

The maid looked away, same as she had for the previous forty-three days. "Well, m'lady."

Well meant her mother was still pretending Flick didn't exist. *It was only a ring*, came the petulant thought.

There was a time when Flick and her mother were close. They had meals and fittings for the latest gowns together because Flick's mother took great care in her appearance. They would pick out furnishings for the estate and take evening walks in the garden. Lady Linden had always wanted to know what it was like to have a child, she used to tell Flick.

She had experienced and accomplished almost everything else, including founding the East Jeevant Company, before she'd adopted Flick as a young girl. But as the Ram colonized country after country, business improved more and more, and eventually when Flick was eleven the EJC swept Lady Linden away.

She spent longer hours in her office than with her daughter, and when she did come home, she was distant and almost bored by anything Flick said. Like a child with a new toy, it seemed as if her excitement at having a daughter had been replaced by the excitement of a bustling business.

In time, Flick found herself searching for something to fill that void. For when one loved as much as Felicity Linden did, it was difficult to not be loved in return. It didn't matter that Flick had the best governesses, seamstresses, private tutors, and a full year of finishing school. She tried painting, she tried embroidery, she even tried her hand in the kitchen, to no avail.

The forging started innocently enough. When her maid urgently needed a doctor and their housekeeper refused to let her go without Lady Linden's approval—which was impossible to get since she was never home—Flick tossed and turned the entire night until the idea came to her. After all, Flick had grown up mimicking the upper class around her, so mimicking was what she did best.

By daylight, her maid had a letter written in Flick's mother's scrawl. The footman's young son had a note in the housekeeper's handwriting a few days after that. She told no one, yet word began to spread. Soon people were trying to make appointments, and the housekeeper became suspicious. It was her maid's idea to set up shop in an abandoned warehouse near the prestigious tearoom known as Spindrift.

Flick had replicated identification cards, prescriptions, and even bank records, discovering that many members of high society were simply frauds in top hats. The signet ring was supposed to be another forge for yet another awkward nobleman with his head ducked low. Flick had been careful, but signet rings were used to seal letters and approvals, and held as much power as the ones who wore them. And unfortunately, unlike bank records, they were almost impossible to misplace. In hindsight, she should never have agreed to the job; the ring belonged to a high-ranking official, and the nobleman drank his tongue loose at parties.

He outed the secret himself.

A nobleman swindling a high-ranking official was newsworthy on its own, but throw a forger who happened to be a lady into the mix and the reporters went wild. The scandal made the front page of every newspaper in White Roaring, and it was only because her mother pulled a string or two that Flick's name wasn't printed. Still, the whispers carried loudly enough, and Lady Linden cared about her image over all else.

She had to. She was a woman in a man's world, where every slight was a sledgehammer, and her daughter had gone and made things difficult. Now Flick would do anything to return to what they'd had. A busy mother was far better than one who was angry with her.

But Flick had no way to undo what she'd done and earn her mother's forgiveness. It wasn't as if she could reach out to the papers and ask them to run articles lauding her mother on the front page. It wasn't as if she could give them a story worth printing when she was trapped in here.

"Perhaps I can speak to her," Flick suggested. "For reparations' sake?"

"Miss Felic—"

A horse's whinny cut her maid short, followed by the yank of a carriage brake out on the street. Flick rushed to the window and pressed her hands into the sill. Several carriages were halted on the wide street in front of the Linden Estate. They were draped in black, the silver sigil of the Ram filigreed front and center.

"Out of the way!"

"By order of the Horned Guard!"

The maid gasped. Flick's hand flew to her throat as men leaped out, uniformed and stern. Sweat dampened her palms. This was exactly the display Flick had meant to avoid.

Her mother would be furious.

Her gaze fell to one of the guards pushing a pair of tinted spectacles up the bridge of his nose. She thought she recognized his gait and the surety that none of the men on this side of White Roaring possessed— but that couldn't be who she thought it was. How silly of her to think she could recognize someone just by his walk and the crooked tilt of his mouth.

"Oh, whatever will we do?" her maid sobbed, yanking Flick back to the matter at hand.

The Horned Guard was here. *Here*. At her house. Panic began to set in. Flick dipped her hand into her pocket, pressing her fingers around the square of her lighter. Downstairs, the door flung open. A buzz of noise rose, and Flick heard the butler's thin voice sounding aghast before a guard's proclamation rang out:

"—for the arrest of Lady Felicity Linden!"

Her spirits plummeted like the heavy hem of a terrible gown. Her maid began to cry.

"Come now," Flick said gently, wondering if she shouldn't be the one being consoled. "It's not as if they're here to kill me. I'll be all right. Mother will get me out."

Her maid looked up, and Flick thought her dubious expression was a little unfair. Lady Linden could call in a favor, like she had done with the papers. Flick would be in there but one night. Two at most. Right? She didn't know how arrests worked. It wasn't something anyone had taught her in between lessons about needlework and penmanship and how to keep house. Goodness, she was being *arrested*.

Flick flung her bedroom door open. The hall looked hazy, distant. *You're in shock*, she told herself. Her feet were moving, the stairs diminishing one by one. She searched the faces of the guards for the one she thought she had seen. She really had imagined him. Why would he be here anyway? He wasn't a guard, he was on the opposite side of the law.

She heard hurried footsteps and glanced behind her, expecting to see her mother with an anguished gaze, the stern lines on her face looking suddenly soft. Flick always thought her mother had remarkable eyes, a shade of blue like the sea beneath the sun. But it was only Flick's maid with her gloves. She was carrying a bag over her shoulder.

"I packed you some clothes and necessities, Miss Felicity," the girl said, handing the bag to a servant.

Clothes were the last thing on Flick's mind. She peeked at the second-floor office, but her mother's door was still closed. She might not even be home.

It didn't matter. Flick was eighteen years of age. She didn't need an escort. She wouldn't allow her mother to further embarrass herself on account of her daughter's misdeeds.

It is for the best, Flick thought to herself numbly. That was what her mother would say. Flick had done wrong, and this was only right.

A stern-faced captain led her through the front door. *Chin up*, she told herself. She was leaving. This was what she'd wanted, wasn't it? She stepped outside for the first time in forty-three days. The sun warmed her skin, and the cobblestones were pleasant beneath her feet.

The captain stopped in front of one of the carriages. "In you go, miss."

A servant tucked her bag of belongings inside, and a footman dropped a platform for her, then headed for another carriage before she could reach for his hand to steady her step.

She looked back at the estate, at the fawn-colored bricks, and the white-shuttered windows, and the roof that matched the pristine walnut floors inside. Her home, her prison. *I'm sorry, Mother. Come for me. Let me make things right.*

"Watch your head there, love."

Flick froze at the voice that came from inside the carriage, but then the footman was slamming the door behind her, causing her to lose her balance and fall straight into . . . a lap? Slowly her eyes adjusted to the dim light, and she saw the face above her. It *was* him.

Flick knew that voice from the nights when he would stop at her warehouse and drop those hands on her table, something clever in his eyes, which were as dark as the delicate tattoos winding up the side of his neck.

"I'm used to women throwing themselves at me, but really, there's a time and place," he said. A current zapped right through her. His peaked hat was pulled low and he wore tinted specs over his eyes, but she recognized his mouth. It was the kind that was hard to forget and equally hard to stop thinking about.

"Jin?"

His lips curved. "Hello, Felicity. I've missed you."

Flick knew they had turned out of Admiral Grove when Jin reached across her to part the curtains over the carriage window. His elbow brushed her chest just enough to make her breath shudder. A tiny sound escaped her throat. Goodness. She needed to distract herself.

Outside. Yes. Outside, the Old Roaring Tower rose like a skeleton imposing over everything in its vicinity. The bricks were a sandy brown and stacked into something ornate that surrounded a round clockface. Massive, sapphire-blue hands ticked away, each minute passing like a sentence. Painted glass tiled the arching windows, reflecting sunlight as prettily as the balcony's gilded railing.

The Athereum was beside it. Its many windows were dark, and shadows pooled between the five fluted columns set atop sculpted plinths. Flick shivered at the words carved into the architrave: *mortui vivos docent.* The dead teach the living.

Jin leaned back, a whiff of bergamot, tea, and the sea lingering in his wake.

"Flick," she said. She always was correcting him, and it had become a half-hearted attempt at this point. "My name is Flick."

"Right, and I'm Jefferson the third," he replied haughtily, pulling off his specs.

Flick growled, but something about the way he said her real name made her breath catch. She crossed her arms. "I know you're a lot more versed in criminal than I am, but you're looking especially suspicious right now. Where are you taking me?"

This carriage wasn't en route to the Horned Guard's headquarters, not when a Casimir was inside of it.

"Oh, didn't you hear?" he asked, dropping his voice. "You're under arrest because you've been a bad, bad girl."

She felt heat rise to her cheeks. And then she just about erupted on the spot when he started unbuttoning his shirt.

"You'll have to put in a little more work to see me undressed, love," he said with a low laugh, peeling off the Horned Guard uniform and revealing a pair of black suspenders over a snug shirt. Had he no decency?

He reached under the seat and pulled out a black umbrella and a sleek jacket, then yanked on a lever between his end of the seat and the door. With an awful sound like something was breaking, the carriage ground to a halt. Shouts echoed outside. Flick heard one of the guards ushering the others to carry on.

Jin gave her a grin. "We're going on an adventure, you and me."

"You've got a job for me, don't you?" Flick asked. "If I'm not in my prison cell—"

"So smart *and* so eager to be in prison," Jin drawled. "Never put it past a Casimir to make something out of nothing. You will have a cell with bars and a bed and food, and a guard who will attest to your presence. You simply won't *be* in it."

And the cost, Flick knew, was this job that he mentioned but hadn't elaborated upon. Her pulse fluttered like wings, heart racing in anticipation. "And when my mother comes to visit me, what then? She's going to get me out, you know."

Jin had the same expression of pity and discomfort she had seen on her maid, and Flick knew he was going to say something she didn't want to hear.

"By the time mummy fills out the paperwork and strolls through the halls with her parasol, we'll have whisked you in and locked you up," he said, surprising her, and her heart swelled at his words.

"How?" she asked, but she knew he had his ways. This was Jin; lethal smiles, artful hands, and one criminal voice.

He threw open the carriage door and held out his hand, and Flick wondered if her mother would be even angrier if she could see her now. Had he ruined her life even further? As if he could read her thoughts, he said, "If it makes you feel any better, you *were* going to be arrested next week. Arthie and I pulled some strings to make it happen today, and then we pulled a few more to borrow you for a bit."

Flick tamped down her relief. She couldn't deny her gratitude for the freedom—albeit very likely temporary—the Casimirs had given her, but she was still wary. Especially if Arthie was involved.

She took Jin's hand. The leather of his gloves was warm in the satin of hers. Goodness, she could scarcely breathe.

"Borrow me for what?" she asked, voice tight.

"Forging, of course. If you want the job, it's yours. If you don't, well"—he tossed the Horned Guard hat into the carriage and shook his hair loose while the sun glossed each inky strand—"it's yours anyway."

Jin pulled her into the morning crowd of Stoker Lane, throwing her sack of possessions over his shoulder. The gray-uniformed guard driving the carriage peered at them, a little uneasy.

"Mr. Jim—"

"Oh, Ollie, I look more like a Jin, don't I?" he asked, then angled closer to Flick to murmur, "It's as simple as names go, unlike, I don't know, Sir Archibald Cornelius. What will it take to get some respect around here, eh? A group of us getting together and singing about self-love and butter?"

He spoke so fast Flick could barely follow.

The guard looked apologetic. "I only wanted to say that my captain will ask why I took a different route, and—"

"How is your sister, by the way?" Jin asked, like the two of them were old friends. The guard's brow furrowed in confusion, but he didn't seem as concerned about his captain anymore. "I hear she was selected as a tutor at that school. What's it called again? Ashton, or some such."

Flick had worked with the Casimirs; they liked to learn everything they could about the people they ran with, and the way Jin said *Ashton* sounded like he knew the actual name of the school, but was fumbling on purpose.

"Uh, no. Adley, actually," the guard corrected. "It's the Adley Academy for Boys. A large school, way up on—"

"Right, right," Jin said. "That's a true win, and certainly cause for celebration, innit? Tell her to swing by Spindrift. We'll give her a treat."

The guard seemed to have forgotten his concern altogether. "That wouldn't really be—"

"On the house," Jin added with a smile that made Flick forget her last thought, and she wasn't even the recipient of it.

A man shouted from the carriage that was stalled behind them, and the guard named Ollie appeared overwhelmed.

"I had better move," he said, thoroughly flustered now. "But that's—that's very kind of you. I'll be sure to let her know. Thank you."

"Of course," Jin said with a nod. He started to turn away. "It was nice seeing you today, Ollie. Always a pleasure."

Before the guard could say anything more, Jin started walking, his umbrella rapping along the cobblestones. Flick didn't know what to do besides keep up. When she looked back at the guard, he was spurring the horses away and tipping his hat at her as if he'd never seen her in his life.

"He—how did you do that?" Flick asked.

"I have no idea what you're talking about, Felicity," he said, but when he turned to give her a grin before she was swept into a hubbub of overskirts and tailcoats, it was obvious he knew exactly what she was talking about.

Flick had practiced her forgery for three years in an abandoned warehouse, but she'd only met the Casimirs several months ago, when Arthie needed a letter forged in the handwriting of one of Ettenia's many officials.

Arthie must have been content with the work, for she and Jin came often after that. She was never friendly or talkative, but Flick got to see Jin, and she enjoyed the jobs they gave her. To the Casimirs, what she did wasn't shameful or vile. It was work. A talent, even.

A crime, her mother's voice insisted. Her mother ruled the EJC the way the Ram ruled Ettenia. She dealt with right and wrong all day, when her men acted out of order in the colonies, when they stole from the inventory they were sent to sell. Mother knew all.

Eventually, Jin started coming alone. He would linger, making sure Flick hadn't forgotten anything. She never did, of course, and it made her wonder if he liked spending time with her as much as she liked spending time with him. She would study him in those moments, when she wasn't bent over her table, as he read over her work several times and bid her goodbye. *Farewell, Felicity*, or, *Try not to miss me too much*.

She always did. Flick had never been very bold when it came to making conversation with Jin Casimir. Every woman and her sister knew of him, so how would Flick stand a chance?

Something pulled at her skirts now, and Flick looked down to find a young boy with a tattered cap and grease on his cheeks.

"What's got you, then?" she asked.

"Please, miss!" he said, a quiver to his bottom lip. "Spare a coin, miss. The Lovelyn Foundry docked my pay."

"Oh, you poor thing." Flick started digging in her pocket, but Jin leaned over and stopped her with a hand to the arm. It was barely a sweep of his glove over her sleeve, but heat shot through her, every nerve ending zapping with a current.

"Let me tell you a secret, eh?" he said to the boy.

The boy's eyes lit up. He was rolling a wrapped toffee between his fingers.

Jin pointed with his umbrella. "See that alley over there? There's a woman standing in front of a door with a bag full of treasures. Tell her *gobsmacked* is the answer to the riddle."

"Gobsmacked?" the boy asked.

Jin nodded. "Say the word, and you'll get a gift out of it. Got it?"

"Got it!" the boy yelled, and took off down the street.

"You—" Flick started. *Lied.* She was certain he had lied, but he spoke with such candor that even Flick had a hard time not believing him. "He believed you!"

"It's a skill, love," Jin said, straightening.

"But you lied to him. That was positively churlish. You've ruined his day!" she reprimanded, and Jin tossed something at her. It was the boy's toffee. "Jin! You stole that from him!"

"Sticky fingers, sorry," he said, not looking the least bit sorry.

"You—you're—"

He lifted his brows. "Superbly striking or savagely clever? That boy was a crook. He filches for a smaller gang."

"That was a child," she protested, swallowing her frustration when he sighed. "And I—I don't forge anymore."

The words burst out of her, surprising them both.

Jin's forehead scrunched. "But you're good at it."

The raw honesty in his voice struck her. She *was* good at it. Flick had been searching all her life—for what, she didn't know. She thought she'd found it when she began forging and people sought her out, but now, as she clutched her beret against a gust of wind, she thought perhaps that wasn't true.

They stopped at the intersection. Her old warehouse was two streets down. Spindrift would be just a little farther ahead, right where the slums of the city began with buildings tumbling one after the other.

"Why would you stop?" Jin asked, pulling her back to the present.

"Because—" Flick trailed off, unsure, until the weight of his scrutiny pried the lid off of her frustration. "Because it's illicit. It's wrong."

She couldn't expect him to understand, but Jin was only half listening. He was watching a passenger in the window of a passing carriage, giving the older man's dark hair and monolid eyes more than a shallow glance. He looked old enough to have been Jin's father. On rare evenings when Flick would summon the courage to ask Jin questions, she'd once learned that his parents were gone. *Not dead*, he had said with some uncertainty.

She was a fool for thinking he couldn't understand.

"It might be all those things, Felicity, but *I* can make it worth your while," he said in a voice that made her shiver, presenting her with a lilac ribbon. They were two paces from a woman selling hair adornments. She didn't think he'd even *glanced* in the direction of the stall.

Then he gestured to the top of Stoker Lane, to Spindrift, home of the Casimirs.

He said nothing of the job or how he would make it worth her while, and yet she followed him, her steps slowing as she neared the deep red building. She gaped at the smooth curve of the lettering on the frosted glass of Spindrift's double doors, the kinds of flourishes she'd once excelled in creating before her penmanship dragged her down a different path.

She'd been here once before, during the day, when her mother had finally allowed it. She could still remember the taste of the extraordinary tea, the reason Spindrift drew crowds from around the city.

It was easy to assume Spindrift belonged in the better part of the capital. It carried itself that way. The tearoom was bright and alluring, the filth of the streets obscured by the cluster of fancy carriages and folk dressed to the nines, top hats gleaming and dresses heavy with embroidery. As if this were a lord's estate and his prestigious ball. As if it wasn't slotted in the midst of foundries and pleasure houses and slumping homes. As if it didn't serve blood to the undead.

Ignorance had always been a defining feature of the privileged.

"What if I'm seen and someone tells my mother I'm here?" Flick asked.

Jin had the same expression as he did earlier. "We employ a lot of snitchers, Felicity, but none of them report to Lady Linden."

The doors to Spindrift swept open in a jangle of bells, and a dark-skinned boy in a tailcoat and black gloves dipped a bow.

"Reni, my boy!" Jin called, saluting him. He passed Flick's bag to a young girl and spread his arms in welcome as he turned a full circle and sauntered inside.

"My lady," the boy named Reni greeted.

"Thank you, young sir," she replied, before fascination took hold at the scene before her: Spindrift, in motion.

There was harmony in the way the Casimir crew handled the floor, one jotting down orders as another glided by with polished trays. She inhaled deeply. The smell was rich and robust, fresh and malty. The wainscot walls topped by dark wallpaper lent a cozy air to clinking crockery and tittering patrons, biscuits crisp between teeth, sugar dropping like magic in pools of tea as deep as the night. It was a melody of sounds complementing a visual feast.

Jin's gaze cut to her. "It's been a while since you've visited, eh?"

She flushed under his scrutiny. He remembered her visit from three years ago. She hadn't thought he'd even noticed her amid the sea of customers on Spindrift's busy floor.

Flick cleared her throat when he pulled off his coat in the middle of the room. It was suddenly very difficult to breathe, but no one else seemed to notice his bawdiness as he slung the jacket over his shoulder.

"Enjoy it while you can." He winked as if his words had nothing to do with Spindrift, and then he sauntered away before she could say anything more. Flick stifled a cough as a heavy perfume wafted off a pair of ladies with haughty expressions who had just entered the tearoom.

Reni eyed them, whispering to a younger boy who was scribbling something furiously into a notepad stuffed every which way. Somehow, Flick didn't think they were orders for refreshments.

To the public, Arthie Casimir dealt in tea. To those who paid enough attention, she dealt in blood too. But Flick had read every letter and document she had forged for the girl and knew the truth: Arthie Casimir dealt in secrets.

Secrets.

That was it. That was how Flick would earn her mother's forgiveness.

She didn't know anything about the job yet or what Arthie and Jin needed from her, but they were bound to give her *something*.

She needed to repair her mother's image, and nothing was better than a good word in the press. Flick could give her the very same front page she had disgraced her with, and it would all be thanks to Arthie Casimir. Flick would simply need to hear them through and then go back and tell her mother of it. And if what Arthie needed Flick for wasn't worthy of the front page, she'd dig around their collections and see.

Maybe. Flick didn't know if they had collections. She didn't even know if anything could be as scandalous as Lady Linden's daughter being a forger, but she would try.

That was when Flick saw her.

Arthie stood with her hands on the railing of the second-floor balcony, surveying her domain with eyes that might have once been warm, the light long devoured by calculation. She wore trousers and a suit jacket as if they weren't made for men, lace-up shoes instead of button boots, a waistcoat instead of a bodice, and a pistol in lieu of a parasol, bright at her hip like a knight's sword.

Arthie Casimir was a maestro commanding the room. A queen at her throne. The hangman at the gallows.

Above all, she was Flick's last chance at redemption.

But when Arthie's eyes fell on her, Flick didn't feel so certain. Arthie's hair was a halo, but her expression made Flick feel as if she were tiptoeing on knives.

"Welcome, miss."

Flick pulled herself away from Arthie's gaze to find a girl in a ruched bodice gown with raven hair and a red mouth. She was beautiful in a way that came from being a melody of sharp contrasts.

"Let me lead you to your table."

"Oh, I'm not here for leisure," Flick said.

The girl was demure. "The house insists you join us for elevensies."

Flick snuck a glance up, where Arthie watched and waited. It felt like a test somehow, and when the girl started through the maze of tables, Flick hurried after her to the vacant seat. She perched in the chair and did her best to smile at the gentleman eyeing her over the day's paper from the next table.

"Royal or supreme?" the girl asked. "I like to suggest orange pekoe if you're fond of adding milk and sugar, but it could take a smidge."

Flick reached for her lighter, gripping the comforting weight before she set her hands on the polished wood of the table. "Oh, I wouldn't know. I'll take what you think I'd like best, please."

With a nod, the girl bounced away and returned with a full spread that Flick's mother wouldn't even offer her closest associates. Steam curled from an ivory teapot, and biscuits fanned along the curve of the plates. Toothpicks speared a pair of sandwiches layered with butter and sliced strawberries atop fresh preserves. The sugar bowl and creamer were rimmed in silver and boasted patterns too detailed to discern without leaning in. Before Flick could drool at the display, the girl set a cup on a saucer and poured her a stream of tea as if the act were an art.

Flick scanned the balcony and floor. Arthie had vanished, and Jin was nowhere to be seen.

"Cream?"

Flick beamed. "Yes, please. I do love myself a good dollop."

"Here you are, the Royal Rouge." When the girl stepped back, Flick lifted her cup for a sip. Flavor burst along her tongue, warming her with its earthy undertones. It tasted of rose petals and sweet caramel, reminding her of the cake bites her mother's ships would bring from Jeevant Gar.

"This is downright delightful," Flick declared. It was smooth and sweet, with something that she couldn't quite place even when she let it linger, something mysterious and ardent. It was everything Flick wanted to be.

The girl gave her a look and Flick knew she was overdoing it. High society tittered over her personality every chance they got because they didn't understand that the little things were meant to be appreciated too.

She set the cup down. A card was tucked beneath the saucer, making her pulse pitter-patter at her neck. Inside was an address written in an impatient, slanting scrawl.

337 Alms Place.

9

ARTHIE

In her room, Arthie clipped the chain of her watch and tucked it in her pocket. She buttoned her vest before throwing on a tweed jacket and adjusting the lapels, remembering her mother, who always dressed her best for everything—even death.

When Arthie closed her eyes, she could picture her mother lying in the sand, the sea-foam meandering around the beaded trim of her sari. It soaked through the fibers, turning them the same deep red of her blood until Arthie couldn't tell where her mother's beauty ended and her wounds began. She sometimes imagined herself beside her mother on the shore, the water lapping at her skin. *Wake up, wake up, wake up,* the waves seemed to whisper.

Arthie met evil when she was only a child, and the great big Ettenian ship came ashore in Ceylan. The Ceylani had gone out to greet the Ettenian soldiers, offering sweets and a place to stay in the shanties by the sea. Not long after, the clear island skies billowed with smoke and chaos as the invaders turned peace into madness. *Colonists,* they called themselves. The Ceylani didn't have a word for that yet because they'd never faced people like that before: kind on the outside, greed and devilry on the inside.

They wore scarlet uniforms, sharp and commanding, as if they were righting the world's wrongs. Their weapons were the stuff of cowards, allowing them to kill from a distance, rifles firing faster than their enemies could run. Some Ceylani fought back, some succumbed, others fled on boats, escaping to the neighboring country of Jeevant Gar, which, at the time, no one knew had already fallen to the Ettenians.

But it was monsoon season, and Arthie's mother did not think her sickly eight-year-old daughter would survive the journey, so she took her to the village healer, who had toured the world beyond Ceylan and acquired the knowledge of it. The man had taken one look at Arthie and claimed they needed a miracle.

"Anything," Arthie's mother had said in her red sari, so focused on saving her daughter that she didn't realize her own window to escape was closing. "Anything."

Anything. Anything.

In the years that followed, Arthie sometimes heard that fervent plea in the dead of the night. She could hear the bullet that struck her father. The three it took to stop her mother.

She slammed her bedroom door closed, shutting the memory inside. The death. The blood. It was ironic that she was in the business of the same substance that haunted her past.

From the shadows of the second-floor balcony, she watched the way Flick devoured Spindrift, her hunger at odds with her sweet demeanor. The girl was taller than Arthie, buoyant curls framing warm features and a pert nose, her skin a deep, dusky brown. She was skilled beyond reason, enough that Arthie could overlook the fact that she was the daughter of one of Ettenia's vilest women alive.

Arthie watched as Flick clutched the address like a lifeline. Whether she accepted the job or not was to be seen, but Arthie had her guess.

"Your guard is here," Jin announced, rapping his knuckles on the wall behind Arthie. "I can see why you said yes."

Arthie didn't take her eyes off Flick. "I will not ask you to elaborate."

"Mm-hmm," Jin crooned, and she knew that if she looked his way, he would waggle his eyebrows. "You had to have some reason to shake hands with our enemy."

The two of them had spent the remainder of the previous night running through the probabilities and risks. Their alliance with Laith would be tenuous, but they were on equal footing, for if *he* was dangerous and unpredictable, so was she.

Jin leaned against the railing and peered down, following Arthie's line of sight when she shifted her gaze to Laith. He looked different in the daylight, more boyish and youthful. He looked like much easier prey than he did last night.

"Think we can get this ledger in two weeks?" Jin asked.

"We have to, and we will," Arthie said.

"We'll need to close Spindrift though. Neither of us will be around, and we'll need all hands on deck."

Arthie pulled her gaze away from the crowded floor, a kaleidoscope of color and aroma, of money trading hands and secrets spilling like rain from broken skies. Reni and Chester together had uncovered a scandal from the Afton sisters—apparently, their brother had carried on an affair with a maid, and their father had fired her, resulting in an accident that cost her life.

That made Lord Afton, by all convoluted counts, a murderer—a useful bit of information in the face of an impending betrothal between one of his daughters and the son of the late viscount that neighbored them. It was a union that would make Afton a bit too powerful for Arthie's tastes, particularly since he ran the shipping warehouse where she stored her cargo.

Chester was on his way to the viscount's house now, where a footman or two would learn the news and pass it onward and upward. Chaos kept the world in order. Not bad for their last day open.

"Then close," Arthie said.

Jin was watching her. "It's okay to feel something about it."

She cut him a look. Oh, she felt something about it all right.

Jin looked like he wanted to say more, but Arthie didn't want to hear it, so she descended the stairs and made her way through the bustling tables.

Laith lounged by the windows, a portrait of stillness amid the mayhem of the patrons filing in and out. He was in those snow-white robes again that tapered off at his mid-calf above fitted pants. A broad sash secured around his middle boasted a curved dagger.

"What's this?" Arthie asked.

He rose and presented the bouquet in his hand like a dead rabbit. "I heard that the custom here is flowers."

He was giving her flowers while she was planning his funeral. "We're working together, not courting."

"Are they not one and the same?" Laith replied.

She took the bouquet. The wax paper was smooth beneath her fingers, the flowers fragrant, the gesture altogether unexpected. She clenched her jaw.

Laith was devouring every second of it. *Nope.*

"Chester," she said, stopping him on his way past her. "Be a dear and take these flowers outside, will you? Toss them in the dirt where they belong."

Laith's tiny, knowing smile reminded her of what he'd said in her office, when her eyes had betrayed her by following the shift in his throat.

"Aw, Arthie's first flowers," Jin remarked, joining them. "Pity they're from you."

"No need to be hostile. I brought you a gift as well," Laith said. "Apple?"

There was a weight to his accent, so the *p*'s sounded like soft *b*'s.

Abble. Jin stared at the offering. It was the shiny kind he liked, the skin a plum color near black.

"Pretty sure there's a fairy-tale analogy for this moment," Jin said, taking it from him. "I'm Jin. Jin Casimir."

"I wondered about that," Laith said, tilting his head. "You don't look related."

"We don't really care for lineage on this side of White Roaring," Jin said, but what he didn't say was that he had spent days looking over his shoulder when Arthie and he had first linked hands, fearing whoever had come for his parents was coming for him too, until Arthie gave them a last name of their own.

It wouldn't do much, really, but when one was young and lost, almost anything made you feel powerful. A new surname promised a new start, a new future they could forge for themselves.

Laith *hmm*ed but didn't comment. He dipped his head. "Laith Sayaad."

"Welcome to life as a criminal," Jin said. Laith began to protest, but really, one couldn't ally with the Casimirs and *not* get a little tarnished. "Can't say we have your kind around here. Where from?"

Laith's gaze dimmed. "Far enough that two became one."

That was new information. Had he left someone behind, or had they died? Arthie inched away, turning her back on Laith, and Jin followed.

She could sense the smirk on his face.

"I take it your mission to Admiral Grove went well," she said before he could speak, heading for the stairs.

That did the trick. He sighed and straightened a frame, oozing reluctance.

"You know she's the best forger there is," Arthie said with a sidelong glance. "So stop whining."

"You didn't even let me start whining." He followed her upstairs. "She doesn't forge anymore."

"She will for me," Arthie said. Flick was already invested. Arthie had seen it on her face. "You never complained about working with her before."

In fact, he'd always wanted to—offering to go down to her warehouse before Arthie could, taking more time than was necessary. He'd even offered to pick up Flick today when Arthie had planned to go herself, knowing Admiral Grove loomed with the ghosts of Jin's past. He was the reason they'd even trusted Flick to begin with, given who her mother was.

"It's one thing to go out to her warehouse and hire her for a job. It's another to involve her in a dangerous scheme. She's not cut out for this," he said. Flick was innocent, that was true. Untried and untested. The girl *looked* as though she were made for decorating pastries, but looks were meant to deceive.

Arthie opened the door to her office. "If only her mother was as concerned for her well-being."

Jin was still scowling. "Did you at least tell her about the job?"

"I don't make a habit of talking twice, Jin. So no, not yet," Arthie said. "We've only got four in our crew right now."

Jin picked up the vase on her desk. "Should have kept the flowers. Poor captain boy."

"They matched my hair quite well, didn't you think?" Arthie asked, turning away when his eyebrows shot up. She pulled on her baker boy hat and stepped back out to the balcony hall before he could tease her again.

Laith was still seated at the same table, strands of that unnaturally bright white hair dusting his forehead. Arthie wasn't naive. He spoke with an accent, he wore the clothes of his kingdom, he walked with a distinct pride many foreigners shed like a coat—he was new to Ettenia. Too new to be so invested in the ledger and taking down the Ram. Too new to care for a country such as this.

She didn't like the idea of him breathing down her neck, privy to her every word, but this was White Roaring. Comfort was hard to come by—even coffins were made of stone.

"Waiting on you, habibti," he called as she started down the stairs. She didn't know what that meant and didn't want to ask. It was likely an insult. He stood up, and the sun cast his eyes in honey and spice. "Where to?"

Arthie pulled up her collar, and Jin picked up his umbrella. "We're going to 337 Alms Place to recruit our fifth."

10

FLICK

Flick glazed her lips with a fresh coat of pink as she crossed the street. She had missed it. The carriages rattling past, the horses trotting away from the newsboys waving papers with the day's gossip, the hustle and bustle and how insignificant it made her feel. How she could walk and laugh and twirl and no one would scrutinize or rebuke her. She passed a few Plodders with the lurid yellow popped collars common to the gang, and then a stand displaying flowers in the same color as her lavender dress and lopsided cap.

Everyone knew who lived at 337 Alms Place, but Flick didn't know how Matteo Andoni fit into Arthie and Jin's plans. Surely he hadn't allied with them. Flick unlatched the gate and stepped onto the cobblestone walkway, where Arthie, Jin, and someone she didn't recognize were waiting.

What would her mother think if she saw her now? Did her mother even know she'd been arrested? Had it only made her angrier, or did she miss her? It would be over soon, Flick told herself. She was going to fix everything.

Jin turned at Flick's approaching footsteps, and she wondered if she imagined his eyes brightening at the sight of her. "I knew you couldn't resist an invitation."

"Hello, Jin," she said.

"Flick." Arthie inclined her head. "Glad you could join us. I thought you could use some fresh air. I'm sure mother dearest will forgive you for it."

Flick froze, but Arthie turned away almost instantly. They were just words, Flick told herself. Arthie couldn't know what Flick was planning.

"We haven't met," the boy she didn't recognize said. He was far more cordial than she had expected. "You must be the talented forger I've heard much about. Honored to make your acquaintance."

"My name is Flick," she said, abashed.

"Laith," he said, tipping his head.

Jin scowled. "I don't think you want to get chummy with the Horned Guard."

Flick gasped, stepping away from him. "You—"

"Your secret is safe with me," Laith said. His voice had a calmness to it that settled her nerves. "As far as I know, Felicity Linden is locked behind bars."

Up ahead, the manor door opened and a butler stepped out.

"Afternoon, Ivor," Jin called. "It's your favorite dashing duo again!"

The man called Ivor looked disdainful.

"Here to see Matteo," Arthie added.

Though Flick hesitated to call Arthie graceful, there was precision in her movements. She lived and breathed a type of fluidity born from confidence, and Flick was envious of her boldness.

Ivor drew himself up to his full height, which was really only a smidge taller than Arthie, and his mustache puffed out with his chest. "Master Andoni is not taking visitors."

"Remember our meeting last night? He'll want to see me," Arthie said. It sounded like a threat, though Flick didn't understand how Arthie could threaten someone as well-loved as him. "Go on. We'll wait."

Ivor glared and turned on his heel. Arthie leisurely pulled out her watch with one hand, the other hand in her pocket.

"Matteo Andoni?" Laith asked when they were alone. "Is that how you intend to fetch the ledger? With a rake?"

Arthie looked back. Her eyes were molten honey beneath the brim of her cap. "We'll have our ledger without you insulting my methods."

Something small squeezed through the gate and stumbled to the guard's ankle. "There you are."

It was a kitten. Her fur was dove gray and mostly white, as bright as his hair. Her tiny claws dug into the leather of his boots, and both Arthie and Jin looked skeptical when he crouched and picked her up with gentle hands.

Flick gasped. "She's adorable! Where did you get such a precious darling?"

"I found her cornered and pawing at a snake. Poor thing would have died if I hadn't found her in time," Laith said, and then his gaze turned distant. "I know a helpless soul when I see one."

"I want to know what the skinny bloke mixes in his tea," Jin said under his breath, flummoxed. Flick had to admit the guard's words were a tad sanctimonious.

"Of course the saint would have a cat," Arthie said.

Laith rubbed the kitten's chin and looked at Arthie. "You know, criminal, I'd prefer if you called me by my name. The sooner you treat me like a member of your crew, the easier it will be for all of us."

She smiled, sweet and amiable and threatening, and Flick stepped between them before they could snap at each other's throats. She scratched under the babe's chin until her yellow-green, marble-like eyes fell to slits. "Does she have a name?"

Laith looked as if he hadn't even considered that she might need a name. Flick thought names were important. They told you a lot about someone, which was why she felt she was more of a Flick than a Felicity. She'd outgrown her name when her mother had outgrown her love.

The front door swung open again, and the butler appeared.

"Aren't you going to invite us in, Ivor?" Arthie asked, like they were vampires who needed inviting.

Ivor hesitantly stepped onto the threshold with a frown so deep it looked right about ready to slip off.

"Come in," he said, in as much of a grouse as a respectable butler could muster. "Welcome to the Andoni Residence."

Flick's heart was racing in her rib cage as the butler led them through the house, first past a receiving room, then down a hall lined with cabinets stocked with antiquities. The air felt rich and homely all at once, making her wish for a blanket and a book to curl up with on one of the oversize armchairs they'd passed along the way.

She was pulled from the fantasy when Arthie murmured something to Jin, who proceeded to turn a keen eye to their surroundings— and not, it seemed, to appreciate the decor.

Was Flick wading into something she should not be involved in? *You were arrested*, she reminded herself. Even if she wasn't in a prison cell, she couldn't wade much further than that.

Still, she was a sheep among wolves, dainty and colorful compared to their sharp lines and dark cuts. She was meant for needlework and gossip, not pistols and blackmail. Young women of her age and status were swooning over suitors and naming future children, not marching with the likes of the Casimirs.

Flick liked that about Arthie. She not only defied society, she owned that defiance. She had forged a crown for herself when the world told her she was not meant to have one. Flick wondered if Laith saw the same in Arthie, and if that was why he watched her so intently. For it wasn't the scrutiny a guard gave a criminal, no. She wondered if Arthie shared Laith's interest. If there was ever a type Flick didn't want to involve herself with, it was the Horned Guard. She had too many crimes to her name.

"Almost done giving us the tour then, Ivor?" Jin called as they turned down yet another hall. "Can't wait to see the kitchen pantry."

Not that I'm here to involve myself with anyone, she reasoned when Jin closed in beside her and she had to remind herself to breathe.

The butler ignored him, leading them into a wide and well-furnished parlor, its drawn drapes standing in contrast to the chandelier bathing the room and its crimson baroque walls in gilded warmth. It was as rich as her mother's estate, but it oozed comfort and warmth.

"No," a voice was saying. "I'd rather not."

A figure stepped through another door, more statue than man, far too beautiful to be real. Matteo Andoni. A girl was beside him, insisting on something, and noticing her flushed skin and low-cut bodice, Flick could tell what he was turning down. Matteo was widely desired, but it was well-known that he kept to himself. He wasn't the rake Laith said he was.

Flick's hand flew to her throat when the girl turned around. It was Beatrice MacArdle. She had snickered at Flick's gown last season, and now here she was with her own mostly undone. The girl said something else, but Matteo shook his head, and she turned with a screech before stomping out of the parlor.

"A little warning would have been appreciated, old boy," he said, voice low. He was a lot younger than Flick thought he'd be. "I was quite busy."

Ivor didn't bat an eye. "Apologies, sire."

"Did you just turn down Miss MacArdle?" Jin asked with a whistle as the butler closed the doors behind himself. Flick didn't like that he knew her.

"The voices and faces blur together when they all want the same thing," Matteo said almost tiredly, but then he saw Arthie, and a grin curved his mouth. "Two visits in less than a day? Oh, darling, I knew you would miss me."

"Sit down, Andoni," Arthie said. "We have to talk."

He looked at her through hooded emerald eyes, the slow drawl of his voice making Flick feel as if she was listening in on something she shouldn't. "That tone gives me shivers."

Arthie bristled. "Sit down, or I'll put another bullet in you."

Flick sputtered. "You shot *the* Matteo Andoni?"

"That would be me," Jin replied, leaning against a wall and crossing his arms. Flick didn't understand how the pose made him even more attractive.

"The emphasis is a nice touch." Matteo sank into a velvet settee and slung his arms across either side. His legs were splayed indecently. As a matter of fact, his entire appearance was indecent, and Flick didn't know how Arthie remained utterly unfazed. "But we did more than that, Arthie and I."

No, not unfazed. A vein twitched in her jaw, her shoulders had stiffened, and there was a hint of color on her cheeks. Matteo observed every bit of it and then some. His very presence needled Arthie, and he knew it.

"Indeed," she agreed, sweet as a bird. "After he declared his love for me, I had him shot in the heart."

Flick's laugh died in her throat. "He's—you're . . . you're still alive though."

Jin was enjoying this. "Alive? Matteo here's been dead a long time."

Matteo did nothing to refute the words. Laith's eyes flared wide, and Flick's thoughts ground to a halt.

A vampire.

Flick slipped her hand into her pocket for the comforting cold of her lighter. It was a reminder of another time, a time before the East Jeevant Company had drawn lines across her mother's brow. Before it had stolen all her time and made her harsh, armoring her with animosity.

Matteo Andoni's work was lauded across Ettenia, his youth and looks as much an allure as the timeless genius of his skill. There were portraits in her mother's office commissioned from him, and she was the lady who refused to stand in the same room as a vampire, let alone shell out duvin for one.

"Is it true?" Flick asked him. It wasn't as if vampires were easy to differentiate from humanfolk. They didn't need to breathe, but often did out of habit. When well-fed, they had pulses and heartbeats. When cut, they bled the blood they'd drunk.

Matteo tilted his head as if he could see the confusion warring in her: to lean into her mother's prejudice, or to see for herself if he was worth hating.

"Is there any reason it should or shouldn't be?" he asked.

Flick bit her cheek. How did it feel to never die? To lose count of the setting suns and the fattening moons? How did it feel to watch the living, born from nothing, turn into nothing once more? Given enough time, a vampire could learn all there was to learn. Discoveries could be made, coffers filled to the brim and then some. Flick assumed it would feel powerful, to be immortal, to never age, to revel in the knowledge that only a wooden stake or prolonged exposure to silver and sunlight could kill you.

But at the end of the day, Flick thought, it must get very lonely.

Unnatural, her mother's voice echoed in her skull, and Matteo's beauty faded, the ivory of his skin dulling to the same pallor of a corpse. She set aside her astonishment and thought about how the secret could benefit her mother.

This was good, she convinced herself. This was exactly what she had hoped to find. *I think.* Her mother would be gobsmacked to learn what Matteo Andoni really was. She ignored the unease in her stomach and looked up to find Arthie watching her.

Speak, Flick.

"What about the job? Why am I here?" she asked, clearing her throat and changing the subject.

"Job?" Matteo asked, lifting his brows. "What job? And who is she?" His nostrils flared with an inhale, and she felt as if she was being sized up by a predator. "I've seen you before, haven't I?"

Flick knew where, of course: in her mother's parlor, years ago. She'd found it strange that the painter set appointments at unseemly hours, but it fit her mother's equally unseemly schedule, which made everything perfectly all right.

"This is Flick," Arthie answered. "Also known as Lady Linden's daughter."

Matteo looked to Arthie warily. "And why do we need the daughter of the EJC?"

Flick *was* the daughter of the founder of the EJC, so she didn't know why the comment stung so much. She was like the moon, she told herself. This emptiness was merely a phase she needed to traverse in order to be full again.

"Because she happens to be a master forger," Jin said, stepping closer to her. At his compliment Flick's heart caught like a lighter snapping shut. "And we can't do this without her." He brushed his fingers against her exposed wrist, calming her for a beat before sending her pulse into a frenzy.

Jin passed a roll of paper to Arthie, who unfurled it across the glass table between them and Matteo. There were notes scrawled along one side, a wide space left blank on the other. Laith stepped closer, the kitten in his arms. Arthie centered herself in front of the paper, and suddenly every man in the room was as enraptured by her presence as Flick was just then.

And Flick could all but taste her mother's forgiveness when Arthie spoke, giving her the ammunition she needed on a silver platter.

"We're breaking into the Athereum to steal the Ram's ledger."

11

ARTHIE

Arthie made herself comfortable in one of the armchairs at a perfect viewing distance from Matteo and his disbelief. She knew she'd bagged Flick by the way the girl's mouth had dropped open, and now it was only a matter of time before the painter came around. His secret was too precious for him not to.

"Say that again, darling?"

"Don't call me darling," Arthie said, sitting back and willing away the stupid goose bumps conjured by his voice.

"Arthie, dearest," Matteo amended with eerie calm, giving her a glimpse of the beast that lay beneath his nonchalance. "Say that again, will you please?"

"We're breaking into the Athereum. The Festival of Night is around the corner. We'll use the auction as cover to find the missing ledger."

Matteo dragged his hands down his face with a groan. "Firstly, no. Secondly, absolutely not. *Especially* not if the Ram is involved."

"Oh, he isn't," Arthie said. "His incriminating ledger is, and we're going to get it."

Matteo looked perplexed. "And let me guess, you plan to expose the Ram with it."

Flick looked very interested in her answer. Arthie pursed her lips to the side. "Something like that."

"Which is exactly why we shouldn't do this," Matteo said, and it didn't slip her notice that he'd said *we*, including himself. "How do you even plan to meet the Ram if you were to retrieve this ledger?"

Arthie didn't want to discuss her post-retrieval plans in front of Laith. "We'll figure something out. Maybe secure an invite to a fancy ball. Aren't they usually attended by anyone of importance?"

"The Imperial Square Gala," Flick said. "They only invite the top of the top to that one."

"Not the Ram, sweet," Matteo said.

"None of this is important right now," Laith asserted.

Matteo gave him and his kitten a proper look.

"Laith Sayaad," he said before Matteo could ask.

"Of the Horned Guard," Arthie added. "And that's his unnamed kitten, because he's one of those monsters who doesn't name his pets."

Matteo rose and paced several feet, then sat down again. "You brought the Horned Guard inside my—no. Arthie?" He looked as exasperated as she often felt, and it filled her with glee. "I believe you have much to tell me."

"Much *has* transpired since we last met," Arthie agreed.

"We've had *quite* the night," said Jin.

Arthie recounted the events of the past day and night, leaving out the finer details of her first exchange with Laith. If the intensity of Laith's gaze on her now was any indication, he had taken note of the omission.

"I can't help you," Matteo said when she was finished.

"And let me guess why," Arthie said. "Because you know nothing of the Athereum?"

Matteo gave her a crooked grin. "Exactly."

Jin strolled closer, making a show of the coin dancing across his knuckles. She had known he would find it during their walk through the house. It was pewter, twice as big as a duvin and far prettier— engraved with an obscure *A* surrounded by vines and thorns, the words *mortui vivos docent* following the curve.

The dead teach the living.

"One Athereum marker dedicated to one Matteo Andoni," Arthie announced. "One personalized ticket to the inside. If anyone had a way in, it would be you."

The Athereum had very likely begged him to be a member, what with his social standing in White Roaring.

"How . . ." Matteo started before deciding otherwise. He sighed.

"Jin has—and how can I put this nicely—fingers that are slightly more adhesive than most," Arthie explained. Flick laughed with a tinkling bell of a sound, and Arthie, watchful as she was, saw how Jin lit up like a lighthouse at sea.

"Right, now that that's settled: Flick, are you in?" Arthie asked.

Flick didn't miss a beat. "Yes."

She didn't ask for payment, she didn't even give it a moment's thought. Everyone stared, and Arthie could tell that Jin had immediately written off her quick tongue as her being overwhelmed. But Arthie wasn't so sure.

"What—what will I receive in return?" Flick asked too late.

"Excitement," Arthie answered. "Now sit down. Let's put that penmanship to work."

Flick sank into the matching armchair a good distance from Matteo.

"Did you fail to notice the part where I hadn't agreed to help you?" Matteo asked. There was a smudge of black paint on the side of his neck and another on the inner shell of his ear.

"As sure as you failed to notice the part where I hadn't asked you to," Arthie replied.

He slumped back. "I'm going to miss our chats when all of you turn up dead."

Laith sat down on the rug in front of the coffee table and crossed his legs, an eye on his kitten as it curled up in a corner of the parlor. "You are going to ascertain it never comes to that."

"Ascertain?" Matteo repeated. "Where did you say he's from again, the dictionary?" But Matteo looked as if he knew exactly where Laith, with his kohl-rimmed amber eyes and curved dagger, was from.

"I think you might know," Arthie said. He struck Arthie as the sort who knew so much that they had no option but to act the opposite.

Matteo tipped his head. "From a kingdom hewn of desert and strength, sprawling palaces and sparkling mirages. You're Arawiyan."

The description alone made Arthie imagine she felt a little bit of that relentless heat and enchantment that Ettenia did not have. Laith ran a finger absently along his exposed collarbone, pulling her gaze to the lean muscles outlined by his fitted sleeves.

"Cursed to remain secluded, are you all not?" Matteo asked.

"No longer," Laith said distantly. "We are now free to access the remainder of the world."

Were they really free, if triumphing over their curse had simply moved them into a new circle of prey?

"Next on Ettenia's list, I can imagine," Arthie said.

Matteo laughed. "I do not think Arawiya can be written off so quickly."

Apt, Arthie thought, looking at Laith.

Flick leaned forward. "Have you been there?"

"The kingdom was corralled by an impenetrable forest for a near century," Matteo said, affronted. "I'm immortal, not ancient."

"A discernible difference for sure," Jin said, rolling his eyes.

"I'm curious why someone from that far away has taken interest in Ettenia," Matteo continued, following Arthie's own line of thought. "And so keenly, at that."

"I like to excel at whatever I do, vampire," Laith replied, an edge to his voice. The air went cold as they regarded one another, two predators in a pen.

Arthie heard the shift of Jin's umbrella, the rise of Flick's breathing that Matteo, being a vampire, registered with a flare of his nostrils. She studied Laith's calm, the steady beat of his gaze that missed nothing. He was hiding something as much as Flick was—but Flick wore her secrets on her face, plain as day.

"Indeed, I am a vampire, though if I had to choose a descriptor for myself, I think I'd use *gorgeous* or *tantalizing*." Matteo lifted one leg over the other. "Anywho, it's an ingenious idea, infiltrating the Athereum during the Festival of Night. They expect a full house for the charity auction, and you'll be able to bypass the issue of your pulses causing suspicion. Blood companions will be roaming the halls, and the vampires in attendance will be well-fed.

"But if you haven't heard, vampires are going missing. At least thirty have been reported across the district in the span of a few days, several of whom are members of the Athereum. It's believed the vampires are still out there and not piles of dust, though you won't be hearing much about any of it."

Arthie wondered if he was more worried about the disappearances than he let on. With no known correlation between any of the cases, there was every likelihood that he could be next.

"My point is," Matteo continued, "the Athereum is on high alert, which doesn't bode well for your little adventure."

"I decide when we pull off this heist," Arthie said. He didn't seem to understand that she wasn't asking him. "And that's now."

"Where's the fire, darling?" Matteo leaned forward, and her retort disappeared off the edge of her tongue.

"We don't do this, we lose Spindrift," Jin said finally. Flick gasped. Arthie cut Jin a look. Laith didn't look too pleased either.

Matteo's brows shot up. His concern almost looked genuine. "And who is threatening Spindrift?"

When Arthie said nothing, Matteo sighed.

"I'll take that silence to mean it's the Ram. Fine. Since you asked so nicely," he said. He took the pencil from Flick and smoothed the paper down with a gentle hand. The very air seemed to relax with the gesture. There were canvases propped against the walls, paintbrushes holding their breath in half-full glasses awaiting his return.

"Now, it's not that breaking in is impossible as much as it is obscenely difficult." Matteo held out the coin. "Let's start with the Athereum marker. As everyone knows, there's no getting in without one."

Everyone leaned close when he pressed a notch on its side, and a layer of the coin popped open on a tiny hinge.

Jin whistled. "Now that's sexy."

"See these numbers?" Matteo asked. They were stamped along the marker's inner curve. "Each coin has a unique set. Without a match of numerical code, you're not only denied access, you will suffer the very, very, *very* minor inconvenience of being impaled with a blunt stake through the heart." He pursed his lips. "A lot more painful for the living to die in such a way, but this is the Athereum, a society that cares oh *so* deeply about human suffering."

Arthie had always known how the Athereum dealt with trespassers, but when Laith slid a furtive glance at her now, uneasiness slithered through her. Did he know what she planned to do once they located the ledger?

"Think of it as their lex talionis," Matteo added.

Arthie saw Flick shiver. Perhaps she *was* too green for the job.

"Tit for tat," Jin explained, knowing Arthie needed the definition. He picked up Matteo's marker and flipped it, the coin winking out of sight for several seconds. "There's a flaw—the marker might have a unique identifier, but anyone can use it to gain access."

"Given how difficult it is to obtain a marker, from needing to be a certain age to holding a good standing in society, no vampire leaves it lying about."

"Except you?" Laith asked.

"You know, I'm not sure I like him," Matteo said to Arthie.

"If I needed to like everyone I worked with, I'd have to do everything myself," Arthie said.

"Hey!" Jin said.

Arthie bit back a laugh.

"Well," Flick ventured. "At least we have one marker. That's a start."

"We do," Arthie said.

Matteo's mouth curled slowly, and she knew he was going to refuse. "Your gaze upon a man, dearest, it's—"

"I have some of the fastest runners in White Roaring. I should think your secret's worth more than your marker," Arthie said.

"Start with the *Hanging Cliff*. They're quick at the press," Jin said, tilting his head to Arthie.

"The *Gold Rudder* prints faster," Arthie said, tilting her head in return. "Especially given the magnitude of the news."

"Mm. You have a point."

"Or," Flick said, "you can steal his marker and let him beg his way in."

Arthie and Jin stared at her, both equally impressed, and Flick blushed under the scrutiny.

"You really are quite adorable, regaling me with such heinous threats. Do you think I find them frightening?" Matteo rose from his seat, leaning closer to Arthie. She inhaled sharply. His next words were low, for her alone. "You know, darling, not everyone needs to be threatened to work for you. It's possible for someone to simply *want* to."

Before she could make sense of his words, he straightened. "Short of tossing you in through the window, I don't have a way to get you inside, and contrary to what you might think, threatening me in increasingly creative ways won't make me produce ideas."

Flick sputtered and pointed at his marker. "But—"

"This?" Matteo laughed. "This is worthless, sweet. No more than a paperweight. You'll find I don't care much for the Athereum. But I'll help you on one condition: Take me with you."

"No," said Laith without missing a beat. He rose to his feet.

Arthie lifted a brow at him. "No?"

"We're not striking deals with questionable parties. If he won't help you, we are leaving."

"He says *help* as if you weren't just threatening me," Matteo said.

Jin, still leaning against the wall, barked a laugh. "Are you hearing yourself? You jumped in through a second-story window and she said yes."

"Khalas," Laith said. "We will do this my way—"

"Or what?" Arthie asked, going still. "We can end this deal right now and let them blow Spindrift to the seas. I'll build it back, better and bigger than before."

Fire beat under her skin, tumbling like the sea that brought her to these shores. Through the corner of her eye, she saw Jin stiffen, but he was smart enough not to put his mouth where he shouldn't and call her bluff.

"If he fails to—" Laith began.

"If he fails, we all do," Arthie said. "So you had better pick up the slack."

"Now sit down," Jin said, and the tension rose as his grip tightened around the handle of his umbrella, even as the rough grind of his voice gave away his distress.

Laith remained standing.

"That's settled then. We might as well get the ducks waddling after us too," Jin said, glaring at Arthie as if she'd gone and destroyed Spindrift herself.

"Why is it worthless? Were you exiled?" Flick asked.

Matteo squinted an eye. "'Exiled' isn't the right word. My entrance would cause quite a scene, and I don't think I nor the Athereum is ready for it. Especially while they're strung tight with the disappearances."

"Why?" Arthie asked.

Matteo winked. "A story for another night."

Flick still looked confused. "But you said you wanted to get inside."

Arthie drummed her fingers on the arm of the chair. She didn't know what he'd done to be not-exiled, but she would find out, she always did. "He wants us to sneak him in. You want to see someone in particular."

"You have a very big brain for someone so small," Matteo said, genuinely impressed. Jin smothered a snort. "Do we have a deal?"

Arthie's lips thinned. "I seem to be striking deals with every questionable man I see. I'll get you in."

Jin cast her a look. She knew she made it sound as if getting inside the Athereum was as easy as swinging by the nearest eatery. As if they'd already hammered out their plans and secured their way in.

She nodded at the pencil in Matteo's hand. "Now, tell us about the Athereum."

12

JIN

Jin watched Matteo draw a line down the length of Arthie's paper, and slowly the stately profile of the Athereum on Ivylock Street began to take shape. Was there really no other way to save Spindrift? Jin thought of his mother's stern love, his father's easy smiles, and wondered what they would do.

The Athereum was old money paired with old families. It was born in the Wolf of White Roaring's massacre, when the government approved the creation of the society that was part authority, part revelry, where members spent their nights enjoying the Athereum's dark delights and Ettenian gossips flocked to its stone walls, hoping for a glimpse.

Though the Athereum never found the Wolf of White Roaring, it did its part in keeping order among vampires, from apprehending those that breached vampire-human laws—like drinking blood without consent—to those who violated basic Ettenian laws—like burglary. But as the Ram continued to step on toes with a widespread anti-vampire agenda, it seemed to Jin that the Athereum maintaining order was more tolerance than not. And as Arthie would say, tolerance suggested something had an end—when would the Athereum's patience end? How long was it before the Athereum decided it didn't want to heed the Ettenian monarchy's wishes?

"Here we are," Matteo said, presenting his sketch with a wave of his hand. "Stripped of its fancy corridors and furnished nooks, the Athereum is comprised of three essential parts. The parlor leads to the central ball-room where parties and events like the Festival of Night's charity auction take place. Next we have the right wing, with living spaces that double as a home for debauchery. And then the left wing, used for matters of business. Offices, the library, et al."

He drew a cushion of space around the offices and shaded it in.

"Why is it shaded?" Flick asked. "And you draw very nicely, I dare say."

Jin wondered if he should take up drawing.

Matteo laughed. "Haven't heard that one before."

"You don't hear it nearly enough though," Arthie said, forever observant. Matteo's hand slipped, the only indicator he'd heard her. It seemed her words had landed a little too close, for he had no quick comeback. "I know a thing or two about being recognized for the wrong reasons."

For Arthie, it was her skin tone over her brains. For Matteo, it was his beauty over his talent. Outside of 337 Alms Place, his name was more often associated with titters and temptation than respect.

"It's"—Matteo cleared his throat—"shaded because it's a secure area. There are two ways to get into this bit here, but both are restricted to authorized members only. No guests of any sort. Necessary, as it's home to the vaults and several high-profile offices. If your ledger is anywhere, it'll be in here."

"Authorized members *and* anyone being sent to confinement," Arthie said, gaze keen on his sketches. "How does that work?"

"Confinement?" Matteo asked slowly. "Get rejected at the doors, and one of the Athereum's two bouncers will whisk you away, depending on who'll be working that day. But the entire point of this operation is to not get caught, isn't it?"

He pointed at his sketch. "Anywho. We'll need to get *into* the building first, which is through a single entry point, fortified by our doorkeeper, Elise Thorne."

His quick yet winsome sketch of Elise told Jin what Matteo thought of her.

"To maximize time, two members can get through at once. Each of them inserts their marker through a slot"—he sketched a little box on either side of the doorkeeper and connected them to channels that ran inside the Athereum—"and then those markers are propelled through these two metal chutes to this room where her sister, Eleanor, verifies them. The chutes themselves are set into the floor, but visible through a glass covering. In case they need to spot jams and the like."

Or to show off their workmanship, Jin thought. That was what he'd do. Matteo drew a small room at the end of the chutes and a tiny stick figure inside of it. Someone didn't like Eleanor.

"She matches the numerical code," Arthie said.

Matteo nodded. "If matched and approved, the marker returns through the chutes marked in green. If rejected, it'll be marked red. If you ask me, the markers seem to have us in a predicament, seeing how we don't have any."

"Hence why I'm not asking you," Arthie said. Matteo studied the parlor molding with a sigh. Surprisingly, his walls were devoid of art, even his own.

Ivor came and went, metal soles clicking, his disapproval of Arthie and Jin spelled out in his frown. He didn't offer them food, and that drove Jin's disapproval of *him* up drastically.

"If Andoni's doesn't work, we'll be in need of five markers," Laith said as if that was Jin and Arthie's fault.

"The markers aren't our concern," Arthie said.

Flick clutched her beret. "You can't possibly mean that. They'll stake us through the heart."

"Death by the stake does sound like a fancy way to go," Jin agreed.

"Stake is a type of Ettenian meat, no?" said Laith.

"No, the letters would be arranged a little differently," Flick said.

"The peakies eat it mostly raw as homage to the cannibalistic carnage they commit throughout the world," Arthie snarked. Matteo choked. She looked at Laith. "You should try it sometime, since you're chummy with their lot.

"The markers aren't our concern because Flick will be forging them," Arthie continued. "She'll create new ones with new identifiers and have them added to the log. We'll only need one actual marker to get her in."

"I've never forged anything that complex," Flick said.

"Group project," Jin said. "I'll study the marker and give you the plans. You can work your magic after."

If she thought she was quick about hiding behind those curls when his words made her smile, she was sorely mistaken. And if he had thought every pretty girl's smile was created equal, he too was sorely mistaken.

"Do you still have access to casting materials?" he asked, clearing the knot from his throat.

Flick nodded. "A foundry not far from here."

"Good," Arthie said. "And how long will you need to add an entry into the log over in the Athereum's archives?"

"It's hard to say without seeing it," she said eventually. "Maybe three minutes?"

"Wonderful," Jin commented, jabbing his umbrella in the air. "Just enough time for them to grab a stake and personalize it with your name."

Flick ducked her head, and Jin decided then and there that teasing Felicity Linden was a delicious sport.

"He's right," Arthie said. "And it's not just one numerical sequence that needs inserting."

Flick looked over Matteo's marker. "I may be able to halve that time."

"Better," Arthie said with a nod. "But it'll need to be a fraction of that. The Athereum is efficient, and any distraction we pull to get you inside that room won't hold for long."

"Without studying both the layout and script in the log beforehand, I don't think I can."

Arthie raised her brows, and Jin read the words in that look: It took a certain kind of confidence to air one's incompetence before an audience. "I didn't ask."

Matteo rose and strode to a cart by the wide curtains where a decanter sat in crystal, narrow glasses rimmed in silver beside it. "Can I interest any of you in a drink?"

It wasn't tea or even liquor in the crystal bottle but something a lot more red. Arthie stared at him, her gaze unreadable. Flick's eyes were wide, while Laith looked uninterested.

"Suit yourselves," Matteo said with a shrug.

Jin turned his attention back to the sketches and the marker they needed to replicate, hinged lid and all. Still, he heard the vampire's swallow, his subdued yet relieved exhale, the tiny tinkle of the glass returning to the cart.

"I know where the sisters live. If you can study their penmanship, it might speed up the forging. I can give you the address, and you can swindle a sample or two that no one will miss," Matteo offered. He gave Arthie a look. "If you ask nicely."

Arthie's lips curved upward. "Please, Matteo, give me the address before I take your paint and redecorate your walls."

"You would never," Matteo said with a sharp gasp. They had just threatened to expose his secret, and *this* was what scared him? "That is heinous."

"I can be heinous, I can also be worse than that," Arthie promised.

"Enough," Laith said. Poor sod was feeling left out, more like it. "You're forgetting something. How will Flick get to the marker archive room *inside* the Athereum without a valid marker herself?"

"The original plan was to use Matteo's marker," Jin said, tapping his umbrella on the floor. "Before we learned that it's unusable."

Arthie shifted her focus to Matteo's sketch, more specifically, the two chutes that ran along the floor from the entrance to the archive room. Jin knew what she was thinking.

"If I get in first, we can rig the chutes," he said. "You said they're covered by glass, we'll just have to break it."

"Cut the chute open and approve the marker yourself?" Matteo asked. "Rejected by one sister but unbeknownst to the other. Smart."

Arthie was nodding, deep in thought, studying the drawings and missing nothing. "Right. So, here's our play. Jin goes in as a blood companion."

Jin wasn't excited at the prospect of calling in a favor, but he would do what was needed for Spindrift. He tapped the entrance with the point of his umbrella. "Flick follows with your marker."

"It gets rejected in the archive room," Arthie answered right on his heels.

"But I'll approve the marker on its way back through the chute," Jin said.

"And I'm in," Flick said, joining in.

Arthie's brow pinched at the interruption. Jin almost laughed. "Yes, you are, love. Once you're in, I'll cause us a distraction, as I usually do by walking into a room."

"Which Flick will use to get into the archive room," Arthie said before Flick could.

"She inserts the numerical codes and our forged markers are now the real deal," Jin finished, rapping his umbrella on the ground.

Matteo pursed his lips. "A solid plan, but you still can't use my marker. Just like sending forged markers through before they're added to the log, my marker wouldn't trigger a regular old rejection. They're typically for renewals or suspensions, not violations. Mine will create more of a ruckus than help our cause. We'll still need an actual marker. Even an expired one will do if Jin can get to the chutes."

Arthie looked deep in thought before she glanced up at Matteo. "Make me a list of as many Athereum members as you can remember. Someone's bound to have a secret they don't want shared, and they'll need to let us borrow their marker for an evening if they want to keep it."

Matteo pulled out a fresh sheet of paper to begin his list. He looked a little too eager for the task, and Jin had a feeling it was going to be full of vampires the painter didn't like. "So vicious, so ambitious. I like it."

13

ARTHIE

Arthie wouldn't commend herself until the ledger was in her hands. The Festival of Night was a weeklong event beginning with an auction, the proceeds from which the Athereum gifted to the public to better their image. They were the *good* vampires, the high-class, enigmatic, impressive ones.

She wasn't fond of how the living treated vampires, but she loathed the Athereum's distaste of *lesser* vampires even more.

"Speaking of a full house," Matteo said, rearranging his decanters and casting Arthie a look, "you won't be able to enter the Athereum armed. Not even with a renowned pistol such as yours."

Renowned and, what Matteo wasn't aware of, *special.* She drew her pistol and shifted it in the light. Gold pooled into the dark abysses of its filigree. Flick was staring; Laith pretended he wasn't. But they didn't have to worry about Calibore being seen or getting them kicked out.

"This?" Arthie asked, pointing it at him. "He'll dress up nice enough for the occasion. Just like the rest of us will."

"You'll be recognized either way with that hair, you know," Matteo said.

Arthie shrugged. She was counting on it.

"Why *do* you go through the trouble of dying your hair?" Flick asked.

"What's the first thing people notice about you?" Arthie asked.

"My skin."

"And what's the first thing you notice about me?"

"The hair," she replied without missing a beat.

"Exactly," Arthie replied. Everything else, like the brown of her skin and the disparities that stemmed from it, came second. "And then there are the whispers. Her skin's like caramel, they say. Or tea steeped too long and doused in milk. Strange that it's food they see when it's anything different than the norm, no? It's not much, but I like giving them something else to talk about."

"Well, if it's any consolation, darling, I think you look dangerous even with that fairy floss hair," Matteo said, returning to his seat. "Now please put that away."

She spun the pistol around her trigger finger, and Matteo's eyes bugged out of his skull. She wondered if he was recounting the previous night, when Jin had shot him. Arthie dropped a glance at his exposed chest. Spotless, not a bruise or blemish marred his creamy skin. He had to have drunk quite a bit of blood to heal so quickly.

Matteo cleared his throat, and Arthie looked up to find him watching her. He winked.

And Arthie had no way to explain why she'd been staring at his naked chest without alerting the rest of the crew to that fact. She decided to keep her pistol out a little longer.

"No weapons, khalas. No one's risking anything besides the clothes on their person," Laith said. For once, he and Matteo were in agreement, and it was clear the vampire didn't like it.

"Oh, we can omit those too, if you're concerned," he simpered.

"I would prefer to omit you altogether," Laith replied, then pressed his lips thin, looking irritated at himself for engaging.

Arthie holstered her pistol. She knew Jin didn't like going in bare. He had as many as ten different tools on his person at a time, usually a lockpick or a knife, and always, *always* his umbrella.

"Don't tell me you have no trouble setting foot in the Athereum unarmed," she said.

"Darling, gleefully reading the occasional obituary is the most violence you'll ever see me partake in," Matteo said, not the least bit apologetic.

Laith sighed, but Arthie supposed there was skill involved in abhorring violence. He had to make use of other methods to stay safe.

Like make a name for himself as a painter.

"What about the Athereum wall? We have to get past that before we can be concerned about the front door," Flick pointed out.

Laith's gaze drifted across the buildings Matteo had begun sketching along the lower half of the paper beside the Athereum, giving them a view of the street. "We can scale it."

"No one in a city of crooks builds a wall without precautions," Arthie said. "It's fortified and impenetrable. You can't climb it."

But Laith was not without pride. "I was trained to master walls far more difficult and cover distances just as great."

"He's right, he definitely has the look of a cultist," Jin said, biting into the apple Laith had given him.

"It is not a cult. Being a hashashin is an art. Our creed shapes bodies into blades, though none can ever be as great a killer as our kingdom's crown prince."

"Your crown prince is a murderer?" Jin asked.

"At least he's up-front about it," Flick pointed out. "What leader isn't a murderer?"

Laith looked insulted. "He is a changed man now."

Arthie attributed Laith's self-assurance to his training. To whittle a man into a blade required stripping away fear and misgivings and apprehension, leaving ample room for pride to bloom.

Matteo cleared his throat. "*Regardless*, the wall won't be of concern."

"We're going to blow it up, are we?" Jin asked, tilting his head. "You know, I didn't think that was your style."

"I forged for someone in possession of dynamite," Flick suggested, looking a tad too excited at the idea. "I'm sure we can arrange something with him."

Matteo frowned, as if realizing for the first time that he was in a room full of people unlike him. "What? Goodness, no. The gates will be open for the event. The Festival of Night is as much a display of the Athereum's generosity to the public as it is a party. Press will be there, possibly even adoring fans—enough of a crowd for us to blend in, both through the gates and in the gardens.

"What I'm more concerned about is this guard here." He tapped at a spot above the left side of the entrance, where a chunk of the roof had been cut for a dormer balcony. "It extends to a mezzanine inside, designed so he can survey both the gardens and the Athereum foyer. He'll spot Flick heading into the archive room."

"A single guard for both inside and out," Laith said, studying the sketch. "I can take care of him."

"These are Athereum vampires. Don't get cocky," Arthie said. "I'll scope it out first."

"Wonderful. And who are we stealing from again?" Matteo asked.

"Did you miss the past hour or so?" Jin asked.

"Oh, but who *within* the Athereum are you stealing from?"

Arthie narrowed her eyes. "I don't see—"

"A vampire by the name of Penn," Laith cut in.

"Penn," Matteo repeated slowly, his gaze narrowing on Arthie. "As in Penn Arundel, head of the Athereum?"

She refused to meet his eyes, pulling his sketches toward her and running a finger over the building rising to the Athereum's left. It was beautifully rendered. Matteo's work was much like him, timeless, refined, and sensual in a way she didn't have the right words for.

"The head?" Flick asked. "Does that make the job harder?"

"Not exactly," Matteo said, reminding Arthie of last night. He knew far more about her than he should.

"Why not?" Jin asked, and Arthie felt his eyes on her back, no doubt trying to decide if she'd known this beforehand. "He's the head of the Athereum. Seems like someone forgot to mention an important detail."

"Head of the Athereum means he'll be involved in the charity auction," Matteo pointed out. "He won't be guarding his office."

Jin continued watching her for a good long minute.

"Well, good." Flick leaned closer. "Isn't it funny how the Athereum shines even beneath the Old Roaring Tower's shadow?"

"Ah yes, the peakies' greatest invention yet: a very, very big clock," Jin announced, finally looking away.

Laith scowled. "Invention? It is a minaret they adapted to include a clock. What is the purpose of a tower if not to magnify a voice?"

"To magnify the passage of time," Arthie replied, tracing the tower as it tapered to its knifepoint peak. "Unfortunately for all of us, those with voices in this fair country are loud enough." Arthie rolled up the plans and pulled on her cap. "Let's scope the place."

Matteo went to a box on the side credenza, where he pulled out a pair of supple gloves and tinted spectacles. He took Jin's umbrella and propped it open while Jin sputtered a protest. "It is a perfectly gloomy day for a stroll."

"It *is* a good day for a stroll," Flick agreed.

"Ivylock Street will be clear of the lunch crowd right about now," Arthie said, pocket watch in hand because there wasn't a single clock in the house. Matteo regarded the little instrument. Vampires weren't fond of noting the passage of time. Arthie supposed it was an unwelcome reminder that they were here forever, cursed to watch generations rise and fall, destined to be forgotten.

The clock tower's position beside the Athereum was a cruel joke indeed.

"Don't frown," she simpered. "I'm not letting you out of my sight until this job is done."

He slipped on his tinted spectacles. "You certainly know how to motivate a man, darling."

On their walk back after surveying the Athereum, Arthie began putting together the first stages of her plan. Jin announced he was about to die of hunger, and Flick looked ready to keel over, so they stopped at a coffeehouse.

"A coffeehouse instead of Spindrift?" Matteo drawled. He sat under the shade of the awning and set Jin's umbrella across his leg, tipping his head back to the skies.

Arthie wondered how often he left his house during the day. It *was* excessively gloomy today, as most of White Roaring's days tended to be with its smog-filled skies, but not every day was like that. Not only did direct sunlight harm vampires, but it would have been impossible for Matteo to have kept his secret this long, as the undead didn't cast shadows. Someone would have noticed.

"What will your patrons think when they see you here?" he asked.

Arthie shrugged and pulled out a chair for herself. People were always hungry, and hungry dogs were never loyal. "Our patrons come to Spindrift because they wish to, not because we drive them there through ulterior means. Greed will get me nowhere."

Spindrift had the best tea and a crew that brewed and baked the best in turn. If people wanted to spend their hard-earned coin on something inferior, that was fine by her. One can only learn from their mistakes.

"Morals," Laith scoffed. "What of those secrets you collect? Do you pay for them?"

"I pay the same for Ettenian secrets as Ettenia has paid for its atrocities. Nothing," Arthie said, her voice tight.

"You'll find Arthie's morals to be quite like the sea. They choose upon whom to enact their wrath," Jin said as he disappeared inside the coffeehouse.

"So we've noticed," Laith drawled.

He exasperated her, and she didn't quite understand why. He seemed to enrage every part of her that her typical anger did not. It seared her chest, burned low in her belly. It confused her.

A waiter brought him a tray with a cup of coffee, a spoon, and a bowl of sugar.

"What do you think of Ettenia?" Flick asked him.

Laith gave it a moment's thought. "It is industrial, crisp, and yet everything about it is bland. Especially the food."

Arthie remembered very little of her life outside Ettenia. When she closed her eyes and dared to think of Ceylan, that place she once called home before she was thrown into a little boat and thrust out to sea, she didn't think of fiery foods or the sticky heat or the lush foliage—she saw red. On her hands. Flooding the shore, dyed across uniforms, smeared on the leaders who had been held less accountable than a refugee on the streets.

Jin returned with a half-eaten pastry oozing raspberry jam dark as blood and a paper bag marked with the buttery imprint of a strudel. He peered at the teacup on a passing waiter's tray and sighed. "Imagine falling in love with someone and learning they make tea the color of bone."

As he finished the first of his pastries and sat down, Flick's stomach growled like a beast. Jin folded the bag back on its crease with a frown and inched it toward the center of the table, wiping his fingers on a handkerchief monogrammed with a *J*. The corner was singed black. It had been years since the fire, yet he still clung to the hope that his parents were alive.

Arthie never shared in his hope—outwardly. She'd scoured the remains of his parents' house and threatened enough officials to know the fire at the Siwang Residence was no accident. But until she had proof that they were alive and an actual lead to follow, she'd continue acting as if she didn't believe they could have survived. Arthie wouldn't give Jin more hope until she was certain. She knew what it was like to have that ripped away.

"Are you not having anything?" Laith was watching her as he piled two cubes of sugar into his cup and fed a third to his cat.

"I have very refined tastes," Arthie said.

"You're a snob, you mean."

"Better a snob than someone mistaking sugar for flavor," she replied.

A slow smirk curled the side of his mouth, and he made sure she was looking when he added a third cube into his cup, stirring it thoroughly before meeting her eyes and dropping in a fourth.

"Can't blame me for needing a way to work with something so bitter."

"Can't make a choice without meeting its consequence."

Laith lowered his gaze to her mouth to irk her further, then he sat back and set the spoon on the table.

"Our high captain seems to be keeping a close eye on you," Jin mumbled.

"The way Flick can't stop staring at you?" Arthie asked.

"If anything," he said, folding and tucking his handkerchief away, "it's because you terrify her, and I'm the only decent one around. You, however"—he gave her a look—"don't forget that he's a Horned Guard. Don't stray from the plan."

Arthie rolled her eyes. Him and his tieless club collar shirts and tender concerns.

"I'm serious, Arthie," he said.

"As am I, more often than you, Jin."

He left the paper bag on the table and pushed his chair back, nearly toppling over a young lady, who clutched the wide hoop of her skirt as she regained her balance. Her chaperone fumed before he saw the look on Jin's face and decided he would rather live another day. Arthie hadn't meant for him to get *that* upset.

"I really believed you were the more charming of the Casimirs," Matteo remarked.

Jin slipped his hands into his pockets. "Oh, I live and breathe charm, vampire. Sometimes one needs a knife to drive a point home."

Arthie ignored the weight of Laith's gaze, left the table, and crossed the street in the direction of Spindrift. For whatever reason, she glanced back at the coffeehouse. But neither the high captain nor Matteo were there, only Flick, picking up the paper bag with a streusel Jin had left behind for her.

14

JIN

Though Jin had flipped the OPEN! sign to CLOSED on Spindrift with a heavy heart, reassuring himself that they would only remain closed until they retrieved the ledger, not a single member of the crew had a moment's rest as Arthie delegated tasks in the lead-up to the Athereum's Festival of Night.

Today he was getting those handwriting samples for Flick. He hopped out of a hansom cab in Admiral Grove, tipping his hat as the horse trundled away. He glanced at the address Matteo had given him a few days ago. The trees swayed in greeting, the *hush hush* of their leaves flinging him back years and years. He straightened the lapels of his coat and double-checked the laces on his shoes, swallowing to make sure the buttons of his shirt were all up. As if Admiral Grove was still his home, and not the grave of a child long gone.

When Jin was a little boy and Arthie was a little girl, she taught him the secret to survival. It wasn't food or a warm place to huddle every night. It wasn't coin or clean water.

It was preoccupation. He couldn't cry for his parents if he was busy running for his life. He couldn't panic if his hands were busy swiping coin.

There were days when Jin thought Arthie had engrossed herself so deeply into their new life that she'd forgotten the one she had before it. It was why she never spoke of it. It was why there was no sorrow in her eyes, nor fear. Only anger, bright and vengeful as a fire, boiling hotter than Spindrift tea.

Movement up ahead caught his eye. Flick was waiting on one of the many benches placed beneath the street's arching trees. Were those . . . pants she was wearing under her calf-length dress? *Well, well, Felicity, what a surprise.* He was fairly certain those were Arthie's pants, but the outfit was far more suited to their impending task than her lavender one from the other day, even if the lovely moss green was still too bright. Any more vibrant, and he would have feared arsenic poisoning just from being near her. A twill, mid-length coat in a soft brown completed the ensemble.

Jin was like her, once. Oblivious, innocent, shoes shined by someone else, clothes pressed before he woke, never a concern for the roof above his head. He had no grievances about what he'd become, but he missed what he had been.

Perhaps *missed* was the wrong word, because that meant he was ready to up and leave Arthie and Spindrift and everything else behind at first chance, when he wasn't.

He had *changed*, and that was what he wasn't proud of. He'd allowed the streets to rip a young boy apart and put something else together in his stead. The same happened to anyone who was displaced, to Chester, to Reni, to Arthie, but change, for Arthie Casimir, was a finely tailored suit that fit all her edges well. She sought it out.

Flick didn't.

And though she wasn't his to force back into a mold she might have outgrown, he wouldn't allow his world to be the reason why she felt she needed to break free of it.

He stopped.

A flame danced from a brass lighter in her hand, growing like a beast threatening to jump down his throat.

"Hello, Jin," she said, and his heart did something funny, but maybe that was because she pocketed the lighter as she spoke.

"Felicity," he replied, dipping his chin. She started to correct him before he peered at her through the curls shrouding most of her face. "Why are you hiding?"

"This is Admiral Grove." She ducked deeper into her coat. "What if I'm spotted?"

Because people like them didn't blend in with the tone of their skin, the shape of their eyes, the texture of their hair, or the lilt of their tongues. *We're meant to stand out*, Arthie would say, but Jin would be lying if he said he didn't sometimes wish for anonymity.

"Sitting still will ensure that, you know," Jin replied, gesturing with a hand. "After you, m'lady."

"Have you heard from your snitchers?" she asked, and the hope in her voice made it hard to hold her gaze. "Has my mother come to check on me?"

Jin started walking. He didn't want to lie, but he *had* heard from their snitchers, and Felicity Linden's mother had not, in fact, checked on her. She hadn't even sent a footman. Flick shot him a look, surprising him with the flint in her gaze, and marched ahead in the direction of the Thorne sisters' house.

"I asked you a question," she said eventually, keeping to the white-bricked wall beside them. She was careful, despite her guile, and Jin felt she knew, deep down, that her mother might not have even thought of her. But admitting something was far more difficult than knowing it.

She tilted her head again. "Did my mother say something . . . distasteful?"

Jin sighed. *If only, love*, he thought to himself.

He double-checked the address for the umpteenth time just to give himself something to do. Flick watched him.

Lie, he told himself, but when he opened his mouth, the fib wouldn't form. Irritation took hold instead. Irritation at Arthie for dragging Flick into their mess. Irritation at Lady Linden for abandoning her daughter.

"Jin, answer my—"

He wouldn't. He *couldn't*, and because he couldn't use his words, he closed the distance between them. Flick took a step back, and then another, until he had her caged between him and the wall. She smelled of sunlight and wildflowers, underlined by her soap, a peachy scent that was as sweet as his pastries. Jin had to stop himself from leaning in and burying his nose in her hair. He tossed his umbrella to his other hand, wishing he could take her back home and tuck her into her quilts and slippers and the care of maids.

"I know what you're doing," she whispered.

"Oh?" he asked. "And what is that?"

Only a tiny sound answered from the back of her throat, half whimper, half growl.

"You were given a job, Felicity," he said. "A job you agreed to undertake, and when we work, we don't let distractions come between us."

He bent closer, just in time to catch her gaze sweep across his lips like a touch. His pulse jumped. Her breath tangled with his, rough and surprised and as shocked as her hooded eyes of deep, dark gold that glittered like black diamonds.

"You—" Jin knew he was damned when he had to clear his own throat. "You understand me?"

"I understand," she whispered, and he should not have followed the bow of her lips shaping the words. He should not have let his eyes wander over the gentle curve of her cheek, the lush coils of her lashes, the anticipation clinging to the air between them.

He ground out a breath and straightened. "Now come. Criminal activities await."

Then he rapped his umbrella on the pavement and walked away.

"Such a pretty house," Flick said, when they stopped before a handsome dwelling with more stories than were necessary and a pitched roof. The awning rippled in the breeze, rosebuds swaying in the trim garden.

A hopeless laugh slipped out of him. "So insouciant."

"I beg your pardon! Doesn't that mean I'm childish?"

"You're a toff, Felicity," Jin said. "Didn't you learn your words?"

She ducked her head. "I prefer the art of them. The way they're written."

"The . . . art of handwriting," Jin said.

Flick nodded. "The way we can deduce a thousand things about the person who wrote a word just by studying the way they wrote it. The way they dot their *i*'s or cross their *t*'s, the way their script might loop or slant. Were they angry? In love? Harried or at leisure? Frivolous or perhaps conceited, and so their rhetoric was better ignored than heeded? Words themselves can't always unfold a person the way their writing can."

It was the most romantic way of looking at the world, which meant it fit Flick and her pastel hues and fierce curls just right.

"Why are you looking at me like that?" she asked.

Jin hadn't even realized he was staring. *Get yourself together, man.* And why was he having a hard time finding what to say when he usually had no trouble stringing together exactly what a woman wanted to hear?

Flick was suddenly shy. "Let's just—" She stopped and gestured to the house.

"Right," Jin said quickly, nearly tripping as he turned around.

Most of the windows were closed, their curtains drawn. Only a single one on the second floor was propped open. Why couldn't it have been the balcony doors, just several yards away? Jin ignored the drainpipe in favor of the frills that jutted in enough places that the house was a fancy ladder itself.

"Hitch your skirts, love," Jin said, gripping what he could.

Flick didn't reply. Jin reached for another handhold and then the next, relaxing his toes on a windowsill before he looked down. Flick hadn't even moved. She was standing by the house, watching his ascent with uncertainty.

Her face scrunched in confusion, and she said, quite sweetly, "But why hitch your skirts when you can open a door?"

Jin screwed his jaw shut. He hadn't seen the door. *Because you always overthink*, Arthie commented in his head. "Didn't know you could pick a lock."

"Oh, I can't," Flick admitted. "It was open, actually."

Jin sucked in a slow breath. "Were you going to wait until I got to the top?"

She tilted her head. "I wasn't sure how to tell you."

He sighed and dropped to the damp grass, then followed her inside the house. It was cool and almost sterile, if not for the fresh planks of cedar stacked on the counter of an unlit kitchen. Barely a kitchen, really, for it was devoid of food, and Jin didn't think the crystal glasses lining the shelves were used for juice. Light cut through the curtains and fell across Flick, illuminating a single eye in a shade of deep gold that reminded him of a sunlit meadow with sunflowers wide and wild.

"Jin?"

Right. The mission at hand. This was already going splendidly.

"Anything of use will be on the upper floors," he murmured, creeping out of the kitchen. He held out his umbrella to stop her from parading onward. "Careful."

She pushed past him. "Matteo said the house is empty."

"Still—"

Flick froze on the second-floor landing then whirled to him with wide eyes.

Jin didn't think. He bounded up the stairs three at a time and shoved her into the nearest open room with him, ignoring her surprised yelp. The sisters supposedly worked at the local bank until nightfall. Jin glanced at the draped window where the sun was pressed against the heavy fabric. It was barely noon.

Matteo had lied.

Which meant anything he'd told them about the Athereum could be a lie too. Jin was going to sharpen a stake and sharpen it some more and then finish the job he'd begun when he'd shot him. He pressed a finger to his lips and peered around the doorjamb until he heard what Flick had.

Well.

Measured sounds slipped out of the bedroom at the end of the hall. Jin relaxed his hold. He snuck a peek at Flick and immediately regretted it when a moan slithered beneath the closed door.

"Aren't we going to see?" Flick asked, eyes wide.

"To—" Jin stopped and faced her fully. "Oh-ho, Felicity. What have we here? A voyeur?"

"A what? No!" Flick said, too mortified to bristle at his use of her full name. "Why would you say that? Whoever that is could be hurt!"

Ah. He reconsidered her. Despite her days on the streets, with a mother like Lady Linden, Flick was even more sheltered than a typical girl of high society.

"No one's in pain besides me. Let's go."

Flick didn't move, the vexing girl. "What do you mean?"

"They're in a bedroom, love. What do you think vampires do to pass the time?" he asked pointedly.

She paused, and he knew the right answer had dawned upon her by the way her skin flushed like the sky before sunset and her gaze settled to the ground.

"Oh. I didn't—I didn't know it sounded like that," she murmured to herself.

Jin found himself unable to leave her be. "Well?"

"I didn't know what they did to pass the time!" she sputtered. "Take up knitting!"

"Oh, they're knitting all right. And you really need to dress more appropriately for jobs like these. You could have been seen. You stand out like a flag."

Flick gasped. "Better a flag than to dress like someone's dead."

Jin laughed. He scanned the hall and found the glass doors of an office. Empty house or not, he was going to get her those samples. At the door, he dug out a lockpick and gently worked it in until Flick bumped his arm and it struck with a *tink* that rang as loud as a blast.

"I may be irresistible, love, but I'm also claustrophobic," he whispered. She shuffled a few steps back, and Jin listened as the pins fell beneath his ministrations, the lock finally giving way with a pleasurable click.

"Not through yet," he murmured, tugging his gloves off with his teeth. He withdrew a tiny case out of his pocket and swiped at the gel with his finger, rubbing it down the hinges and coating the metal nice and slick. Flick stared. Jin had to bite his cheek against a thought.

He pulled open the quiet doors with a flourish. A heavy oak desk sat in the center of the ample office littered with papers and files. There were pens scattered among open books, and a monocle dangled off a lamp. A cart similar to Matteo's was off to the side with a decanter full of blood.

"Grab yourself a drink and get to work," Jin instructed.

"Very funny," Flick whispered.

She tiptoed around, her hand hovering over the desk, reaching but touching nothing, a shadow of fascination on her face.

"In your own time," he added.

Flick scowled. "I can't work with you standing over me."

"Would you prefer I sat down?"

She flung open the curtains with a tiny growl then, realizing they could be spotted, closed them back up. Jin watched as she pulled out her supplies, focus slipping into the crease of her brow and the planes of her face. She layered a graphite sheet and then a slip of paper under a diary page, slowly tracing over it with a pen.

Jin released a breath and dug out a clove rock. It was only after it struck his teeth and settled on his tongue that he heard it.

Footsteps. Someone was coming down the hall.

He scoured the room for a place to hide, but these were vampires. His pulse was erratic, his heart like a horse gone wild. Hiding wouldn't help. He added Matteo's name to the growing list of people he'd enact vengeance upon when he was dead, right there beneath Arthie's.

"Do you trust me?" Jin asked. He flicked a look at the window and mentally mapped the perimeter of the house.

Flick's laugh was like brittle glass. "Not entirely."

"Good girl. Grab a few samples and, at my command, run to the next room and jump from the balcony. It's time for plan C."

She stopped gathering her things. "What? We're on the second floor! What's plan B?"

Jin shrugged. "Just not fond of the letter. Jump, Felicity."

With that, Jin straightened the lapels of his jacket, smoothed back his hair, and strolled into the hall.

15

ARTHIE

Arthie pushed through the crowds on Stoker Lane just before noon, feeling good about their plans. When Matteo had handed her his list of Athereum members in his tenacious, looping scrawl, he had warned her that the task would be difficult. Athereum members benefited from having time at their disposal. They were patient and covered their tracks, and as a result, they were careful with their dealings. Blackmailing any one of them would be an arduous endeavor.

But she hadn't expected to see the name of the official in charge of public works. She didn't know he was a vampire, and she never would have pegged him as a member of the Athereum.

His name on Matteo's list had made her job infinitely easier. By tonight, she'd have a valid marker in her hand.

She passed the dye shop and the tannery, then Fat Anvil's florist that wasn't a florist at all. There were folks who waved at her, some who complimented the tea they'd drunk at Spindrift, and others who made their distaste for her establishment known.

At last she reached the stretch of road beside the cemetery where gravestones were plunked down like afterthoughts because no one ever remembers they're going to die.

Clutching her cap against a gust of wind, she stopped when something white disappeared into an alley across the street, a kitten strutting into the shadows after him. *Laith.* He was supposed to be meeting her at noon, not wandering through backstreets.

Arthie crossed over, keeping her distance. A ladder was propped up to the sawtooth roof of a building, and Laith scooped the kitten onto his shoulder before he began his ascent, swift and languid. Arthie clenched her jaw and looked ahead to the street she should take.

And yet, there was something to be said about a girl who knew everything about everyone and a boy more mysterious than the moon.

Exhaling through her teeth, she started up the rungs, reaching the top as Laith made quick work of the roof's dips and rises like a phantom passing through fog. She could barely follow his lead.

When she finally made it past the narrow ledge near a chimney, she stopped, clutching her hat against a gust of autumn air.

Yards ahead, Laith was watching her. He wasn't even surprised to see her, and she remembered Jin's warning.

"Arthie," he said. *Almost despicably*, she thought. But she knew she was lying to herself; his voice was as soft as it had been that night in her office, and little embers raced down her skin.

Here was a boy who knew his worth, the pride on his face said, but unfortunately for him, she was a girl who knew hers. She lifted her chin.

"Shadowing me, hmm?" he asked. "One might think it's because you don't trust me."

Oh, she didn't, but there was more to it than that. A pretty face wasn't enough to raise her interest. She needed a puzzle, an enigma. A challenge. They might have formed an alliance, but neither of them trusted the other. This wasn't merely a deal. It was a game.

"You were to meet me at the Office of Public Works," she said. "Not plod around abandoned alleys. Of course I'd tail you."

"You'll find I don't break my promises." There was something deeper to the words, a message she couldn't fully grasp.

"You will this time, because the traffic on Stoker Lane will double in about three minutes."

The breeze ran fingers through his hair. "Not on my route."

Arthie glanced at the foot traffic four stories below. It was a long drop, and the next building was a street's width away. This was his route? He couldn't jump that.

He twirled a sprig of rosemary between his fingers. Arthie wondered if he knew that Ettenians spoke with flowers when they were too prim and proper for direct conversation. He very likely did, for every corner sold a pamphlet with a list of which weed meant what and what blossom to say why.

"You don't fear death." His words weren't a question but an observation. He breathed a laugh. "Or maybe you're simply not afraid of heights."

"What mattered of me died long ago," she said, and started for the drainpipe.

"You and I aren't much different in that regard." He didn't elaborate, and she wasn't about to ask. Asking meant interest, and interest would suggest she cared.

She didn't. "You can risk a leap. I'll take the street."

"Or you could let me show you how."

Surprise flared in his eyes because he hadn't expected her to turn back. In this game between them, she had scored a point in her favor.

"Go on then," she said, stunning him further by closing the distance between them. His throat bobbed, and she delighted as his confidence crumbled.

She could see the flecks of bronze in his dusty brown eyes, matching the jewel set in the hilt of his curved dagger. She could see that his nose was a little crooked, and his hair was wavy where it had been allowed to grow out a little.

"Hello, criminal," he said, stepping behind her.

"Teach me, saint," she replied.

He reached for her arms, straightening them with a gentleness she didn't expect. It unnerved her. His touch struck flint down her skin, forcing the *tick, tick, tick* of her watch to be as silent as a vampire's pulse.

His exhale feathered the back of her neck, and then his hands slipped to either side of her ribs and fell to her waist. She heard him gulp.

There was that exasperation again. Vexing her. Strangling her. It was as if she couldn't control how she felt, and that terrified her. She was aware of the weight of each of his fingers through her shirt as if he was carving her with a knife. She wanted to press into him. She wanted to snarl at him. She wanted—

His hand brushed her pistol.

The world rushed into focus.

Arthie whipped Calibore free and shoved Laith onto his back. He fell with a surprised *oof*, boots scrambling to gain purchase. His kitten leaped away with a startled cry. Then Arthie pressed the barrel of Calibore to his brow, and he went absolutely still.

If she didn't need him to infiltrate the Athereum, she would blow his brains into the shingles of this roof.

His breathing was loud, rough. Wind ruffled the back of her jacket, warning her that she was at the edge of a four-story building in front of a boy she barely knew, a high captain of the Horned Guard she had just gotten far too comfortable with.

"Calm down, Casimi—"

She dug the barrel farther in until it scraped bone. "Don't 'Casimir' me."

He pushed back against it, voice low. "I can't decide if you're trigger-happy or easily intimidated."

But his words tripped, his accent heavier. His veins bulged, blood gushing, roaring. *Afraid*, she thought, until something shot through his eyes, goading her. She shoved him flat and got to her feet.

"We're going to walk," she said, and started back the way she came.

It was half past noon when Arthie and Laith made it to the Office of Public Works.

Laith sat beside her in one of the chairs arranged near the entrance. He hadn't spoken a word since they'd descended from the rooftop, and neither had Arthie. The silence wasn't an amiable one. They were temporary acquaintances, and once their deal was done, they'd go their separate ways.

As they should.

The Office of Public Works was three stories high, with fancy corbels and a pair of double doors inlaid with a mosaic of glass, though its beauty was overshadowed by the dilapidated building to its left. The inside was just as quaint and obnoxiously happy, the walls a bright and springy yellow. It looked as if Flick had done the decorating.

A man on a ladder rifled through records on the shelves built into the far wall. A maid dusted a wide curio. The official's various certificates were pinned behind the secretary's curved desk, scraps of yellowed paper meant to signify brilliance. A clerk worked by the light spilling from the window, a mess of papers on his desk that made Arthie absolutely certain someone was going to get an approval for the wrong project. She tipped her hat at him.

"The window on the uppermost story is open," Laith said tentatively, breaking the silence between them first. He stroked his cat, and Arthie uselessly remembered the feel of his long fingers on either side of her ribs. "We could bypass this and hop in."

"The only way to access it is through the window of that abandoned warehouse next to us," Arthie said. "Not even you can scale a wall that slick."

"Is that a compliment?" Laith asked with a hint of a smile.

She flicked a brow at him. "Don't push your luck. Besides, we're not here to steal."

Semantics, as Jin would say.

The gap above the front doors let the cold inside because the official didn't have the money required to fix it. He would, if he hadn't siphoned it into his own coffers. When the last of the official's appointments left the room, Arthie rose from her seat, and Laith started to do the same.

"Going somewhere?" she asked.

He looked down at her. "I'm coming with you."

"No, you're not."

He opened his mouth, but she wasn't here to argue. She gave the sigil embossed on his lapel a pointed look.

"You will wait, or I will cause a scene like the criminal that I am, and imagine what the office will think when you fail to arrest me."

"No one has to know what will happen when I put you in handcuffs," Laith said, voice dropping low.

Liquid heat curled into her veins, flooding down her skin, making her hiss through her teeth. "You're mistaken if you think I'll let you. Sit down."

He sat, his dark eyes igniting with the same murder burning in her.

At the sight of Arthie, the secretary sank into her daffodil day dress like a turtle. "Deepest apologies, miss, but Official Lambard is not currently in."

Arthie gestured to the exit. "So that surly-looking woman who just left had been sitting alone in his office?"

The secretary blustered, trying and failing to find an answer. "He doesn't want to see you," she admitted at last.

"Oh, but unless he wants to stop seeing altogether, he will."

Heads turned to look at her, murmurs buzzing. The secretary didn't move. The orchid in her coiffed hair bobbed with her swallow. Arthie could feel Laith throwing his judgment into the ring too.

Arthie lowered her chin. "Now get."

The secretary shot to her feet and hurried up the stairs, disappearing through the oak door on the third floor. She returned almost immediately and nearly toppled the pile of mail on her desk.

"Official Lambard will see you now," she said breathlessly. Her face was flushed, and not in a good way.

"Much obliged," Arthie said, giving Laith a final glare.

Official Lambard was a little man with a big desk and nothing on it. She didn't know how she'd missed the signs the first time she'd been here. He was pale, with eyes that bore the slightest tint of crimson, and he smelled faintly of blood, a scent she'd grown accustomed to in the bloodhouse.

The flask beside him suggested he was looking forward to a good break—one of hundreds of breaks he took every day until his plan was thwarted by her.

A guard stood at the door, well-built and stern-eyed. Judging by his size and street attire, Arthie was fairly certain he was for hire and not Horned Guard–ordained. *Interesting.*

He shuffled his bulk toward her.

"Oh, I'll have black tea, please. No milk, less sugar," Arthie told him. "Got to save the teeth."

The guard turned red and looked ready to swing a punch, but when Arthie switched gears and produced a shiny duvin with two fingers and said "I won't be long," he took the coin and closed the door behind him.

Clayton Lambard sputtered in indignation, but he should know: Loyalty was easily bought in a country that valued profit over all else.

"Lambard." Arthie inclined her head. The wallpaper was a sickly shade of yellow that made his sickly pale skin look a tad more . . . well, sickly. "You're looking alive."

Jin would have laughed at that one.

"Casimir," Lambard replied, displeased. "Why are you here?"

Arthie sat in the chair across from his desk and crossed a leg over her thigh, watching Lambard's discomfort rise as she made herself comfortable.

She couldn't expect to be convincing by twiddling her thumbs at the door. It was the first requirement of any good swindle: Make yourself belong. She picked up the little brass bell from the edge of his desk and rang it.

Lambard looked distressed.

"I thought we were settled," the balding official said. "After last time, there—"

"Did you stop finding extra duvin in your pockets?" Arthie asked. His mustache twitched with her disrespect, but his silence was what she'd expected. "As I thought. I need your Athereum marker."

"You cannot have it!" he blustered with unfounded indignation. "I refuse to do any such thing."

Arthie let his words echo in the silence. The four wood-paneled walls spewed his words back at him until he shrank into his curved chair.

"I was more expecting you to deny being an Athereum member or even a vampire, but you're as pathetic as ever. I do appreciate you saving me the time, however, so there's that."

He shook his head, too embarrassed to even try saving face. "I—"

"You forget, Clayton Lambard, whom you speak to. You won't even need to use what little brain you have left to give it to me."

"You're a monster," Lambard whispered.

"A monster would shove a barrel down your throat until you handed it over. I like to think I'm quite civilized." Arthie regarded her fingernails. "Oh, and I also don't steal. So please don't insult me."

Lambard huffed a wet sob. "You did your damage and swore you'd never return."

"I'm not a plague, Official. You broke your oath, and here I am. Your reckoning." Arthie had enough to keep track of without poring over Lambard's books again and looking for figures that didn't tally, but she knew the man. She only needed a single glance at him to know he hadn't stopped skimming the funds allocated to the Office of Public Works.

Bad habits worked that way.

"Why?" He was drowning in anguish. "Why must you do this?"

"We break bones and accept the consequences, Official. And that makes me better than you. You lack culpability. That doesn't warrant an office but a cage in a menagerie." She consulted her watch. This was taking too long. "Is it in your pocket?"

He looked down at his trousers as if a scorpion had dropped into his lap.

"I have every press on Stoker Lane under my thumb and a runner on every street." She didn't want to be a broken record threatening to expose every vampire's secret, but he was a gold mine of secrets. "Ettenia loves a good story, especially when it has to do with their hard-earned money."

She didn't think it was possible for him to pale even further, but he did just that.

"Your luck will run out," Lambard began quietly, dangerously. Arthie went still. "No one is immune, no one is without secrets, and you are a loveless, soulless girl."

Arthie swallowed. She had not always been loveless. She had searched every street, every swell of the ocean's waves, and every patch of blue sky for a mother's love before she learned she would never again have it.

"It is human nature to err, Casimir, and you'll find yours soon enough."

"Ah, but I'm a monster, remember?" Arthie held out her hand. He rose to his feet and dropped the marker in her palm. She ran her thumb along its crisp embossments before pressing the notch on its side. Sure enough, it was stamped with a numerical code. "Smart man."

"It won't do you much good, because I haven't renewed my membership."

Arthie held back a sigh. Of course he hadn't, but she wouldn't let her disappointment show.

Lambard didn't sit back down.

Arthie narrowed her eyes. "You can get back in your chair."

He ignored her, mumbling something under his breath as he exited through a second door. She started to follow him and froze when the lock turned.

The doors behind her flung open. *A trap.*

Arthie spun around, only to have the wind knocked out of her and the marker snatched from her hands. She blinked to catch her bearings, staring into the face of her assailant. It wasn't the guard for hire. This man was *huge.* Tall and just as stocky, clad in all black and surprisingly light on his feet.

Bloody Lambard.

Laith slipped in before the man slammed the doors closed. With far more strength than Arthie thought he possessed in his lithe frame, he threw their assailant against the wall and extended his gauntlet blade, stopping just before impaling him through the throat.

Arthie was beginning to think *hashashin* sounded much like *assassin*.

"I'll have my marker back," she said to the man quietly, straightening her cap. "Or my friend here will get a little more friendly."

"Him?" The man barked a surprised laugh and slammed his boot on Laith's foot, breaking his hold. He shoved a knee into Laith's groin and reversed their positions, pinning him against the wall in an instant.

Arthie cocked a brow. "This is what happens when you learn from a manual, saint."

"Teach me better, criminal," he said with a hiss. This was White Roaring, where fights were dirty and no one held out a hand unless it was for a shovel to a grave.

But Laith wasn't breaking free.

The man closed his hands around Laith's throat, digging nails into his flesh. Laith gasped for air. She dropped her hand to her holster, but she couldn't shoot. Calibore was no ordinary gun and fired no ordinary bullet. She wasn't in some back alley no one would find. And the man was too tall for her to knock out with the butt of her pistol—or anything, really, unless she had a club.

Which she didn't.

Oh, but you do, said a whisper in her head.

She curled her fingers around her pistol's grip. Calibore was special in a way no one but Jin and Arthie truly knew.

The man grunted, and Arthie saw the fight leaching out of Laith, fear blowing his pupils wide.

You need him, she told herself. That was why she felt a twinge of alarm when his skin began to bruise. They still had to break into the Athereum.

He couldn't die, not yet.

She pulled Calibore into her hand and ignored the world. She ignored Laith dying in front of her. She ignored her rage toward Clayton Lambard and Ettenia. She thought of her mother's saris, she thought of racing through the streets with Jin, and the pleasure of a newly tailored suit.

In her hands, the pistol shifted, twisted, and *changed*.

16

FLICK

Flick wasn't fond of having work done for her, much to the dismay of her household staff. And now, hiding behind the desk and watching Jin saunter through the glass doors as if he owned the place, shoulders thrown back, one hand in the pocket of his trousers and the other swinging his umbrella, Flick wished she could do something.

"Who are you?"

It was a woman's voice. Flick's pulse thundered in her ears. Was it the same woman from the bedroom down the hall?

"I might ask you the same question," Jin said coolly. Flick wondered how he could do that. If she'd been out there, she would have sputtered herself to death already. "I was told to wait in the office for a Miss . . ."

Flick held her breath.

"Eleanor Thorne," the woman finished. Her voice was low and husky. Flick thought back to the discussions with Matteo. She was the vampire sister stationed in the marker archive room, and not the doorkeeper. Flick was relieved they wouldn't have to worry about her recognizing him at the Athereum entrance.

Don't waste this, Flick told herself. She peeked over the desk and pulled whatever loose sheets she could get her hands on, pocketing anything with that neat and pretty script exhibiting a sense of meticulousness and certainty.

"Miss Thorne." Jin smacked his lips. "See, I've been waiting far too long, and now I must make another appointment, so please inform her that I will need—"

The footsteps started again, and Flick peered over the side to find the woman circling him. She was barely dressed, her silken robe slipping down one shoulder with sensual confidence. Her hair was bold black, sea-glass eyes bright in the dark, skin a rich brown. Flick had seen more and more vampires since Arthie and Jin had allowed her into their fold for this job. She was beginning to recognize their sculpted bones and ethereal features.

"Who allowed you inside?" the vampire asked.

"Your sister, I'm guessing?" Jin asked. He was facing Flick now, so she could see him scrutinizing the woman. "Looked a lot like you." His gaze slowly traced down her form with a grin that quickened Flick's pulse. "Though I must say, you're far more my type."

The woman tittered and stepped even closer. She pushed a hand into his hair, and Flick thought she would combust. Surely she should look away. The vampire tilted his head back and slid the bridge of her nose along his jaw with a hum. Jin's eyelids fluttered. Flick touched her lighter to her scalding neck and looked away when his lips parted with a rasped exhale.

"What a coincidence," the vampire cooed, "because you just so happen to be mine. I'm only trying to decide if I should kill you here, or let you run. Blood always tastes better freshly pumped."

Flick straightened, accidentally bumping the lighter out of her hands. It tumbled slowly through the air. Her heart collapsed. She scrambled and fell on the rug with a soft thud, catching it just before it clattered to the floorboards.

The vampire stilled. Flick could have sworn her ears twitched.

Jin's mouth feathered along the woman's jaw, and this time *Flick's* breath shook.

"Murder is a crime, but I must say oxygen makes everything better," he drawled in the vampire's ear in a low murmur. His smile turned lazy, and somehow, Flick knew it was for her. "Now would be the time to jump, love."

He took off down the stairwell.

The vampire hissed and shot after him. Flick's heart leaped. He couldn't outrun a vampire. *Stop thinking, start moving.* Shoving the lighter into her pocket, Flick stood up from behind the desk and nudged open the office doors. Downstairs, glass crashed to the floor. She winced and ran for the next room.

She flung open the curtains leading to the balcony and unlatched the doors. The balcony was narrow, curved balusters giving the illusion of more space. A neatly tended garden sprawled beneath it, a little too far down for her liking.

"Jump?" she asked, panicked. No one answered. She climbed over the railing, the iron slick beneath her hands, toes cramping from the inch of space. "Easy as pie, Felici—*Flick*."

She carefully crouched, gripping the spires like her life depended on it. She laughed. Her life *did* depend on it. One leg at a time, she lowered herself off the edge, heart between her teeth. She craned her neck to look—still too far off the ground. But what could she do now, grow an inch or twenty?

A muffled shout came from somewhere in the house, and footsteps crashed up the stairs. Flick had no choice. She dropped, her leg twisting painfully when she hit the damp ground. She heard a door burst open and noises spilled into the garden as she got to her feet.

"Oh, wonderful," she muttered, limping ahead. A brick wall surrounded the garden. She found footholds where chunks of the brick had broken off. Stone ground into her legs, ruining her dress as she hoisted herself to the top of it. She'd felt scandalous when she'd worn it this morning and her hem had fallen just above her knees, trousers hugging each leg, but now she wished she was wearing a shirt like Arthie did.

Something crashed. Flick nearly toppled. Jin emerged from the house, hair sticking out on end and eyes bright with mayhem. He was stunning.

"Jump, Felicity!"

She jumped, tumbling to the cobblestones. Seconds later, Jin landed on his feet beside her and grabbed her arm, half dragging her down the backstreet. Footsteps echoed behind them.

"Jin?" Flick asked shakily. She didn't dare look back to see how many were on their tail. "They're following us."

A sound rang out, like rapid rain pinging a metal roof, and Jin swerved. Flick ducked. *Goodness, gunshots.* She knew guns were meant to be triggered, but she'd never *heard* one, much less been the target of one.

"Now they're firing at us!"

She could die here, and then her mother would finally know Flick wasn't in a cell.

"Really, love. You ought to be a fortune teller," Jin said, hurtling over another wall and into someone else's garden. He let go of her hand, trusting her to follow. Flick scrambled over it as another shot pinged the stone, sparks marking her sleeve. On a bench in the garden, a couple in the midst of a heated conversation leaped apart.

"Pardon us," Flick exclaimed without breaking stride. "We truly don't mean to intrude."

Jin laughed.

"A little concern would be nice," she shouted at him.

They tumbled through a gate into the next yard and paused to catch their breath. "You know, it's quite possible to laugh *and* be concerned at the same time."

She met his dark eyes, noticing the smears of blood on his face, and her heart fluttered in a way she recognized. *Stop it, Flick.* He was wild and dangerous, and she should not be attracted to either.

"Aren't you afraid?" she asked.

"Fear stops life, not death," he said, and when she looked at him in surprise, he paused, and the world seemed to pause with him. "I tell myself that anytime I think a fire's going to swallow me whole."

Flick wondered if that had anything to do with that patch of burned skin on his arm. "You're bleeding."

"Oh, it's not mine. I might have shattered a blood reserve or two." Jin pulled her up, and the air was suddenly too tense between them, too . . . *real.* She almost swooned when Jin leaned down and winked at her. "You're so sweet."

"Just you wait," Flick snapped at his teasing tone. Whatever Jin had done to give them a head start was wearing out. The vampires were catching up. Her arm screamed as they hurtled over a line of hedges and another round of shots rained down on the wall behind them. He chuckled at her yelp, and the words flew out of her. "You're going to eat a bullet and then—"

And then he threw himself in front of her and fell to the dirt with a startled hiss, blood blossoming from his side.

ARTHIE

Every so often, Arthie felt the same pinprick panic as the people whose secrets she exposed. Like now, when quick as a trick of the light, Calibore the pistol became Calibore the knife, black filigree scrawling down its hilt, silver blade sharp.

Laith froze in the midst of his struggle, and for a harrowing second, she thought he might have died, but it was only a beat of surprise before he started clawing at the man's grip anew.

From a knife, Calibore shifted again, this time to a sword, and then finally into what she wanted: a club. Arthie rushed at the man and swung, throwing all her weight into it. She slammed the club against his skull. The impact jarred her teeth. He released Laith with a shout and stumbled back, blinking as he looked from Arthie to her weapon.

And then he collapsed.

Laith gasped for air. "How . . . how?"

Arthie holstered her pistol again. "He won't be down long. We need to go."

There was a tremble in her fingers, and she wasn't sure if it was because she'd revealed her secret or because the high captain had nearly died. She toed the man before digging through his pockets for the marker.

Laith rose unsteadily to his feet and hesitated. For a moment she thought he might thank her, but then he turned away, and *she* was thankful. With a wheeze, he reached for the doorknob. It didn't budge. He threw his weight against it, and something rattled on the other side.

"They've locked us in. Drat it all," Arthie growled.

Their assailant twitched.

Laith gestured to where the curtains fluttered from the open window. "There. It's too long a drop, but we can escape through the abandoned warehouse."

But the warehouse window was closed and too far out of reach to open the latches from here. "It's not—"

Laith sprinted past her, whispering to his kitten to hold fast before he leaped through the window. At this rate, she would need to spend time making sure he *didn't* die before they got the ledger.

He landed almost soundlessly. *Landed* was the wrong word, because he was defying gravity. One of his hands clutched the window's ledge as the toes of his boots dug into the grooves on the stone wall. With the other hand, he worked at the latches using his gauntlet blade.

A groan rose behind her.

"He's waking up," Arthie called.

"Oh, I'm sorry, I thought I had time for tea," Laith snarked. The first latch clicked open. He turned to the second.

The man huffed, and Arthie turned to find him sitting up. He shook his head and blinked at his surroundings before he fully came to.

And stared straight at her.

Laith shoved the window open as the man rolled onto his feet.

"Jump, Arthie," Laith shouted.

She tucked the marker into her pocket and braced herself. The ground shook. The man was charging toward her. She ran. Jumped. Her eyes locked with Laith's for the barest of moments before fingers closed around the heel of her shoe, breaking her momentum. She wasn't going to make it. *When will you acknowledge that you're in way over your head?* Why was the window so far out of reach? *Reach, Arthie.*

Her fingers brushed the ledge.

Her fist closed around air—before a warm hand engulfed hers.

Arthie opened her eyes.

She was dangling yards above the debris piled in the alley—she wasn't a heap of bones on the ground.

"I've got you," Laith rasped.

He moved to secure her with his other hand, but she gripped the ledge and pulled herself up to the dusty wood beside him. She huffed, trying to pretend away the panic that flared in his eyes when she'd lost her footing. Laith rushed to close the window and growled.

"I can't close it. The latches are jammed," he said. "We need to move. We're four floors from the ground."

Their assailant was struggling to brace his own footing in the office window.

"He'll be across soon enough," Laith said.

Arthie dusted off her clothes on shaky legs. The warehouse had been long abandoned. It was oddly built. Each of the four levels were more balcony than full floor, though there were no railings to keep anyone from toppling, rickety and rotted stairwells connecting each one. Far below on the ground floor, tatty tables were arranged in rows, moth-eaten manuals spread beside hammers and screws the length of her hand. Giant barrels lined the left wall.

"The stairwells are all shot," Arthie said.

Laith gagged. "That *smell*."

Arthie was well acquainted with the rotten, smoky stench. Sulfur and charcoal. *Gunpowder.* Sure enough, one of the barrels was broken, and a pile of gray-black powder was strewn beneath it. It was everywhere, dusting the floorboards, trailing the corners of the upper story where they were now.

Chains swayed eerily, most suspended from the ceiling, some dangling from under crates stacked along the upper floor.

"Wait," Arthie said. Laith turned back, and she struggled to meet his eyes. "This makes us even."

He chuckled darkly. "For now."

"Forever," she deadpanned.

"We'll see about that." He glanced at the window before gesturing to a broken stairwell. It looked like a mouth that had been punched in and was now missing teeth. "Follow me, I can lead us down."

He tucked his kitten into his robes, letting her paws and head stick out, and leaped across, glancing back every ten seconds as if Arthie was a child. She started after him and nearly lost her footing again when the man jumped over in a cloud of dust, disturbing the wood beneath them.

Arthie whirled to face him. He swayed, gripping the back of his head with one hand before he pulled out a knife, swinging it artlessly at his side. Arthie pulled out Calibore, shifting it into a knife of her own before the man could see.

He lunged first, nicking her shoulder. "Give me the marker."

"This was my best seersucker," she growled. The man swung again and she evaded, cuffing his chin and catching the sickening bite of his tongue. She slipped and righted herself, nearly tumbling from the narrow shelf of space.

She was backed into a corner. *No.* Trapped. *Never again.*

The chains suspended from the ceiling drifted to her side, feet away, enticing her with an idea. It wasn't too long, falling just to the level of the floor beneath them, but it would allow her to get away from the man. *Don't even dare*, came Jin's voice in her head. If she missed, she would be a pile of bones on the first floor. The wood beneath her shook again as the man trundled toward her. Waiting here was by no means safer.

Arthie jumped, legs kicking air until she grabbed one of the chains, rust in the links snaring her fingers. The musty air rushed through her limbs when she propelled herself forward—

Her arc was cut short, jarring her teeth. Her attacker was gripping the chain in his hand like she weighed nothing.

"Are you trying to prove a point?" she yelled as he started pulling her up. She scanned her surroundings, but the third floor was worse for wear. The stairs were shattered and there was very little ground to stand on, and that was saying something, considering the rest of the more intact floors. She vaulted to the next chain and shimmied up, swinging onto a plank jutting out of the fourth floor. She tasted dust, no, the gunpowder.

It gave her an idea.

"Get out of here, saint," Arthie shouted. She couldn't see him, but knew he was waiting for her somewhere.

"Are you s—" Laith began to shout back.

"Don't finish that question," she snarled.

The man laughed at her. "Give me the marker and you can go home to your mother, girl."

"You'll have to send me to the sea, then," Arthie replied, shuffling her feet and gathering as much of the gunpowder together as she could. She jumped to another plank.

He vaulted toward her, landing a few feet away.

She slammed her leg down. The wood snapped, splinters falling to the clutter below. The man's eyes met hers, a flash of fear in the depths of his because any moment now they were both going to join the broken remains beneath them, or possibly fall all the way to the ground floor, breaking both their necks.

Arthie darted along the narrow ledge. There was no stairwell at the end, no chain to rappel down from. Only a large window coated in soot.

The boulder of a man thundered after her. All this for an expired marker.

"Come and get me," Arthie said. She plucked a match from her pocket and struck it on the bricks of the wall as she ran, tossing the tiny flame into the trail of gunpowder behind her.

The match fell with a hiss and the gunpowder caught fire, the hiss growing into a roar as it struck the pile she'd collected, quickly growing, swallowing everything around it. The wooden board beneath it crumbled, careening to the ground below.

To the shattered barrel of gunpowder.

The man's eyes flared in realization. He flung back, rappelling down one of the chains. And Arthie leaped, crashing through the window and hurtling through the air as shards of glass exploded into the evening light.

18

FLICK

With Jin against her side, Flick cut across Alms Place and spotted Matteo Andoni's manicured lawn and kiss-red door at last. If this job had been so woeful, she could only imagine what breaking into the Athereum would look like. Before a couple crossing the street could get a good look at Jin, she worked the gate open and the two of them hobbled up the walk.

He was bleeding all over the cobblestones, all over her shoes, and all over his clothes. How much blood did a body have? She dumped him unceremoniously on the grass near the house's side porch.

"Oh goodness, I am so sorry," she rushed to say when he winced. With a wounded look, he eased himself back against the bricks and pulled up the end of his shirt. It was soaked through, the blood nearly black.

"It looks worse than it is," Jin said, half to himself.

That didn't stop her insides from churning weakly. There was a sheen along his brow despite the chill, and Flick startled when he laughed.

"Do you find this amusing?" she asked incredulously, shoving her hand into her pocket. A bird chirped in the jeweled trees, the harmony cut by her erratic pulse.

Jin peeled back his undershirt with a hiss, and Flick averted her gaze, hearing her maid's and her mother's voices chastising in her head.

"On the contrary," Jin said, "just passing time until you help me stop the bleeding."

She looked about helplessly and remembered Abe's General Store two streets up. Abe would have something. Bandages, gauze, tape to hold it all in place. Flick didn't know much about fixing up wounds. She was dusty and spent, her perfectly good gown tattered and grass-stained. She could feel dirt on her cheeks, her curls as wild as the streets they'd run through. She didn't have money on her either, but the old man liked a good conversation.

"I'll get something from the store."

"There's no time to toddle around, Felicity," he rasped. "Undress me."

Flick's jaw dropped. "I beg your pardon."

"Please," Jin tried again tiredly. "Help me rip up my shirt so that I may staunch my bleeding. Is this Matteo's house?"

Mustering as much self-encouragement as she could, Flick dropped beside him, rethought her life ten thousand times, and then reached for his shirt.

He smiled weakly. "I knew you couldn't resist."

She huffed but said nothing, too concerned with the blood darkening the grass. Too diffident about touching him. *Undressing him.* One by one, she worked the buttons free to expose the undershirt beneath.

"I need scissors," she said, after attempting to rip it. She couldn't remove it without making him move too much and risk losing more blood.

"And I need a raspberry streusel drizzled in dark chocolate," Jin remarked, "but since we have neither, Felicity, use your teeth."

"Teeth? Oh, right."

But that meant getting impossibly close to him. *The alternative is letting him die*, Flick chastised herself. She lowered herself to the clean edge of his shirt. She wasn't sure what compelled her to hold his gaze while she did it. She heard the unsteady draw of his breath. Felt the heat of his skin graze her cheek. She gripped the fabric between her teeth, and tore.

His gaze bled black as he watched her. Shining. Delirious. This silence was going to make her explode.

"Why did you do it?" she asked.

"Do what?" He shifted with another sigh that she felt down to the tips of her toes.

"Take the bullet." Flick straightened the edge of his shirt. It was easier to rip now, and she carefully tore off a strip long enough to cinch around him and set it aside. She shook as she peeled back the soaked end of his undershirt and cleaned away as much as she could with gentle hands. The creases of her fingers were stained in red, and she had to force a few steady breaths as her insides churned. *Is it only the blood?*

"It barely grazed me," Jin said.

"You could have easily escaped through the balcony with me. You could have easily swerved away when they fired," she said, barely listening to him. She was rambling now, and she didn't know how to stop.

He was bleeding because of her. He had tried buying time because of her. She had accepted this job for her mother, and she had been prepared to do anything for her mother's forgiveness. She never thought anyone would do anything for her.

But Jin had nearly died for her.

"I've seen you and Arthie and your ridiculous jobs, but today you seemed to have left your brain in whatever empty teapot you could find at Spindrift before you sauntered over to Admiral Grove, didn't you? You were careless, and witless, and—"

He was staring at her. His gaze fell to her mouth, then to her throat when she swallowed heavily. It was too cold for the sweat on her brow. She wrapped the fabric around him and was suddenly acutely aware of his body heat and the rise and fall of his chest. She had never been so close to a boy before. A thousand nerve endings exploded when she knotted it tight to staunch the bleeding as best as she could and her fingers brushed his skin. His muscles constricted at her touch, all lean and taut lines. *What had you expected?* He spent his nights keeping vampires in line, his days commanding the streets by Arthie's side.

Jin arched his back, leaning close. "Go on," he murmured sleepily. "Don't stop now, love."

"Reckless," she finished quietly. Hummingbirds fluttered against her rib cage. She wondered how delicious and warm it might be to splay her fingers over his broad chest. Did it matter? She planned to betray him.

Jin, who had nearly died to save her. Jin, who believed in her when no one else did. It had seemed so simple when she was locked in her bedroom: She would do whatever it took to regain her mother's approval. But if Flick convinced a maid to let her into Lady Linden's office now—*please, just this once*—and then convinced her mother that *here is the Ram's missing ledger* or even *here is what the Casimirs have planned*, where would she stop?

Her mother would go to the press, and Arthie and Jin would lose more than Spindrift. Lady Linden *could* leave their names out of the story. She could pull some strings the way she had with Flick and the signet ring scandal.

"You did good today, Felicity," Jin said quietly, interrupting her thoughts. He was watching her with a gaze too perceptive, too *raw*, and she wondered if he saw her turmoil and indecision.

A door slammed. Flick straightened.

"Please do continue." Matteo Andoni stood in the shadows of his side porch, watching them with a grin. His ivory skin was offset by the dark topcoat he'd pulled over a half-unbuttoned white shirt and black trousers. Decency was still not in his vocabulary. For the amount of exposed male skin Flick had seen this past week, one would have thought she'd gotten married.

Before Flick could gasp, Jin vaulted to his feet. He shot up the stairs and shoved Matteo against the brick wall of his manor.

"You lied, Andoni," Jin rasped, teetering from the pain.

His voice was lethal. All Casimir. For a moment, Matteo only squinted down at him, stunned and confused.

"I don't recall doing any such thing," he replied calmly. When he spoke, Flick caught flashes of white in his mouth that she hadn't noticed before.

"You said the Thorne sisters worked at the bank," Jin hissed, scrunching Matteo's shirt in his fist, and Flick was certain it was to keep from falling as much as it was in anger.

Matteo's nostrils flared, his eyes darkening and falling to slits. He seemed at war with himself, fighting against something. He was slowly beginning to appear less like a painter and more like a . . . hunter.

"I did," he replied, the tenor of his voice dropping a notch. His chest heaved, and he sounded almost breathless when he said, "It would be wise to let go of me now, Jin."

"I don't think I will." Jin laughed, even as his blood fell onto the wooden slats in heavy drops. "I'll let you guess at where they were today, vampire."

Jin's blood. *Fangs.* Those were what had lengthened in Matteo's mouth.

Flick knew the moment they were in danger: Matteo relaxed. His restraint disappeared. Then he hooked a leg behind Jin's and dropped him, pinning him to the porch with his weight. The vampire moved with liquid grace, a carefree sort of sprightliness. Flick could only watch as he ran a finger along Jin's cheek. No, not a finger, a *claw*.

"At home," Matteo answered softly in a voice that sent shivers through Flick's core. She could have sworn Jin's gaze glazed with the lure of the vampire's voice. "Where most people usually are."

They were in terrible, terrible danger. A vampire like Matteo wouldn't go around using his lure on a human. Not unless he was giving in to his more animalistic impulses. Any moment now, Jin was bound to be his midday snack.

Flick looked about helplessly before she picked up Jin's umbrella. What could she do? Whack him over the head with it? If Matteo had lost control, they were both in danger. *Flee*, came a voice in her head. No, she told herself. Not after Jin had risked his life for her.

A shadow fell over her.

"Don't make me cut you out of this deal."

Arthie. She was framed against the sun, her hair a halo, Laith behind her. She was dusty and beat, the hard press of her mouth warning them that her patience had worn down to a thread. Flick opened her mouth to alert her that Matteo might not be thinking all too clearly, but this was Arthie. She surely knew that much already.

The quiet was the sort where Flick could have heard a pin fall.

At last, Matteo opened his mouth.

"Oh, how I missed you, darling," he said, but there was nothing light about the words. No tease, all bite. An edge that was half warning, half plea. Arthie held her ground. Matteo turned his head toward her, and Flick knew the moment their eyes locked because it drained the air from the world, cementing them in time.

It was an eternity in which her heart felt submerged in syrup, each beat as slow as its drip, each blink of her eyes as if she were underwater.

At last, Matteo released Jin's bloody shirt. Jin fell back against the porch, heaving breath after breath while Matteo's throat worked in a series of calming swallows. Jin, who had been running on anger and nothing else, crawled to the wall.

Arthie looked at the scene like she wanted to set fire to them all. She didn't seem to care that Jin was bleeding on Matteo Andoni's porch.

"He lied," Jin gritted out, dropping his head back against the bricks.

"No, he didn't," Arthie said with barely restrained calm. "Andoni, get out of my sight and find someone else to drink."

"With pleasure," Matteo said almost gratefully.

She looked at Jin. "If you had paid attention, you wouldn't be making an embarrassment of yourself right now."

"What do you mean?" Flick wasn't fond of the warble in her voice, but Matteo was only straightening his sleeves and yawning, not a fang in sight now. "The bank closes at seven bells every day."

Laith stepped to Arthie's side, and they almost looked like allies then. No, not allies, *equals*. She was either beginning to trust him or beginning to learn her way around him. Knowing what Flick did about Arthie, it was likely the latter.

"Except when it's closed," Laith said. "It's a holiday."

19

ARTHIE

Arthie opened the cabinet by her desk later that evening and swished her decanter. The murky coconut water sloshed forlornly around the glass. Each rotation conjured Matteo's fangs and Jin's bloody body. Each splash summoned the memory of Laith's hand gripping hers.

A snip drew her attention to an armchair on the other side of the room, where Jin had finished stitching himself up. He set the pair of bloody scissors beside a growing pile of candy wrappers that verified his sour mood. Arthie moved the Athereum marker she'd filched today like a pawn across a chessboard before forcing herself to stop.

"You're fiddling." Jin was watching her.

"And?" she asked. His pale, blood-drained face was still seared behind her eyelids.

"You don't fiddle. Go on, tell me again what a fool I was for not remembering today's a holiday when I can barely find an hour to sleep anymore and the roof above my head is in danger of being blown to smithereens, my eye won't quit twitching, and you're—"

"Not remembering it's a holiday isn't the problem, Jin," she calmly cut him off. She had known it was a holiday when he set off to do the job today. She thought he'd known, too. "We've done plenty of jobs in full houses. We don't get caught."

He looked away.

"And we're lucky the sister you ran into isn't the Athereum's door-keeper, or our entire plan would be shot and it's far too late to come up with a new one."

He slumped back with a growl.

It was the same way Matteo had growled when his fangs were inches away from Jin's throat. Arthie clenched her jaw. "Nor do we throw ourselves at a vampire while bleeding all over his porch."

Jin's eyes flashed. "Like you don't act with the same level of reck-lessness I merely adopted for a half hour."

Arthie shot to her feet. "I know I won't turn up dead. You think Matteo would have stopped with a kiss on your cheek?"

Jin rose too. "I could have—"

"No!" She whirled on him. She knew her emotions were spelled across her face by the stricken look on his. "You could have died, Jin. You could have *died*." The fight broke out of her, cracking her voice to a whisper. "And one day, I won't be there to stop it."

He looked away. In the lamplight, the skin of his arm shone like leather, wrinkled and glossy. He'd shaken death's hand more than once, felt the skim of its scythe. Arthie had stepped between them every time. Before the fire could consume him. Before a bullet could claim him.

In the silence, Arthie closed herself back up again and circled to her desk. The chair sighed softly.

"This—" Arthie started to say.

Jin stopped her, peering over the gunmetal rim of his teacup. "And no, this had nothing to do with Flick."

"Never said it did." Arthie returned her scrutiny to the marker, though she'd thought exactly that.

"She's—she's not my type." Jin sounded adorably embarrassed. *The Jin Casimir*, expert flirt and charmer of anything that moved, made bashful by a girl.

"Mm-hmm," Arthie said, indulging him.

"She can't dress inconspicuously to save her life."

And he couldn't lie about his true feelings to save his.

Arthie nodded. "She's green as a tea leaf is what she is."

He made a displeased sound. Ah, so only he was allowed to make up reasons to whine about her. "She's a toff, through and through," he continued. "What kind of name is Felicity anyway?"

"The kind you shorten to Flick." Arthie snapped the light away and made a note. She knew he didn't believe a word of what he was saying. "Don't go with her to the foundry."

"What? Why?" he asked, fully concerned now.

Because a foundry was full of what he feared. Fire and heat and smoke in a dark, yawning chasm.

"Because," she said instead, "you have enough to do before the festival. We're cutting it close as it is."

The door flung open on his protest and Chester squeezed through, all red-faced and out of breath.

"Boss, boss, I told them not to let him in. It was Reni, that bugger," Chester exclaimed, baring his teeth like a kitten playing lion as Matteo stepped in after him, cool and amused and not a vein of violence on display. "You couldn't pay, you shouldn't drink." Arthie scrunched her mouth to the side as he parroted her usual words.

"It's quite all right, Chester," she said.

Flick stepped in behind him, followed by Laith, with a glance in her direction that sent a zap down her spine. His kitten dashed to the windowsill, where the moonlight bathed her fur in iridescence beneath a blue-and-black, star-peppered sky.

"But . . ." Chester's brow notched with that trio of lines everyone jested him about.

"Seems your boss has taken a liking to me," Matteo said with pride.

Chester tilted his head, considering him with fresh understanding on his way out. "Boss likes anyone with secrets."

Arthie almost laughed at Matteo's pout. "He isn't wrong."

Flick snorted and clasped her hands to her mouth in horror at the sound. She then proceeded to stare at the ground like it was the most riveting thing in existence, brightening Jin up considerably.

"Did you get the marker?" Matteo asked, then frowned. "Your jacket's torn. Are you all right?"

It was a tiny detail to notice, but Arthie wasn't accustomed to anyone being so attentive to her. So caring.

"Perhaps you should stop looking," Laith said, shifting closer to her.

"Someone's getting a little possessive," Jin whispered in her ear.

She belonged to no one, she wanted to say, but a little thrill ran through her, and she couldn't decide if it was from Matteo's attention or Laith speaking out on her behalf.

Matteo didn't reply with his usual quip. He stepped to the window and ran his fingers down the kitten's back, blowing fluff off his fingers with a frown. "Jin, I apologize for earlier."

Arthie was surprised by the apology, and it made her respect for him grow.

Jin tipped his head to the side. "And I to you."

"Though calling someone a liar isn't nearly as bad as drinking someone dry," Flick pointed out, anger dipping into her brow.

"No, sweet, it is not." Matteo let out an embarrassed laugh. He turned to her and bowed. "I deeply regret nearly drinking from Jin."

"And yes," Arthie said, "we did get Lambard's marker, but it's expired, and we don't have time to find another, so Jin will need to go in as a blood companion after all."

"As you originally intended," Matteo said. "There is hope."

Arthie narrowed her eyes at him. "What's wrong?"

Matteo looked surprised she'd noticed something was amiss. "There's been another disappearance."

"Was it someone you knew?" Flick asked, concern quickly overtaking her anger. A siren wailed in the distance, shouts echoing through the night, and Matteo shook his head. The unspoken questions hung in the air: Who would be next, and why were vampires being targeted at all? Arthie hated not knowing, but they couldn't afford any distractions.

She led them to the room connected to her office, once a hidden bedchamber when this was the Curio. Back then it was governed by a man with a fat mustache and equally fat greed. Now it belonged to a small girl with an equally small heart, as Jin liked to tease.

Jin switched on the lights, illuminating his worktables on one wall, their collection of secrets and records hidden behind the shelves along the other that Flick turned a keen eye toward, and a table at its center with Matteo's sketches of the Athereum.

Chester followed them in, toting a tray with goodies and a tea set that clinked with his steps. The woody, earthy scent of the warm tea enveloped the room, and Arthie breathed deep. She had missed it.

"Not now, Chester, we're busy," she said.

"Jin asked for 'em," he said with a frown. "Reni brewed it just now."

Arthie pulled out the chair beside Flick and looked to Jin for an explanation.

He shrugged. "The pastries are going to be thrown out anyway."

"Thrown out?" Chester asked. "I bought these for you!"

"I think you should leave now, little man," Jin said mock-sternly. "Besides, you know I can't think on an empty stomach."

Matteo gave him a look. "I hate to say it, old boy, but it's always empty."

"Because it's never not pastry o'clock," Jin said, and then glanced at the others. "But don't act like I'm hoarding them. Go on. Anyone else care for a spot of tea?"

"It has been an age since I had a Bakewell tart," Matteo said wistfully, eyeing the tart with its candied cherry that looked like a drop of blood atop white icing. "Ground almonds, rich butter, cherry jam."

He punctuated his list with a dreamy sigh.

"Have one, then," Arthie said.

Matteo balked. "And taste ash? Losing the ability to taste food is a curse, really."

Jin looked mournful on his behalf. Flick leaned over and examined the platter of pastries and biscuits. There was grease on her fingers from rifling through her tools. The girl was becoming more and more unladylike by the minute. Arthie had to admit that she was pleased.

"I'll take a bourbon biscuit, please," Flick said. "And tea, of course."

"Saint?" Arthie asked, gesturing to the tray.

"Some of us like being nimble," Laith said, shaking his head. He was fiddling with his gauntlet blade. She didn't like how closely he was watching her.

"Some of us are lucky enough to eat what we want *and* be nimble," Jin said, sipping his tea. "I'm sorry you're not so fortunate."

20

ARTHIE

Long after the others had gone to bed and the rain had petered to a stop, Arthie made herself comfortable in an armchair in an apartment on the highest floor above the Nimble Street Bakery. Here, the lamps were doused, and only the soft, cool breath of the moon fell through the wide windows.

She wasn't fully certain why she'd come, only that her limbs were restless and wanted to move and now she was here.

On the table by her wrist, a small glass held a number of flowers, none of them chosen for their beauty, but for their significance, telling a story. Sprigs of rosemary for remembrance, a pair of gladiolas for pride and victory, asters for patience.

Water splashed in the room just beyond. She tried not to listen. She tried not to imagine the way it would pool in the hollow of his collarbones and cascade down the nape of his neck, the way it would trickle down the length of his arms when he lifted them.

"Arthie."

Laith was framed in the doorway, bone-white hair wet, a pair of dark trousers slung low around his waist. There was a cuff on his forearm that sat loose, a winding length of silver that swelled to the head of a snake with blue jewels for eyes. He wasn't wearing a shirt. Arthie didn't know what to do with her hands or where to look. She wondered if it was as difficult for him to stand there without a shirt as it was for her to witness him.

"Why are you here?"

Not *how*, only *why*. In the short time he'd spent with her, he'd learned that she had her ways. He was careful, but so was she. Felix had followed Laith to his apartment the day they'd met in her office, but she never thought she'd ever actually visit the address.

"Put a shirt on," she said. It took effort to keep her voice light and nonchalant. "We have to talk."

He stepped into the room, forcing her to look at him. His feet were bare on the knotted-fringe rug. The moonlight ran fingers down his skin, drawing shadows, and Arthie resisted the urge to lean over and light a lamp beside her, not to better her sight, but to see what he would look like bathed in gold instead of silver. Why was he coming toward her? Closer and closer still, each step like a bullet falling into a chamber.

If he was trying to intimidate her, then he—

"My shirt," he explained hoarsely, reaching for the armoire behind her. He tugged open the door and pulled one out, a swallow shifting in his throat before he drew it over himself, muscles rippling from the movement. "Well? Appropriate for you?"

She wanted to tell him to put his robes on too. It wasn't about him being appropriate. She wasn't an Ettenian prude who fainted at an exposed ankle. She didn't care if a man wanted to walk bare in the middle of White Roaring Square.

With Laith, she simply couldn't think. She couldn't focus on the desperation in his eyes and the pain set into his features. She studied him, the steadiness of his limbs, the relaxed stance. *Always looking for a lie where there isn't one*, Jin said in her head. And she was. It was why she'd survived this long. It was how Arthie had climbed from the filth beneath someone's shoes to scraping it off her own.

"Sit down," she said.

She had saved his life, and he had saved hers.

"I think it's time you tell me the truth."

Laith brewed himself a cup of coffee, and Arthie shook her head when he offered her some. She didn't care for its bitterness. It had none of the comfort of tea. He shrugged and stirred in five sugar cubes. At that point, he was having coffee with his sugar.

He tipped his head at her waist. "Why don't we begin with that?"

"This?" She pulled out her pistol and focused. It blurred when it shifted, the silver shimmering, the black beckoning. She heard the catch in his breath as Calibore the knife became Calibore the hairpin, pretty enough for her hair, sharp enough to kill. It became a pair of scissors, a bladed star, silver dusters, a dagger—always a weapon, always bearing that fine dark filigree that reminded her of Laith in a way.

"How?" he asked as he sat down on the rug, coffee mug in hand.

The first time it had happened, Arthie had been on the run with Jin. She remembered him joking about needing a quieter weapon than a pistol. Arthie wished for it too, and seconds later dropped the sword between them. They each stared down at the thing as if they'd been duped by the other. Neither of them had known how it happened.

If anyone were to open up the pistol and look inside, there would be a single bullet in its chamber, despite the fact that she had used it and never once reloaded it. Not only could it shift into any weapon, the pistol could *kill* anything too.

Even vampires.

Arthie had learned that the hard way when she'd stumbled on Reni, young and orphaned and under attack in a derelict alley, screaming for help. Arthie had shot at the vampire hoping to buy time for a getaway, but she'd gotten more than that. Reni had been too traumatized from being turned into a vampire to remember the incident, but he remained with them after that, and Calibore had never left her side.

Over the years, Arthie had cared for Calibore in a way no one really cared for a pistol. It made her stronger, not in the way a weapon typically did, but because it was proof she'd outsmarted an empire. In that way of his, Jin claimed that perhaps, because of how Arthie appreciated it, the pistol had begun to fancy her back. Enough that it would shape itself into whatever weapon she needed. She'd never told a soul aside from Jin.

Until now.

"Don't concern yourself with how it worked as much as the fact that it did," she answered.

Of everything Arthie expected of him, she did not think he would look away, eyelashes sweeping downward like knives relinquished.

"Thank you," he said finally. "For saving me."

This time, *she* looked away. She hadn't expected him to forgo his pride and thank her, and she certainly hadn't expected him to sound so earnest.

She bit down on her tongue until the pain made her angry. That was the state she had lived in for the past decade, and that was what kept her moving forward. But since meeting Laith, it felt as if she'd lost control of herself. Something was forcing her to suffer one emotion after the next—exasperation, confusion, distress, and now this: *guilt.*

"You ought—"

"What you said to the man at the warehouse," he interjected. His kitten crawled into his lap, purring louder than a motor. "When he spoke of your mother."

"Funny that was what you focused on." Arthie didn't want to talk about her mother, not here and now in the dead of the night when memories crawled out of their graves.

"Have you no family?"

Her pocket watch thrummed against her stomach. "Jin is my family. My crew is my family. Spindrift is our home, if you haven't noticed how dedicated we are to getting that ledger."

Disappointment flickered in his eyes, and something about the gesture gave her pause.

"I watched my mother and father die," she said, softer this time. Perhaps it was the night that made it easier to unwrap truths. "I had no one else."

That last sentence was a lie. Between her parents and Jin, there *had* been someone else, hadn't there? Someone who had cared and taken her in and called her his own. Until she'd run away.

Did Laith know? When he had voiced the name for a second time in Matteo's house, had he known its significance?

The clouds drifted in front of the moon, rearranging him into something darker, less *good*. She waited, knowing he wouldn't draw information out of her without an even exchange. She might not have known him long, but somehow, she knew this. It was his turn.

"I've never liked thrones and those who sit on them, digging graves with a swipe of a pen." He spoke the words with a quiet vitriol, reminding her that she knew very little about him. "My king was responsible for the death of my sister. She was all I had.

"I know what it's like to watch kin die," he continued, in a voice that reminded her of the sea lapping the shore. Quiet, barely restrained in its resentment. "To be left adrift, a fraction of a whole. To be surrounded by others and no one, at once. We are the same, Arthie. We understand what it's like to grieve with fire and not tears. What it's like to do anything for those we love."

To grieve with fire. She did not grieve. Her family, childhood, *life*— they were gone. What point was there in grief?

"But you have no one left."

He looked at her with a small, sad smile. "Is that not grief? The act of keeping one alive in whatever way that we can?"

He slid the cuff up his forearm until it fit snug. "She was everything I had in this world. When I see you and Jin together, it reminds me of what I'll never again have."

She had nearly lost Jin more than once, and then again just today. She had stood on the threshold of loss and stared it in the face, but could she have survived that fall?

"She was a hashashin too," he said, twirling a blossom between his fingers. It was too dark for Arthie to tell what it was and what significance it held. "And the reason I myself joined the creed. She excelled at everything she touched, rising up the ranks swiftly as a flower unfurling beneath the sun's light.

"Too swiftly," Laith amended. "Our new one-eyed king is clever and ambitious, but most of all, sharp."

Arthie liked this king already.

"With the fall of the trees that once cursed our borders, he knew that another danger would fill its place: conquest."

"You mean colonialism," she corrected him. *By the people you worked for*, was what she almost said.

He met her eyes. "Is there much of a difference?"

She thought of the boats teetering on Ceylan's shores, the blood that dyed her mother's sari a deeper shade of red. She thought of the people who remained there now, foreigners in their own homes. No, Arthie decided, there wasn't.

"He vowed that Arawiya would not fall the way the rest of the world did," Laith said, "and dispatched hashashin to retrieve hilya, artifacts that could be weaponized against us and used to challenge him. My sister's talents caught the king's interest, and he sent her here, to Ettenia. One girl, barely of age, out on a quest to save his kingdom."

Arthie didn't share his sentiments. If she had been in that girl's place, she would have thought this the opportunity of a lifetime. It would have meant that her efforts had not gone to waste.

"She thought it was the opportunity of a lifetime," Laith said bitterly, and Arthie bit back a smile. "But she was too young to go so far on her own, and though I was still suffering an illness, I joined the voyage. She'd never been to sea. Most Arawiyans had not, but she caught sickness quickly. By the time we reached Ettenia's docks, she was gone. Death is slower across the sea, but he came eventually."

Laith turned the mug in his hands, swishing the remains of his coffee. He blamed his sister's death on his king. He didn't live for the future, but for days departed.

It seemed a wasteful way to live, burning fuel over something long gone.

"You still want that artifact, don't you?" she asked. "But not for the same reason."

"Yes. There's something symbolic about killing a man with what he wants," Laith said, and Arthie caught a glimpse of a darkness she hadn't thought him capable of possessing.

It seemed to her that the king of Arawiya had wanted the artifact to protect his people. Laith's sister's death was an unfortunate accident that Arthie wasn't sure warranted the king's murder, but she wasn't about to involve herself in politics.

She went still. "And you thought the Ram could deliver if you did as you were told."

He nodded. "I rose up the ranks quickly, and the Ram took note."

She thought back to how strange it seemed that he was so loyal to Ettenia. How dedicated he was, to the point where it was obvious to her that he had another reason for serving on the guard. Did that sense of purpose extend to retrieving the ledger? Or had he reached the point where he decided the Ram had too much power?

Arthie couldn't bring herself to ask him. It occurred to her then that the Ram might even know the ledger was in the Athereum, that Laith was partnering with Arthie to retrieve it.

When she had left Spindrift for his apartment, she'd been torn about her plan to let him take the fall at the Athereum.

Now, she'd never felt so certain.

When Arthie returned to Spindrift, she found a tiny yellow blossom in her lapel loop, fragrant and lonely. A marigold, for the heart that suffered grief. Later still, it gave Arthie the courage to knock on Jin's door. By the time she heard the soft laugh followed by his chuckle on the other side, it was too late. She'd already knocked. It was Laith's fault for letting the ghosts in.

The door swung open, its wrought iron accents catching the light. Jin propped a hand against the doorframe and looked down at her with a lazy smile. His shirt was mostly undone and his hair stuck up every which way.

"What are you doing?" she asked with a frown.

His brows flicked up. "Well, I work at this place called Spindrift, and my boss is a tyrannical girl who leaves me with barely an hour that I can get off."

Arthie glanced at him sidelong. "'Get off' quite literally? Who is it this time?"

"Arthie!" Jin exclaimed. "It's Flick! You know it's not like that. Couldn't you have stayed ten years old?"

Arthie flinched. Ten years ago was exactly what she had come to talk about. That past that she hadn't told him about. That family she could have had if she hadn't been afraid and run away. But he was in a hurry and had company. This was a different Jin, and now simply wasn't the time.

He sighed. "What's wrong?" he asked, leaning closer in her prolonged silence. "What did you want to talk about that couldn't wait until sunup?"

Hello, brother, did you know there's an entire chapter of my life I've never told you about?

She didn't think he would take that well.

"Take your hour off," she said finally. She'd been on the fence about talking to him anyway. He'd only helped sort that out.

She started back down the hall, fingers gliding along the banister to her right from which she usually overlooked Spindrift's mayhem, tearoom or bloodhouse. The quiet unnerved her. Laith had left his sadness on her shoulders like a coat.

"Arthie," Jin started hesitantly.

"I'll see you in the morning."

And still, she was a little disappointed when he closed the door. She returned to her desk. Sat. Plans and notes and the wax paper layers of Matteo's sketches stared back. She had learned the layout of the Athereum inside out.

A crop of white-blond hair bobbed outside the glass-paneled doors of her office.

"Chester," Arthie called.

He threw open one of the doors with more force than was necessary and bounded inside, rubbing an eye sleepily. His suspenders were slipping down his arms. "Yeah, boss?"

"Everything good to go on the tungsten?" she asked. He nodded. "Ace. Come close. I have a special job for you."

He perked up and puffed out his chest, automatically looking around.

"But you can't tell anyone," she said, because she knew what—or rather, whom—he was looking for. "Not Reni, and certainly not Felix. Can you do that?"

Chester hesitated.

"You're still one job ahead of Felix and two ahead of Reni."

He nodded.

"You can't tell Jin, neither."

His deep brown eyes widened a fraction. Good. She needed him to take the job seriously.

"It's a good thing Jin's busy, then," Chester remarked.

Arthie decided she didn't need to discuss Jin's activities with a nine-year-old. She passed him a slip of paper with an address.

"Go there at sunup and wait. Keep an eye on the mansion across the street. At six bells, the housekeeper will leave for the market, and she'll take a boy with her. They should both be wearing the crest of the Arundel house. It's a letter *A* flanked by two standing eagles. Follow them. Don't be seen, all right? Talk to the boy; get friendly enough to get the answer I need."

"What's the answer you need?" Chester asked, following along.

"Nothing big. Just find out how the master of the house is doing. I don't think he's been home in a while, but I want to be sure."

Chester frowned. "That's it? Why? Do you know 'im?"

"Unfortunately."

"Got it, boss." He clutched the address against his chest as he left.

Arthie leaned back in her chair with a sigh, twirling that yellow marigold. The room spun, her desk distorting before her eyes.

Just a sip, she told herself, pulling out the decanter from her cabinet and holding it up to the light. There *was* only a sip left, and she felt as if even nature was her enemy just then. Arthie downed the last of the coconut water and dropped the glass on her desk with a melodic *thunk*. The fog cleared.

What was one more odd stacked against her?

21

FLICK

When Flick left Spindrift the next morning, the Casimir crew was still riding high after retrieving the penmanship samples and Athereum marker. It might have been expired, but it was still a valid marker, which they would need once Jin got in as a blood companion. Despite her true intentions, Flick found herself feeling just as buoyant as the crew, as if she were a vessel in the ocean intent on going one way before loosening her sails and letting the wind carry her along the waves of its jubilation.

I can't, she reminded herself. She was here for her mother, as hollow as the words were beginning to sound. It didn't matter if Jin made her feel things and Chester treated her like a doting older sister. Jin did that to every girl on the street, and Chester looked at Arthie that way even when she was holding a gun.

She told herself to focus. She had a job to do now. Markers needed forging.

Flick cut down an alley, navigating laundry hung to dry. The building ahead was much like the one next to it and the one next to that and on and on down the street; red bricks with cracks running up the mortar, a bell at the very top for shift changes, weeds overgrown and snarling across what was once a paved path. Smokestacks rose every so often like fingers in the mist.

The foundries of White Roaring.

Young ladies her age marched nowhere without a chaperone, but once Flick had begun forging, that had changed. She couldn't have a chaperone tagging along the backroads of White Roaring. And though it had been years since those first escapades, Flick still hadn't grown accustomed to being alone.

She swept through the muck, remembering the last time she'd come here, for the signet ring that had ruined her life. The place was doorless and dark, like the many glassless windows cut into the brick face, but the sound of metal on metal clashed with men and children yelling over roaring fires from deep inside.

Workers of all ages, down to boys and girls no older than eight years old, carried shovels and hefted crates. They scattered coal and passed about green sand. The place glowed orange and gold as smoke and steam rose in equal protest above vats of angry red. The weight of her clothes itched against the rivers of perspiration dripping down her skin, and Flick gagged from the fumes.

White Roaring was pumped full of foundries, enough that the entire city smelled faintly of them, but here it was concentrated. The stench would take days to get out of her lungs, as attached to her skin as the memories of the day when she'd last come around.

"'Scuse me, miss," a boy exclaimed, squeezing past her with a bucket of water sloshing by his side.

"Wait," she called, but he was already limping away, leaving little puddles that reflected the many pulleys swaying from above. She searched for the foreman, hurrying past a bellowing furnace before she stumbled on the man she needed.

"Raze!" She was relieved to see a familiar face, even if it was his.

He wiped his sooty hands on the front of his apron and turned.

His face contorted almost immediately, blistering anger rearranging his bold features.

"You," he snarled. His salt-and-pepper mustache quivered.

Flick took a couple steps back, nearly tripping over a boy scooping coal out of a barrel. Terror shot through her. Raze wasn't the most pleasant of men, but he'd never been vehement.

"Raze, it's me. Flick," she said. "You helped me not long ago, and I'd like to use your machinery again."

He barked a laugh, the sound dragging a chill down her spine. A willowy man came up beside him—Too Tall, his second. He was tapping a poker against his palm, and Flick took another very careful step back. She did not think she'd ever felt fear this acute, turning her sweat to ice.

"You got some cheek, showin' up 'ere again," Too Tall hissed. Without warning, he swung the poker with enough force to shatter her ribs. Flick threw up her arms and shrank away, but she knew it was hopeless. She knew she was a fool for taking on this job, for thinking she could trim her name to something worthy of the streets and do something as grand as double-cross Arthie Casimir for her mother's forgiveness.

The steel struck something with a clang.

"Now that's no way to treat a lady."

Flick opened her eyes at the low words to find Jin towering between her and the two foremen, his umbrella holding back Too Tall's poker. He wore a black surgical mask over the lower half of his face, dark bands looped around his ears. What she could see of his features were set in stone, the glow of the factory lighting his profile gold.

He was looking at her as if there were no angry, violent men before him. As if it was only the two of them in the world. "Did he hurt you?"

Flick didn't know how to respond to the pure fury in his eyes.

"Did he *touch* you?" Jin asked again.

She shook her head.

"Casimir?" Raze said, voice mellowing with what Flick realized was respect. "This . . . this isn't no lady."

He lifted his right hand and wriggled his fingers—four of them, because the smallest was missing. Flick gasped. Jin tilted his head.

"This is what she did after taking advantage of my kindness," Raze continued. "I let her use my facilities, and this is how I was repaid."

Flick lowered her arms. "That isn't true! You're mistaken." The words rushed out of her. "You helped me forge that ring. Why would I hurt you in return?"

Only her mother knew she'd come here. Flick had been careful not to leave a trace behind, and she'd assured her mother as much.

"You can't hurt a fly, woman. Those cloaked fiends did your dirty work. I'd have lost worse if it hadn't been for my men," Raze sneered, and Too Tall pulled back the poker for another attack. Flick was about to scream before Jin swung his umbrella again. Up until this moment, she'd assumed the umbrella was a part of his attire, part of his spruce and snappy look.

What a fool she was.

Jin cracked the umbrella across Too Tall's knuckles, breaking his hold, then struck him twice more, too quick for Flick to follow.

Too Tall screamed and dropped to his knees. *Broken.* Flick's breath shook, and Raze went still. Too Tall's rod rolled across the stone floor, and the shadows cutting through the coppery trusses above drew an *X* on his face.

Jin waited until his howls quieted.

"Now that we can see eye to eye," he said, "listen well. She"—he pointed at her with his umbrella—"is under my protection." He looked around at the men that had gathered around them. The foundry exhaled and bubbled eerily without the voices to accompany it. "Touch her, and you will all die. Have I made myself clear?"

No one breathed.

"Have I made myself clear?" Jin repeated, louder this time. She flinched at the cold menace in his voice. He rapped his umbrella on the side of a barrel sharply, and the murmurs were instant.

Flick saw the way the foundrymen looked at her then, the shift in their gazes, the anger glittering beneath the respect forced upon them. She didn't want to be regarded with fear. These were good, working men. If she'd brought danger to their doorstep by replicating something as frivolous as a signet ring, she owed them an apology.

Yes, an apology will undeniably help them sleep at night.

Flick paused at the new voice in her head. It was Arthie's, dry and empirical, and it was right. She bit her tongue.

Raze pulled the newsboy cap off his bald head. "Yes, Casimir." He snapped his fingers at a boy dragging a pair of crucibles out of the way, suspenders slipping down his shoulders. "Toddy, give her what she needs."

Jin gestured after the boy disappearing into the orange-tinted darkness. "Ladies first."

Legs trembling, hair sticking to her neck, Flick followed him. "How did you find me?"

"You weren't at Spindrift, and the markers hadn't been made yet. It was obvious. As for how I knew which foundry to find you at, everyone knows which workshop forged the infamous signet ring," Jin said, and the words roiled in her stomach, making her think of her mother.

Toddy gave her a crucible and helped her gather the things she needed to set up a miniature foundry in Raze's second-floor office, privy to the collective heat of the furnaces and the bellows of machines and men alike. He lit a pair of lanterns and stepped back, adjusting his suspenders and clasping his small hands in front of him.

"Thank you," she said. She knew she should thank Jin too. For saving her. For letting her walk out of this place alive. The boy didn't respond to her thanks the way she expected him to. He jerked a fearful nod, struggled to meet her eyes, and then darted away.

Jin laughed darkly. "And that's how you know you're one of us."

Flick dabbed at her forehead with a kerchief. If that was what it meant to be respected in the underworld, she wasn't sure she liked it. She dipped her hand into her pocket, pressing her fingers to the edges of her lighter. She didn't *dislike* it either. She brushed her fingers down her side, feeling each of her ribs with newfound gratitude. When she looked up, Jin's gaze was following the movement.

She drew out her lighter and toyed with the flame. *On, off, on, off.* Again and again until her mind was fire. She had always believed there was something beautiful in the way a fire could start from nothing and rise into a beast. It told her that anything was possible. It told her that no matter how dark the world might be, all it needed was a spark.

She would start by thanking him and regaining some sense of humanity. She raised her eyes to his as the lighter snapped on.

He flinched.

Flick paused at that flash of something old and bruised. She tucked it back into her pocket and got to work, pulling the Athereum marker from her pocket and easing it into a fresh mold.

I'm sorry, was what she thought she should say, but Raze was wrong. Too Tall was wrong. It wasn't because of her that Raze had lost a finger. How could they see a slew of cloaked men and make that connection?

Jin rounded the table, leaning down with his palms on either side. She waited for him to speak of her mother. She waited for him to tell her what she refused to believe.

"Are you hurt?"

Her hand slipped at the gentle words.

Molten metal hissed like liquid fire. Jin yanked his hands away from the table and exhaled a careful breath. Why was he jittery? It was making *her* jittery. She smoothed the imprint of the numbers from her molds before they could set and stood back, waving the heat from her face.

What if Raze had connected the incident to her for no reason other than because he could? Flick stopped and faced Jin, hoping he wouldn't see the sting of tears in her eyes.

"I know what you're thinking, and I can't bear it." Her voice broke midway, but she forced the rest of the words out of her mouth.

"I'm thinking I might go back down there and break some bones," Jin said.

Oh. She didn't condone violence, but perhaps because she was shaken and not entirely herself, the words—and the anger with which he spoke them—gave her an exquisite thrill.

"No—no. It's all right," she said. "Let them be."

Jin said nothing.

Flick completed the rest of her work in silence, melting, casting, and degassing each piece. It took hours, and though Jin waited patiently with her, an eye to their surroundings, it would take longer still for the markers to be ready, so she gathered what she needed on a tray and left behind what she hoped was enough duvin as payment.

Jin gestured toward the doorway and followed her down the open staircase, metal steps clanging beneath their footfalls. The foundrymen fell quiet as she passed.

Raze stared after her. Too Tall did the same. Jin's umbrella was loose in his grip, and she wanted to tell him it wasn't her. She wanted to tell them all it wasn't her. It was only a ring. Her mother would never react in such a way.

But deep down, she knew that wasn't true.

———

That night, Flick dreamed about her mother's forgiveness. Pressing the ledger into her mother's hands. The sound of newsboys on every street: *Lady Linden exposes the Ram!* The dream careened quickly, flinging her into Raze's foundry. She saw his four-fingered hand. Too Tall, who might never walk again.

Flick woke up drowning in guilt, reopening that gaping emptiness she hadn't felt in days.

She sighed and dressed herself in her room in Spindrift. The markers she'd replicated were spread across the surface of the writing desk in the corner. She oxidized and rubbed each one down until they looked naturally aged, trying to distract herself with the work.

They were her best forgeries yet, and she tried to take pride in the results as she headed downstairs to the others.

Arthie said hello, Matteo sipped blood from a teacup, and Jin glanced up from his work. It was a heavy glance, too serious and too concerned. Had he changed his mind and sided with the foundrymen? Was there even a side to choose here? She selfishly wished they were alone.

Flick set her markers on the counter beside the real one, where the five glimmered beneath the midday sun.

"These are remarkable, Flick," Matteo said. He ran a thumb along the Athereum motto. "I can barely tell the difference."

Flick warmed at the compliment.

"That's because there isn't one," Jin called. Flick warmed even more, and felt tears prickle behind her eyes. Perhaps he didn't hate her. But that wasn't the only thing that was making her emotional, was it?

He had done more than save her life. He'd made her a part of something. For the first time, she felt truly appreciated. Recognized. *Needed.*

His tools ground to a halt over something that was gunmetal silver.

Stray sparks dusted the plate of pastry crumbs next to him, and painted the elegant tattoos on the side of his neck in gold. She couldn't see much of it, but it looked mostly like a bird. A stork or a crane. Maybe even a heron, but the design was more stylized than realistic, so it was hard to tell for certain.

"Thank you," she said to him. "For yesterday."

He looked like he wanted to ask her a question, but the last thing she wanted was to explain what had happened to the others.

To her relief, he only winked. "I'll let you know what you owe me."

Her cheeks heated, and she stepped away before she made a fool of herself. She straightened the markers and snuck another glance at him.

"Specs," Arthie explained, even though Flick was looking at Jin and not what he was making. "Jin will wear them. If we can't bring anything inside with us, we'll have to find another way. The frame will be sharp enough to cut through the glass covering the chutes transporting the markers."

"That's very smart," Flick remarked, imagining Jin in glasses. Her face was suddenly even hotter.

"That's very Jin," Arthie said as she weighed each marker against the real one, but she ought to have known that Flick was good at her job. Arthie met her eyes, and it was like Flick had said her thoughts aloud: "I like to be careful."

Laith brushed past, observing Arthie with the intensity of a hawk. Flick saw Matteo noting it.

It was hard *not* to watch Arthie Casimir. The way she worked and schemed, at times as still as stone, other times as restless as a bee. For the most part, Arthie obscured her femininity. She was, after all, a girl in a man's world, but it snuck through every once in a while. When she turned a certain way. When she lit up at Jin's words or countered Matteo's provocations or slid a glance at Laith. When the waves of her hair caught the light, illuminating the copper of her skin and making her gaze come alive with mischief.

"Don't worry," Flick said to Matteo. "They hate each other."

He said nothing for a long minute. "Neither knows it yet."

Flick didn't know what that meant, but she was pleased to see Arthie setting the markers away with care, her inspection complete.

Laith surveyed them, glancing from Arthie's desk to Jin's. "Seems everyone's contributing but the vampire."

"I'm elevating the crew with my looks," Matteo said matter-of-factly. "*You*, on the other hand. No one likes a baby tyrant breathing down their necks."

Something fell with a *tink* on the other side of the room, then a tool clattered onto the table.

"Will the lot of you quiet down?" Jin snapped.

Arthie wasn't fazed by his outburst. "Anything to help you return to serenading Flick."

Flick flushed. "You shouldn't tease."

"I shouldn't do a lot of things," Arthie said, and nodded at Laith. "This one would be out of a job then."

"You flatter yourself too much," Laith said.

This time, something shattered. Jin went still. Glass glittered on the floorboards by his feet.

"What part of keeping mum do you not seem to understand?" he snarled.

"You never said *not* to talk," Matteo pointed out.

Flick peered at Jin's worktable. Narrow tools were scattered near a shallow bowl of water and a small pile of glass disks, the lenses for his fake specs. She was fairly certain the ribboned length of angled metal he was trying to wrap around each one was tungsten carbide. She'd worked with it before.

Jin angrily grabbed a dustpan. "Well, listen here, you overgrown mosquito: Shut up."

This time Arthie laughed, and Jin immediately softened. She turned to Matteo and Laith. "We're done here for now. I'll scout out the tower tonight, and we'll reconvene tomorrow for the job."

"Ouch, darling. I know a dismissal when I see one," Matteo said, but he didn't tease her beyond that and turned to Laith.

The guard scowled. "Don't touch me."

"Easy there, captain boy. That's the last thing I'll ever do, trust me," Matteo said, and Flick thought she caught a flash of fangs again before the two of them finally left the room.

Arthie crouched beside Jin and picked up a fallen pair of pliers.

"You've got this," she said gently, and Flick was surprised by this tender side of her. She wondered if Arthie knew she was still in the room with them.

"Do I?" Jin asked.

"The specs?" she asked. "Yes. The only reason you think you don't is because you're worrying about everything else."

"Like how we might die tomorrow?" he asked.

"Precisely," Arthie said lightly. "Doubt is of the devil."

"More often than not, *you* are the devil," Jin replied.

Don't stare, Flick commanded herself. But it was hard not to—his sleeves were rolled up to his forearms, which were corded with veins charting a path to his hands. He ran his fingers through his mussed hair and cleaned the intact lens with the edge of his shirt. Her throat made a funny sound when she glimpsed a sliver of skin.

He slid the specs on his face, one finger adjusting them up the bridge of his nose. He was always stately and trim, but goodness the specs were something else, possibly because he'd fashioned them himself.

"*Dulce periculum*, brother," was all Arthie said, poking her finger playfully through the empty half of the frame.

He sighed but lifted his right hand and knocked the back of it against the back of hers, their knuckles rapping. "We were made for trouble, you and me."

Flick envied them. Their camaraderie, their friendship, their love. They were bound without blood, a bond not unlike hers and her mother's, and yet they couldn't be more different. And it made Flick wonder, then, what exactly she wanted from her mother, if not this.

22

ARTHIE

There's a way to manifest insignificance: Stand on top of the world.

On the balcony at the top of the Old Roaring Tower, less than twenty-four hours before the Festival of Night, Arthie unzipped the maintenance uniform that had gotten her through the guarded entrance and tossed it aside, readjusting the cuffs of her shirt and smoothing out her trousers. Jin had only winked when Arthie asked how he had managed to swipe it.

Far below, the city lay awake even this late, gaslights glowing like abandoned wishes. People turned in circles until they found an eternal home of dirt—or a pair of fangs. Buildings tumbled in chaotic disarray, balustrades like sentinels, stone carved upon stone, ending where the sea spilled into the mist far beyond or emptied into the River Tamesis, winding through half of Ettenia. Wind whipped at her hair, ruffling the panels of her suit jacket and tugging at the laces of her shoes.

The moonlight bathed half of her in white, the other half in stark shadow. Fitting, for what she was. Half here and now, the other half lost at sea. Ravaged by an ache that could never be dulled.

Please, the ripping wind seemed to beg. *Please, please, please.*

Below her the clock ticked on, counting through the second hour. A bird took flight from a nest on the number nine, and she shivered as the tower's pulse became her own. It was a mechanical heartbeat that measured life in seconds, counting time the way mortals rarely did.

Tell me, do you remember what it's like to live?

Those words had pierced her skin and burrowed under her muscles, settling into her bones. Just like the boy who had spoken them.

And there, in the indiscernible silence, she heard it: the low draw of a breath.

Arthie spun. A figure was silhouetted behind her. She sprang forward and shoved him against the brick wall, finger dropping to the trigger of her pistol. He broke her hold and reversed their positions within a single strike of the clock.

He tilted his head, locks of white falling across his right eye. "Your aggression grows increasingly violent."

There was a reason for that aggression: the fact that he was in her head before he appeared behind her. The fact that she couldn't stop thinking of him and how he'd held her, touched her, looked at her.

How she planned on getting him killed.

"Let go of me," Arthie said quietly. Her arm was caged beneath his, his knee pressed between hers, locking her in place. Her body itched to lean closer, to brush against him. A current was shooting through her veins. She was angry, that was it. There was no possibility of the low, silken thrum of his voice having any other effect on her.

"Or else?" he asked, slipping closer until the tip of his nose almost touched hers. His smile was the edge of a knife, and she was ready to bleed. He smelled like smoke and wood and spice, a mystery twined with enchantment. "You're in no position to make threats, Casimir."

The night gusted between them. She drew her lip between her teeth.

Was it the shift of the moon, or did his eyes darken? Was it the clock that thrummed down her body, or was it something else? Arthie let herself linger in the heat flooding through her limbs, feeling powerful when his gaze dropped to her mouth.

She shoved him off her, immediately curling her fists against the feel of his skin beneath his clothes, the solidity of his chest. It wasn't hard to conjure the image of him at his apartment, his torso bare, skin glistening with stray drops of water. He had discarded his robes today in favor of a linen shirt in royal blue that fit snug across his shoulders with billowy pants slung low. He looked even more bare without his kitten curled on his shoulder.

Arthie rounded to the other side of the balcony, biting her tongue to force herself back to her senses.

"What are you doing here?" Arthie studied him, the smooth mask of indifference, the bow of his lips that made her skin prickle—*there*. The quick twitch of his eye every few heartbeats. A ruptured peace, an unsettled heart. Strangely, it eased something inside of her, made her less hostile.

Which wasn't a good thing.

"I thought it would be smart to survey the Athereum from above," he replied. "I didn't expect to find you here."

She wondered if he'd used his rank as a captain to get inside or if he'd scaled the tower itself. She wouldn't be surprised if it was the latter.

"Oh, because I'm not smart?" she asked.

He started to protest before he caught sight of her teasing smirk and laughed, rich and warm, and she latched on to the sound as if it were the sequence to a vault.

He studied her with something like respect, throwing her off-kilter once again. Nothing about Laith slotted into place, and perhaps that was why she found herself thinking about him again and again. Puzzling him out, trying to decipher the secrets that lurked behind the tenebrous dark of his eyes.

"How did you find such confidence?" he asked.

"Finding it suggests I had no part in its making." When she had.

She'd fed it into her veins, nurtured it from stilted first steps to a wizened stalk.

The Athereum spanned across the tower's shadow, the wall carving a white perimeter, narrow and slick. The establishment dripped decadence, from the details carved into the stone to the roof glinting like duvin ripe for the taking. Vampires lingered in the garden, aglow with the light from inside, their conversations as low as they would be in Spindrift.

Closer to Arthie and Laith, a guard paced in the dormer balcony cut into the Athereum roof. Half of his platform extended out of the Athereum, giving him a view of the gardens, and she could see the other half, a mezzanine that extended farther inside, where Matteo said he surveyed the entrance.

"Now there's a guard who doesn't slack off," Laith said.

A glint of metal hung from the guard's waist beside a spool of silver.

Arthie gestured to it. "We'll have to take him out with his own weapon."

Athereum guards were equipped with barbed wire and specially designed guns that fired without a sound. They were meant for vampires. The bullets dissolved shortly after contact and unleashed a toxin that would knock one out for a good ten minutes—and a human indefinitely.

She nodded at the gates, where two guards monitored the crowd gliding in and out. "We'll pilfer a gun from one of them and shoot the dormer guard. That gives us ten minutes. Once Flick gets into the Athereum and inserts our identifiers, you'll follow, scale the interior wall, and secure him with his own coil of barbed wire before the toxin wears out."

"Barbed wire," Laith deadpanned. "What good will that do?"

"Wrap it tightly enough and it will keep him immobilized and quiet until the shift change comes looking for him the next morning. They move, they bleed. He opens his mouth, it cuts into his lips. Vampires might be powerful, but the bullet drains them, and they won't risk bleeding dry. Vampires can't produce blood."

"And how do you know all this?" he asked.

"I listen. Spindrift was designed to pacify, and people like to talk when they feel safe," Arthie said. "I would—"

"Shh," Laith cut her off.

Footsteps. They echoed behind the clockface. Voices called to one another. The tower guards. She had known her maintenance ruse wouldn't last, but with Laith here she'd overstayed.

The balcony was one flat bed of stone corralled by a balustrade, and there was no place to hide. They couldn't jump without breaking their necks or make the climb down before they were spotted.

Laith gave her his hand.

"What?" Arthie asked.

"You don't have to trust me."

"I don't."

The doorknob rattled. The auction was less than a day away. She didn't have time to take chances. She had prepared too much to let it fall apart.

She took his hand as the door flung open. "You're ludicrous."

"You would know," he said with a quick grin, and swung her over the ledge of the clock tower balcony. The world toppled. She was hurtling through the air, a shout cramming into her throat.

She was held aloft by nothing but Laith's arm around her middle until he dropped them both into the nook of a narrow window, just beside the curve of the first hour.

Arthie bristled. "Was there—"

"Hush," he cut her off again, clearly enjoying himself. Him and his flowers and his white kitten and those wretched flecks above his brow.

The narrow nook, Arthie belatedly realized, really was very narrow.

He brought his fingers to the small of her back, then leaned into the star-studded sky and peered up to the balcony.

The guards' voices echoed, but Arthie couldn't hear them. Not with her body pressed against his and the breadth of his shoulders engulfing her. Not with the hammer of his heart inches from her ear so she could count each beat.

"They won't find us here," Laith murmured, pulling back into the shadow of the nook, and his pulse quickened like horses beneath a whip, a vein thrumming at his neck. Fissures of amber shimmered in his irises. "This is the part where you thank me."

"If I ever do, you'll know that something is very wrong," she replied, fighting to remain in control of herself.

The rumble of his responding *hmm* echoed down to her toes. He was studying her, and Arthie had the sinking realization that he knew exactly how he was affecting her. Why else did a smirk lift the side of his mouth when he leaned even closer?

Quick as a shot, his thumb brushed the swell of her lower lip, leaving fire in its wake, and she thought she felt the hand at the small of her back tug her closer. She thought she allowed it.

"What are you doing?"

She told herself she asked because she needed to know. There was no other reason why she sought out the sound of his voice when every space in her mind was already allotted for, each one working through a task, a job, mulling White Roaring's secrets.

"What *are* we doing, Arthie?" he murmured with half a groan, and the night lit a fever in his eyes.

She didn't know why his use of the word *we* made her shiver. She wondered what she had to do to hear that barely restrained hint of a groan again.

"Is it mayhem or desire?" he asked, slowly sliding his hands up her arms.

It was both. It was something kindred. For Arthie, one was often synonymous with the other, but right now, she couldn't breathe. Every inch of her wanted to throw herself at him, every inch of her wanted to put as much distance as possible between them.

Up above, the door to the balcony slammed closed.

Soon, she told herself. She'd retrieve that ledger and be done with him. Be done with this. And if any part of her did not look forward to the fact, she buried it deep.

right wing

left wing

rooms

vaults

offices
& rooms

auction
hall

parlor

prison

locked
& guarded

glass
chutes

dormer
guard

stair

guard

guard
house

in

*

mortu
vivos
docen

locate the
the wretched
in way over her
is why I didn't
ly dreadful, she

Athereum
marker

numerical
code
inside

left wing

vaults

offices & rooms

parlor

prison
locked & guarded

dormer
guard →

right wing

auction hall

rooms (mostly debauchery)

marker archives

glass chutes →

'winsome' sketch of a female vampire

gardens

ACT II

PAST AND FUTURE

Athereum List

- Edward Prior
- Sanjay Bhatt
- Oliver Tan
- Daisy Vincent
- Clayton Lombard
- Ronnie Humphries
- Faulk

ARTHIE didn't let me finish adding roses

23

JIN

Jin had planned his outfit for the Athereum job days ago. His jacket was finely spun velvet in the deepest green he could find. It would seem colorless to anyone who was tasteless, fashionable to anyone who mattered. He had even dabbed on cologne, more so to find comfort in the blend of bergamot and cashmere, but still.

The heist was tonight. There was a chance he might die, but there was also the utmost certainty that he would do so in style.

He set his umbrella against the sideboard with a heavy sigh, already feeling like he was missing a limb, a little part of his childhood that made him *him*.

He wasn't excited to call in that favor, to see Rose Ashby and be reminded yet again of how he'd killed for her. He could lie and steal and coax without hesitation, break bones and shatter jaws as quickly as a shot, but killing was killing, and Jin wasn't fond of it.

The Ashbys were a family of vampires, and not by choice—as most vampire families tended to be—but by actual kinship. Once the patriarch of the family had turned, Jin guessed he couldn't bear the thought of his spouse and children aging without him, and so he turned them one by one, waiting until each child reached the age he wanted to preserve.

To some, it was romantic—a family forever united. To Jin, it was heinous. It was one thing to be born without the privilege of money and standing, it was another to live without the power to make a decision for oneself. To have control forcefully taken from one's hands, to understand the true meaning of helplessness.

Rose Ashby was nothing like her father. She was kind and *real*, a rarity in a world made up of superficial and materialistic people. When she'd come to Jin two years ago, asking him to make sure her still-human, critically ill brother never left the hospital a vampire, he couldn't say no—not when there were fates worse than death.

So no, he wasn't excited about the reminder of what he'd done, but if there was any way to get into the Athereum as a blood companion and bypass the vetting process, it was with Rose Ashby.

She was the closest thing to vampire royalty.

It was a little past eight when he left his room in Spindrift and went downstairs to where Laith and Arthie were running through the plans one last time. Flick was in one of the booths by the window. Her gown was as pretty as a garden at dawn. It was a warm shade of cream, like well-made milk tea. A heavy smattering of flowers were embroidered along the hem, gradually fading up to a laced bodice that cupped her every curve in a way that made Jin jealous, ending with a delicate collar around her throat. She tilted her head and peered at him as if she were compiling his chapters into a book and something didn't tally. As if he were broken, and only she could see it.

But Jin was the one who fixed things. He knew what was broken, and it sure wasn't him. It couldn't be. Nope.

Moonlight pooled in Flick's hair, tracing each ringlet like the hand of an earnest lover, gradually drifting to outline her profile in dusky silver. She looked at the stars as if they were home, and he wished, impossibly, that he could take her to them.

"Oh, hello," she said when he neared. "I, er, like your glasses."

Jin couldn't stop a boyish smile. "Why thank you, Felicity."

Flick nodded, barely holding his gaze. "Also your tattoos. Why—what are they?"

His smile turned into a grin. "Going to ask all the questions now, are we?"

She ducked adorably into the collar of her dress, and then that damned lighter was in her hand again. She slowed her movements but didn't tuck it away.

"I've seen your arm," she said softly. "I can tell you're not fond of fire."

Jin gritted his teeth.

"But it's okay." She looked up at him. "It really is."

Jin latched on to the rise and fall of her voice, the measured sounds of her breaths.

She watched him for a moment and finally capped the little thing. "It's funny, I think, how a flame has the opposite effect on me. It calms me. Sometimes I think even vampires hunt for the flame. For the light. It's what we need to live, undead or otherwise, isn't it? I know it marked a terrible part of your life, Jin, but that doesn't mean you can't overcome it."

"Perhaps," Jin said.

"For certain," she said, and the belief in her voice soothed him.

Jin released a slow breath. "It's a heron."

Her brow pinched in confusion.

"My tattoo," he said, tugging his collar away so she could get a better look at it. "It's a heron. When I was a child, I had a stubborn tuft of hair right at the back here that would never stay down, and my mother joked that I looked like a black heron they'd seen on one of their voyages. My father would always call me Little Heron after that."

"Do you still miss them?" Flick said.

"Every day," Jin said quietly, and saw the notch between her brows. "You're the same. You miss your mother."

That notch deepened. "I thought I did."

Spindrift's doors swung open in a jangle of bells, and a figure stepped inside with a satisfied sigh, wiping something dark from his chin.

Chester darted forward. "We're closed! Bugger off!"

But Jin knew that swagger, even if he didn't recognize the rest of the man.

"Matteo?" Arthie asked.

Flick rose to her feet. "Bang up the elephant, I almost didn't recognize you!"

"I do clean up nice, don't I?" Matteo asked, his lips curling a crooked grin at Arthie. "Don't stare, darling."

He hadn't cleaned up, he had *changed*. His hair was as bright as Chester's now, bound loosely at the base of his skull. A pair of gold-framed specs sat on the bridge of his nose, his signature half-open ruffled white shirt now as dark as sin and matched by his trousers.

Laith crossed his arms. "Can the two of you focus? Yalla."

Flick lifted a hand to her mouth, chagrined. For once, Jin agreed with the high captain.

But Arthie would never admit to staring. "Your drawings had better be right."

Matteo *hmm*ed. "This will work. Trust a little."

That was the problem, wasn't it? She didn't trust anyone. Jin sometimes wondered if she even trusted him.

"The auction begins at ten," she said, striding for the door. "We reconvene at three-quarters past. Laith, you are not bringing that kitten with you."

"Oh, I am," he replied. "After me, she's the stealthiest in our crew."

Jin studied Arthie. She was off. Her eyes looked almost hollow, something wild and hungry lurking in the umber.

"Our ten-minute window begins once I take down the dormer

guard. And no, Matteo, he won't die. I'll be knocking him out. Flick then needs to enter the archive room and get everyone in. Laith follows. Matteo brings up the rear, distracting the entrance crowd so Laith can scale the wall and apprehend the guard before he wakes up and sounds the alarm for *being* knocked out. Then he and I will search for the ledger while Jin and Flick keep the auction going."

"Are we clear?" Jin asked.

Nods went around.

"Listen for the bells," Arthie reminded.

"And don't die," Jin joked.

"That's the one thing I haven't mastered," Matteo said with a dramatic sigh.

When Matteo and Flick turned for the door, Arthie pulled Calibore from her waist. Jin watched as it shifted into a sharp-edged hairpin, that strange magic unsettling him even now. She flipped it over in her hands and held Laith's gaze for a fraction of a second too long before she secured it through her hair.

Laith knew. She had told him. A thread of uncertainty snaked through Jin. It was not jealousy, but fear. Worry. And, finally, apprehension.

Because Arthie never revealed a secret unless she had a bigger one waiting right behind it. She saw Jin watching her.

"Ready?" she asked him.

"No," he answered honestly, swallowing his many questions because now wasn't the time.

"Perfect." Arthie smiled, and it shouldn't have made it easier for Jin to breathe, but it did. She stepped out into the night. "It's teatime, scoundrels."

24

ARTHIE

The Athereum cut a startling figure in the dark, tucked behind its alabaster wall. Arthie hadn't run a large job in a while. She'd never run a job *this* large, and she'd almost forgotten what it was like to move from plan to execution. That rush of emotion, that fear and excitement warring with each other.

She watched as Jin disappeared through the Athereum's imposing iron gates with a saunter in his step, looking every bit like he belonged in the swarm of vampires lounging in the gardens. No one spared him a glance.

Tiny lights were strung from the trees, illuminating the latest in undead fashion, with necklines deeper than what was decent, skirts slit sharp as knives. Vampires left shame in the grave when they returned, their attire more provocative than what high society would even deem appropriate for sleepwear.

Flick followed, tucked between two members of the press as instructed, and then Laith. Behind them all, Arthie fell in step with a group of vampires making their way to the Athereum. She kept her head low, spirits rising as she got closer and closer to the gates.

The cold nipped at her ears, but she wished the moon would tuck itself behind some clouds right about now. One of the guards was attentive, the other was deep in conversation with a guest. All she had to do was bump into the distracted one and slip his gun out of his holster.

She veered closer to him.

"Oi!"

It was the attentive guard. *Drat.* Arthie kept walking, pretending she couldn't hear.

"I know you."

And if he kept yapping about it, everyone else would too. Gritting her teeth, Arthie broke away from the group and detoured to him.

"You're that Casimir." He was yellow-haired and dark-eyed and fully irritating.

Arthie recalled everything Chester had gathered on him. "And you're Barclay."

The guard narrowed his eyes, but he'd quieted down, and they weren't getting as many stares anymore. Still, he would know she wasn't from the press or even an enthusiast, and the last thing she needed was for him to demand he see her marker and ruin the job before it even began.

She came prepared.

"You'll have to tell me if these sound familiar," Arthie said, stepping closer to him and the gun at his waist. "Prussic acid. Lead carbonate. Arsenic. Tough stuff."

He drew himself to his full height and bared his teeth.

"Ah," she warned, seeing through his thick skull. "You don't want me to go missing."

"It's a side job, all right?" he said. "I stock the local apothecary. Not everyone here oozes money."

"Strange," Arthie said with a frown. Through the gate, she could see the Athereum gardens and the crowds thickening. She needed to move. "Madam Mabel didn't own an apothecary last I checked."

The vampire stilled, an effigy under the moonlight. There was more than one grifter on the streets of White Roaring, and if Arthie culled secrets, at least she duped her patrons with something healthy in a cup. Madam Mabel Ever killed them. Slowly. She couldn't care less about the effects of the toxicants she used in her cosmetics—so long as they had immediate results and took long enough to rot her high-paying customers.

"How much does Beautiful For Ever pay you for the poison Mabel uses in her opulent cosmetics, stripping Ettenia's beauties to their bones?" she asked.

He huffed. "Enough."

Arthie nodded. "Thought so. But I'm not one to get in the way of a good transaction, so if you'll turn around, I'll be on my way."

There really was little difference between Ettenia's undead guards and the living ones. One had bones that could be snapped in two, the other boasted bones well-nigh made of stone. Both were small-brained folk in tinsel suits.

"You think I'm going to let you through?" He sounded baffled.

"As a matter of fact, I *know* you are," Arthie replied. "Unless you want your work history to find its way out. I'm just here to be a part of the excitement."

He clenched his teeth and glared, but finally relented. And he was so busy seething that he didn't notice Arthie striding past the gates with his now-missing gun.

25

JIN

Jin kept an eye out for Rose Ashby. Though a line had begun to form at the door, most of the vampires loitered beneath the fractured stars, deep in conversation. Jin had seen his fair share of the undead on Spindrift's floor, but he'd never seen *this* many and in so posh a setting, no different than a ball on Admiral Grove.

He bit his tongue to stop from spiraling down another memory: his mother in a dress as pink as the sky's first blush, his father in a suit sharper than his cheekbones, their hands clasped, their conversation rife with blood and needles and bacteria and teasing, even en route to a dinner party.

A hush fell when a girl of twenty started up the path to the Athereum doors, her hair the same vibrant red as her voluminous skirts, drawing every eye that wasn't already on her. Jin's heart squeezed. This was it.

"Rose," Jin said, stepping past a pair of vampires to catch her eye.

She stopped walking, the billow of her skirts coming to a halt. Dread fleeted across her brow. "Jin? Are you turned?"

"Not yet, love," Jin said. "I don't like the idea of never savoring a pastry again."

Had she been any other vampire, he would have chosen his words with more care.

"Oh," she said, envy wrapped around the word. "Are you here with someone, then?"

"I'm not," Jin admitted, and cast a glance around the garden. "Or rather, I was, before I was abandoned."

Rose laughed, a tinkling that drew them unneeded attention. "I find it hard to believe anyone would leave you, Jin."

The words struck him with a pang.

"If you can give me a name, I can go looking," she offered.

"That wouldn't be necessary, really," Jin said, and then, as if he'd just had the thought, he added: "Although I am much more in favor of seeing the sights than leaving without the night I was promised."

"Sweet Jin, I would be your date if I didn't already have arrangements," she said, and Jin didn't think the sympathy in her tone was false. That was what he liked about Rose. He looked away, mustering as much of a sulk as he could.

He could almost feel Arthie's gaze from the crowd, counting every precious second. The line into the Athereum shuffled forward, and if this took any longer, they'd be the only ones left for the doorkeeper to scrutinize.

"But if you're here for the night you seem to be alluding to, you wouldn't need me, would you?" Rose asked. Her expression spoke of devilry. "You only need to reach the right wing."

"So I've heard," Jin said. He had every intention of avoiding the right wing and its dedication to debauchery. He cast a look at the light spilling from the Athereum's double doors. The hope and longing he conjured was only partially a lie. "I need to get inside the Athereum for that."

She paused, a furrow in her brow. He'd spoken the words too quickly, hadn't he? It was the pressure, the worry, the weight of this night as heavy as the clouds in the sky. She knew he was a Casimir. She knew the mischief he and Arthie were about.

And if someone like Rose Ashby could get him inside without a hitch, no one would doubt her if she sounded an alarm either.

Come on, Rose. Come on.

With a sprightly laugh, Rose held out her arm, and Jin exhaled in relief. "Well then, allow me the honors."

He took it, calming the restlessness in his limbs as they joined the slow-moving line. Before long, the pair of them were bathed in gold before the doorkeeper, Elise Thorne, and Jin was once again grateful that he'd run into the other sister at the Thornes' house on Admiral Grove.

Matteo had been spot-on with his descriptions and depictions. It was exactly as Jin had imagined. He watched as Rose dropped her marker through the slot and introduced him as her human date for the night. Elise chastised her for not having him vetted, ignoring him like he was some brainless arm candy, and Rose apologized in good form. When the bouncer finally frisked him down, he had to bite his tongue against a comment or two.

And then he was in.

Jin stopped just inside the doors to leisurely button up his jacket and scan the space at the same time. The area was lit by lamps shaped like open palms gripping bulbs, the walls a deep, dark crimson patterned in damasks. Eerie, but fitting. Farther inside, there were silk-wrapped settees, tufted cushions, and scattered armchairs. He saw vampires sitting far too close to one another, others lounging with flutes of crimson. There was a quartet playing cards and another tittering over an engagement ring.

Wicked knives, he was inside the *Athereum*.

Something clinked beneath his right foot. He glanced down to the lacquered wood floors and saw the pair of channels set feet apart and covered in glass, just as Matteo had said. As he stood there, two markers shot in the direction of the archive room. A lone, freestanding accent wall rose up ahead, bedazzled with pearled tiles behind a massive flowerpot.

The marker archives room was just beyond it to the right. The mezzanine extended high up on his left, letting in the cool night air. On it, the dormer guard was pacing back and forth.

There will be at least one blind spot, Arthie had said. *They're not worried about anyone messing with the chutes once they're already inside.*

Easy for her to say.

Jin tracked the guard's line of sight, trying to find Arthie's blind spot. He needed to get to the other side of the freestanding wall. If only that toxin lasted longer than ten minutes. She could shoot the guard now, and Jin would have more freedom to wander around.

"Don't worry about him," Rose said, following Jin's gaze to the guard. "He can make the foyer feel like a prison. Let's get to the party."

Jin laughed. "I think I ought to sit down for a bit. Feeling a tad overwhelmed. Never thought I'd be here in the Athereum, you know."

That, at least, wasn't a lie. She gave him a look. *Ah,* she'd forgotten he wasn't a vampire.

"This way," she said, gesturing toward the small alcove beneath the guard's mezzanine. Perfect.

It'll be empty ninety-nine percent of the time because the fun is inside, not in the foyer, and no one likes to be watched, Matteo had said.

At least not by a guard, Jin had thought.

Rose led him to the settee and released his arm. Jin held on.

"Thank you, Rose." Of the emotions he'd displayed since meeting her tonight, this one he meant, and he hoped she could see as much.

"No," she said with a bittersweet smile. "I will always have you to thank, Jin."

Such a strange thing, to be appreciated by a woman for killing her beloved brother.

He sat down. Rose disappeared down the hall.

Jin took off his specs and got to work.

26

FLICK

Flick left the cover of the gardens and touched her pocket, berating herself one more time. If she didn't want her lighter confiscated, she couldn't keep drawing attention to it. The others hadn't thought to ask Flick for her weapons. She was armed with a longing that was killing her, and no one knew.

She willed her feet to work, her arms to remain still, her blood to stay whisper quiet. No one was looking at her, but it certainly felt as if they were. Her awareness was slowly narrowing to obscurity.

This was it.

The line crept forward, giving Flick her first glimpse of the door-keeper at the entrance, and she was once again relieved to find that it wasn't Eleanor Thorne. This sister's gaze was a dewy brown, her nose more pert than her sister's sharp angles.

Flick caught sight of Jin crossing from one end of the foyer to the other. She flipped the expired marker in her hand, digging the grooves into her palm with each turn. She felt the weight of her lighter in her pocket like a stone. The line moved and then moved again. The vampire behind her glanced down the length of her dress and called it pretty. Flick thought she said *thank you*, but she couldn't remember.

Then it was her turn to stand before the soft light of the Athereum entrance and remember how to breathe.

27

JIN

Using the tungsten carbide frame of his specs was simple enough, and Jin cut through the glass that cased the chutes within minutes, right where they disappeared beneath the freestanding wall. If anyone looked, the notches would appear to be design flaws. Neat ones.

He popped the lenses out of the frame and positioned them above the chutes, readying for when he needed to shove them into place and stop the markers from returning. He would swing the arm of his glasses to propel the markers forward again after.

For now, he leaned back against the freestanding wall, out of sight from the dormer guard.

Time to wait.

Wait for Arthie, wait for Laith, wait for Matteo.

He popped a clove rock into his mouth. Lovely.

28

ARTHIE

Arthie hid behind the Athereum's rosebushes and lined up her shot, watching Flick get closer and closer to the entrance. The wind blew east in intermittent bursts forcing her to adjust her trajectory more than once. The dormer guard paced in and out of the Athereum, vigilant and out of reach.

Laith opened his mouth.

Arthie thought this conversation had already gone twice as long as it should have.

"He might hear the bullet," he said at her side.

"They're designed to be silent, but I'll take that chance," Arthie murmured, keeping her eye on Flick and her finger on the trigger.

Laith opened his mouth again.

"Nope," Arthie said, watching the door as Flick inched closer and closer.

She inserted her marker. Arthie fired. The bullet slung through the night, flashing once before it disappeared. For a moment nothing happened, then the guard teetered against the iron balustrade and collapsed.

"Ten minutes," Arthie whispered, tossing the gun into the bushes. Ten minutes before their guard awoke and sounded the alarm. Ten minutes for Flick to get in and out of the marker archives.

Arthie flipped the forged marker in her hand and joined the line, Laith and Matteo behind her.

29

FLICK

Flick stared blankly at the doorkeeper at the entrance to the Athereum. Elise, Flick told herself. Referring to her by name made her less formidable.

Flick paused. "Do I—"

First step to a con, Arthie had told her, *act like you belong. Look sharp.*

She squared her shoulders and pressed her marker into the slot. Her *expired* marker, Flick's nerves reminded her. It fell with a heavy plink into the channel below, and then something clicked, propelling it into the hall behind Elise.

To her right, another vampire did the same, and that was when Flick heard it, just as Arthie had promised: the *zing* of a bullet hurtling through the air. Flick's pulse soared the same way.

Elise was watching her.

"You've gathered quite the crowd tonight," Flick said, the words bubbling out of her. "It will be exciting to meet everyone."

Arthie would have advised against chitchat, but that was what Jin would do. Flick might not possess his charm, but she knew how to be kind.

Elise softened. "Indeed. The charity auction attracts vampires from around the country."

The chutes rattled with a sound. Flick knew her marker would trigger a rejection, that it was all part of the plan, but that didn't make it any easier to stand here. That didn't mean nothing could go wrong. Jin couldn't charm an inanimate object into letting her through.

A cold sweat dampened Flick's palms. She touched a hand to her breast, already feeling the stake with her name on it, splinters making little rips at her skin while blood gushed free. She'd bleed to death, and her mother's forgiveness wouldn't be as important anymore.

Stick to the plan, and we'll be fine.

Easier said than done, Arthie, Flick thought.

The bouncer shuffled beside the door, his coat bulging around his muscled frame. Flick had never seen such a large man. She blearily wondered how much blood he needed to consume to maintain such a figure. *That's not what you need to be thinking about,* she chastised herself.

The markers returned with a tinny sound that could have been a siren for the way the noise rang in her ears. Flick gulped, but Elise only handed her marker back, blotted in something green that was already fading. She had to refrain from inspecting it, pressing the marker's grooves into her palm, spying the faint smudge of red beneath the green approval. She snuck a glance at the marker of the vampire beside her; the green was much brighter. Had Jin . . . rubbed some off of it to approve Flick's? The doorkeeper looked like she knew precisely what Flick had done but didn't know how.

Flick didn't know either.

"Enjoy your time at the Athereum, miss."

Flick thanked her and stepped into the lavish opulence of the Athereum. The walls dripped in sinful decadence. The heels of her boots clicked on the tiles like bullets in a glass. The chutes rattled as another pair of markers shot through. She didn't look back to see who it was. It wouldn't be anyone in the crew—they had to wait for her.

She inhaled, grounding herself in the rich and earthy scent. It was amber and spice, old books and cloves, and . . . perhaps blood, but it was very lovely. Up above, the ceilings were illustrated, dark designs almost invisible in the swirling black.

Keep walking, Arthie had told her. *Don't stop for anything.* She didn't. *Don't draw attention to yourself.*

Flick kept walking.

30

ARTHIE

Arthie approached the entrance of the Athereum repeating the plan to herself, every angle and every leg, each of the possibilities they'd predicted where something could go wrong.

And Arthie knew, *knew* Flick hadn't yet added the forged markers into the log, but she did it anyway: She dropped her marker into the slot.

Elise Thorne sneered at Arthie in recognition, fangs coming out in earnest as tension spiked the air. But the Athereum put its members first, and she wouldn't say a word, not until Arthie's marker returned.

Which it did, smeared a different color. Not green, not red, but yellow. A violation, as Matteo had warned.

Across the foyer, Jin stared. Fear and concern were rampant on his features. *It'll be okay,* Arthie willed him to understand, holding his gaze. She could handle herself, and he knew it.

"Unsurprising," Elise spat, gesturing the bouncer forward. Neither of them noticed Flick tucking herself into the nook behind the archive room or Jin hovering near the chutes in preparation to smash through the glass.

The bouncer bent to frisk her, moving his meaty hands across her spread arms, along her waist, and then down each of her legs. It took everything in Arthie to not kick him off of her.

"Come with me," the bouncer demanded.

Arthie held her ground. They knew who she was; they should

know she would never give up without a fight. He stared for a senseless minute before he dismissed her petulance with a grunt and swung.

She ducked clear of his punch. "Think you can rough me into obedience?"

The bouncer grabbed her by the arms, locking her in place. Too many eyes were on her. Too much attention. Laith's jaw tightened, Matteo gave her a reassuring nod. Arthie bit her tongue, saying nothing as the bouncer dragged her through the doors and inside the Athereum. She'd been through worse, she told herself. This was nothing. This was *necessary*.

But as far as plans went, there was no backing out now.

31

JIN

Focus, Jin murmured to himself. Arthie could handle herself. He pulled his tie free and wrapped it around his gloved fist, waiting until a pair of vampires disappeared into the halls. Then he crouched and slammed his fist through the glass chutes. It took two more punches before it shattered and Jin carefully pushed the fractured pieces into the chute until there was enough to obstruct the markers leaving the archive room.

If only he could use the tungsten carbide again, but he needed a mess. A proper distraction that didn't look like it had been perfectly planned. He stepped back and surveyed the broken glass.

That should draw her out.

He backtracked to the settee where Rose had left him and sat down with a view of the archive room.

The door swung open, and Jin heard the vampire's sigh as she rounded the corner, a sequined, gray-green dress clinging to her figure. Eleanor Thorne. She slipped several small disks that resembled weights into her pocket as she walked, her sea-glass eyes missing nothing. For a moment Jin was afraid she'd see him lingering in the dark, but her attention was on the obstructed chutes.

"What is it?" Elise called from the entrance. Jin tucked himself deeper into the alcove.

"Some imbecile shattered the glass," said Eleanor. Imbecile? He had shattered that with care, thank you very much. He had taken the time to flirt *once*, and it was biting him in the arse relentlessly.

Keep talking, Jin goaded, one eye on the vampire and the other on the door to the archive room as it slipped closed again, the hem of Flick's gown disappearing inside.

32

FLICK

Flick was almost surprised when she made it into the marker archives intact. She was grateful that Arthie had knocked the dormer guard out. She couldn't fathom trying to slip under both his *and* Eleanor Thorne's noses undetected.

The clock was ticking; Laith still needed to apprehend the guard before he woke up, and she had little time to waste. The room was more bare-bones than the vampire's fancy gown had suggested it would be. There was a wide ebony desk and chair in its center, then a comfy armchair and a sideboard by the door atop which sat a brass scale, polished from daily use.

"Now," Flick said, tugging the silk gloves off her hands, "where is that log?"

An indignant meow responded, spooking her half to death. It was Laith's kitten.

"Oh, hello there, little one." Flick didn't know how she had snuck in after her, but she wasn't about to shoo away company.

And she had found the log.

It was on the desk, opened to a page with rows of numbers just as Matteo had described. What he had failed to mention was the reason why the vampire didn't bother locking the door behind her each time she left her room.

The log *itself* was locked. It lay beneath a glass case whose latch connected to a series of levers that ran all the way to the brass scale on the sideboard. It was indeed used daily: Every time Eleanor accessed the log, she balanced the scale to unlock the glass box. She didn't have to do a thing to lock it either—just grab the weights on her way out. The scale was still wobbling from her recent quick exit.

"No time to panic," Flick told herself. The sideboard was too far from the desk for her to press down on the scale with one hand until the case unlocked while entering the numbers with the other. She searched the room for something she could use to balance it. The weights had to be with Eleanor. They were every bit a key, for there was no chance of someone finding the exact weight quickly enough to tamper with the log. And whenever Eleanor anticipated being gone for longer, she simply had to lock the door behind her.

It was smart. Flick thought Jin would appreciate it.

She plucked up the pen holder beside a fountain pen in a delicate stand and set it on the scale. It barely tipped.

The kitten meowed. *Aha!* Flick snatched her up and set her in the pan, which promptly fell with a clang. Too heavy.

Think, Flick. The weights had to be a reasonable load to be carried around. Something easy enough to slip into the indecently small pockets of a woman's gown. Something as small as . . . a lighter.

Holding the kitten in one arm, Flick fished the lighter out of her pocket and set it in the pan. It was worth more than its weight in brass, more than the liquid gas inside its chamber, more than the wheel that kept it working. It was the love her mother once had for her. And it was enough.

It had to be.

The seals exhaled, unlocking the glass case with a sigh. Flick flipped over a single luxuriously thick page, fountain pen in hand, then froze at a sound. Laith's kitten looked up at her with a curious tilt of her head.

And then the door swung open.

Flick grabbed her lighter off the scale and dove under the desk. She held her breath. The vampire stilled in that terrifying way, motionless and statuesque.

Don't breathe, don't breathe.

But there was one advantage to Laith's kitten having followed her. She bounced away from where she'd been swatting at the throw tossed over the side of an armchair. The vampire relaxed, the sequins of her dress catching the low light when she crouched and crooned at the kitten.

Flick held very, very still.

If she so much as turned her head, Flick was—*no.* She was not going to let herself think that far.

"Duty calls, little one," the vampire said, and rummaged through the sideboard. She emerged with something smooth and flat—*to repair the chute,* Flick realized—and disappeared back outside.

Flick had seconds. She hurried out from under the desk and slammed her lighter back on the pan, barely waiting for the seals to release before she pried open the glass, snatched up a pen, and started scribbling the first identifier into the log.

3–9–3–4–2–2–0. Her hand shook, forcing her to round out the curve of the nine more than once. *Done.*

"One down," Flick murmured, moving on to the next one. *3–9–3–4–2–2–1.*

The silence broke with a rattle—markers. If markers were being sent through, the chute had been repaired. Jin's distraction had come to an end.

"Come now, Flick," she spurred herself on. *3–9–3–4*—she stopped, narrowly saving herself when ink swelled from the fountain pen's tip—*2–2–2.*

Flick dropped the pen with a flourish. *Wait.* She picked it back up and jammed it into its stand, grabbing the tin beside it to dust sand over the wet ink and nearly inhaling it in her rush to blow it off. She tidied up the space until Laith's kitten rubbed against her ankle. Flick picked her up and hurried for the door.

Her lighter.

She rushed back to the sideboard and shoved it in her pocket. Then she ran, hair falling over her face. She certainly looked the part of a lost girl when she flung the door open and came face-to-face with the cruelly beautiful Eleanor Thorne.

Flick took a few steps back.

"My deepest apologies, miss," she blustered with a smile that felt more like a grimace. "I thought this was the lavatory."

33

JIN

Jin heaved a sigh of relief when Flick exited the archive room with a charming smile and a minute to spare. He didn't have to worry about her anymore, but he was still worried about Arthie. When he was certain Eleanor Thorne wasn't about to reemerge again, he left the cover of the alcove and joined Flick by the accent wall, her sweet sunshine scent soothing his nerves almost immediately. It took everything in him not to pull her into his arms.

The chutes rattled with the markers hurtling through, and then Laith was inside, stalling near the alcove beneath the dormer where the guard's toxin-induced catnap would begin wearing off at any moment.

Matteo needed to hurry up with that distraction.

A voice rose from the doors. *At last*, Jin thought, nearly forgetting the painter was in disguise when a blond man in tinted specs began insulting the vampire beside him in Matteo's voice.

"Nice suit, old boy. Does it come in men's sizes?"

Ouch. It was no wonder Matteo saw no need for violence. His jibes were brutal enough. Jin gave Laith a nod.

Laith flexed his limbs and began his ascent to the mezzanine, but everyone was looking at Matteo, too riveted by his audacity to notice a hooded human crawling up the wall.

When Matteo had made the suggestion back in Spindrift, none of them had believed an argument over style could distract anyone, but Jin stood corrected. There was good sense and then there was affluence.

"Who are you? Do you know whom you're speaking to?" the other vampire hissed at Matteo.

Jin was only half listening. He was watching Laith. They had seconds before the guard woke. Seconds before he sounded the alarm.

"I do indeed," Matteo intoned solemnly, leaning toward the other vampire. "Someone who left his fashion sense in the grave."

There was a scuffle of shoes out on the steps and raised voices. And then Laith was finally out of sight and everything was quiet.

Jin waited. Flick made a sound.

"Do you think he's all right?" she asked, eyes locked on the shadows of the mezzanine.

"Done and dusted, love," Jin said, guiding her deeper into the Athereum. The room would be a lot louder if Laith *hadn't* reached the guard in time. "Time for phase two."

34

ARTHIE

The bouncer had Arthie's elbow in a viselike grip. He led her to the Athereum's prison, where the vampire standing guard sneered at her. What was with all the sneering? He threw open the gate with far too much excitement and locked it behind her and the bouncer, leaving the two of them alone. The room was sterile with a set of empty cells and another reinforced door at the end.

Arthie jerked free before the bouncer could continue the ploy and throw her in one of them.

In every discussion of her plans with the others, Arthie always faced pushback on one particular part of it: the bit where she got caught. It was dangerous and risky, and Jin tried talking her out of it more than once.

But Matteo had warned them that getting into this secure area was impossible without possessing a key or being imprisoned, so she had no choice, really.

"Was that really necessary, Theo?" she snapped.

Especially when she realized she knew one of the two Athereum bouncers.

The bouncer looked chagrined. It was a look she recognized from his brief stint as a Spindrift employee, during which he'd accidentally thrown out the wrong patrons multiple times. She should have realized he would still be difficult to work with, but it wasn't as if she had another option.

"You said make it believable!" Theo said, perplexed.

Arthie sighed, feeling bruised all over. "*Believable*, Theo, not *kill me*. Now let me through."

"But you promised you'd pay—"

"How would it have looked if I'd carried a bag full of duvin in here, eh?" Arthie asked. "Exactly. Go see Felix tomorrow, and you'll have your pay."

He thought about what she said then nodded once and let her through the second door.

Arthie straightened her coat and then her hair, carefully closing the door behind her. The corridor was long and empty, thrumming with the din of the festivities on the other side. Arthie reached the bend, where the Athereum's vault was fit snug into the corner, a massive structure of brass with an elaborate lock she wished she could crack simply for the fun of it.

If Arthie were looking to hide an important document, that was the last place she would store it, because it would be the first place anyone looked. Eventually, the corridor branched into the hall of offices. The second entrance to the locked corridors was at the end of it. A seating area spread out to her left, a glass wall to her right, where she caught a glimpse of the society in motion.

And a figure waiting for her on the other side of the door.

Arthie turned the lock and opened it. Moths fluttered in her chest.

"Hello, darling," Matteo said, tipping a fluted glass at her. Even disguised, he looked every bit . . . himself. The way he walked, the way he smiled. The way that damned dimple taunted from his cheek. "How are you finding the Athereum?"

"Every night, when the foundries go dark and the patrols get lax, men shed their shirts, wrap gauze around their fists, and throw sweaty punches in a ring," Arthie replied, dropping her hands on the back of a chair. She pursed her lips in thought for a second. "This feels about the same."

Matteo laughed, and the sound made her wholly aware of herself. "You never fail to surprise me, and yet you behave exactly as I expect."

He looked at her as if she was something special, something more than a criminal with a gun, something more than a monster with a timer running out.

He swept his tongue across his lower lip, and she mimicked the movement across her own. He swished the blood in his flute, stirring up the scent of it with a soft sigh. Her head swam. His gaze missed nothing.

"Are you quite all right?" he asked, watching her every motion.

"Of course I am." She clenched her jaw. It was the stress getting to her. Yes, they'd forged coins, thwarted sisters, and gotten into the Athereum without losing their heads, but the Ram's ledger was still out there. Spindrift still hung in the balance.

"You know what you have to do," she said.

"I do," he said with a nod, and she turned to leave. "So. Penn Arundel, hmm?"

She turned back, suddenly acutely aware of everything around her. The brush of air on the nape of her neck, the footsteps on the polished wood floors, the hum of a violin somewhere in the Athereum.

Please, please, please.

Matteo swayed in front of her. Her limbs felt leaden, her head light. She had known what she was getting into, but she'd still chosen to do it. For her tearoom.

"You and I have much in common," he said almost gently.

Arthie bit out a laugh. "How would you know?"

"Penn is, well, he was the only one who was there for me when I first turned," Matteo said. "He's told me a lot about you."

Arthie regarded him, trying to decipher how much was *a lot* and it made her realize: She cared what Matteo thought of her. It was a scary epiphany she did not wish to dwell on.

"That means—wait. He's whom you wanted to get in here to see," Arthie said.

Matteo nodded, barely surprised she had figured him out. "When I learned he hadn't been seen outside the Athereum for weeks, I knew something was wrong. He might be head of the place, but there's very few vampires here that he can trust. I never thought I'd get the chance to possibly see him again, but I knew that if anything had happened to him, he would have wanted you to know."

The concern in his voice struck a chord inside her.

"That's why you were racking up a tab at Spindrift," she said as his plan slowly fell into place in her mind. "That's why you wanted me to come to your house."

He laughed softly. "You are extremely difficult to arrange a meeting with, Arthie."

"But you didn't tell me," Arthie said, refusing to believe him.

He looked contrite. "Can you blame me? You were quite intense that first night and then you showed up with the Horned Guard in tow the second time. Anywho, what matters is that you're here now."

"Here," Arthie repeated.

"Here," Matteo agreed, "at the crossroads of your past and your future."

35

JIN

The corridor wound artfully before spilling into the massive main hall where the auction was to take place. Rows of lacquered chairs lined the room, many already occupied by vampires. Jin plucked one of the bidder numbers from the table and found himself a seat. Beside him, Flick did the same, Laith's kitten snug in the crook of her arm.

The room was filling up. Vampires had come from all across Ettenia. Many of them, to Jin's surprise, seemed to be immigrants who had retained elements of their home cultures. There were vampires in form-fitting qipaos and others in wide-sleeved agbadas. He caught sight of the flowing folds of Hanfu, the regal skirts of an anarkali, and saris in sapphire, emerald, and onyx, each one beaded more heavily than the last.

On the stage up ahead, the auctioneer's assistant propped open a stand while a vampire with silver hair and skin the same shade as Arthie's swaggered down the aisle, a cravat knotted at his throat. He was carrying something large and rectangular and draped in beige.

Look for whoever brings in the auction piece, Matteo had instructed. *That's the pocket you'll want to pick for the key.*

Sir Silver Hair was their man.

The assistant straightened at the sight of him. "Sidharth, what took you so long?"

"Apologies," he drawled. "I was unaware you'd finally learned how to read a clock."

The assistant fumed but took the parcel from him and set it on the stand with care, unveiling the object beneath an angled light. Sidharth gave it a wistful look as if it were his, but Jin had stolen and studied enough art to recognize its artist.

Matteo Andoni.

His work had a distinctness to it, an urgency that didn't quite match the vampire himself—or any vampire for that matter. Time held no meaning for them when their limbs worked eternally. Perhaps that was where the Athereum saw the value in Matteo's work: that reminder of time passing, that longing, even if they'd never admit to it. Everyone yearned for what they couldn't have.

This particular piece featured a single stroke of shadow, obscure enough to be anything but defined enough to be a woman. She stood in a blurred street, lamps scattered like souls, her head tilted toward a full moon as if she were a wolf calling for her love. There was something hollow about the piece, haunting and lonely.

"Until later." Sidharth inclined his head with a flourish. When he lifted his hand for a wave, Jin saw the keys Matteo had promised would be there.

There were three of them, made of brass. Jin barely caught a glimpse before Sidharth slipped them into his right pocket and turned to leave. Jin turned too, leaning closer to Flick, who looked at him as if he'd lost his head when he emptied a pocket of keys into her lap.

"Jin!" she exclaimed as he shuffled through a mess of silver and gold until he found three brass keys that he slid onto a ring. "Oh, this is marvelous. Wherever did you find all this?"

"Under my pillow, love," he answered. He'd meant for the words to be innocent, but her breath caught, and he curled a crooked grin. "You'd be surprised what all can be found on my bed."

Truth be told, he had been picking pockets since he'd stepped into the Athereum in preparation for this. In that time, he'd learned it was a lot harder to pull off a believable sneer when one was missing the keys to their own house.

"I—" Flick looked up sharply. The auctioneer's assistant tapped his gavel on the podium, and the thrum of voices turned down a notch. "Oh."

Jin followed her line of sight to a new vampire taking the place of the assistant.

Every inch of him demanded attention, from the length of his dark hair to the aristocratic planes of his face. He was a mix of races, that much Jin could tell. Not quite Ettenian, not quite foreign, and he looked vaguely familiar.

He surveyed the room and bent to murmur in his assistant's ear.

"Keep an eye out," Jin told Flick, and hurried after Sidharth, who was lingering at the entrance as a flock of vampires in dark gowns and netted hats filed inside, hands at their throats and fangs bared beneath bayonet smiles. Making a fool of himself in front of a lady wasn't in his nature, but the job was the job.

One hand in his pocket, Jin stumbled on the rug with an *oof*, pitching himself at Sidharth. He slammed into an unexpected wall of muscle and hooked a finger around the vampire's suspender to shift his focus as Jin swapped the keys and righted himself.

"Someone's had a little too much to drink," Sidharth said, none the wiser as he observed Jin through hooded eyes.

He made to catch his hand, but Jin released him and pulled back with a *tsk*. "Sorry there, I'm already spoken for."

Flick's face popped into Jin's head at the words before he plunged into the crowd of vampires, slipping through a cloud of perfume and jeweled skirts. If he somehow found himself in possession of a pearl-studded silver barrette and a carved jade fountain pen when he finally made it to the empty foyer, it wasn't his fault.

After getting the keys to Laith, Jin made his way back to the auction hall. He wasn't certain whose bidder number he snatched on his way back in, but he sent them a silent apology as he drove up the price of the auction again and again and again.

"Four thousand duvin," the dark-haired vampire called from behind the podium, "once more from the gentleman in the back."

That *once more* sounded belligerent. Beside him, Flick's paddle went up with excruciating hesitance. Was she worried she'd truly have to pay?

"Five thousand," he announced. Jin saw the crimson in his eyes, betraying his age.

"Andoni's work isn't even worth half that," someone murmured.

"I daresay I agree," murmured another.

"Appreciation of the arts is an acquired skill," Jin said, insulted on Matteo's behalf.

"I wholly agree," Flick echoed, prompting others to pick sides.

Another gentleman lifted his paddle, followed by a lady with a cane. The vampire behind the podium called out the next figure.

"Nine thousand duvin," the vampire announced. "Have we any others?"

He began a spiel about the piece and the cause it supported. Jin's paddle went up and then a slew of vampires followed, paddles rising and falling.

A figure started down the aisle, and Jin narrowed his eyes. *Matteo.* The vampire at the podium paused too, scrutinizing him as if he knew him but couldn't quite see past the disguise. What was he doing?

"Jin?" Flick dragged out his name.

"I see him," Jin murmured.

Matteo climbed up the front of the stage, eliciting murmurs from the crowd and wrenching the auction to a halt. He leaned close and whispered in the dark-haired vampire's ear, and Jin was filled with a sense of foreboding too late to act upon it.

Then the dark-haired vampire set down his gavel and looked straight at Jin.

Damn it all.

"Time for plan C," Jin said. He didn't understand. The man was stepping away from the podium, moving *toward* them. What had Matteo told him?

"What's plan C?" Flick asked nervously.

Jin looked down at the vampire beside him. "Have you ever been hit with an auction paddle?"

"I beg your pardon?" the vampire sounded flabbergasted.

"No?" Jin asked, and slammed his paddle across the vampire's face. "You're welcome."

The vampire shot to his feet, swinging his paddle with such force, Jin barely had time to duck before it slammed into the head of the vampire beside him. The woman leaped up.

Chaos erupted.

"Come along, Felicity," Jin shouted, snatching her hand, fully aware of how perfectly it fit in his. The two of them wriggled their way out of the row of chairs.

"So sorry," Flick shouted at someone, and when Jin looked back at Flick she wasn't stricken with fear or worry, she looked delighted, *excited*.

As if, perhaps, she could get used to this life.

He pretended not to notice the way she looked at her hand when he released it, ignoring the sparks that echoed down his own. What was he, a schoolboy? It was her *hand*.

"Come now, the paddle can't have hurt *that* much," he yelled as they ran.

Really, the vampires ought to be thanking him for bringing some much-needed energy to their undead lives. More chairs screeched and an uproar ensued, but when Jin stopped at the entrance to the main hall and looked back, neither Matteo nor the dark-haired vampire were anywhere to be seen.

36

ARTHIE

Arthie's head spun again. She threw her hand against the wall to steady herself, grateful neither Jin nor any of the others were here to witness this. It was getting worse.

She was getting worse.

The hall seemed to extend without end, doors upon doors on either side of her. Had Matteo said Penn's office was the fifth door from the right or the seventh? Footsteps sounded on the carpet and Arthie had an excuse ready on her tongue for whoever turned the corner, but it wasn't a vampire.

"Laith," she said.

"The auction's begun." He tossed her the keys and paused. "Are you hurt?"

Every curt response she'd used in the past rose to her tongue, but every single one faded when he scrutinized her. She didn't want his care. She didn't want his coddling. *Focus*—he was toying with her, trying to get under her skin again, to make her trust him. The ledger was close, and he knew it as well as she did.

"Did the bouncer go too far?" he asked, insistent.

"If he did, he'd be dead," Arthie replied. She gritted her teeth. It simply felt, at times, that his concern bordered on doubt of her capabilities. Perhaps she was being too harsh, too critical. "But no, he—he didn't hurt me."

His brow furrowed at her reply. "Good. I'm—I'm pleased you can still hold up your end of the bargain."

That was enough of . . . *whatever* this was, Arthie decided. She continued down the corridor, and that was when she smelled it: something pungent and sweet, a whiff of leather and wool soaked in spice. A handful of chapters of her life bottled into a scent. Arthie had never needed Matteo's directions; she could have found Penn Arundel's office by smell alone.

She paused before the door.

"Who is he?" Laith asked, and his voice was almost kind. Again, a ploy. He was a high captain. He worked for the Ram.

"A vampire," Arthie said. She knew that wasn't the answer he wanted. She turned the key, the click as jarring as a gunshot.

"Is that why you pause before the threshold as if it's the gallows, then?" Laith asked.

The past had been known to hang a person.

She said nothing as she stepped inside. A massive desk was placed in the center with an imposing chair behind it. The fire burning in the hearth angled shadows down the paneled walls, a dark contrast to the sepia rug spread over the floorboards. Maps lined the walls, pins tacked on destinations Arthie had never heard of. A pair of armchairs were accented by vases and fresh flowers. Despite the amalgamation of trinkets and goods on the bookshelves, two mirrors stood out strangely.

"Start looking," Arthie said.

You'll find it, Matteo had told her. *You're keen enough.*

She began at the desk, where another tiny mirror was attached on a swivel, but there was nothing out of the ordinary. She turned to the walls, searching the panels for one that could open into a recess for storing valuables. Laith took down a painting and did the same but came up empty.

When he hung it back up, Arthie recognized it as one of Matteo's. Only he used color in such an arbitrary way, brushstrokes chasing the value of time, grasping on to what he no longer had. She despised sorrow. It was a futile emotion, not actionable like vengeance and anger were. And yet his art made her sad.

In one of the mirrors on the bookshelves, Arthie saw Laith shove a hand through his hair. He didn't look like he was preparing to do anything drastic, like leave her behind. But then again, Arthie was pretty good at masking intentions herself. Another mirror was set into the wall behind him, doubling the fire's warm glow on his features. It was strange that the hearth was lit, and she wondered if it was only to make the vampire feel human again.

No, Penn had been a vampire for a very long time. Long enough for the novelty of being human to wear out.

Long enough to know that vampires couldn't see their own reflections in a mirror.

"The mirrors. It's a puzzle," Arthie murmured, something buzzing to life under her skin.

She swiveled the little mirror on the desk to face the fire. Its surface shone, casting a glow to the area around it. She was filled with a giddy emotion. Nothing spoke to her more than a puzzle, a disparate collection of pieces that promised a correlation not so different from the satisfying *click* of a lock beneath her brother's careful picks.

"Get that one," she called to Laith, nodding at another small mirror that stood like an ornament on an end table by one of the armchairs. He frowned but adjusted it, turning it to and fro until the mirror in her hand shot a line of fire into his.

She met Laith's eyes and grinned before she could think better of it. He stared at her almost blankly.

"Now what?" he said, a hush to his tone. Her head swayed, that hunger rising, ravaging. She needed to think, and it wasn't letting her. Shouts echoed outside the office walls, a world away.

She studied the remaining mirrors—one on the other end of the desk, two on the bookshelves, and then a third one on the far side of the office, glinting inside an eight-pointed star cut into the wall. It was directly in line with one of the mirrors on the bookshelves.

There. A lock.

Arthie adjusted the first of the bookshelf mirrors until it caught the firelight cast by Laith's mirror. He matched her actions without instruction, swiveling the mirror on the other end of Penn's desk until the light slanted onto its surface. Arthie tinkered with the last of them.

Light catapulted from one mirror to the next, pooling into the eight-pointed star until the glare was almost blinding. Then she heard the low exhale of a seal followed by the rumble of gears. The back wall split in half, retracting to either side to reveal a space just beyond, illuminated by a plume of light.

She had expected a safe or lockbox, not an entire chamber.

In that room was the Ram's ledger. In that room lay Spindrift's salvation. The ground rumbled and the lamp above them swayed. Voices echoed outside the walls, loud and disorderly. Laith touched the vault doors. They made a sound like glass but seemed far more solid.

"We don't have much time," Laith said.

Arthie wanted to correct him. *You* don't have much time, she wanted to say.

"If Jin doesn't reach us before Athereum security does, we—"

That was more than reason enough to leave him to the wolves. "Let's not doubt my brother," Arthie said, recalling his description of the ledger while leading him into the vault. It was as cold as a grave, windowless and uninspiring.

Journals were lined up on plain shelves beside stacks of letters that wore a fine layer of dust like sugar granules by an empty teacup. She saw a collection of pistols and a tarnished astrolabe, bound books with ribbons in crimson and sapphire and violet. Arthie opened all of them. Against a wall, two more pieces of Matteo's art lounged as leisurely as the painter himself.

Several chairs were arranged in the room too. If there was space allotted for leisure, there was bound to be a way to lock the vault from the inside.

To hide inside the vault.

Are you sure you want to go through with this? came Jin's voice in her head.

"Arthie."

Laith stood before a desk. Beside that desk, Arthie saw a lever he appeared not to have noticed. That was exactly what she had been looking for.

In his hands was a book marked with a violet ribbon.

"The ledger."

Oh, and that too.

Arthie walked up to him before he could flip open the cover. She studied the way he held it and planned her next actions, eagerly leaning in to try and make sure it was actually the ledger he said it was.

"Violet ribbon, standard leather casing," Laith explained, letting the flap stay closed. Men did love explaining the obvious. He looked at her. "Now, where's Jin?"

What was more curious, Arthie thought, was the way he gripped the ledger: tight, away from her. How he hadn't allowed her to give it a closer look. How he didn't trust her. He didn't know she'd already thumbed through the pages, ensured it was what they were looking for.

It was his loss that he hadn't done the same. Or her cunning.

Still, he didn't look for a weapon to kill her. He didn't look like he was about to leave her. Trepidation whispered along her veins, doubt rippling through.

And Arthie rarely entertained doubt.

Laith strode back into the office and froze. The door to the office rattled, shouts echoing from the other side. Arthie took half a step back into the vault and half a step closer to the lever by the desk.

"Get behind me," Laith said to her, tucking the book into his robes.

The door flung open. Vampires flooded the room, stakes at the ready, fangs sharp. And as a pair of vampires grabbed his arms, Laith glanced behind him, only to find the office wall staring back, the secret chamber gone.

And Arthie watched it all from the two-way mirror inside Penn's vault.

37

ARTHIE

Arthie reached under the desk and pulled out the real ledger. Its violet ribbon looked almost exactly like the replica she had tucked into the book Laith had pocketed before he was dragged away.

Get behind me.

She had the ledger at last, but she could barely summon triumph. She couldn't stop repeating that moment in her head, when Laith's alarm and fear morphed into the realization that she had betrayed him.

It was him or her.

And yet, he hadn't done the same to her. He hadn't said a word when the vampires apprehending him had asked him if he was here alone. He hadn't even looked angry, only heartbroken.

He'd taken the fall and the false ledger, and now he would die.

Arthie pulled on the lever, and the vault doors slid open again with a forlorn sigh. She snapped her pocket watch closed. Jin would arrive any moment now. No sooner had the thought crossed her mind than the office door swung open.

She saw Jin first, then Flick. Both of them had been expected. She hadn't expected Matteo, blond and pale and almost ghostly. And certainly not the figure before them: a vampire with a trim beard and dark, shoulder-length hair tied at the base of his skull. He had a cravat set with a ruby knotted at his throat and a gold hoop in his right ear that glinted in the lamplight.

For this very reason, the plan had always been to leave before the auction concluded. But it couldn't have been over yet. Not unless— *Matteo*. She should have known he would do this.

Arthie faced him. "Penn."

He smiled at her. "Hello, daughter."

Arthie caught a whiff of the cigar in his hand and she was eight again, standing on his ebony doorstep while silver needles of rain pelted the cobblestones, clouds heavy and gray. Her cheeks were still stained with the death of her parents, blood still crusted under her nails.

"I'm not your daughter," she said, forcing herself back to the present.

The firelight lit his half-Arawiyan skin. She used to envy anyone who could pass as a peaky before she realized such a wish was a betrayal to herself. The easy route was never for her.

"You were the only one who came close. Good word, look at you," Penn said, almost surprised, as he closed the door behind him. His voice made her feel safe and comfortable, two illnesses she never allowed herself to catch again.

Please, please, please.

Jin made a sound in his throat. It seemed she was betraying everyone tonight. She had *meant* to tell him when they'd first found each other. It would have been easier to process the horror on his face when he learned the truth, to watch him pull away and disappear forever. But later became tomorrow, and tomorrow became next month, and next month became a decade.

Arthie loved secrets, but love was a feeling much like hate—so full, so heavy, so laden with everything. And for all the secrets she collected, she hated her own.

She loved Jin in a way she would never speak aloud, in a way that made her feel weak and foolish. In a way no one but he loved her back. She hadn't wanted that to end. But one secret had slowly become another, each tangling with the last, and when he looked at her now she realized that somewhere along the way she had pushed him away herself.

"All that talk of your parents dying in Ceylan," he said, the words rushing out of him in a mix of anger and hurt. "It was—it was—"

"True," Arthie finished. "Penn took me in for about a year after I got to Ettenia. Before you. I've never lied to you, Jin."

"No," Jin agreed mockingly. "You only left out just about everything."

Penn set his cigar on an ashtray and swiveled the mirrors on his desk, sealing his vault back into obscurity. "I'm afraid I can't let you leave."

Jin huffed a laugh. "Oh, we're leaving all right."

"And how do you intend to do that?" Penn asked, tilting his head to the door. "You step out of this office, and you will die. Just as your friend soon will."

"Which friend?" Flick asked, searching about the room. "Arthie, where's Laith?"

Jin looked at Arthie. He was the only one who knew she had never intended for Laith to leave with them. There was that guilt again, knotting her tongue and stifling her conscience.

"He was apprehended," Penn answered. "Arthie was lucky enough to have been sealed in the vault."

Lucky enough. It wasn't luck that had saved her, but her own quick thinking. Arthie would have been insulted if she didn't feel so horrible.

"Oh, Arthie," Flick breathed, whirling to face her. "I am so sorry. You must be devastated."

Arthie was irked that Flick thought *she* might be more devastated than the rest of them.

"There are rules that must be followed," Penn said sternly. "Break them, and there are repercussions. Now give me the ledger, and tell me what this is about, little lion."

A memory rose in the quiet. Her hands bloody, her skirts dripping red. He had drawn her against his side despite the mess of blood.

She clutched the ledger tight to her chest.

"The Ram has too much power, and we're going to challenge it," Flick said, stepping to Arthie's side.

Jin stepped to Arthie's other side. She could tell he was angry and hurt, that he had an endless list of questions to ask her, but his presence gave her comfort. "It's the only way to save Spindrift."

A knock sounded at the door.

"Come in," Penn called. Someone new entered the room. "I've apprehended the intruders. Don't look at them, look at me. Placate our guests and resume the festivities." The vampire nodded and finally left, and Penn turned to address Arthie. "You and your friends have caused quite a stir."

"And exponentially increased the value of my work," said Matteo.

"Don't talk," Jin snapped. "Don't pretend to be one of us."

Matteo looked at him coolly. "As if I was in search of a reason to disgrace myself."

"Open the ledger," Penn said. A line jumped in his jaw.

Arthie slipped the ledger from its case and flipped it open. There were notes, but it was mainly an account, tracking exports and imports and commodities. She flipped to the page marked by the ribbon. It was the same export, over and over again. The first few hadn't gone far before being returned.

Flick read over Arthie's shoulder. "What's an *EJC Corpus*? Are these weapons?"

Ettenia lacked the resources to produce anything on a large scale. It

was why they'd dug their claws into places like Ceylan for tea and cin-
namon, Jeevant Gar for spices and textiles, Qirilan for silk and opium,
far-off Morubia for gold and ivory. In many ways, the East Jeevant
Company was as bad as the Ram.

Penn's voice was tight. "Of a sort. Starve the lion long enough,
and no force can vanquish him. By my definition, that makes one a
weapon, doesn't it?"

"Starve?" Flick asked with a frown. "I thought we were talking
about the EJC's exports."

Penn picked up his cigar. His face was grave when he nodded. "We
are. The exports are vampires."

38

FLICK

Flick was still getting over the fact that they'd broken into the Athereum and lost one of their crew. And now she had to wrap her head around the idea of vampires being the cargo listed on that ledger. As if they could be fitted into crates like weapons and sent across the sea—by her mother's company, no less.

"Why?" Jin asked, his arms crossed. Flick could tell he had his emotions on a leash.

"At its most distilled level, hatred. Because fear unchecked too often festers into loathing. It's easy to look at the errors of a few and blame an entire kind," Penn replied. "But why destroy when you can utilize? Place a starved vampire in a battlefield, and what choice do they have but to feed? Their only concern is staving off that hunger—they'll attack anything with a pulse."

"What is a monster if not a man pushed to the brink?" Matteo murmured.

Arthie looked grave. "Weapons on a mass scale with none of the cost."

"Much like the peakies forcefully enlisting Jeevani and Ceylani to fight against their own in Ettenian wars," Jin said.

Penn tilted his head. "If the reason for the Ettenians' animosity toward any minority in this country could be compared to vampires, then yes. But those are people. Vampires are predators."

"So this is why vampires have been going missing. None of this could be possible without help from the inside," Jin said. "From the vampires themselves."

Penn nodded. "From the *Athereum* as well. For many, aiding the Ram and the EJC is their only security against being taken, while others are simply looking for a cut. I can't fully blame them, for I've lost some of my best vampires."

Arthie laughed bitterly. "If the EJC is transporting them to the battlefields, then it's making a cut itself."

Flick sat down in one of the armchairs by the hearth, letting the warmth of the fire sink into her bones. As frightening as vampires were, Flick didn't think they ought to be drugged and used. Even in the throes of hunger, when whatever innate, vampiric instincts took over like with Matteo on his porch, they were still conscious of their actions. She tried to imagine being driven by a blinding hunger, trapped inside her own body as she tore through masses of people.

No one deserved such horror.

Matteo turned to her. "Mommy's been a very bad lady."

Flick sank deeper into her chair. She knew the EJC wasn't entirely clean, but this was beyond acceptable. And as she sat there, she felt like a kettle left too long on the stove. All her insides were roiling, raging, and bubbling out, hot and angry.

Jin tossed his jacket on the back of the other chair. His exhale was heavy with a decision. "Let's go back to the beginning, shall we? Starting with how you, Mister Penn, know everything, and why we should trust you. You might have taken Arthie in a decade ago, but that's plenty of time for a man to go dirty."

"The beginning?" Penn asked with a laugh. "Very well. It began with an expedition. My father was Ettenian, but my mother was Arawiyan and an adventurer, more so after his passing. She was eager to join the voyage to Ettenia, and so I accompanied her on the trade ship that was carrying artifacts of immense value—and not the monetary kind."

"Sentimental then?" Flick suggested.

"Not quite. Arawiya is a kingdom of enchantment. There is magic in the very land beneath their feet, fueling conjurers of flame, hunters capable of finding anything they set their hearts to, dreamwalkers, healers who can stitch wounds with a touch."

Penn continued wistfully. "The kingdom was cursed to isolation in recent years, but even before that, magic was limited to Arawiya alone. Stand on enchanted land and you may borrow a bit of its magic. Leave Arawiyan soil, and any affinity you have will no longer work, *except* in the case of hilya, artifacts charged with magic and memory, capable of immense, immeasurable power."

Flick saw Arthie's gaze light up in recognition.

"They can be used anywhere, with the right words," Penn said. "Creation has since been forbidden, but in the old days, when Arawiya was at its cusp, they were traded to the kingdom's advantage."

Flick sensed an *until* somewhere in his story. Jin and Arthie listened keenly, albeit warily. Matteo, on the other hand, looked as if he'd heard the story before and poured himself a glass of blood from a decanter opposite Penn's fireplace.

"My mother and I boarded that ship along with several of the ruling Sisters' trusted immortals."

"Were they vampires?" Arthie asked.

Matteo waved a hand. "They're elven. Immortal, vain, think they're better because they've seen it all."

"Sounds familiar," she said pointedly.

He lifted his glass at her.

"Can we go back to our bedtime story, please?" Jin asked.

"I should like that," Penn said, amused. "Our ship docked here in White Roaring, and I remember thinking it fitting that the skies were so wan and gray in a way Arawiya's were not, for my mother was frailer than ever. The days crawled by and her condition worsened. Hygiene was not commonplace here, soap almost impossible to procure. Not long later, she passed."

Flick noted the way he spoke the words, unaffected and unafflicted. There were days when she missed her mother as if they had been parted by death, not a wing of their estate.

"I buried her myself. The same evening, we learned one of the Arawiyan elves hadn't been so trustworthy. One of the hilya was a glass heart filled with what was argued to be blood. He thought he could make a profit of his own, and in the midst of trading the piece, it shattered. Without the right incantation, a hilya cannot be used, but no one knew the procedure for one that broke, disappearing into the land itself, too far from the one that birthed it."

"Let me guess, the immortals said it would be fine," Arthie said.

Penn nodded. "It created some twisted mutation of magic. We were by the graveyard when it happened. Corpses started rising from the dirt. To be a vampire, one must be turned within seconds after death, before the heart and brain cease to fully function. These weren't vampires, but ghouls. The same concept, but they were heartless and brainless, possessing nothing but an endless hunger."

He looked down at his desk as if he could see his past in the smoke from his cigar.

"My mother was one of them. She attacked me, and what sort of son would injure his own mother in turn? Before I knew it, darkness was tipping into my vision. The others were shouting, the ghouls were letting loose terrible, throaty growls.

"They pried her away from me, but I couldn't move. I was so overcome with emotion at the sight of what she had become that I wished for physical pain. *More* of it. Anything to distract from the pain of having to see her die again.

"Another corpse attacked from behind. Squeezed my windpipe. I was dying. And at some point in those few seconds before my death, I drank blood. I don't know whose, or how they even *had* blood when they'd been dead so long, but when a hilya was involved, anything was possible.

"I woke up a vampire. I hadn't known what I was, only that I hadn't been dead long enough to become a ghoul. I was as terrified as the others were, and to this day I cannot fault them for attacking *me* in turn. And no one can fault a body for its innate sense of self-defense.

"You've heard of vampires that wake with powers, yes? I had the power to make others feel pain with nothing but my mind. It was an illusion. In the midst of their screams, I realized they were *imagining* pain, that their bones were breaking, or their spine was snapping."

Flick stared at Penn, the crinkles by his eyes from an eternity of smiling, the compassion in his gaze from an age of understanding. More and more, it seemed that every person she met had something terrible in their past. Whether they'd seen it or inflicted it, everyone walked with a burden.

"That very power has seen me through the decades. Not the use of it, because I'm no monster, but the rumor alone," Penn said, then laughed. "When the Wolf of White Roaring went on his rampage, I was asked to establish the Athereum and helped craft the vampire-human laws we have in place.

"It did little to appease the public's fear of vampires, and the monarch was too busy scrambling. Not long after, we had a new one, who knew exactly what the people wanted."

"What are you getting at?" Arthie asked.

"The Wolf of White Roaring attack was fabricated *in order* to instill fear," Penn said. "Vampires had lived in relative secrecy. For decades. Until the Ram decided otherwise, forcefully turning the Wolf of White Roaring into a half vampire and unleashing him upon the city so that the Ram could sweep in and save it. But no one knew that was only the beginning."

39

ARTHIE

"The Ram controlled the chaos to gain the people's favor," Arthie said. Just when she thought the government couldn't get any worse, the Ram had found a way. "Pacify the people to keep them in check, and no one notices you furthering your own agenda."

"First power, now profit," Jin said, disgust dripping from his tone.

Arthie didn't know how the Ram had managed to work in a personal cut in the deal between the government and the trading company, but here they were. Flick looked as if she was sick to her stomach.

"Felicity? Are you all right?" Jin asked.

She rubbed at her chest, her gaze distant.

Arthie snapped her fingers. "Flick."

Flick looked up with a gasp. "What do you do when you're angry?" Her voice was tight, and the way she asked the question made Arthie think the emotion was foreign to her.

Arthie understood. "I let it fuel me and everything that I do, but it's important to note the difference between fuel and dictate."

Flick nodded, half to herself, deep in thought.

Jin looked up from the ledger. "What does this mean?" he asked, taking it to Penn. "The Ram's been logging each transaction with some sort of shot. The earlier ones failed, but the later ones have had a good success rate."

Penn drummed a quick hand on the desk. "They discovered a way to formulate silver into an inoculation for the betterment of the human population, but silver is detrimental to a vampire's physique. Inject them, and they're immobilized for long enough to starve and seal in a crate and ship off to the front lines."

They knew the stories of the Wolf of White Roaring. Of the horrific attacks that cropped up from time to time across Ettenia. A vampire starved beyond reason was a machine with a single purpose: carnage.

"A second half dose is administered just before the drop point," Penn continued, "so that once the vampire reaches the battlefront, they will ravage the enemy until either the vampire or the soldiers are overcome."

"Despicable," Matteo said.

Penn tilted his head. "Ettenians were being enlisted, and vampires refused to do the same. We are predators and refused to partake in unfair wars spurred by colonization, and the country capitalized on that."

Refusing to take no for an answer was certainly a peaky thing to do.

"We always knew the ledger was damning," Arthie said to the others. "Nothing has changed. And so long as we have it, the Ram won't know peace."

"Nor will we," Jin pointed out. "We came here to retrieve the ledger and save Spindrift. I warned you that this would be bigger than us."

The fireplace crackled in the silence spurred by his words. It stretched shadows across the room, lengthening already concerned faces and heating the atmosphere of dread.

"I'm afraid I can't let you have it. The ledger is the only proof I have in the case I'm building," Penn said. "I'm waiting on leads to a few of the vampires who've gone missing before I appeal to the court."

"Appeal?" Jin repeated with an incredulous laugh. "Are you serious?

If the Ram could fabricate his way to a crown, I doubt the evidence you gather will go anywhere."

He was right. They were weaponizing vampires. Arthie didn't think proof would make a lick of a difference. There were too many variables in his plan, and almost all of them ended with the ledger being destroyed.

"You are young and jaded, and in many ways correct, but some of us refuse to use unethical avenues." Penn gestured to a leather folio on his desk. "If I have enough proof, they'll be unable to refute it. As such, I've also uncovered a lead to the laboratory where the scientists first produced the silver doses."

"Wait," Jin said, a hush to his voice. "Scientists?"

Penn nodded. "Old friends of mine."

And then he tossed Jin a clove rock.

40

JIN

Jin caught the candy and the life drained out of him. It was him. Penn was their weekly visitor who had argued with Jin's father the night before the fire. Jin made a sound that was half laugh, half sob, and all hope.

You've always known they were alive, he chastised himself. But believing his eleven-year-old self had gotten difficult as the years went by.

Do you want to know a secret? his father would say whenever he and his mother were in the thick of their research. They would tell Jin of their findings but make him promise not to tell anyone else because they weren't proven yet. They'd spoken of coconuts and transfusions, nerve endings and viruses, but he'd never once heard them talk of a silver inoculation.

A hand touched his back. Flick, reminding him to breathe.

"I'm sorry, Jin," Penn said.

Jin almost laughed. Ten years, and no one had ever expressed their condolences for what had happened. No one besides Arthie even knew, or knew enough to care, really.

"Do we know if they still live?" Arthie asked.

Penn worked his jaw. "Not for certain. They've been missing ever since they formulated the inoculation. It's been years. There's every likelihood that they are—"

"No." Arthie thought on it for a moment and shook her head. "The Ram is too smart to waste a resource."

A resource. That was what his parents had become. Not a mother and a father and a friend and a loved one, but yet another commodity for the Ram to exploit.

Everyone was staring at him.

"Let the poor boy be," Matteo said.

Jin looked everywhere and then finally at Arthie. He was supposed to be mad at her. "We haven't learned anything new. I'd always known they were alive, and now I'm just hearing it from someone else. Spindrift first."

Arthie hid a smile, and he knew then: He wasn't the only one who'd held out hope about them being alive. Knowing her, she would have kept quiet about it to give *him* less hope. In case the worst was really true.

"Spindrift first," Arthie repeated with a nod, then she turned to Penn. "Gathering proof doesn't guarantee the court will listen."

Jin tried to focus on the conversation and quell his racing pulse. He was grateful to Arthie for redirecting the conversation, but also selfishly wished they could dwell on it a little more. His parents! Alive!

Arthie was still talking. "We don't know how many of them work for the Ram."

Penn smiled. "We?"

Arthie faltered, and Jin saw her uncertainty. In the decade he'd been by her side Jin had rarely seen Arthie hesitate. Nor did she ever involve herself in anything outside of the wrath she wanted to enact. The world was full of suffering, she would say, and it wasn't her job to fix it.

"Yes," she said to Penn, meeting his eyes with finality. "This is my problem too now."

"Our problem," Jin corrected. "We're bound to have dirt on some of the officials. We can coerce enough of them to see Penn's case through."

"And I might be able to get you a court roster," Flick offered.

Jin and Arthie exchanged a glance. Spindrift was founded on blackmail and threats. It only made sense that they would save it using the same.

41

ARTHIE

Exiting the Athereum was a much easier affair when Penn escorted Arthie and the others through the halls like they were royalty. On the street just outside the gates, Arthie inhaled the night breeze. The night had deepened, and in the darkness, she let her thoughts crash, one after the next.

Laith and his words before he was taken away. Jin and the betrayal in his eyes as he left her to walk home alone. Flick and the secrets she was bursting at the seams to spill. Penn warning them that Spindrift might no longer be safe. His offer to relocate them to his house on Imperial Square only rubbed salt on the wound.

White Roaring carried on as if nothing had changed. Lone carriages trundled, pleasure house doors slammed shut on rusty hinges, coins jangled in the hands of workers after a long day. It was only Arthie's view of the world that had sustained another crack from a hammer since she'd broken into the Athereum. Weaponizing vampires—*people*, for all intents and purposes—wasn't an ignorable evil.

Nor was leaving someone for dead.

There was that guilt, coiling thick in her throat. If she hadn't stepped back into the vault, she would be sitting with Laith in that cell right now. If the vampires hadn't burst through Penn's door first, Laith might have slit her throat. Or he might not have.

Get behind me.

The words haunted her every step. Trundling in her ears like this wretched carriage beside her. Was there no other road in the city? Arthie shot a glare at the wagon's unmarked covering and turned down another street, suddenly certain she'd seen the same pair of horses lingering outside the Athereum when she and Jin had gone their separate ways.

She paused and listened. Silence.

The carriage hadn't followed her. She was being paranoid. She started walking again and heard the neigh of a horse followed by the sound of wheels rolling over cobblestone.

Drat it all.

Arthie ran her hand over her pistol and walked straight into the middle of the street, forcing the carriage to a halt. She held her hat against a gust of wind and circled past the horses, eyeing the driver as she went. He didn't look her way, nor did she recognize him. If Jin was here, he'd give her a thousand different warnings as she marched to the door of the carriage, but she'd spent the last few hours breaking into the Athereum.

A carriage was nothing.

She heard a latch lift inside and thought, fleetingly, about the vampires being kidnapped. The door swung open to a yawning pit of darkness. No one emerged, nor did any sound. Arthie touched her pistol again and stepped inside.

"Arthie Casimir."

The voice was modulated, muffled by something in front of the speaker's mouth. *Like a mask.*

"And there's the first reason I should kill you," Arthie said. "You've been following me since Ivylock Street. What do you want?"

"You have something of mine," said the voice.

Arthie tilted her head and narrowed her eyes. "You'll have to be more specific."

She heard a shuffle and the figure leaned into the moonlight, illuminating a gilded mask, shadows pooling into the pits of its eyes.

The Ram.

Fear dropped like a stone inside of her.

"My ledger."

"Are you demanding or bargaining?" Arthie asked, willing her voice to remain calm.

"Give me the ledger, and you can keep your establishment."

"That's mighty generous of you, but it was my establishment until you threatened my proprietor," Arthie said. "Wearing a mask doesn't make you a better liar."

There would be no end, Arthie knew, even if she handed over the ledger. It was as Laith had said: The Ram disliked Spindrift, and as long as Spindrift existed, the threat to it would remain. For as long the *Ram* existed, the threat would remain. This wasn't only about Spindrift anymore. She couldn't be a thorn in the Ram's side anymore.

She needed the Ram gone.

For herself, for her crew, and for the vampires being snatched for a war that wasn't theirs.

"My ledger for Spindrift," the Ram repeated, and the carriage door swung open again.

Arthie stepped down, the weight of her pistol heavy at her side. If only it was as easy as firing a bullet through that pathetic mask.

42

FLICK

Flick tried to see the best in everything. If that couldn't be done, she was sad or indifferent. Never angry. Or rather, never *this* angry. This was rage. She'd spent the entire night tossing and turning in her room at Spindrift. She couldn't forge a signet ring or a document or even a doctor's note without being treated like a dirty criminal, but her mother could do *this*?

There was a voice in the back of Flick's head that said Lady Linden might not know. The EJC was large, and there could be any number of supervisors looking to make extra profit on the side. But louder than that voice was the certainty that her mother did know.

And that was how Flick found herself standing in front of the Linden Estate on Admiral Grove in the early hours of the next day. The trees were going bare, their leaves lightly carpeting the cobblestones in gold. Amid that rustle and dry tumble, Flick thought she heard another sound: the whisper of small footsteps, the crunch of a shoe across leaves.

When she whirled around to look, no one was there.

"Chester?" she called. "Felix?"

No one replied.

"Stop looking for excuses," she chided herself, and marched up to the basil-green door of the estate, ignoring the quiver of her fingers when she rapped with the iron knocker. It looked stately before, but now it reminded Flick of the horns of a devil.

The door swung open and immediately closed again, leaving only a sliver of space through which Flick could see a brown eye surrounded by full lashes. Her Mother only hired the prettiest.

"Miss Felicity," the young maid stammered out.

Flick held herself together. *Act like you belong.* "I need to see my mother."

The maid paused at her tone, and Flick peeked inside. Nothing seemed any different than when she'd lived there. "I . . . I . . . of course, miss. It's just that I don't know if—"

"Now," Flick enunciated.

"Yes. Of—of course," said the maid, brown hair bobbing with her nod. "She's in her office."

Flick took several deep breaths and dipped her hands into the pockets of her periwinkle wool coat to grip her lighter. Then she tugged her beret tight over her curls and stepped inside her house, hurrying up the winding stairs.

She threw open the door to her mother's study without a knock.

"Felicity!"

Her mother's surprise was punctuated by her pen rolling to a stop against a stack of books. Lady Linden stared at Flick from behind her oak desk, her remarkable cerulean eyes filled with shock. She was dressed in a gown she typically reserved for business—a fathomless shade of blue with fitted sleeves that flared from the elbows and lace that folded at her throat. It made her look regal and commanding.

"What . . . what are you doing here?" Lady Linden asked. Was it the light streaming in through the shuttered windows behind her, or did she appear annoyed? Her daughter, who had been arrested and supposedly was now rotting in a cell, had returned, and she had the audacity to look vexed?

Flick straightened her beret. She was so caught up in her anger and wanting to confront her mother that she hadn't thought about what to say.

It's important to note the difference between fuel and dictate.

She wasn't being dictated by her rage. It wasn't all-encompassing. She missed the cedarwood scent of her mother's office. She missed having tea and biscuits every evening in front of the wide windows facing the garden. She missed the sharp, sophisticated lines of her mother's gowns.

The harsh crease across her mother's brow softened.

"Why did you do it?" Flick asked.

"I loved you, Felicity, but you did this to yourself," she said with a resigned sigh.

Loved. Was that in the past tense? She didn't hear it over the thundering in her ears.

But there was something to be said about children and their knack for knowing. Flick knew her mother's love had been real. What she hadn't known was that parents could stop loving their children and tire of them the way someone tired of a pair of shoes.

It didn't matter how much wrong Flick had done. It didn't matter that she'd made mistakes spurred by her mother's growing distaste for her. No matter what, Flick was her daughter. She clutched her lighter as if etched somewhere in the brass was the reason why she had gone from her mother's little spark to a stranger.

But this wasn't about Flick.

"I'm talking about what *you've* done," Flick said, and it took everything in her not to recoil at the anger twisting her mother's face because of her tone. "Oh, I need to be more specific, don't I?"

Her mother's neat blond bun was dull, and new wrinkles were carved into her skin. Was it because she'd been worried about Flick, or did she know the Ram's ledger had gone missing and that word of her involvement could spread?

"You will not speak to—how did you get out of prison?"

"I was never in it, Mother," Flick snapped. "Which you might have known if you'd come to check on me."

Lady Linden looked like she'd been slapped, but Flick wasn't finished.

"How could you partake in something so evil? How could you treat vampires like any other cargo on your ships?"

Her mother froze, but recovered quickly. She rose, towering over her. Flick used to feel safe in her shadow. Now, she felt a quiver of fear.

Fear. That was why she'd rarely experienced anger. She'd never been allowed to—she was always afraid to. Afraid to speak out, to feel anything but gratitude and appreciation and happiness. It was funny how she'd spent over a week with Arthie and Jin, running the streets and breaking into the Athereum of all places, and the fear she'd experienced then was entirely different.

Exhilarating. It had felt like *living.*

"Where did you hear of this?" her mother asked. There was no remorse on her face, no shame. Only cold assessment. This was business to her, nothing else. A transaction.

Flick cracked a sad, sad laugh. "And to think I wanted to give you the benefit of the doubt. To think I was ready to do anything for your forgiveness."

She was ready to steal that ledger from under Arthie's nose, risking Spindrift, risking her alliances, risking *Jin.* Just to give her mother the front page of every paper in White Roaring, in Ettenia even.

Just for her mother to love her again.

"Answer the question, girl," Lady Linden snapped.

"Or what?" Flick asked, a bit of Arthie creeping into her voice. "You'll confine me to my room? No, I think I'll take my leave, Mother."

Flick turned to leave. She knew her mother would ring for help, but Flick had learned a thing or two from Jin. She'd disconnected the wire on her way in.

"That won't be necessary," Flick said, as Lady Linden reached for the cord. "I know the way out. This is my house, after all."

She had a few extra seconds to spare, which was more than enough time to leave her brass lighter on her mother's desk and close the door behind her.

left wing

right wing

vault

offices & rooms

rooms

parlor

auction hall

prison

locked & guarded

glass chutes

dormer guard →

stair

guard house

guar

ir →

*

mortu
vivos
docent

locate the
the wretched
in way over her
is why I didn't
lly dreadful. she

Athereum
marker

numerical
code
inside

left wing

vault

offices
& rooms

right wing

parlor

auction
hall

rooms
(mostly
debauchery)

tone
all →

prison

locked
& guarded

glass
chutes

marker
archives

dormer
guard →

'winsome'
sketch
of a
female
vampire

gardens

ACT III

A FIRE IN
SLUMBER

ers

ARTHIE didn't
let me finish
adding roses

43

JIN

It took Jin a few moments to remember he was in Spindrift when he woke the next morning. He'd dreamed of his house on Admiral Grove, his mother talking about certitudes and his father talking about theories. Still, when he tumbled out of bed, it wasn't with the optimism at having outsmarted a foe or the excitement of a possible lead to his parents, but dread. He didn't even get to bask in the comfort of being back in Spindrift again.

Something felt wrong.

He knocked on Flick's door, and it swung open beneath his knuckles. The room was empty. His brow furrowed. Strange.

The doors to Spindrift flung open downstairs before Jin could think more on it, and he hurried to the balcony. Arthie stood at the threshold, and he wished her every emotion didn't bleed into him. He wished she didn't look unkempt and wild, warning him that something was wrong.

"Get everyone to Imperial Square," she said. She was breathless.

Jin wasted no time. He crossed the balcony and tugged on the rope, ringing the bell to alert the others. Arthie's panic became his, and then everyone else's as urgency swept Spindrift's wooden walls. Doors flung open across the tearoom.

Jin darted down the stairs to meet her. "What happened?"

"The Ram knows we don't plan to hand over the ledger," Arthie said.

Jin swallowed a laugh. What had been the point of breaking into the Athereum? Of everything they'd risked their necks for?

"What about my things?" Chester shouted, swinging his blanket from the upstairs balcony. He shrank back at Arthie's look.

"We're coming back," Jin said gently, ushering him down. The boy brought his blanket anyway, telling Reni he trusted no one. They all had a little bit of Arthie in them.

"You, get word to Matteo Andoni on Alms Place," Arthie ordered someone. "The rest of you, leave in groups. Don't need a row of ducks waddling ten blocks over."

Jin rounded the flip-top and pulled out a box from under the counter. "How do you know—"

"I met the Ram last night. Felix saw men mobilizing this morning."

Cold dread settled in his limbs and he nearly dropped his umbrella. "You *met*—"

"We don't have time for this," she said in a low hiss. "Has anyone seen Flick?"

"Her door was open," Jin said with a shake of his head. "No one's seen her."

The Ram would not be so bold as to utilize the Horned Guard to attack them, but there were plenty of others who hated them. Plenty waiting for an excuse. The Ram only had to point, and one of White Roaring's gangs would rise to the occasion with cheer.

"Find her," Arthie ordered. "I want to know where she's been."

Somewhere behind the kitchens, a window shattered.

Everyone stopped.

Jin wished he was asleep and this was all a bad dream. He wished he could roll over and leap into a new one with pastries and candies.

Arthie moved first. She turned to Chester and shoved a map in his hands. "You remember the house on Imperial Square, don't you?

It's a safe house. Knock and tell the housekeeper Penn would like hot chocolate with his pie, and they'll let you in. I'm counting on you, eh? Good boy."

Three sinister shadows fell across the frosted glass doors, each holding something long and wicked.

"Plodders," Jin said. They were the only gang who couldn't afford guns. They weren't the brightest of the lot either, but they made up for it in brute force.

The sudden silence inside Spindrift was starker than a gunshot.

Arthie swept a look across their crew. "Line up against the wall by the entrance. At Jin's signal, file out."

Then she squared her shoulders and threw open the doors.

The Plodders were dressed like the streets they ran, a terrible shade of brown like they'd rolled about in mud before showing face. Faded trousers, ratty sashes, dusty bowler caps, yellow collars bright. Arthie feigned surprise, taking several steps back to draw them inside.

Jin waited until the Plodders cleared the entrance, then gave Chester a nod. He squeezed past them and through the doors, grabbing hold of the hand behind him, each of them doing the same until a Plodder turned around and broke the line, throwing the new girl to the ground. Several more Plodders trundled inside and slammed the doors shut before anyone else could escape.

"Boys, and girl," Jin said, inclining his head. He swung his umbrella up to his shoulder beside Arthie. "Long time no trouble."

The leader of the gang, Davison, tapped a bat against his open palm. He looked half drunk.

"Let me guess, someone told you there was a party to be had," Arthie said, pulling back the panel of her jacket to flash her pistol at him.

Davison swayed. "I've always wanted to wipe those smirks off your faces. Now I'm getting paid to do it."

Arthie reached for the teapot Jin had set down on the counter earlier. "Might I interest you in a cup of tea first?"

He only stared blankly, then jerked his head. His filthy lot converged.

Arthie swung the teapot, shattering it against Davison's head before she grabbed him by the scruff of his jacket and swept the counter with his face, teacups shattering, teaspoons scattering. She threw him at the bricked column, where he struck his head and fell.

Pitiful fellow.

Jin sighed. "You didn't have to go and ruin my favorite tea set."

"You said that about the last one too," Arthie replied, straightening her jacket.

The rest of the Plodders looked at one another.

"Oh, don't look so disappointed, lads," Jin placated. "Plenty of tea to go around." He picked up a stack of saucers. "Fancy some biscuits too? You can't come into our home and expect us not to treat you with proper Casimir hospitality."

The Plodders came at them all at once.

Jin moved toward the tables, flinging saucers at throats and shoving chairs out of his way. A Plodder lunged when Jin's stack ran out, and he swung his umbrella, toppling him with a calculated strike to his leg. He kicked another Plodder out of the way and swung for the third one's hand, but the girl grabbed the end of his umbrella and yanked it out of Jin's grip.

"Gently. Gently!" he chided when it struck the wall.

She lashed out with a wicked knife dulled with rust and dirt. Jin swerved, and when she lashed again with startling speed, he grabbed a chair and threw it up as a shield. The force of her arc drove the knife through the seat, snapping the wood in two, but not before Jin slammed it—and the end of her blade—downward through her thigh.

He cringed. That was going to leave a mark.

A burly Plodder came at him with another knife, and Jin whipped out his own, landing a strike that bought him time to whirl the fellow against his body when yet another one came at him with a club. The club struck the Plodder on the head, knocking him out cold, and Jin rammed his knife between the other's ribs as a thank you.

Jin tugged the knife free, tossing the club up and into his hand. "Much obliged."

"Jin!" Arthie yelled. His blood spiked, and he nearly tripped when he ran, flinging the club at another Plodder. But after all this time, he should have known he didn't need to worry about Arthie.

He found her bashing the heads of two Plodders together, both far taller and larger than she was. In the beat of calm, she wiped a smear of blood from her cheek, her eyes wild and cold in a way that gave Jin pause.

"Get the others out," she said, her voice strained.

He stepped closer. "I'm not leaving you here."

"I didn't ask."

"Neither did I."

Arthie leaped back and thrust her knife into a Plodder's gut with one hand, hurling it at another in the same move. She clenched her jaw as if struck, swaying as if she were losing blood. Something was wrong.

He started toward her before he jerked to a halt at a sound he knew well. Too bloody well.

A hiss.

A sputtering *whoosh*.

Fire.

Flames ripped across the counters where rags had been stretched to dry. Terror struck every part of him. Held him captive. The fire crackled, roared, reached with angry protests.

No. Not Spindrift. The adrenaline from the fight disappeared, leaving only stone-cold dread.

Arthie fought to get by his side. "Breathe, Jin."

He opened his mouth and a sound came out. He couldn't form words. He couldn't think past the chant in his head. *Fire, fire, fire.*

"Stay calm," Arthie hissed in his ear. She was struggling. Why was she struggling? She didn't fear fire the way he did. With a growl, she turned away. Her knife caught the light as she lobbed it again, then she nabbed his and disappeared. Through his tunneling vision he saw her parry a Plodder double her size.

Get the others out, she had said.

He swallowed. He could do that. He rubbed at the scarred skin of his arm. Breathed past the claws digging into his chest. Dropped to his knees and scrambled for his umbrella, tightening his fist around it after what felt like forever.

He turned to the others pressed against the shadows. Reni was bent over a Plodder, his fangs in the man's neck. A couple of the others were helping Arthie.

Jin threw open the doors. *Too slow, too slow.* He ushered the others out, counting heads, then losing track and counting them again. He lifted one of the younger ones into his arms and hurried into the street, prying her hands from his neck.

He swayed under the open air, his knees threatening to give out under him. But he had to turn back. He gulped down fresh air, blinking away the darkness before turning back to the angry, orange mouth of Spindrift. Arthie couldn't hold off the Plodders on her own. He couldn't be afraid of his home, of his everything.

One foot in front of the other, he made it to the doors before an explosion shook the street.

And Spindrift went up in flames.

44

ARTHIE

The *tick, tick, tick* of Arthie's pocket watch echoed between her ribs. One second the flames were small and taunting from the shadows, insignificant in the face of her hunger, gasping and tumbling into ashes.

The next, her ears rang with a sound.

Arthie had been so careful, so meticulous. And her careful planning was what had ruined everything. She yanked her knife out of someone's spine and holstered her pistol. The walls shook and trembled, and as she begged them to hold, to be strong, to *keep going, my loves, keep going*, they gave up.

They gave up, and after all these years, some part of her did the same.

Splinters flew, glass shattered. The world's wrath came, a reminder that she was a little girl playing at something too big for her to hold. She had tried though. She had tried so, so hard. And for what? Her life unraveled as she watched, because of a single act of defiance.

Because that was the nature of man. Born to nurture, determined to destroy. *Fitting*, Arthie thought. At least Jin wasn't here in this nightmare returned.

All her life she'd spun a slow dance through a burning room, and the inferno had caught up to her at last.

45

JIN

Ashes never really went away. A fire doused was a fire in slumber, waiting for its next feast, its next unsuspecting mark. Jin had thought nothing could compare to how helpless and hopeless he'd felt a decade ago.

Spindrift was the culmination of half his existence.

Blood, sweat, tears. Laughter and anger. Home in every way the estate on Admiral Grove was not. That was the home that had been given to him. This was the one he had made himself, with the family he had chosen for himself.

"One day, you're going to need to face that fear of yours," Arthie had said years ago.

Jin had been annoyed. "Why?"

"Because you can't afford the weakness."

He hadn't spoken to her for days after that. Not everything needed conquering. But now he saw that she was right, that this weakness could cost him her life. Bystanders were beginning to gather, toffs pointing fingers from afar, gangs snickering from the shadows. No one offered to help.

Jin kicked open the doors.

Smoke charged at him, a horror without fangs, worse than one awoken from a grave. It gripped him in invisible shackles, held him hostage beneath an invisible pistol. *Yellow. Orange. Red. RED.* His breath was coming out in tiny rasps. He gripped the doorframe.

"Arthie!" Jin yelled. The banister he had leaned against day after day to watch the dance and flurry of Spindrift groaned and collapsed, taking with it some piece of his heart. The walls were scorched black. Those beautiful dangling orbs had all shattered, swaying like abandoned souls.

He was suddenly overcome with wrath. He had never known such rage as he did now. It lit him up inside. It swallowed his panic and his fear, if only for a moment, and gave him strength. He sidestepped a line of Plodder corpses and fallen teapots and searched behind the counter, but saw no sign of Arthie. Most of the tables had toppled, but no one alive lay beneath any of them. He tucked his nose under his collar and powered onward.

It was easier not to think of what the fire was doing to him—no, it was not easy, it was impossible.

"Arthie!" Jin called again. He couldn't summon anything more. The Siwang Residence was astronomical. How could he find her in time? *No.* This was Spindrift, *this* was home.

Embers floated down onto his clothes, and Jin slapped them off in a fit of panic. *Panic.* Panic had wound through his muscles and, like a string pulled taut, he could no longer move.

"Arthie," he said uselessly. He could barely hear himself. Smoke clogged his throat, and he broke into a series of coughs. His eyes were watering, his lungs burned. "Where are you?"

Stop thinking, he told himself. A thud echoed from the direction of the stairs, a shuffle that couldn't be an act of the fire. The panic eased, allowing him to move. He skirted past more fallen bodies and broken chairs, Arthie's voice a chant in his head that changed to Flick's when she'd twitched that lighter.

And there in the gloom, he saw mauve. Jin ran.

Arthie was trapped under the remnants of a bookcase, slowly prying herself free. She looked up at his approach, soot on her skin, determination sharp on her jaw. By the time he reached her, she had shoved the bookcase off and risen to her feet. She said something, her voice bubbling as if underwater.

Spindrift darkened impossibly, and Arthie stumbled, reaching blindly and swaying from the heat. Jin rushed closer and lifted her into his arms. He couldn't breathe. Why couldn't he breathe? His head throbbed. Sound. Fire. A nightmare of memory.

Something swayed above Jin—*wicked knives*, that was the second story. He leaped out of the way of the collapsing stair rail but not before it struck his back. Arthie went limp, impossibly heavier in his arms.

He squeezed his eyes closed for a beat and saw Flick, vividly alive and unafraid, a queen in her gown sculpted from a piece of the unblemished sky.

She was sunshine in a bottle, and he was a storm in a boy, drawn to clear skies, reaching for her hand. *Just a little farther*, she told him. Just a little farther.

And then Jin collapsed.

46

JIN

Jin went from imagining Flick guiding him out of the fire to feeling her hands on his arms, helping him to his feet. *You saved me*, he almost said, but that would be the delirium speaking. She wasn't real. The smoke had conjured her.

The cobblestones outside Spindrift were littered with debris from the blast. An audience of Ettenians in vibrant skirts and wool coats had gathered as if this were the latest play at the theater. Horror was muffled by excitement, by fingers jabbing at the smoke curling thicker than the smokestack plumes, the fire brighter than the Ettenian sun.

Not one of them had come to his aid. He wanted to yell at them all.

"Jin."

He blinked down at Flick. She *was* real. She pulled him away from the fire and into safety, dragging him from the bones of his home. He was still holding Arthie in his arms. Barely.

Flick hailed them a carriage. She helped him carry Arthie inside. Gave Jin water to wet his parched throat. Sat beside him as the driver spurred the horses in the direction of Ivylock Street. Arthie needed care, and as outlandish as it sounded, the Athereum was the safest place for them right now.

"Jin," Flick said again, concern heavy in her voice. "Say something."

"You came back for us," he rasped at last. He could barely move his arms. His legs felt just as weak. The rumbling of the carriage made him want to hurl his insides. He wanted to retch, scream, sob.

"Of course I did," Flick said softly.

The carriage trundled onward, the sounds of the city slipping through the seams. Newsboys shouting, horses whinnying, people going about as if this was any ordinary day. And it was, for them. Buildings rushed past the carriage window, each of them intact and untouched, bricks as perfect as Spindrift's had been this morning.

Flick took her handkerchief and wet it, using it to wipe the soot from his skin. His eyes burned. He wanted to pull away from her touch. It was too caring, too tender.

It ripped away the last of his resolve.

And Jin couldn't hold them in anymore. The tears fell, and he did nothing to stop them. He could *do* nothing to stop them. He had bottled them up since the proprietor had given them the news.

"Oh, Jin," Flick whispered. She pulled him against her and adjusted herself so that his face rested in the crook of her shoulder, enveloping him in wildflowers and sunlight, everything the remains of Spindrift was not. His tears fell onto her skin and dampened her dress, but she held him firmly.

"It's gone," he managed to say.

"I know," Flick said, eyebrows pitched earnestly. "And I'm sorry. I know how much it meant to you. It was a horrible, horrible thing to do. A dirty move on the Ram's part. But your crew is alive. You and Arthie survived, and in this war against the Ram, you're already winning."

He angled his head to look at Arthie stretched out across the double seats across from them, frail and unconscious. Flick was right.

She swiped at her own face, and then breathed a little laugh because he noticed. "When I—I didn't see either of you at first, I was worried I had left my old life behind only to lose my new one, too."

Her new life. Was that what she thought of them? Of him?

"Killing us is no easy task," Jin said. "We're annoying like that."

Flick laughed again, louder this time, drowning out a sob.

He sat back and dragged a thumb up her cheek, wiping away the stray tear, freezing her in place. Jin remembered the last time they'd been in a carriage together, when she'd tumbled into his lap. That felt like forever ago.

She must have been thinking the same, for she tilted her head at him. "And this job had its victories—we have the ledger. The truth. You learned something about your parents."

He had so much to tell them . . . which made him realize something else. He had spent so many years fixated on the past, worried and afraid of what might befall him again, that life had up and happened without him.

Arthie twitched but didn't awaken. It was as she'd said, time and time again. He was always so worried about taking risks and potentially losing Spindrift that he rarely took time to fully enjoy and appreciate it.

"Don't overthink," Flick whispered.

Jin clenched his jaw. She leaned closer and brushed ash from his hair. His breath caught. Flick froze too, realizing how little space there was between them.

Classic Flick.

If he tilted his head forward a fraction, he could brush his nose against hers. If he tilted his head to the right or left, he could kiss her soft, unblemished cheek. If he dipped even closer, he could kiss her lips.

"Jin, I—" She stopped, eyes dropping to his mouth. Her hands had been all over him moments ago, funny how it was her gaze that made him shiver now.

He leaned closer, running his tongue over his lips, pleased he didn't taste like soot. Her fingers curled into his thighs, as if she was bracing herself. If only she knew what that was doing to him. Wicked knives, it was doing things to him. And neither of them noticed that the carriage had stopped until the door was flung open.

Flick made a little squeak. Jin wrenched away, adjusting his trousers as discreetly as he could.

The dubious face of the driver peered between them, the Athereum behind him. "Uh, we're 'ere."

47

ARTHIE

When Arthie opened her eyes, she couldn't remember the last time she'd closed them. She sat up and everything rushed back. Spindrift. Her home, her joy, her life—gone.

There was an armchair by her bed and an unlit hearth beside it. She knew this place. She recognized the illustrated ceiling and those ornate walls: the Athereum.

She slumped back into the pillows and ran her hands down her ribs, making sure everything was in place. She'd felt every crash and shatter of Spindrift as if it were her own body. As if she had been tethered to it by a thread, and the Ram had come and snipped it clean, leaving her bereft.

The emptiness was as loud as the hunger gnawing at her insides. She almost laughed. She almost gave in to the mayhem thrashing beneath the surface. She was tired of powering forward. She was tired of outsmarting the next hurdle.

Her pistol was on the bedside table. She holstered it, tucking a piece of herself back in place, and forced herself out of the bed. She needed to check on Jin and her crew. But she was an animal pacing in a cage. Something was rippling through her, begging to be unleashed.

Please, please, please. A sob tore out of her, draining the last of her will, forcing her down to her knees on the rug in the room's center.

In this game between her and the Ram, she had lost.

Lost her home, lost her life, and worst of all, lost the control she had so carefully cultivated.

A whisper of a sound pulled her out of her thoughts. Something white drew her attention—a white orchid that symbolized missing someone. That hadn't been there before. A figure drew near, silhouetted against the curtains. She recognized the shape of him, his scent that heightened her senses.

"Laith."

That couldn't be right—he couldn't be alive. He couldn't be roaming free in the Athereum of all places.

"Arthie." He spoke her name on a twisted exhale, stepping into the lamplight. She shivered in anticipation and gritted her teeth against it.

It *was* him.

"You're . . . you're alive."

She should have apologized, but the words refused to form on her tongue. She could barely form coherent thoughts.

A shaky laugh broke out of her instead. "You're here to kill me, aren't you? After what I did to you."

His gaze swept down her body, and he took a step closer. "If only that were true. I loathed you, Arthie. I hated you for the span of a heartache before I realized how much I craved you. And I know you yearn for me the same."

Arthie did, she realized. She'd looked for him at every turn—when learning the truth about the Ram's ledger, when the flames tore through Spindrift.

"And I understand why you did it," he said. "I wasn't as forthcoming as I should have been. I apologize."

He spoke the words too quickly. He *forgave* her too quickly. If only Arthie could think clearly. There was a piece she was missing, and she only needed to rearrange the puzzle that was him for it all to click into place.

"I heard about Spindrift."

"It's gone," she said, and her voice broke.

"I know," he replied softly, too calm for her chaos. "I know. I'm sorry."

"The others—"

"Safe," he said. "Your crew is at Imperial Square. Jin, Flick, and Matteo are here. I learned about the ledger, too. It is safe to say I don't work for the Ram any longer."

She glanced at his breast pocket. Sure enough, his robes didn't bear the badge of the Horned Guard.

"Why don't you let go?" she asked suddenly. The words burst out of her. "Why live for the dead when you have a life of your own?"

Laith paused, taken aback. "The past cannot be forgotten."

No, it could not. Only death would take her past from her. "But can it be forgiven?"

"My heart seeks a peace I may never know," Laith said. "Until I find it, I do not know how to live any other way."

"Lex talionis," she murmured. She knew what peace he spoke of, even if she'd never considered it as more than a wound in her chest, a hole she could never fill. "How long can vengeance last?"

"An eternity. Until they suffer the same fate, until justice is struck."

Her thoughts bled into one another. She needed to stuff all her broken edges back into a tailored suit and return to what she was. Nothing made sense but her hunger.

His clothes rustled in the silence, and then she felt the ghost of his fingers at her jaw, lifting her chin. He lifted his hand slowly, waiting for her to pull away. When the light from between the curtains dipped his fingers in gold, it held her in place. When it danced across the smooth curve of his cheek, she stared. He traced a swoop of her hair, curling it behind her ear, his gaze following the movement like a beast tracking its prey.

He pressed closer, and impossibly, her head tilted without her consent. "If there is anyone who can endure an eternity, it is you."

When she felt the feather of his breath along her skin, she felt dangerously like giving in. His finger swiped her lip, and that hunger amplified. It wanted to ravage and destroy. It wanted, and she couldn't stop it.

"I know what you are, Arthie," he whispered. His voice held the barest of tremors. "I've known since the day I met you."

She pulled away from him, freezing as she searched the planes of his face. How? How could he know?

Tell me, do you remember what it's like to live?

He grazed his fingers down the side of her arm, depriving her of her ability to think. "Let me help you."

She inhaled, devouring the scent of his blood, the fervor in his veins. It assaulted her. Drove her mad. She wanted to unleash her rage upon him. She wanted to crack open his rib cage and crawl inside of him.

He loosened the sash of his robes and let them fall to the rug with a soft hush. He undid the trio of buttons on the top of his linen shirt and bared the unmarred skin of his throat. His eyes were as dark as her heart, a sea at dusk.

"Let me bleed for you."

When that healer in Ceylan had told Arthie's mother that only a miracle could save her daughter, he had taken Arthie in his arms as if she weighed no more than a sack of rice and set her down in the back of his hut, with its coconut palm leaf–thatched roof and snaking wisps of incense smoke. He moved with impossible speed. One moment he was there, considering her. The next, he was striking himself like a viper. When she gasped, he pressed his wrist to her mouth.

She didn't know what made her drink.

A fire started in her limbs, sweeping through her veins in invisible torrents, consuming her, draining her, filling her with hunger even though she had just eaten.

"What's happening to me?" she had asked, voice rising.

"You must live for those who will not," he said.

And then the darkness swallowed her up, only for an instant, an eternity, a minute or many, and when she opened her eyes, the healer was gone. Or maybe she had left his hut. She moved too quickly, every sound rang too loudly. Around her, people were screaming and running. Ettenian soldiers were coming, they said. Angry waves swallowed bobbing boats. A storm was coming, too.

"Arthie!"

She ran in the direction of her mother's voice, feeling stronger than she could ever remember. She looked down at her black-stained hands and sticky fingers. She angled them toward the sunlight creeping through the smoky skies and realized they weren't black, but the darkest shade of red.

Blood.

Hands gripped her, pulled her close. The embrace was warm, a feast to satisfy her hunger. *No!* She reprimanded herself. This was her mother, shouting at her to hurry, and her father, steering her in the direction of their boat.

Arthie ran for the crashing waves, unafraid because she loved the sea. But when the water lapped at her limbs now, she hissed at the way it burned her skin, like a thousand needles piercing into her. Still, Arthie powered forward. She reached the boat. There were two girls in it already, their eyes wide as saucers.

She turned back, her hand outstretched, but neither of her parents was behind her. They were back at the shore, and as Arthie watched, they died at the hands of the Ettenians.

Death bleeds red no matter the color of one's skin.

They called her father kalu Asoka because there was another Asoka in their village who was lighter-skinned. They called her mother netta Dasaka because she was the tallest one of the three in the village. But when they lay on the sand, eyes glassy, riddled with holes large enough to see the glint of the bullets, it was all the same. A pool of red. A pool of injustice. A pool of death.

To this day, Arthie remembered her hunger at the sight of them. She did not mourn, she did not weep. That craving engulfed her. The villagers mistook her wild abandon for grief. They pinned her to the boat. Perhaps it was one of the girls, or the man who joined to turn the oars.

Arthie lashed out against them, angry tears rivaling the torrents pouring from the dark skies as they pushed out to sea. They couldn't understand.

And then she stopped. The boat rocked on the waves in silence, her three companions looking grim and guilty at their own relief.

They didn't know she'd come to realize something: She didn't need her parents to feed her. No one could care for her now but herself.

Later, much later, once the skies had cleared and she'd put enough distance between her and Ceylan's shores, an Ettenian ship found her.

One lone girl in a boat full of blood.

She was too small and too brown and too dirty, but she somehow found herself on the threshold of Penn's mansion weeks after the Ettenians had found her bloody boat, where they'd nudge one another while spooning slop into their mouths and share quips she couldn't understand but knew for certain were jibes at her.

At that point, she was oscillating between pain and anger, wishing her hunger hadn't disappeared so that she could unleash the monster inside of her. Wishing she could stop reliving her final moments in Ceylan.

She remembered bits and pieces after that. Setting foot on the Ettenian pier. The damp cold she'd never known before. The carts and the horses and all those voices and buildings. She remembered the way her footsteps echoed in Penn's foyer when she entered with her water-warped shoes. It sat behind a trim lawn carved with a winding path where a carriage had been parked, a pair of horses waiting patiently.

The housekeeper was telling her something. Arthie didn't understand what until she demonstrated, getting to her knees and scrubbing at the floors. She didn't see a single speck of dirt on the glossy floorboards, but she nodded. She didn't know what else to do.

At home in Ceylan, her mother would only make her clean once she'd returned from school and had gotten some time to play in the sea with the other children. No one asked about her studies here. No one seemed to see her as a child, only another pair of hands meant for work.

The doors swung open for a pair of guards with rifles against their shoulders. Arthie shrank back with a strangled cry and squeezed her eyes shut.

The house fell silent.

Arthie remained very still as a shadow engulfed her.

"Open your eyes, little lion."

It was a language she understood. A man was crouched in front of her. He was about her father's age, but carried himself in a statelier fashion. Aristocratic, she would later learn. His hair was tied at the nape of his neck, and a brilliant red ruby sat in the ruffled knot of fabric under his throat.

He looked Ettenian white, but he spoke her language. That was why they brought her to him, he said. When he smiled, she saw something sharp, and she touched her tongue to those sharp thorns of her own.

He laughed. "Fangs."

He lowered his voice, and it felt as if they were sharing a secret. "Draw them in and no one will know."

He regarded her oddly and held a finger under her nose, where her breath came out in fearful, tiny sniffs.

"Fascinating," he said, more to himself than to her. "You're alive, but also a vampire. I've been trying to find someone like him."

She still didn't know of whom he spoke, and it would take her a long, long time to realize she'd been abandoned in an in-between state. Half here and now and alive, the other half lost at sea. Half human, half vampire. Her growth trickled to an end when she neared sixteen. Her heartbeat petered to a halt. She cast a shadow but not a reflection.

For she wasn't near death when she was fed a vampire's blood.

That was why she'd wreaked havoc on that little boat, eerily similar to what the Wolf of White Roaring had done years before her. Perhaps if she'd stayed with Penn, she would have learned all that and more.

He told the housekeeper that she wouldn't be part of the staff. Instead, he gave her a room and a maid and care. But a man like Penn Arundel couldn't always be home, and a growing girl could not always remain sated. Not long after she moved in with him in Imperial Square, that hunger returned, consuming Arthie's consciousness until there was nothing else.

Penn found her that night in the bathroom, staring at her maid in a tub full of blood.

It was his reaction that scared her. His face scrunched in pain, and

Arthie braced for a reprimanding, but he drew her against him, enveloping her in a wall of comfort and safety. It would be all right, he said. He would help her.

She only needed to trust him.

Months later, her hunger struck again, and he wasn't there to stop it. Arthie stumbled into the kitchens, gripping the doorframe, claws digging into the wood. Everyone but the cook's young daughter ran. She cornered her. It didn't matter who the girl was, only that she was breathing, that blood pumped through her veins, frenzying at Arthie's approach.

"Please," she begged. "Please, please, please."

Arthie spent hours shivering near the kitchen door. The cook screamed. Penn didn't come. His household began whispering and whispering until she couldn't take it anymore.

She ran.

Arthie spent days huddling in the alleys of White Roaring's streets. She saw other vampires bewitching humans into baring their throats, just for a taste. She didn't trust herself to hold that same restraint, and so she starved. She vowed never to drink another drop of blood again. She clung to the humanity she remembered, the remains of what had been stolen from her.

Some nights, she screamed into the darkness until her body felt numb. She found other ways to stay busy, other emotions to feel. The color bled from the world, and life became a curse.

Until she met a boy with a coconut.

48

ARTHIE

Arthie shook her head when Laith sank to his knees in front of her. She had ached from restraint, from holding herself back, ever since that last glass of coconut water.

"I'm dangerous," she said, but she felt herself giving in. She had nothing left to lose.

"As am I," he murmured, and her fangs elongated for the first time in years at the smooth cut of his voice.

This wasn't nearly the same. Once she started, she might not stop. She might not stop until she'd ripped him apart. Laith closed the distance between them, and Arthie was moving before she could stop herself, something carnal replacing reason, something starved coming to light.

She dropped her head to his shoulder with anguish. His warmth made her quiver. His breathing quickened, striking the crook of her own shoulder.

"You need to leave," she whispered. "Before . . . before—"

"No," he whispered back. "Destroy me."

He pulled his head to the side, baring his throat. *Why?* she wanted to ask. What did he want from her in return? Arthie's nostrils flared at the scent of his blood, dark and enchanting. She tilted her face, the heat of him pulsing against her skin, beckoning. Calling. He pulled away, drawing his shirt over his head in one quick move and discarding it to the side. She unclenched her fists and lifted her hands to his exposed chest.

Laith's breathing broke, stopped, started afresh. She thought he said her name. She thought she had forgotten what it was like to feel warm. His skin scorched her hands, muscles coiling as he watched her exploration. She wanted to speak. To tell him she'd never touched a boy like this before.

His whispered laugh wound through her. "When I first set eyes on you with your mauve hair and knife-sharp smiles, I swore you would be a means to an end. When we met for the first time in your office, I realized it would be harder to keep that oath."

"And then?" she asked.

He lifted a hand to the back of his neck, something like torture in his eyes. She wished she knew the reason for it. She wished she knew what was holding him back. She wished she could think straight.

"And then you would use your mouth to cut me down in the most wicked of ways, and I realized I'd met countless men and women but never my mirror."

Was that what she was? They were different in every way, but also very much the same.

She took a step forward. "And now?"

He trailed the backs of his fingers down her cheek. "And now I've found a kindred spirit whose heart beats for the same pain. I don't know what I want anymore."

Kindred spirit.

She slid her nose up the plane of his skin, curling her fingers into his hair. His pulse was a rabid thrum against her. She parted her lips and pressed her mouth to the curve of his neck.

"Arthie." He sounded as starved as she was.

She wondered what it would be like to kiss him. To claim him. To devour the mystery of this boy from some faraway land.

Her mind showed her the maid in the tub. The girl in the kitchens. The refugees in the boat.

"I'm—" *Feral. Wild. Beastly.*

"Hungry," he whispered to her.

She sank her fangs into his neck, twin blades breaking skin. The heat of his blood flooded her tongue, metallic and sweet, a melody in her mouth, coursing down her throat and filling that eternal cold.

She was different now. She was in command of herself. Not a starved, confused little girl.

Laith bucked against her with a rasp, one hand disappearing into her hair, the other slipping down the curves of her body until he gripped her thigh. She gasped at the heat of him, pushing closer to please that dull ache.

"Don't," he begged. "Don't stop."

She didn't stop. They staggered to their feet, locked in a drunken dance. The rumble of his groan shot through her as she retracted her fangs and welcomed this new rush. This ache she'd never experienced before. She kissed the curve of his neck and laved her tongue down the bloody nicks.

She hadn't realized how deeply her strength had depleted until it returned. Fire pumped through her veins, filling her to near bursting, giving way to a different need pulsing through her, a different kind of hunger.

Laith's hands slipped down her body, gripped her ribs, her waist, higher, lower, *everywhere.*

There.

Her pistol.

Arthie wasn't hungry anymore. Her mind was not clouded by starvation, and suddenly, everything wrenched to a startling halt as the pieces fell into place. The way Calibore's intricate filigree reminded her of Laith. Those accidental brushes of her pistol. His keen interest in how it worked. The story of the hilya his sister was sent to retrieve.

It was Calibore. Her pistol was the hilya.

He had never intended on taking down the Ram. He hadn't cared about the Ram or the ledger. He had simply played his part, feeding her lies and sidling closer and closer to the pistol. Touching her, goading her, coaxing her to drink from him when she'd sworn never to do so ever again.

She stared at the twin punctures at his neck, her broken oath.

This would end now.

His chest heaved, still bare and begging for her touch, his lips swollen and inviting. He must have noticed the change in her, because he hesitated. "Arthie, w—"

Arthie threw him against the wall, knocking the breath out of him. She had forgotten how much stronger a vampire could be when freshly fed. She had forgotten how sharp her claws could become.

She pressed the five of them against the delicate flesh of his throat.

"I should kill you," she whispered. "Rip you to shreds. Tear you apart for even thinking you could take Calibore from me."

Understanding dawned in his dazed eyes. He had known it was inevitable.

"Would you not have done the same?" he asked, his voice strained.

And that was precisely why she couldn't kill him.

She had used him as much as he'd used her. Neither of them had expected the raw desire that would bloom between them, angry vines drawing them close. Neither of them had expected to find their match in the other. Mirror, indeed.

"Leave," she said softly, "while your blood is only on my teeth and not splattered on these walls. If I see you again, I won't be so kind."

49

ARTHIE

Arthie watched Laith leave. She was never one to mourn, but here she was, mourning Spindrift, mourning the oath she'd made to herself. Some part of her mourned him too. He had used her, disrespected her, nearly robbed her, and yet.

And yet.

He was a knot of emotion she didn't yet know how to unravel. She was grateful to be rid of him and sad to have chased him away, and she was not looking forward to telling Jin that he had been right. Their high captain of the Horned Guard truly couldn't be trusted, and it wasn't for the reason either of them had expected.

Arthie stepped out of the room and turned down the hall, coming face-to-face with Matteo. He looked different now that her hunger had abated, blood rushing through her veins, bubbly and fresh. Everything looked more alive, vibrant, less tunneled in darkness. He saw her and froze.

"No, Arthie," he whispered. "Tell me you didn't."

He rarely called her by her name.

"You did," Matteo said, stepping closer. His hand twitched as if he wanted to reach for her. "You fed. On him."

"You knew about me," Arthie said.

Penn truly had told him everything. There was pain in Matteo's eyes, something almost like defeat, *betrayal.* What she did surely couldn't affect him that much.

"I've known for years," he said, but he didn't know what she'd done. He didn't know what she was capable of. "Even if I didn't, it wouldn't be hard to assume as much about the owner of Spindrift."

"What I am has nothing to do with Spindrift," she said. The sconces flickered in the hall, drenching him in shadow.

"No? Is it coincidence, then, that the moment you lose Spindrift, you lose the restraint you had cultivated for years?"

Arthie couldn't summon more than a whisper. "How do you know that?"

"Call us kindred spirits," Matteo said softly. His shoulders loosened with his sigh. "I like to observe, Arthie. I knew you were a half vampire, but I noticed anytime the conversation of blood came up, you didn't act as most vampires do. You looked disgusted. Anytime I offered a drink, you looked repulsed."

Kindred spirit. From Laith, the words had sounded empty. From Matteo, something struck her differently, setting her at ease. Like a part of her was settling into place.

Was it true? Had she tied her restraint to Spindrift? Or had the timing of her coconut water's depletion simply coincided with the tragedy? No—she'd downed the last of it before they'd left for the Athereum, and she had handled that entire job well enough.

Matteo was right.

"Why do you care?" she asked, hating that her voice sounded like a plea. Hating that someone could care for a wound she was allowing to fester. "You're a vampire. Would you not want me to embrace it?"

"Embracing and giving in are not the same thing," he said.

The words struck like a blow. Arthie's chest heaved. She slumped back against the wall, her eyes fluttering closed.

"I can't."

It broke out of her in a strangled whisper, hollow and dejected. It was defeat in a teacup, as tiny as a sugar cube, as weighty as a mountain.

"Stop punishing yourself by refusing to accept what you've become. Imagine your chaos, darling. Stop playing their games, and you can do so much worse."

Her laugh was bitter.

"You think I can just let go," she scoffed.

"No. A wound must be tended to before it can heal, but oh my sweet, what you will unleash when you're freed from that tether."

He spoke as if he understood. He'd lived a life sheltered between canvases, immersed in a brushstroke meadow of his own making. But when he turned his face to the lamp, she thought she saw something ruined and monstrous. She blinked, and the light painted him anew in the same beauty as his work. Was there more to Matteo than she saw?

He touched her cheek with a tenderness that made her vision falter. Arthie hadn't cried in years. She wasn't going to start now. Her eyes fluttered closed, and she felt herself lean into his touch, little pinpricks of heat leaping to attention, pooling to simmer low in her belly.

Because of Laith, her brain told her, but it was a lie. This felt different. Heightened. Amplified. Not spurred by hunger.

"I'm sorry," she whispered, opening her eyes. She didn't know what she was apologizing for, just that she felt the overwhelming need to.

"The great Arthie Casimir, apologizing to the even greater Matteo Andoni?" Matteo called out to no one in particular. "Someone fetch the presses."

The presses. That was it. That was how they'd take down the Ram, and they'd do it tonight. As much as Arthie loathed the fact that she'd broken her promise to herself and drunk from Laith, she couldn't ignore the clarity feeding had given her.

She met Matteo's eyes. "I know what to do. Get everyone to Penn's office."

He didn't even look surprised, only proud of himself. There was that damned dimple again. "As the empress commands."

50

JIN

It had been twenty-four hours since Spindrift collapsed, and Jin was surprised by how quickly his devastation was devoured by rage toward the Ram, as if his soul had taken the fires he'd lived through and decided to ignite one inside of him.

Arthie joined him in Penn's office, looking different. Less wild and less pale. More herself. And Jin realized he hadn't seen this version of her in weeks, perhaps months. She looked like a well-sated vampire leaving Spindrift at the end of the night.

"You saved me," she said to him.

"I thought it was time to repay the favor," he said as casually as she did, as if neither of them had nearly lost the other.

"Well," she said, "you're a decade late."

That made him laugh, and he was stunned when she threw her arms around him. He almost didn't hug her back before she pulled away. She straightened her shoulders and turned as Penn, Flick, and Matteo arrived.

"Where's Laith?" Flick asked.

Jin hadn't known how to feel when he saw that Laith was no longer scheduled to be staked through the heart. He wasn't particularly fond of the high captain, but he also hadn't really wanted him *dead*.

Arthie had been the same.

"Gone," she said, barely restraining her anger, and Jin wondered what had changed. "Our deal was for the retrieval of the ledger."

"So he just left?" Flick asked, puzzled, but Jin knew not to push. Matteo looked like he knew more about the situation himself. Jin didn't like this.

"I'm sorry, Arthie," Penn started. "For Spindrift."

Arthie twisted her mouth. "Is the ledger still safe?"

He nodded.

"Give me what you have of your case," she said. "We're not going to bother with the court anymore. We're going to arrange a meeting between the Ram and the press, and neither will know it. It'll be loud and public and not really our style, but that was exactly the hand the Ram played on Spindrift."

Arthie had a way of speaking when a plan was turning over in her head, probabilities and risks and chances running rampant. She'd changed since their fight. Whatever was wrong had righted itself.

"We'll need to hit every newspaper at once," Flick said, clearly speaking from experience.

Arthie nodded. "You're aware this will affect your mother just as much as the Ram, right?"

It was an odd question for Arthie to ask, and even Flick looked taken aback by it. It wasn't as if she would abandon her plans if Flick wasn't on board. To Jin, it looked more like Arthie was planting an idea, and he wasn't sure he approved.

"I am," Flick said with a confident nod.

"And I've got contacts with most of the papers," Matteo offered.

"Good," Arthie said. "Jin and I have a few of our own. We'll invite them to a single location and give them what we know. They can badger the rest out of the Ram, who won't be expecting to be bombarded by the press. Penn, do you have a place? I'd offer Spindrift, but it's temporarily closed."

"The Athereum has a meeting hall," Penn said. "It's not connected to the main building, so entrance doesn't require anything special."

"Excellent," Arthie said. "Send word to the Ram that we have the ledger, and we want to meet. Say nothing else."

"Will the Ram believe it?" Flick asked.

"That the Ram's taken everything from us, and we're relenting because we're afraid of what more we'll lose?" Jin asked. "Yes."

The Ram should have realized destroying Spindrift wouldn't make them cower in fear. They were beaten down, yes, but they were stronger now. There was nothing more dangerous than those with nothing left to lose.

"It will still be risky. We want the Ram to arrive after the press so we can get the first word in, but if the Ram does show up earlier, they might not know whom to believe. I want everyone looking their best," Arthie added, wiggling a finger through one of the tears in the lapel of her jacket. "I won't have anyone thinking any less of us."

"Will going to the press make a difference though?" Jin asked. "The people don't care about vampires, let alone them being abused and weaponized."

"The people might not care for vampires, true," Arthie conceded. "But suffering shouldn't be a secret, and the people will always fear the unknown. Right now, our focus is on the Wolf of White Roaring attack that led to the Ram's rise to power. We won't have proof, but if the press catches the monarch by surprise, they'll discern the rest and there will be an uproar."

"To what end?" Matteo asked. "Do you intend to usurp the usurper?"

Only now did Jin realize they were truly in way over their heads.

Arthie pursed her lips. "If that's what it takes to make sure the Ram doesn't threaten us ever again."

Jin was aware the Council that sat beneath the Ram would just appoint a new mask, as Ettenia always did, but that was a problem for the future. The Ram loathed Spindrift and vampires far too much. Ettenia might not have been the best of empires, but the Ram was far too biased.

"I think it'll work," Penn said, looking proud of them.

Jin nodded. "They'll appoint a new mask soon enough."

"Or maybe Arthie here can take the reins," Matteo teased.

"Nope. I'll be busy rebuilding Spindrift," she scoffed. "Why save the world when you can have tea?"

51

FLICK

When Flick placed her order at the family tailor for a gown, she had to shell out more than was necessary to keep the woman's mouth shut about it. She didn't need all of high society talking.

"My sweetie, it is no good to wander without a chaperone. Especially in this day and age," the woman was saying, setting aside Flick's fabric of choice. It was different from what she usually preferred, and it gave Flick a little thrill every time she thought of it. "You should have come with your mother last week!"

Flick bid her farewell and left before she could hear any more. Of course her mother was having a new wardrobe made for herself while Flick was out there worrying about a stake through the heart.

She sighed. Now she was just becoming bitter.

Flick stopped and doubled back, peering into the window of Hira House, one of the only Jeevani-owned dressmakers in White Roaring. The trio of mannequins on the dais inside the window was wrapped in colorful swaths of cloth, the ends of them elegantly draped over their right shoulders. Saris, Flick believed they were called. Behind the one in sapphire blue, a girl in a tailored suit was placing an order, baker boy hat pulled over her mauve hair.

The woman at the counter smiled, and Arthie, in proper Arthie fashion, didn't smile back as she set her payment on the worn wood and made to leave. Flick hurried away, tucking into one of the alleys as Arthie leisurely made off in the opposite direction.

And Flick began her walk to Admiral Grove once more.

After what Lady Linden had done to her, she deserved to face the same consequence as the Ram: bombarded with questions about her actions.

Flick didn't expect to return to the Linden Estate so soon, and she certainly didn't expect to feel so indifferent about standing at her mother's doorstep again. She was emboldened by the reminder that she wasn't alone anymore.

She felt bad knowing Arthie and Jin had lost something dear to them while she was delighted at what she had gained: a family. As much a family as the Casimirs could be. One day she was an outsider, the next, she was simply included in every meeting, adding to every conversation, and joining every trip.

"Miss Felicity," the maid said at the door, eyes wide as saucers. Flick said hello. Hushed voices sounded inside, and she heard the housekeeper's snicker. "Lady Linden said I'm not to allow you inside again."

She told herself not to be surprised, but it still hurt. "That doesn't seem fair."

The maid looked away. "No, it doesn't. She did say that if you insisted, I could let you in, though I don't think I'm supposed to tell you that."

Odd, Flick thought. She dropped her hand into her pocket for the comfort of her lighter before she remembered she'd left it on her mother's desk.

She didn't need it anymore, she told herself.

Pacify the people to keep them in check, and no one notices you furthering your own agenda.

Arthie's words had been about the Ram, but they had made Flick scrutinize each of her mother's actions in a new light. They had meals together so Lady Linden could monitor how much Flick ate, dress fittings together so Lady Linden could be in control of how Flick dressed. She appeased Flick by taking her on outings that were convenient, when she was heading out for something anyway. Even that very first time Flick had visited Spindrift—she now remembered they went because her mother was to have a meeting with someone, not because she had wanted to take Flick.

It was funny, Flick thought, how something utterly unrelated could uncover a side of her past that she had never noticed herself. Or perhaps it was because she had been removed from the confines of a life she had deemed normal that she could finally see it for what it truly was.

Her punishment hadn't even been a punishment at all. It was what it always had been—Lady Linden doing what was best for her reputation, and in the case of Flick, it meant hiding her away.

"Well, I'll only be in for a little while," Flick said. "And I appreciate you telling me."

The girl paused. "I've missed you, Miss Felicity. The house hasn't been as warm without you."

Flick didn't feel so warm anymore. She was naive before, shielded and sheltered. Her mother had kept her in a cage, and Flick had extended her arms as far as she could every time she forged, until Jin had picked the lock and let her out.

Her mother was in her office again, and Flick knocked, because she wasn't so angry this time. Lady Linden was at her desk. She contained her surprise quickly.

"Felicity. You have some nerve returning after the way you spoke to me."

"I only spoke, Mother," Flick said, which was the problem, she supposed. "I said nothing untoward, or even disrespectful."

Her mother started reaching for the bell, and Flick had to bite her tongue against the panic that flared. She kept her voice calm, her words slow.

"Before you call to have me removed, you must know that all I wanted was to give you the front page again. This time, a praiseworthy one. I wanted to repair the damage you believed I'd done. I wanted your forgiveness so that you could love me again. I see now how foolish I'd been."

Lady Linden had the decency to look away. She felt bad, Flick realized.

No, came Arthie's voice in her head, *look closely*.

Flick did. Her mother's shoulders were tight, rigid. She was unrelaxed, almost as if she was on guard. Almost . . . afraid of what Flick might do.

"Whatever you heard about the vampires, Felicity, you must know there's more to that story," her mother said, more tentative than sure of herself. She was testing the waters. Testing *her*.

It was a ploy. She was trying to get her to divulge what she knew. Flick wouldn't fall for any of it. This was her mother. She knew exactly how to guide Flick in whichever direction she pleased like she was a puppet.

"And no, I'm not trying to get you to tell me what you saw or heard, I'm telling you that I was forced into dealings I'm not proud of."

Her mother spoke as if she wasn't Lady Linden herself, as if she had no sway or control over her actions.

"All this distance between us?" her mother continued. "It's because I was busy trying to make things right, trying to repair the extensive damage that was done to our company."

But they'd begun drifting apart years ago. Flick started to say as much, to counter her, but then she realized that her mother was right. The distance between them had only worsened recently, and it was simply chance that it coincided with the signet ring scandal. It had nothing to do with what Flick had done.

Her mother's hard mask fractured before she pulled it back on again, and in those seconds, Flick saw penitence. Flick understood it deeply, and that almost made her feel bad.

"The Ram used me," her mother whispered, "and it took you away from me."

That was true remorse. It made Flick waver. When Lady Linden looked up, her bright blue eyes were wet with unshed tears. She gave Flick a smile, and it reminded her of when they'd have tea and biscuits in the nook by the window. It reminded her of their walks in the garden.

Flick swallowed, suddenly wishing she hadn't come.

She looked at the envelope in her hand for a moment before she held it out. "Here."

"What is this?" Lady Linden asked.

It was the address to the Athereum's meeting hall, along with a date and time.

"The coveted front page," Flick said. "A way to make things right."

Flick had begun to question herself from the moment the Linden Estate door had closed behind her. Now, back at the Athereum, as she arranged her hair and swiped perfume at her neck, a little bit of sunshine to carry her through the long night ahead, worry wrapped around her shoulders like a coat.

It was the right thing to do, she told herself.

She pulled the gown over her shoulders, with all its folds and layers still weighing lighter than her heart, and soon realized she had never dressed herself for an event before. And after a good deal of time spent trying to tug the laces on her own, she gave up.

She needed help, and the vampires of the Athereum were the last people she'd go to. Flick snatched up her satin gloves and, holding the dress against her chest, she opened the door to find Arthie just about to knock.

Flick almost didn't recognize her.

Arthie Casimir was wearing a dress. The simplest way to describe her wrapped in a length of scarlet was *regal. Beautiful.* She wore a sari made of yards of silk edged in gunmetal silver, wound around and around, covering every inch of her skin except for the sharp contrast of her collarbone and the bold hue of her blouse until it came to a brazen drape over her shoulder. She wore no baker boy cap. Her mauve hair had been teased into voluminous curls framing the dark depths of her eyes.

No, *beautiful* wasn't quite the word to describe her allure. She was cutthroat and deadly, the way a rose appeared entirely different when you saw its thorns.

"I was hoping to find you," Flick said breathlessly as Arthie came inside. The *hush hush* of the fabric echoed her steps. "Can you help me with these laces? In hindsight, I should have thought twice before ordering a dress I couldn't wear on my own, now that I don't have maids."

Flick turned without waiting for Arthie's answer, and it was easier to breathe without the weight of the other girl's gaze on her.

"Thank you," Flick said.

"Did everything go as planned?" Arthie asked, tugging and knotting with deft fingers.

Flick nodded. "I handed her the envelope. I just wish . . . I don't know."

"But you do know. Did you speak to her, as I said you should?"

"Yes," Flick said, and as grateful as she was to Arthie for telling her to prod and pry and pay attention to her mother's manipulations, she was still disappointed by it all. A part of her wanted to return to being oblivious. "I think I did better today than I did the first time. Before we lost Spindrift. And I—"

"Don't ramble," Arthie said, watching her.

Flick sighed.

"She truly did sound remorseful," she tried to reason.

"Did she really though? You're lost, Felicity," Arthie said gently, adjusting Flick's curls with a tender hand. "And no one can find your way but yourself."

52

ARTHIE

Arthie had known from the moment Flick stepped inside Spindrift that the girl was eager to orchestrate a plan of her own. It wasn't difficult to figure out what that plan was, not when Arthie was privy to Flick's circumstance. Arthie hadn't tried to discourage it, no; she'd done the opposite, bringing up her mother often, dropping hints to remind Flick of whatever plan she had concocted—keeping the door open for whenever Arthie needed quick access to the head of the East Jeevant Company.

Like she did now.

Slowly but surely, Flick grew more and more jaded, but that was the cost of the truth.

"I am sorry for dragging you into a fight that isn't yours."

Arthie turned to find Penn in the doorway. It was the Ram's fault though. All of this was the Ram's fault, and she didn't even know who the Ram was. But until she put a face to the one behind it all, the shadowy figure she met in the carriage would be the one she bloodied in her thoughts.

"Red suits you, little lion," Penn said, and she warmed at the compliment.

It felt fitting, taking down the Ram in a red sari. The same red as her mother's death shroud.

"I heard about what happened between you and the high captain," he said. "Matteo told me."

"Of course he did," she said, unsurprised.

"You're different, Arthie. Half vampire, half human. When a person is drained of blood, they die. And if they're turned into a vampire in those precious seconds before the brain and heart cease to function, they're subdued. Hungry, yes, but too weak to do a thing. You were still very much alive when you were turned, weren't you? You had the means to act upon that hunger, an amplified hunger, almost hungrier for the life you had just left than for sustenance. You barely even feasted as much as massacred."

He reached for her hand. "But that part of your life is over."

"Yet I spent the last ten years afraid I would do it again," she said quietly.

She spent half her life fearing herself, fearing what she was capable of, peering into the dark alleys of White Roaring and looking for others like her. It was why she'd opened the bloodhouse, wasn't it? So that a vampire like her wouldn't have to brutalize the streets but could pay to drink from a cup.

"You and Matteo have more in common than you might think," Penn said.

Arthie laughed at that. "Have you *seen* the man?"

Penn chuckled and then turned pensive. "I think often of the day you lifted your pistol from White Roaring Square. The girl who was doomed to greatness."

The choice of his words was not lost on her. This was a burden and not a blessing. She suffered more than she reaped.

"When all this is over," he said, locking his gaze on hers, "we can return to Imperial Square. You and me. Your crew. Make it your new Spindrift."

He gathered both her hands and held her close, pressing a kiss to the top of her hair. She lingered there a beat, allowing herself to feel small, to feel sheltered in his large body, allowing herself to feel her youth in the way White Roaring didn't allow.

He spoke of the same comfort and safety he'd promised a decade ago, but Arthie knew how such things ended, even if she still longed for them.

The voices in Penn's office fell silent when she entered. Flick wasn't here. Arthie looked at Jin first, because that was easiest.

"Oh, Arthie. I can't say I've ever seen you in a dress before," Jin said. "You look beautiful."

Arthie bared her teeth. "How many of your teeth would you like to keep? Two or four?"

Jin laughed, and she could almost imagine this to be Spindrift, slick counters behind him, the smell of tea warming the room.

"Most certainly Arthie under there." He started for the entrance, patting the top of her head with something like pride. "I should get ready too." He gave Matteo a look. "Behave, Andoni. Or we'll have some words."

"Is everything in order?" she asked.

Matteo blinked at her as if he hadn't heard a word she'd said.

Arthie scowled. "I don't take well to being stared at. I believe I'm called *exotic* in your tongue, if you didn't know."

"My tongue is quite capable, darling," Matteo assured her. Something prickled in Arthie's chest. "And I'm more than happy to demonstrate."

He leaned down, green eyes ablaze as they dropped to the exposed stretch of her collarbone. He worked his jaw, and she caught a peek of his tongue between his parted lips.

"You are utterly dazzling, Arthie. Exquisite. A sight to behold because of that brilliant brain of yours."

It was rare to hear praise for her intellect. It was only ever treated as something that was overgrown to the point of recklessness; she was always told she was too cunning, too corrupt.

Never brilliant.

He gave her one last look, adjusted the fold of the sari over her shoulder while searing her bare skin with liquid fire, and left.

53

JIN

Jin thought Penn had gone above and beyond to host the press at the Athereum's meeting hall. Waiters in tailcoats glided about with trays, narrow flutes catching the light of the dazzling chandeliers high above. The gloss of the floors was complemented by the richly patterned rugs from a desert far, far away, and the decor that decked the place was dark and decadent.

He thought he heard a sound and turned toward the shadows, umbrella ready.

"It's me."

Jin's heart leaped at her voice. "The dark is no place for a dove."

"What if I don't want to be a dove?"

Flick moved into a wash of light. Her curls framed the soft beauty of her face, several ringlets draped over her brow. A knot lodged in his throat. "What are you wearing?"

"What are *you* wearing?" she sputtered back, just as surprised.

"You said I dress like someone's dead!" he exclaimed.

"You said I dress like a flag!" she said at the same time.

The silence gripped them.

She looked glorious, clad in crushed velvet in the deepest, darkest emerald. It began with a tight collar around her throat, flaring before a cinched waist where the wide folds of the skirt began. It held her the way she ought to be held, tightly, fiercely. Beautifully. He wanted to sweep forward and do the same. He wanted to bury his nose into her hair and inhale the sunshine of her spirit.

"Lilac," she said stiffly. She'd tugged gloves to just above her elbows, leaving inches of bare skin to taunt him. "You went with lilac."

The color of your beret, he wanted to say, but it sounded stupid of him now, even if it had seemed like a good idea when he was ordering the jacket at the tailor. He wore it unbuttoned over a crisp white shirt, his black-bordered kerchief tucked into the breast pocket, the ensemble completed by cream trousers.

There was a guardedness in Flick's gaze, worry and concern rampant. Her mother would be here, Arthie had said.

"It's going to be all right," Jin said.

"Is it easier to have no heartbeat?" she asked softly. "To feel nothing at all?"

He didn't want her to think of her mother and the horrible things Lady Linden had done. He didn't want Flick to rethink handing her the envelope.

"We're alone in a dark corridor," Jin said, tilting his head toward her, "and you wish to philosophize?"

For the rest of his days, he would recall the way her sunflower eyes went ink black at his words.

"No," she whispered, and surged toward him, backing him to the wall of the alcove and stealing the air from his lungs.

He trailed his fingers up the smooth shine of her gloves. Her breath caught, hooded gaze following the movement and sending a spike through his blood.

And then, with a sweet little sound, she rose up and kissed him. Softly, gently. Driving him mad. He pulled away with a *tsk*, his voice a low scrape of want. "Let me show you how it's done, love."

He cupped her face between his hands and slanted his lips to hers.

She gasped into his mouth, shuddering against him before she matched his push with her pull, pressing the length of her body against his, drawing a sound out of his throat, drowning him in that meadow of wildflowers and sunlight.

"Flick," he whispered, half groan, half prayer.

She pulled back slightly, staring up at him with something like wonder and delight. "Say it again."

He crooked a lazy grin. "Really, Felicit—"

"*No.* Not the name she gave me. The name I made for myself."

And he was so stunned by the force of her words, by the fervor of her spirit, that he did.

"Flick." He pressed a kiss to the bridge of her nose, where freckles fanned like stars in the night.

"Flick." He pressed another to the edge of her mouth, cherishing the sound of her irritation.

"Flick."

He coaxed her mouth apart, and her breath caught when he bit down on her lower lip. Her arms settled to his shoulders, hands reaching for his hair, threading into the strands and pulling him tighter.

He tasted hope in her kiss. Possibility. Jin felt good about tonight, and not only because he was finally kissing Felicity Linden.

The clock tower struck nine. They pulled apart, breathless and dazed.

It was time.

54

FLICK

Flick rubbed the back of her hand across her swollen lips. She buzzed from head to toe, and her skin felt tight. Some sort of adrenaline roared through her, akin to the way she felt when he'd spoken her name. *The name I made for myself.* The name she had chosen after she'd left her home behind. The name that fit her the way the grit and grime of White Roaring did.

When Jin's breath skated her neck, she hadn't been thinking of the consequences; she wasn't worried about what her mother or anyone else might think. Jin had never expected her to be more than what she was.

She didn't know if her mother truly did seek to repair her name or if she was still in league with the Ram, but what Flick did know was that she was done with Lady Linden. Done vying for a love that didn't exist.

Arthie was right. She had been lost, but she had finally found her way. She might be stumbling along it right now because she had never been kissed before, and she certainly hadn't thought she'd ever kiss Jin Casimir, but she had found it nonetheless.

The press was slowly crowding the hall. Matteo had gathered quite the extensive list. Flick recognized badges from almost every one of the papers in White Roaring, despite the late hour.

"I don't think I've ever seen so many news folk in one place before," Jin commented, his voice slightly hoarse. It gave Flick a little thrill, even if she couldn't look at him without imagining his mouth on hers. *Focus.* They had a job to do, and once the Ram arrived—as well as her mother—they needed to be on full alert.

Flick made the rounds as Arthie had instructed, picking up bits of conversation as she passed.

"What is this damning document we've been promised?"

"I didn't know Arthie Casimir was involved. This could be scandalous."

"Are we even to believe anything we hear?"

Flick's heart sped up anytime she saw the ledger in Arthie's hands. In many ways, that violet-ribboned book made Arthie the most powerful person in Ettenia, because with it, she controlled the Ram. But it was their one piece of evidence, their one and only recourse in this country that had taken so much from them.

She stopped to pick up a glass of water, hoping that would settle her nerves a bit. When she set her glass down, something brushed against her leg, featherlight like an insect that might have slipped inside the hall.

"Oh, you're no fly, are you?" she crooned.

It was Laith's kitten, fluffy tail swishing back and forth like a duster, that motor of a purr starting up again when Flick crouched.

"We really ought to give you a name. Something like Snowflake or Alabaster." Those were white, but neither sounded like a name fit for a kitten. She'd never had a pet before. "Cloud, maybe? You are very floofy. Or Snow or even Opal for how regal you are."

Stop distracting yourself, Flick chided. She looked around the hall. If the kitten was here, Laith was bound to be close. Strange. Arthie had made it seem as if she had severed ties with the high captain. Had she changed her mind and invited him here?

Flick picked up the kitten and took her over to where Jin was waiting by one of the round tables piled high with refreshments, where they were to be stationed. He seemed just as confused by the sight of the kitten as she was.

Arthie snapped her pocket watch closed, drawing Flick and Jin's attention. She nodded. At a poised knock, Matteo pulled open the double doors at the end of the hall, and Flick felt each beat of her heart like a smithy's hammer in her ears.

Jin reached for her hand and squeezed. "Stick to the plan. No matter what happens, we protect the ledger."

Flick nodded. The kitten wriggled free and darted under the tablecloth to hide. Flick wished she could join her.

The Ram swept into the hall, wearing a cloak as deeply blue as the sea. The guests exclaimed in surprise, voices stirring to a hum. Every bulb in the chandelier lit a different facet of that nefarious mask, horns curling from the antique bronze like those of the devil.

Only the Ram's eyes were visible, bright and cerulean.

Flick's heart stopped. She could barely gasp. She stumbled back. Jin was asking her what was wrong, but she couldn't hear him. The room faded, the buzz of the press's excited voices winnowing away.

And Flick had a single, harrowing thought: She always did think her mother had remarkable eyes.

55

ARTHIE

In the hushed silence of the Ram's entrance, Arthie heard Flick's gasp and then the single word she whispered, ringing as loud as the crack of a whip. *Mother.* It took Arthie a moment to understand that Flick wasn't looking at her mother, but the Ram.

Lady Linden was the Ram.

That was when Arthie knew her plan had gone horribly wrong. Because the Ram didn't know about the press. Lady Linden did.

The Ram was supposed to be ambushed, but Lady Linden knew what was really going to happen. They had no element of surprise on their side. They'd told her exactly what they'd be doing here, and she had come prepared. The Ram knew they had learned the truth about the ledger and the vampires since Flick had first visited her mother.

Arthie's plan had failed.

"Do not blame yourself. There's still nothing she can do," Penn said at Arthie's side. "The press will report any and all of it."

This wasn't a frightened official or some flustered lord. This was the Ram. Arthie shook her head. "Not if they're dead."

There were four sets of doors in the Athereum's meeting hall. Four escape points.

"Get to the doors!" she yelled over the hushed whispers. "Everyone out!"

But she should have known it was futile. This was the Ram—not only the ruler of Ettenia, but the embodiment of everything Arthie hated. She was head of the East Jeevant Company that had raided her homeland, the woman who had taken her humanity, the tyrant who had struck the match that destroyed Spindrift.

"Get ready," Arthie told Jin and the others.

The doors flung open before anyone could reach them. Men flooded inside, dressed from head to toe in black, masks pulled over their faces. They weren't from the Horned Guard, but they were armed. To the teeth.

The Athereum hall, with its luxurious decadence, erupted in outright chaos.

Knives flashed in the brilliant light of the chandeliers. People screamed, fell. Blood splattered and pooled on the alabaster tiles. It was a massacre.

"The Ram doesn't intend for anyone to leave the hall alive," Arthie shouted.

Matteo looked sick to his stomach, but stepped in to defend a trio of women, narrowly missing a machete that swung straight for his arm. Jin was using his umbrella off to her right, and to her left, Penn was lifting his arms, and it took Arthie a moment to realize: his power.

The Ram's men screamed, some trying to fling away invisible parasites, others curling into balls. Arthie had known Penn was powerful, but seeing the way he brought those men to their knees with nothing but a wave of his hands made her feel a little afraid herself.

She needed to help them. She spotted Flick in the fray and shoved the ledger into her hands. "Protect it." Flick was barely breathing. "Flick! Now is not the time. We've come this far—*you've* come this far."

"Right, yes," Flick whispered. She held it tight.

Arthie ran and helped someone to their feet. She picked up a waiter's tray and slammed it against one of the Ram's men, plucking his knife and stabbing him through the throat. He fell with a gurgle. There were too many fallen reporters, but with Penn's help, they could turn this around.

"You see, Arthie?" a voice asked from behind her.

Arthie felt the blood in her veins go cold.

Laith.

"People in power will never care for those like us." He sounded detached. Far-off. He spoke of the Ram killing her own people. He spoke of the hilya the Ram had promised him. The one he was inching toward Arthie to steal.

"No," she said, taking a step back, "they don't. We established as much."

She took another step back. There was too much happening at once. Too many foes and too little time.

"Forgive me," he whispered, and then he lunged too quickly for her to move out of the way. He snatched the pistol out of the folds of her sari, and took aim.

At her.

They stared at each other, the two of them against the world. Abandoned souls bound by the restless anger in their veins.

"Are you going to kill me?" she asked.

He hesitated, giving her the second she needed, and she leaped at him, the end of her sari a whisper against her throat. They collided, grappled for the pistol. His hands brushed hers, and her focus shifted. They were back in that room, his lips on hers. Her fangs were sinking into his neck, his hand gripping her thigh.

Arthie rammed her shoulder into his chest, but he was bigger, and she was still in shock.

He threw her off him and as Arthie stared down the barrel of the gun, she thought, perhaps, that Laith might not shoot her. She saw it on his face: They were back at that abandoned warehouse again, where she had saved his life before he had saved hers.

But then, around her, the fighting and screams began anew. The men weren't curling up in pain anymore. Penn was there, *here*, shielding her and going for Laith's throat in the same instant.

56

JIN

Jin thought he heard a gunshot. He knew the sound of that pistol and felt a terrible sinking, wrenching, *knowing*. Calibore. Arthie. His other half in this world of destruction. She would never, *ever* fire it herself. Not when they knew what it was capable of.

He ran for her, stumbling over pools of blood and wayward limbs, journals soaked red and shining pens. He pushed past a pair of the Ram's men, swerving away from their attacks, and finally spotted the shimmer of Arthie's sari in the fray.

Don't die, don't die, don't die. He could lose Spindrift a thousand times, but he could never lose his sister.

Jin stopped.

The Ram stood in his path, and Jin knew with sinking clarity that his end was near. She cocked a revolver, small and dainty, and fired.

57

ARTHIE

Arthie was on her knees, the floor's cold seeping through the thin silk of her sari. Around her, the carnage continued. Penn's head was in her lap. There was a bullet hole right above his left breast pocket, for Calibore was no ordinary pistol. Still, Penn did not bleed, he did not shake, he did not gasp out a breath.

She had brought death to his doorstep, and he was looking up at her as if she'd saved him. His eyes were full of love, and Arthie, after all she had done, loathed herself a little more because of it.

"Do not mourn. I lived an eternity and more on this earth."

"We can fix this," she said, like a child, like a fool. "We can be a family together. Like you promised."

For years after running away from his home, she wondered what it would have been like if she had stayed. Would she have met Jin? Would she have made good on her anger and opened Spindrift?

She would have had a father. A family.

"Family isn't who we live with but those we would die for."

Penn lifted his hand to her hair, and Arthie couldn't understand how someone so big, so powerful, so ancient could do this. *Die.* Then he curled her trembling hand into a fist and tucked it against his cold, unbeating heart.

"Stay brave, little lion."

She didn't want to be brave. She didn't want to keep fighting. The damask curtains fluttered in Laith's wake, a purple hyacinth bright in the fray.

I'm sorry, the flower meant.

Arthie threw herself to her feet just as Flick screamed.

58

JIN

The Ram's bullet struck his heart. Jin stumbled. Fell. One knee hit the cold, hard floor, then the other.

He had long wondered what death would feel like. He had lived surrounded by it. Weekends in the morgue with his parents and their research, those harrowing minutes when he'd looked for them in their burning house, then life with the girl who'd pulled him out of the rubble.

Jin didn't know if Arthie was bleeding out somewhere in this hall, just like he was. He didn't know if she was aware of how much he appreciated her. Loved her.

He blinked groggily, because his eyelids weighed more than a barrel of gunpowder. He saw the Ram's men fall one by one at the hands of vampires he didn't know, joining the reporters who had come here for the truth, and then he saw the Ram herself inching away, disappearing before anyone could stop her.

Matteo's shadow fell over him. "Jin. It's fatal. Let me—"

Jin knew what he was going to suggest. What he had to offer. He thought he nodded, but then he was alone again and another pair of footsteps skidded toward him. Flick. She wasn't crying for him, was she? She didn't like him *that* much. She had kissed him. Beautifully. Jin found himself laughing, it made the pain sharper, colder. He liked it. At least he was going to die happy.

"Jin," she was saying. Over and over.

And then she was moving aside. In her place was the girl who had stepped between him and death's scythe again and again and again. She was alive. Of course she was alive. She was Arthie Casimir. She never needed saving.

"At last," he murmured. He still had so much more to do—find his parents, rebuild Spindrift, love a girl who had sunshine curls and pastel berets—but he knew Arthie would track them down and do the tearoom justice. And Flick would find someone else to love her.

"No," Arthie said fiercely, thickly, but not even she could stop this. "No, Jin. Look sharp."

Jin felt his eyes flutter shut. He heard voices shouting, arguing, fading away. *He* was fading away. Then he felt a pain unlike any other, as if the life was being sucked out of him, as if he was being drained, the blood leaving his body. He thought he was screaming, but he couldn't tell.

And then something pressed against his lips, and someone pinched his nose, forcing him to drag a broken breath through his mouth. Metal. Metal flooded his tongue in liquid form. Sweet and tangy and sharp. *Blood.*

And then a whisper.

"Live," said death in his ear. "For me."

Jin's eyes flew open to a halo of mauve, a pair of demon eyes. Arthie. There was something wrong with her.

There were fangs in her mouth. There was blood in his.

And as fire bled through his veins, he thought, impossibly, of coconut. Because that was how denial worked: The brain refused to believe the truth in front of it and tucked it away instead.

Jin remembered it now, like a shock. Hidden behind the lavender aster bushes in the front lawn of the Siwang Residence as the last of his life went up in flames, an eleven-year-old Jin handed Arthie a coconut. Her eyes took on a faraway look when she saw it, and then she seemed sad.

He didn't know her well enough to know that she'd come from the same country as this coconut; he thought she simply didn't know how to open it.

And if coconuts made people happy, he owed it to her to make her happy, didn't he? He rose on shaky legs and found the gardener's tools, cracking open the coconut the way Ceylani coconuts ought to be cracked—divots hacked into the top, not in half like the fibrous brown ones—and poured it into Arthie's dirty cup. "Drink."

She stared at him, wanting to say something. If only he'd known she wasn't sad—she was a vampire. If only he'd known she was afraid to drink because she thought vampires only drank blood.

"Drink," he insisted, rattling the coconut to show her that there was more inside.

Her gaze dropped to the vein jumping at his throat, but she took a sip. She blinked down at the cup immediately and took another sip. Then another. Then she tipped the cup upside down until the very last drop disappeared in her throat.

Jin hadn't thought anyone could move so quickly. Then again, he didn't know what she was. He didn't know he was changing her life by leading her through the unburned side of the kitchen to a barrel full of the same green coconuts. He didn't realize it wasn't because of her love for them that she used her ingenuity to create an icebox to preserve as many of his father's coconuts as they could, until years later when she found her footing and began importing them herself.

For Spindrift, she would say. *For myself*, she never admitted.

"I believe a vampire can subsist on coconut," his father had once said.

"And not blood?" Jin had asked, eyes wide. That explained the plethora of coconuts scattered in his father's study, some cracked open, half-full glasses littering the room.

There was one such glass on the dinner table. It was murky with little milk-white slivers floating about. Jin's father took a sip. "Only the Ceylani coconut seems to do the trick, though they need to have some blood in them for it to work."

"Are you a vampire then, Pa?"

"I think your mother would have sent me back to the grave already, lad," he replied with a laugh, and gave Jin some to try. It was sweet, and somehow made him feel lighter, happier. "Good, isn't it? In addition to making excellent weapons, coconuts make you happy."

How could he have been so blind? It wasn't tea she lived for, but the coconut. He'd only ever seen her drinking coconut water happily—rarely anything else. When she'd insisted on keeping a batch in reserve. When she'd always ask after the status of its shipments more than that of the tea.

She had never told him a word.

You were right, Father, Jin thought now. *Vampires* can *subsist on coconut.*

"Wake up," came a voice, dragging him from the gallows, from that curtain of forever black. "Jin, wake up."

His eyes fluttered open, and he drew away with a hiss. Everything was too bright, too white. And the hunger—good grief, he was hungry. Starved. Ravenous. Hadn't he just eaten? He slid his tongue along his teeth, a sinking, harrowing feeling in his stomach.

Fangs. He had fangs. That hunger wasn't for food, but blood.

Arthie sat back on her heels, the folds of her sari in disarray. Her relief was bare on her face, but she didn't smile because she knew him.

She knew he was not happy with the secrets she'd kept. She looked smaller, frailer. Broken. She stumbled and righted herself. He didn't know what to say, and so he watched as Arthie threw the drape of her sari back over her shoulder, a fan of red and crimson and blood, and then she was gone.

59

ARTHIE

Arthie liked to think that she had a heart made of ice, but ice was like glass—one fall and it shattered. She didn't want to leave Jin, not now, but she had to move. She paused to look at Penn one last time. The other vampires stayed away. How could they not, when they'd seen the abomination of a weapon that had rendered Penn dead within moments? She took his Athereum marker and the revolver from his pocket. It was gold, as dignified as he was.

And then she ran, the doors of the Athereum's meeting hall thudding closed behind her.

She knew what she looked like to anyone who saw her on the street: A girl racing through the dark, a sari slipping from her shoulder, blood-soaked hands gripping a gun, eyes wild as the night had been.

But Nimble Street wasn't far from here.

When she tried the door to Laith's apartment, she wasn't surprised to find it unlocked. He was waiting for her in his armchair, the one she'd been seated in on the night they traded secrets.

They had always been destined for this moment.

"I told you to leave," she said. "I warned you."

"I didn't know what it was capable of," he said, still holding

Calibore. She saw the shock in his eyes. She believed him, but that wouldn't bring Penn back. That wouldn't undo what had happened.

Laith was bleeding from his neck in the same place she had kissed him. If she closed her eyes, they were both on their knees, the truth of what she was bared before him.

He laughed and looked down at the pistol.

"You understand, don't you?" he asked. "We're the same, you and I."

He sounded exactly as he always did, the silken thrum of his voice low and lovely.

"We will never be the same," she bit out. "You're so deluded by your own pride and righteousness that you never stopped to wonder if you truly were right."

"Are you saying the king didn't send my sister to her death?"

"Did it ever occur to you that *you* might be the reason she died?" Arthie asked.

Murder darkened his gaze. She recognized that limitlessness brought on by vengeance. She knew it because it lived in her bones. It was why she was drawn to him, why she'd let him so close to the cage of her heart.

But she *was* like him, and in that, she saw her flaw. She saw herself mired in a past that wasn't driving her forward but holding her back.

She had thought herself feral, when he was the animal.

"You joined that voyage when you were ill, when you knew she would be in close contact with you, when you knew that medical care would be lacking on a ship that was likely one of the first to leave Arawiya in a long time," Arthie said. "You made her sick. She would have been fine if you had seen her potential, rather than lying to yourself that she needed saving."

Get behind me. Those words had troubled her since he'd spoken them in the Athereum. She had thought it was because he had shown care for her when she was moments from betraying him, but that wasn't it.

He had always doubted her.

He had tried to teach her how to leap across the sky. He had tried to put her behind him. He had all but forced her to drink from him when she had made her reluctance known.

"Even that kitten of yours. You saw her toying with a snake, not cowering from one, but thought she needed saving too."

"Do not try to make assumptions about my existence," Laith said coldly. He cocked Calibore.

She drew Penn's gold revolver. "Oh, these aren't assumptions, saint. Now put that down."

He raised his arm. "I truly did grow fond of you, Arthie."

"Says the pistol aimed at my heart," she replied, brushing her thumb along the hammer of the revolver. She hadn't checked to see how many bullets were in its cylinder. She'd never fired one before, but she'd seen Jin use his enough times to know how it worked. "You're ludicrous."

He smiled that smile full of secrets. "You would know."

A shot rang out.

Laith fell back into the armchair, surprise gasping out of him. Blood bloomed in the shimmering white of his robes, petals unfurling in crimson. It called to her, but Arthie didn't feel right. She was numb and cold. Empty. He had killed, and she had done the same.

No, she felt worse than that.

The front of her sari was wet.

Arthie looked down. Blood dripped onto the floorboards by her feet. The gold revolver fell. Pain started pulsing through her. There was a hole in her heart. The blood she had taken from him spilled from her chest, and she wanted, impossibly, to laugh at the irony of it all.

And then Arthie Casimir collapsed.

60

THE WOLF

The Wolf of White Roaring knew what the world saw when they looked at Arthie Casimir: driftwood washed up on a faraway land, lone and assuming. They couldn't have been more wrong.

She was forged of shrapnel words and gunmetal bones. An enigma wrapped in tailored armor and violet-gray curls. She was color in his world that had begun to bleed black and white. Half vampire, half human, more like he once was than any other soul to have crossed his path.

The Ram had nearly taken her from him, just as the Ram had taken everything else.

He found her bleeding in an apartment on Nimble Street.

"She struck the match," she whispered, an oath in her voice as death came for her, swift as a tempest. He should never have left her alone.

"Now we'll burn her to the ground," he swore.

Then the Wolf of White Roaring scooped her into his arms and took her away.

ACKNOWLEDGMENTS

Just as Spindrift would not exist without its crew, the same is true for *A Tempest of Tea*. It isn't my debut, but it was still a collection of firsts. Arthie and Co. stood by my side as I went from re-entering the query trenches to getting married and moving across the country, but through it all, there were more constants that this story could not have happened without. And so, a thank-you is in order.

To Asma and Azraa, the best of sisters. For standing by my side through some of the darkest times. For the long bouts of daydreaming, helping me paint the landscape that soon became White Roaring, tossing *what if*s and *how about*s back and forth, plotting and dismantling until we had a graveyard of discarded words along the way.

To Cayce, roohi. If I begin to tell the world how I feel about you, I may never stop, but here is my attempt to be concise: Every day with you is a joy, and this book couldn't have reached the finish line without you cheering me on. Thank you for fueling me with lattes, for reading my words and cherishing them, but most importantly, for showing this jaded soul that true love isn't a fantasy that only exists in books.

To my parents, for guiding me and always giving me the push I needed. To my grandfather, who would have loved this book and the author I became.

To my incredible agent, Josh Adams, whose patience and support remains unparalleled. You are the ally I didn't know I could have in the publishing world. A true champion. To Tracey Adams, Anna Munger, and the rest of the Adams Literary team: It is an honor to be a part of the family.

To my editor, Janine O'Malley, equally as patient. For challenging me and believing in me even when I don't. For always being a quick text message away. I've called you my publishing mom before, and it remains true today.

To Melissa Warten, there to make this story stronger in the beginning and there at the end. To the loveliest of friends cheering me on: Joan He, the best goat who isn't actually a goat; Kelly Andrew, my favorite agent sister; Huda Fahmy, who understood my torment; and Joanna Hathaway, sweet soul.

To my amazing publicists Chantal Gersch and Samantha Sacks, for opening the door to many new readers. To Melissa Zar and Leigh Ann Higgins, marketing magicians. To Kat Kopit and Helen Seachrist for polishing my pages to a shine, and the copyeditors who scoured through every word. To Molly Ellis and Allison Verost, for making Macmillan feel like a home. To Aurora Parlagreco, designer extraordinaire who *gets* it.

Special thanks to Jon Yaged, Jen Besser, Ally Demeter, Gaby Salpeter, Asia Harden, and the rest of the team at Macmillan. To Anissa de Gomery and Korrina Ede, for your support, always. To Cate Augustin and Sarah Plows, for brewing up magic across the pond. To Virginia Allyn, for the gorgeous map once again, and Valentina Remenar for the astounding cover. To the Zumra Discord and the many fans who have been waiting, oh so patiently, since we left the kingdom of Arawiya behind.

Which brings us to you, dear reader. I write for you, and I remain ever so grateful to you for picking up my books and bringing them to life in a way I never can. Thank you.